Praise for Jamie Ogle

"*Of Love and Treason* is a terrific read, rich in historical detail. With vividly drawn settings and complex characters, Jamie Ogle brings ancient Rome to life in this immersive and heart-wrenching story about early Christians who sacrificed everything for their faith. Fascinating from the first page to the last."

FRANCINE RIVERS, *New York Times* bestselling author

"What a triumph! *Of Love and Treason* is for anyone who's ever wondered why bad things happen to good people. It offers no cliches or easy answers. . . . A tender love story and boost to faith!"

MESU ANDREWS, author of *In Feast or Famine*

"Ogle's novel, based upon the life of St. Valentine, is a beautiful examination of love in its many forms. While wholly transporting the reader into the streets of ancient Rome, the questions posed within its pages hold tremendous consequence for the world today: is God trustworthy? And, if so, just how far does that trust go? Filled with equal parts heartbreak and hope, this is one debut novel not to be missed."

JENNIFER L. WRIGHT, author of *Come Down Somewhere* and *The Girl from the Papers*

"A moving, memorable debut, *Of Love and Treason* overflows with heart and hope, courage and conviction. Fans of Francine Rivers's Mark of the Lion series will welcome this well-researched, timeless novel set in third-century Rome."

LAURA FRANTZ, Christy Award–winning author of *The Rose and the Thistle*

"*Of Love and Treason* is a feast for the soul. My heart filled to overflowing as I savored this story, and I came away completely satisfied. Jamie Ogle has breathed pulsing, throbbing life into third-century Rome in this profoundly moving episode in the saga of the early church. Fans of Amanda Barratt's novels and Francine Rivers's Mark of the Lion series will rejoice over this astounding debut. It's one of the best novels I've read all year."

JOCELYN GREEN, Christy Award–winning author of *The Metropolitan Affair*

"A fresh, evocative look at a character everyone has heard of, but few truly know. *Of Love and Treason* is the perfect blend of historical research and depth of character—a beautifully wrought tale. I could not tear my eyes from the page once I'd started, and I've never read anything quite like it. I come away with a completely new view of an ordinary holiday, and the man behind it. New author Jamie Ogle is a brilliant storyteller with original, heartfelt stories to tell! I cannot wait for more of her novels."

JOANNA DAVIDSON POLITANO, author of *The Lost Melody*

"Jamie Ogle's vivid novel takes us to the gritty streets of Rome in AD 270 and paints a picture of the price early believers paid for their faith in Christ. The unforgettable characters in *Of Love and Treason* touched my heart and made me thankful for the religious freedom we enjoy. I will never view that freedom—or St. Valentine's Day—in the same way again."

LYNN AUSTIN, bestselling author of *Long Way Home*

OF LOVE AND TREASON

OF LOVE

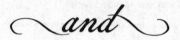 *and*

TREASON

JAMIE OGLE

Tyndale House Publishers
Carol Stream, Illinois

To my courageous brothers and sisters in the faith
who stood for truth and endured to the end.

City of Rome
Ides of Februarius, AD 270

When they drag him to the center of the ring of sand, the stands rumble with jeers and shouts and the restless hum of fifty thousand Romans eager to be entertained with blood. They do not recognize him at first—the man they spoke of with reverence and excitement. The man who went head-to-head against the emperor and will now lose his. He does not look like the hero they imagined, this shortish, gap-toothed scribe.

But someone recognizes him and shouts his name. The stands fall eerily silent. The sun is high. Beneath his feet the sand is hot. The waiting makes his knees shake. He will die, and they will make it painful. He isn't afraid to die. Yet he carries an ember of hope in his chest that he will be saved like the three in the fiery furnace. A miracle that would cause all in the stands to believe in the One God. He scans the arena, taking in the blur of the tens of thousands here to watch him die.

In the rustling stillness, a cry rings out. A single word. Then another voice joins the first.

And another. And another, until the stands roar in unison.

"Vita! Vita! Vita!"

Life! Life! Life!

I

The merchant promised a miracle if Iris wore the pendant.

"It restores what has been lost." His voice dropped, thick with secrecy, as if afraid he'd be overrun by every careless citizen looking for misplaced purses and apartment keys. "I watched it grow a full head of hair on a bald man and add two inches of height to a stooped old woman. I am certain the pendant will work for you."

Iris fingered the thumb-sized piece of stone strung on a chain. It was heavy in her hand and the temptation to purchase it equally weighty. This day marked seven years of blindness. Some called it a curse of the gods. Iris called it unfair.

She bit her lip. She had to decide before the Markets of Trajan closed and her father came looking for her. "You're certain it will work?"

"*Absolutely*, my lovely one." He smelled of sweat and onions.

This merchant was new. Iris had bumped into his makeshift booth by accident as she left the bakery after her morning shift. He occupied most of the wide aisle between Yanni's Silk Slippers, which were no longer made of silk, and the Fine Falernian Wine Shop, which now sold cheap watery *posca*—but with class.

As if sensing her hesitation, the merchant continued. "These stones are special. Dug from enchanted mines high in the Alps where

2

few dare to tread. Only priests who have undergone extensive purification rituals can enter the mines, and fewer make it out alive. This stone is enchanted, kissed by gods and blessed by priests. It will give you what you seek, if you are true of heart and belief." Fingernails scratched against stubble. "It's a small price to pay for your sight."

Iris still hesitated. Past experience shouted that it would not work. But what if it did? What if this stone was what she'd needed all along? She'd long endured the whispers of neighbors and passersby, all murmuring about the poor jailor's daughter and speculating about what heinous sin she'd committed against the gods to be cursed with blindness.

She'd always wonder unless she tried.

"All right." She handed the pendant back to the merchant, shifted her walking stick to the crook of her elbow, and took out her purse. "I'll take it."

"A wise choice."

A strange male voice spoke at Iris's ear. "I wouldn't buy it if I were you."

She jumped and clutched her purse to her chest.

"Sorry. I didn't mean to startle you." He gave her arm a light tap. "Don't buy the necklace."

She lifted her chin and shifted away from him, fighting irritation over yet another well-intentioned stranger who thought she couldn't make her own decisions.

Still . . . she sighed. "Why not?"

"It's a chip of marble strung on a brass chain. He's a swindler."

"Hey!" the merchant snarled. "*This* is an enchanted stone. It restores what has been lost. I'll take you to the magistrate on charges of slander."

"*Asterius?*" The stranger's voice brightened. "I know him well—tell him Val said hello."

"How do you know it won't work?" Iris pressed. Did she dare let a possibly enchanted necklace slip through her fingers at the dissuasion of a stranger? Of course, it wasn't as if she knew the merchant any better.

She caught a faint whiff of sandalwood as the stranger leaned closer to whisper, his breath blowing her *palla* against her cheek.

"He's missing a tooth."

Iris couldn't stifle the laugh in time.

"Get away from my booth before I call over the guard." The merchant's voice rose in elevation as if he'd straightened to his full height. "This is a respectable business."

Ah. There it was. A slight whistling of air between his teeth.

Heart sinking at yet another disappointment, Iris stepped away from the stall, sliding her walking stick along the cobbles. The stranger's footsteps moved in tandem with hers. She looped her purse strings around her wrist and clutched it in her fist. Stopping in the cool shade of another shop front, Iris inhaled the musty sweetness of pears and melons thick in the air. Her stomach growled.

"Here." The man's voice moved low as he bent and scratched at the street before plopping a warm rock into her hand. "Now *this* is an enchanted piece of cobble. It reveals the name of whoever touches it—but it may also carry the plague, so be careful."

Iris smiled as the man continued in a mock salesman tone. "This *particular* pebble has traveled from the ground at your feet all the way to where it now sits in your hand. And that, miss, is a pretty impressive feat for a rock, don't you think?"

She laughed and closed her fingers around the stone with a conceding nod. "Very."

He had a nice voice, mild and cheery, with a hint of firmness. From the sound of it, he was near her height and her age—which, at one and twenty, was seven years past the normal marrying age. She was ancient. He was young.

"I'm Valentine. But my friends call me Valens or Val."

A fisherman passed them, carrying a pungent basket of old fish and fresh flies. Under the awning beside them, two women haggled over the price of pears. Farther off a man yelled something about a thief.

Iris tilted her head. The fringe of her palla, pulled unfashionably low over her eyes, tickled her nose. "I am Quinta Magia, after my *pater*, of course. But everyone calls me Iris."

"Iris." He repeated her name slowly.

She liked the way it sounded, rolling from the back of his mouth to the front, sliding over his teeth like gentle waves.

His voice smiled as he added, "See? The stone *does* work."

Iris smiled in return as the familiar longing swept over her. She rubbed her thumb over a sharp edge on the pebble. "Wouldn't it be nice if miracles like that actually happened?"

"They do."

"I mean real ones."

"They *do* happen." His voice was firm, insistent.

She shook her head. "It's fine. I'm used to being blind—I think it bothers other people more than me." She flipped a carefree hand, lifted a shoulder, and tried a wobbly grin. "Still, you can't blame a girl for trying. It'd be nice to see the hairs in my food before I eat them."

He laughed. "Minotaur's Table?"

"Ah, you've eaten there too?" She shook her head in mock sympathy. The proprietor—and food—of Minotaur's Table were both well-known for being extremely hairy.

"A mistake never to be repeated."

Iris grinned even as the scent of meat pies from the questionable café drifted toward them. "Still." She lifted her chin and inhaled. "They're rather tempting."

"Resist." He chuckled, then added in a dismayed mutter, "I'm going to be late."

"Oh. I'm sorry."

"I'm not. I'll pray for you to see again."

A creaking of wicker announced the passing of a weaver loaded down with a stack of baskets.

"Don't bother." She tried to keep her tone light. "It's about time I accept that the gods don't care."

"Mine does."

Her mouth went tight as the man's motives became clear. "Of course yours does. And at what price?" She held up a finger. "Wait, no, let me guess—there's a special deal for today only." Iris turned away, toward the exit of the market complex that would leave her only a few streets from home. "Thank you, but I said I was fine."

He kept pace with her as her walking stick alternately skimmed and caught over the uneven cobblestones. Iris's shoulders tensed. Just like a salesman not to take the hint he was unwanted.

"There's no price."

"There's always a price." Her voice flattened. "Everything costs something. No gods listen for free." She wished she could move faster through the winding shopping complex. Why did Paulina's Bakery have to be all the way on the far end?

"Yes, I suppose you're right." Valentine's sandals scraped the cobblestones in time with hers. "The ability to pray to my God came at a great cost. Far too great a cost for any one person to pay." He sounded so cryptic, so certain.

Warnings pulsed through her mind. Saved from one swindler by another.

"Posca!" the bartender shouted from the doorway of the Fine Falernian Wine Shop. "Served with class and no attitude!"

"We can pray now if you like." Valentine's tone was casual.

"*Here?* Now?" Her mind shuffled through the pantheon of gods, unable to think of one that didn't require incense. "What kind of god—?" She stopped as understanding dawned. Oh no. "You're a—a *Christian?*"

She whispered the word, too offensive to say aloud, and took a step back, mind running circles around the stories she'd heard about them. *They kidnap children, drink blood, sprout horns at night.* Untrue, of course—she was fairly certain.

He sucked in a quick breath as if to answer but didn't get a chance.

"Iris? Iris! *There* you are. I've been looking all over for you."

Titus.

From the sound of it, her oldest and only friend hailed from the other end of the street.

She lifted a hand in acknowledgment.

"It was nice to meet you, Iris." Valentine's words came in a sudden rush. The sort that accompanied the appearance of a Praetorian Guard. "And I *will* pray for you."

She forced a smile. "Thank you."

Valentine's retreating footsteps were replaced by the clack of Titus's military-issued hobnailed boots as he crossed the street toward her.

"Who was that?"

She dumped the pebble into her purse. "Nobody." Why the hesitance to reveal his name?

Titus's pointed silence told her he didn't believe it. Raised by Iris's father, Quintus, after the death of his own, Titus Didius Liberare had always felt like an older brother to her, though she'd never been quite certain the feeling was equally returned.

"He said his name was Valentine."

Titus's voice strained as if he craned his neck to look for the stranger in the crowded market. "Was this *Valentine* bothering you?"

"He kept me from buying a worthless rock." She sighed and resumed the trek toward the exit.

"So I don't have to hunt him down and kill him?"

She smiled at his teasing and shook her head. "Not this time."

The air hung still and heavy, and the day's heat radiated from the stone street and building walls. At the street entrance, Titus took her arm and held her back.

"Let this litter go by first."

"What are you doing here? It's a rare day you leave your precious office."

Titus's voice went quiet. "I thought . . . it being *today*, that I—"

"Would buy me some honey-roasted almonds?" Iris cut him off, hating the undercurrents of pity and remorse in his tone. She didn't want another reminder of the accident. "If you insist. I accept your gracious offer."

Titus chuckled and shelled out a few coins to the almond roaster, then set a warm palm-leaf bag of almonds in her hand.

They angled away from the market, sharing the treat as the streets narrowed with every turn, cooling as they dropped into shadow. A breeze, warmed by the heat from the brick buildings, carried a pulsing stench from gutters clogged with sewage, rotting vegetables, and bones.

"Puddle." Titus pulled and pushed her around obstacles in the street. "Broken stool . . . Mind the steps." His voice changed, growing deeper and more serious. "Did you find anything in the market today?"

Her thoughts went to the pebble in her purse, but she shook her head.

"Pity."

She knew he meant it. Titus had been with her that horrible day, seven years ago. Iris reached beneath the fringe of her palla and ran her fingers over the scarred flesh rippling out of the hairline over her left temple. The blemish skipped over her eye, ending in a jagged nick on her cheekbone. She dropped her hand. She had long known she would never see again. For all they'd tried, there was no fixing it. And yet she couldn't help the longing that swelled inside. To be able to see the sky awash with the colors of citrus fruit, see her father's eyes crinkle when he smiled, see if Titus had grown into his ears.

They turned onto Cedar Street, her nose assaulted by the smell of dirty laundry and vats of urine collected from passersby and used as bleach. Nearly home.

"Have you seen my pater?"

"I'll see him when I get to the prison. He has someone I need to talk to." Titus didn't elaborate. Didn't have to. Titus only went to the prison when they needed him to extract answers from prisoners. And whenever that happened, her father came home late.

"Christians again?"

"Not this time—broken pot." He tugged her out of the way.

"I met one today."

"A broken pot?"

She dug an elbow into his side. "A Christian."

"Is he the one who told you not to buy the rock? You should have let me arrest him." Titus bent his head close to hers. "Did he have horns?"

"I didn't see any."

Titus groaned. "I keep telling you to be more observant!"

Iris smiled at his good-natured teasing but continued in a serious tone. "He said he would pray for me, so I could see again."

"And did he?" Titus's voice was strained, as if he held his breath.

"No." She tugged her palla further down on her forehead. "I think you scared him off."

"Probably for the best."

Titus opened the door to the courtyard of the five-story *insula*, stepping aside to let her precede him. The walk from the market to the insula was not long, but the stairs leading to the fourth-floor apartment were hazardous. And before those, there was the first-floor laundry to navigate. The laundress, Silvia, bawled at her slaves for scorching bed linens.

"That woman has the arms of a legionnaire," Titus whispered. "Watch out for the urine vat."

"You wouldn't want to trip into that again, would you?" Iris giggled, remembering.

"Telling you that story is my biggest regret in life."

"But your tunic was never whiter."

He inhaled and effectively changed the subject. "Someone's cooking sea bass."

The courtyard was shaded, the sun having long passed overhead, but the cracked paving stones still radiated heat. Quick footsteps slapped across the courtyard.

"My dear, have you seen Priscilla?" Dorma's voice wavered with age and worry. The insula's oldest tenant shuffled about, clunking garden pots on the flagstones.

"Who's *Priscilla*?" Titus murmured in Iris's ear. "Anyone I should know?"

Iris answered under her breath. "Yes. The two of you would get along famously. Priscilla is Dorma's chicken."

Titus chuckled. "I do love a good roasted chicken."

She sent an elbow to his gut, hoping Dorma hadn't heard. One did not joke that way about Priscilla. Iris raised her voice. "I think I heard her on the third-floor landing when I left this morning."

Dorma's voice went weak with dread. "The *third* floor?" She shoved past in a shocking burst of speed, sending Iris stumbling against Titus.

"Falco said he'd eat her if he caught her in his bed again." The old woman shrieked, *"Priscillaaaaa!"*

Titus steadied Iris and slid his hands from her sides, releasing a deep breath. "I'd better go."

She grabbed his arm in both hands, her fingers unable to meet around the bulk of it. "You're not going to stay for the chicken hunt? It's great fun."

"Not unless the winner gets that sea bass." He inhaled again and brushed the palla off her head affectionately. "I'll see you."

She nodded and climbed the stairs carefully, thankful no one was moving or throwing out a husband today. The three flights of stairs were free of debris.

Iris let herself into the one-room apartment, sparsely furnished with an unused cooking brazier, a rickety table, and three stools. Her loom crowded the far wall, and curtains divided the other half of the room into two sleeping areas, one for Iris and the other for her father. When Titus and his widowed mother had lived with them, they'd slept on pallets in the main room. Titus's mother had only stayed a few months before marrying a carter and moving to Ostia, leaving Titus to be trained up in the Praetorian Guard.

Leaving her walking stick by the door, she went out to the balcony, checking the dryness of the herbs and potted geranium. They needed water. Titus was right: someone was cooking sea bass. She closed her eyes and inhaled. Sea bass with lemon and rosemary. Her stomach rumbled despite the roasted almonds. She'd make do with plain bread and olives again.

Iris opened her eyes. The shadow of a bird skittered across the wooden planks at her feet.

Her hair stood on end. She stared, mind reeling.

She could *see*.

Her pulse pounded. She watched her fingers come up to touch the soft skin around her eyes, confirming that they were indeed open. She saw her chest rising and falling too fast, her round toes wrapped in plain leather sandals. She was afraid to blink. Afraid the fuzzy gray shapes and light would disappear. Her eyes burned and watered. Iris reached up again, this time to hold her eyelids open. She couldn't help it.

When she blinked, it was gone. Like a lamp pinched out in the night. That faint glimpse of blinding light and shadow plunged once more into deep fog and swirling darkness.

She blinked again, emotion swelling her throat.

Nothing.

She shuddered, knees going doughy. Sitting down hard, her back against the wall, she struggled to grasp what had just happened. It *had* been real . . . hadn't it? Perhaps it was only a memory of something she'd seen before . . . But no, there was no dream or memory in it, just simple sight.

Simple and glorious, and gone.

She sat on the balcony shaking and frozen in place, hardly knowing whether to laugh or cry. On the other side of the wall bracing her was the *lararium*—their niche of household gods so crammed with deities there wasn't room for another. Had they smiled upon her at last? She pushed herself to her feet and stumbled inside, dropping to her knees before the shrine. Her hands shook as she poured wine into a small bowl to offer as a libation.

But who had done it? Panacea? Hygeia? Aesculapius?

A tiny thought prickled her mind, and she shoved it away. No. Impossible.

The thought came again, stronger. Her insides quivered. *No.* Valentine had not actually prayed for her. She had not made offerings of any kind. Valentine's god had no reason to do anything for her. She did not know his god, and his god surely did not know her.

She replayed the images over and over in her mind while hope and despair wrestled in her heart. Where had it come from? Why hadn't it stayed? Would she ever get it back?

"Thank you."

Her whispered words bounced off the wall, floating away like the curling smoke of incense. Would they reach the ears of the god who had returned her hope?

II

QUINTUS MAGIUS SQUIRMED beneath the tribune's stare. Tribune Lucius Braccus braced his fingertips against each other, the pillar formed by his index fingers tapping against a thread-thin upper lip.

"I'm afraid I'm out of options." The tribune looked down at his desk. "And so are you." He slid a wooden tablet toward Quintus, rows of numbers and dates neatly pressed into the wax covering the surface.

It took Quintus a moment to realize it was a ledger recording the finer details of his financial ruin. A pay advance here and there. Several loans taken from the Praetorian treasury and approved by his cohort tribune—Lucius Braccus himself. Quintus's finger dropped down the long list of numbers to the sum printed at the bottom. *Mars and Jupiter.* His throat went dry. He'd never been especially good at calculating interest rates and fees and—*carry the one . . .*

It added up so quickly. So high.

Quintus's heart sank to the underworld. "I spent every *sesterce* of these loans at the temples." The explanation fell weak. "My daughter—there is nothing to show for it yet, but soon . . ."

Soon what? Even if the gods *did* restore Iris's sight, he would still be swallowed in debts. The money he'd borrowed for charms and incense, physicians, elixirs, and sacrifices in the temples—it would not miraculously reappear once she was healed. *If* she was healed.

His heart leaped to a gallop, familiar worries circling his mind like chariots in the Circus Maximus. He wasn't getting younger. The

12

painful limp from his old battle wound made finding extra work impossible. And Iris? No one would marry a woman cursed with blindness, no matter how beautiful. What chance did she have on the streets? Each thought lashed at his heart like a charioteer's whip. He'd never given the loan repayment serious consideration before, his sole focus on Iris and restoring her sight.

Sweat beaded on his forehead as the office became hot. Too hot. He needed a drink.

Behind the military-issued desk—little more than a box on folding legs—Tribune Braccus tilted his small head and leaned forward, lowering his voice to a compassionate pitch.

"If it were up to me, I'd overlook the whole thing." His hands fluttered as he spoke. "You're a good man, you've served Rome well, and the fates have not rewarded you in kind."

As he paused to draw a deep breath, Quintus's hopes rose just enough to be battered.

"But I'm afraid with the war on, we cannot be so lenient. Prefect Heraclianus has orders from Emperor Claudius Gothicus requiring all loans be repaid in full." He paused again to let the news settle before delivering the death blow. "I called you in because per the signed agreement, you must pay the debt by the first of Februarius or pay the consequences."

"Consequences?" The whip lashed harder, Quintus's lathered thoughts blurring. The first of Februarius? That was only—he tapped his thumb over his fingertips—four months away.

"Any holdings you have will be forfeited and sold."

"But I have nothing of value."

Tribune Braccus drew his mouth in an apologetic line, but his pale-blue eyes held a greedy glint. "Your home, furnishings, slaves, and if it comes to it, you and your daughter."

Quintus slumped in the chair, the air leaving his lungs in a rush. "I gave the money to the gods! How can they do this to me—to my *daughter*? Haven't they taken enough?"

Tribune Braccus straightened a stack of correspondence and adjusted his inkwell. "The gods did not borrow money from the

Praetorian treasury." He flicked his eyes at Quintus, jaw firming. "*You*, Jailor, are the only one at fault in that. And *you* are the one who must pay the price."

The tribune stood and gestured from Quintus to the door behind him. "Four months."

Knees wobbling as if they'd give out, Quintus stood, looking to the tribune. He hoped the leader of his one-thousand-man cohort would change his mind, but Braccus simply waved his hand toward the door again. Quintus slammed a fist to his chest in salute and left, numb with panic and shock. His mind ran with schemes, none of them good. What would he tell Iris? It would crush her to think she was the cause of this. No, he couldn't tell her. Not yet.

The dying sun swathed the city in purple shadow. Quintus did not return to his post at the *carcer*. Instead, out of habit, he headed for the run-down temple of Panacea, goddess of all healing, and the seer who waited in the dim chambers beneath.

The seer's ebony skin glowed in the light cast by dozens of colored lamps littering the niches in the wall behind her chair. She was robed in a gauzy red *chiton*, her bare arms clattering with brass bangles as she gestured for Quintus to sit in the chair opposite her. As he sat, he flipped a few coins onto the round table draped in stained green silk that rested between them. The dank, smoky air held a musty, singed smell.

"You're back." She swiped the coins. "And unhappy."

When he made no reply, she downed the contents of a small goblet, the light glinting off a tarnished turtle strapped to the middle of her purple turban. Setting the goblet down, she locked eyes with Quintus. He shrank back as her gaze seemed to peel away the skin from his bones, probing the very depths of his soul. She leaned toward him and took his wide hand, flipping it palm up and tracing her middle finger over the lines. Her eyes, strangely silver, took on a glassy look and did not stray from his. Quintus swallowed and shifted in his chair.

The seer's lips pricked in a slight smile before drowning in a frown that set her face in deep creases. "You have displeased one of the gods."

This was new. Quintus straightened and licked his dry lips. This might account for his problems, for Iris's curse. "Which god? How? Why?" His voice choked, hoarse and eager.

The seer looked through him as she spoke in a tone that questioned as much as it revealed. "This god has done you a great service, and you have not taken notice."

"Great service?" Quintus racked his brain for anything that might remotely resemble a service, small or great. Trials dogged him like the three-headed hound, Cerberus. His parents and siblings had died during the annual spring sickness that crawled over the city without partiality between young, old, rich, or poor. His wife, Julia, died birthing Iris. The strength of his leg had been stolen in battle. His heart tightened. And then Iris, blinded when girls her age were getting married. A great service? He snorted. Where indeed?

The seer's voice lightened to a wispy singsong. "He waits for you."

Desperation, swift and strangling, swelled in his chest. He gripped the seer's hands. "Who? A god? Tell me which one—I'll do anything!"

Gritting her teeth, the seer pulled her hands free, eyes clearing. "I don't know." The words came out hard, fear barely masked in the tone as she looked away from him. What had she seen?

Quintus leaped up. "What do you mean you don't know?"

"I don't know," the seer repeated, shuddering. "It is not a god I know. I—I do not know his name." Her chair screeched across the floor as she pushed away from the table, gripping her elbows. "Do not return here." She turned away, voice edged with fear. "I cannot help you."

Quintus wanted to shake her. What had he paid her for? He wanted answers—*needed* them—and all he'd gotten were more questions. And now he had to find an unknown god who had done him some great and unnoticed service? He stormed from the room, hobnailed boots smacking against the marble steps. Cool night air washed over him as he emerged from the humid warmth of the chamber below the temple. They were all the same. The priests and priestesses, *haruspices* and seers, charm sellers and healers—*Pay us and we will feed you emptiness wrapped in ritual.*

His bad leg ached, but he didn't slow his pace. Quintus couldn't bear the thought of going home and looking into Iris's blank eyes. He'd done all a devout Roman should—and what good had his devotion done him or his daughter? The gods either were not inclined to help or did not have the power to do so. Iris was cursed, and now they would be destitute.

Quintus stopped the hard march when his leg nearly gave out, shooting pain into his hip and knee. He cursed the old battle wound that had pulled him out of the Praetorian Guard and slapped him in front of the carcer prison cells at discount pay. Breathing hard, he swung into a gritty tavern that advertised cheap posca and, questionably, "fresh clams."

The patrons were spread out and quiet. He lowered himself to the nearest table, the top covered in a gummy film. A clay cup of the cheap, watered wine appeared before him without having to ask. Stellar service. He tried to drown himself in the wine, throwing it back and waving over three refills before his head began to spin. Still, it did nothing to hold back the memories that swamped him. The door of the prison bursting open and Titus staggering in, carrying Iris, her face bleeding and swollen purple. She'd been—and still was—that bright bloom of life pushing back the barren deadness of winter. Hence the pet name, Iris. To see her bruised and broken in Titus's arms had nearly undone him.

Quintus tossed back another cup and grimaced. He should not have allowed her to run as free as she did. Perhaps if he had made her stay home—but no, sitting home had never suited Iris's nature. And forcing her to do anything against her will went against his.

Seven years ago this very day. Quintus took another drink. He'd been at her side when she awoke, screaming for him to light the lamp. She had always been afraid of the dark. But the lamp was lit and next to the bed, and her eyes were wide and empty. He'd shouted for the doctor, begged him, "Do something, please!"

Do something. Please.

The words he'd spoken to every physician, priest and priestess, god and goddess, seer and haruspex. Nothing. That's what he'd gotten in return.

Quintus shoved himself upright, left a few coins behind, and stumbled toward the prison, keys jingling on his belt. He'd nearly forgotten about Titus. The tavern was close enough to the prison that Quintus avoided a mugging on the way. He clumped up the stairs of worn tufa stone and the night guard, Helix, greeted him with a reproving look and the news that Titus had picked the lock to the cells. Again.

The prison office was small and square and dim. A cot squatted in the corner, bordered at its head by the wall of shelves crammed with law scrolls and prison records, writing tablets and prisoner belongings the guards had deemed unsellable. At the foot of the cot, the ironclad oak door leading to the main holding cell stood slightly ajar. Quintus moved toward his desk, set in front of the shelves and held up by three legs and the extra stool. He'd get around to fixing it someday.

Hobnails screeched behind the armored door, faint at first, then growing louder as they ascended the few steps to the office. A yellow light flickered around the edge of the door before it opened fully with a groan. Quintus settled into his chair, twisting slightly so the broken slat in the seat wouldn't pinch. Relief shot through his leg.

Titus emerged from the holding cell, carrying a lantern and a look of tired triumph. In ten years he'd moved through the Praetorian ranks faster than the Tiber fever in spring. If his father were alive to see him, he would have been proud.

"Did you get what you needed?"

Titus shut the door and nodded, stooping over the grimy washbasin to rinse his hands in water that turned pink. "Eventually."

"Long live the emperor."

Titus raised a grim smile. "And now he shall live a little longer . . . if the plague doesn't kill him."

"What do you hear on the street?"

Titus wiped his hands and flung the dingy towel next to the basin. He crossed his arms and settled a wide shoulder against the wall, facing Quintus. "Much the same as ever. The people think Emperor Claudius is a warmonger—that because there is bread and wine in Rome, the war is not as dire as they're told. And now this. Have you heard about his new edict?"

"Rumors only." Quintus rubbed his head. It was beginning to throb. "Is it as bad as they say?"

"It goes into effect in two days." Titus examined his fingernails and went to the washbasin again. "If Claudius thinks he's unpopular now . . ."

Quintus shrugged. "Soldiers have never been allowed to marry; it's never stopped us before."

"But this is a marriage ban on the civilians." Titus skipped the dirty towel and wiped his hands on his thighs instead. "With a draft of all unmarried men to follow." He locked his hands behind his head and paced the room, perusing the "wanted" notices posted near the outside door. "Military duty has always been voluntary—and with no way to marry and get out of it . . . there will be riots like we've never seen before."

"Even so." Quintus leaned back in his chair, shifting toward Titus. "A ban has never stopped anyone from slipping the *notarii* a few coins for a marriage contract."

"A charge of high treason might." Titus skimmed the notices, lifted a few of the sheets to peer at the ones underneath, and let them drop.

Quintus whistled. "He'd go that far?"

"It's already in writing, according to the prefect. Claudius Gothicus wants a bigger military and he'll stop at nothing to get it." Titus's eyes narrowed as he studied Quintus. "You don't look so well."

"I'm fine," Quintus lied. "How was Iris?"

"Her usual." Titus crossed the room to fumble through the stacks of records on the shelves. He shifted several precarious piles and pulled out a small amphora of wine and two cups hidden behind. Quintus waved a hand of refusal, head already spinning, and Titus poured one for himself. "She puts on a brave face, makes her jokes and laughs, but—" He took a drink, caught the despair that must have shown on Quintus's face, and didn't finish. A muscle ticked in Titus's jaw as he tossed the cup back.

"I'd better get back to the Castra Praetoria." He replaced the cup and amphora in their hiding place. "And you'd better get some rest too. Once the marriage ban is announced, this place will be overflowing with rioters."

"Are you sure you don't want to sleep here and go to the fortress in the morning?"

Titus grinned. "You don't think I can take on a few muggers?"

"They murdered that Urban Guard last week."

"That's an Urban for you." Titus shook his head. "I've got to get back. The *trecenarius* will want to hear about this." He jerked his thumb toward the cellblock and moved to the door. "Good night, Quintus."

"Make good decisions."

Titus left with a noncommittal chuckle, and Quintus locked the ironclad door over the dark stairwell to the silent cell beyond. If what Titus said about the riots proved true, Quintus wouldn't be going home for days. With a debating glance at the rumpled cot, Quintus told Helix he'd be back at first light and set off for home. He descended the stairs outside, feet like leaden weights.

The long and pristinely swept Forum stretched before him, lined with temples and public buildings. Moonlight glowed on the smooth marble facade of the Curia Julia where the Senate had met for centuries. Smoke from smoldering incense altars within the temple of Saturn hung close on the still air. Cutting between the Curia Julia and Basilica Aemilia, Quintus wove through residential streets, which, unlike the Forum, were dark and littered with refuse. Before long he let himself through a painted door, dark in the moonlight. He moved cautiously through the courtyard to avoid strangling himself on the now-invisible laundry lines.

The night grew chilly, and while most of the balcony doors were closed, they were thin. A baby screeched. Someone else snored. The old couple was arguing again—something about a chicken. Keys jingling, Quintus trudged upstairs and let himself into the apartment as silently as he could. A thin moonbeam left a patch of pale light on the floor and set the rest of the room in shadow. A soft snore behind the curtain told him Iris was already asleep.

Out of habit, he knelt before the shrine, searching his soul for a scrap of anything that might resemble faith. He lit the incense and watched it smolder in front of the small statue of Panacea, casting the clay goddess in an orange glow. *Goddess of misplaced hopes.* The thought came tinged with bitterness but no remorse. A gray curl of pungent smoke rose around Iaso, goddess of recuperation, and Hygeia, goddess of health and cleanliness.

He didn't pray. He didn't know to whom he should pray or what he could say that he hadn't already said. Quintus just stayed on his knees and watched the smoke. It swirled, pale and translucent, lighter and lighter until it disappeared into nothing. He brushed away a spiderweb connecting the staff and twisted snake of Aesculapius to Aceso, goddess of the healing process, and then sank his head into his hands, overwhelmed. There were so many gods and goddesses. *So many.* How would he ever find the right combination of whom to appease and to whom he should appeal? And what about the seer's unknown god? How would he begin to search him out among thousands? Was he Roman? Greek? Egyptian? Persian?

His head ached, hollowness filling his belly. He should give up and accept the will of the gods but still, he knelt until his knees went numb and his limbs soaked up the coldness of the floor and held it like marble in winter. He stared at the figures, pale wood, clay, brass, stone. He lifted one, studied the frozen limbs and lifeless eyes, and set it aside on the floor, reaching for another. Soon the niche was empty.

Quintus lit a new bowl of incense and placed it in the empty space. He prostrated himself, pleading to and invoking a god he did not know and asking for forgiveness for overlooking a service he had not noticed.

His hope dwindled. A tiny flickering in a murky sea.

The unknown god was silent.

Distant.

Unmoving.

III

VALENS EXITED THE STREET BISTRO eating a pastry filled with honey and pistachios. It was decidedly *not* as good as the raisin pastries from Paulina's Bakery, but he licked the sticky, flaky bits from his fingers anyway and sent a quick glance at the sky. He would be late. Again. He'd hoped that stopping for a few minutes would give the afternoon congestion a chance to ease, but it'd had the opposite effect. One hand over his leather satchel and humming an absent tune, Valens joined the mash of the crowd leaving the Forum.

The air, heavy and hot, was too still to clear the stinging smell of sweat. He shuffled with the crowd for a few blocks, then broke free of the crush, swerving down an alley. Pulling up sharp, Valens avoided a collision with a humped laundress struggling to free a small handcart laden with linens from the clutches of a pothole.

"Here, let me help." He took hold of the handle and gave a tug.

"You're very kind, sir." The woman beamed at him with a round-faced smile.

He sighed, giving in. "Are you going far?"

By the time he'd delivered the laundress and cart to an apartment courtyard filled with kettles, he was really late. He took a moment to orient himself and set off again, this time at a jog, though it would not make a difference. A slave cradling a jar of cheese floating in thin milk struggled with the back door of a café. Valens caught the door for him as he went by.

As the door shut, the café owner poked his head out and shouted after him, "You get a discount for that. Come in and eat."

Valens laughed. "Next time. I'm late."

The man waved him off and Valens continued past the Markets of Trajan and toward Quirinal Hill. His sandals scuffed and scraped the black cobblestones as he trotted by several temples of lesser deities and beneath the triumphal arch of Claudius I. Here, he left the tangled web of side streets and joined the wide Via Flaminia, buildings rising on either side of the road with all the order of a child dumping blocks out of a basket. He wound around insula apartments stretching six levels high and small homes clustered next to each other with scarcely room enough for a man to squeeze between them.

Why was every street in this city uphill?

Wheezing hard, and trying harder to mask it, Valens stopped at a walled villa perched on the edge of the Via Flaminia. The varnished wooden door in front bore a simple painting of a snake draped over a cross. The sign said the physician was out. He knocked once and the door flung open. Valens barely stopped his fist from knocking the nose of the answering youth.

Abachum, youngest of the three Calogarus brothers, grinned. "Right on time." He stepped back to let Valens inside.

Valens frowned and stepped through the doorway. "I am?"

Abachum closed the door and led Valens through a darkened clinic. "I told everyone you'd get sidetracked on the way, so we told you to be here an hour ago—an hour before you're *actually* supposed to be here." Abachum grinned again, teeth flashing. "And here you are, perfectly on time!"

Valens shook his head, unable to suppress a smile. "It's a relief not to be late, but I'm thinking perhaps I need to preach on the dangers of deception at our next gathering."

The boy swung open a door to the courtyard. "We only said to *be here* an hour ago. Not that it *started* an hour ago."

"That's a slippery slope, my friend." Valens followed him into a lush garden filled with potted palms and citrus trees strung with chains of late-season flowers. A marble fountain trickled peacefully, splitting a white granite walkway that wrapped around it and led to a corner where three men played soft Eastern music. Valens raised a hand toward Audifax, the middle Calogarus brother, who had set aside his shipping scrolls and bills of lading to play a flute with ink-stained fingers. He gave Valens a raised-eyebrow nod in return.

"I should have brought my lute."

Abachum slapped Valens on the shoulder, with a firm shake of his head. "Trust me, your talents are of far better use elsewhere."

"Where is everyone? Do I smell?" Valens lifted an arm and sniffed.

"Not too badly. Everyone should be out soon."

"Val!"

Cato, the eldest of the brothers and Valens's closest friend, crossed the courtyard, his unfashionably shaggy black curls bouncing around his chin.

Cato flung his arms wide in greeting and surprise. "What do you know? It worked. He's actually on time." He flagged a servant woman. "Phoebe, tell everyone he's here."

Valens crossed his arms. "You know I'm never going to trust you again."

Cato laughed, then sobered as he glanced around the festive courtyard. "Welcome to the last wedding in Rome."

"Your parents are kind to open their home like this."

The house, while deceptively lavish on the outside, was simply furnished. Marius, a Persian shipping merchant, and his wife, Martha, had moved their three sons to Rome during the reign of Emperor Valerian when they'd heard the church was under intense persecution. There, Marius had set up his house and business, creating a facade of wealth as he funded asylum and escape for those seeking to leave the city. In the relative peace that followed in the wake of a new emperor, Marius and Martha had opened their home to Valens's church.

"You know Father." Cato shrugged and tugged at the neckline of his white tunic. "He will not hoard what God has given us."

The large double doors on the far end of the courtyard opened and a short, womanly figure draped in a saffron-colored veil walked toward them, escorted by a man with thinning hair. Valens's stomach went jittery for a moment. He tried to remember what he was going to say. Following the couple were a few friends and family members and Cato's wife, holding the hands of their two little daughters, who bounced and waved when they saw Valens. He nodded to Marius and Martha, walking arm in arm behind them all.

Valens took a deep breath and unlooped the satchel slung across his chest, setting it on the table beside him. He ran a hand through his hair and tugged his tunic straight, but those simple preparations did nothing to erase the unease he felt over Cato's words. *Would* this be the last wedding in Rome? And if it were, what would that mean for Rome? For *him*?

The couple stopped in front of him and he tried not to wrinkle his nose at the man's choice of scented hair tonic. The man swallowed and fidgeted.

Valens smiled, looking at the eager faces gathered around them. He cleared his throat. "We're gathered here today as friends and family, to witness and celebrate the binding together of this couple in sacred marriage." As he spoke the familiar words, the nervousness faded, but the unsettled feeling remained. The emperor's marriage ban would go into effect tomorrow. Rushed weddings were taking place all across the city tonight. The last few days in the notarii office had been busier than he'd ever seen. He'd been writing marriage contracts until his arm cramped and his fingers molded around the pen. He flexed his sore hand as the couple repeated the traditional vows and the bride received an iron ring signifying that her heart was forever bound to her husband.

Everyone cheered. Valens officiated the marriage document with his signature and wax seal while servants appeared with trays of food.

"You haven't been around much lately." Cato leaned against the table as Valens repacked his things.

Valens stoppered his ink bottle. "Haldas had us notarii working late all week. It turns out the threat of a marriage ban brings out the commitment in people—and the extra coin."

Cato crossed his arms. "The edict won't last. Or the emperor won't." He lurched forward to snag an egg stuffed with olive paste from a servant's tray. It was true, or mostly true anyway. The marriage bans that had been placed into effect in the past were revoked by Emperor Augustus, who, noting that the morality of society disintegrated when women and children were not cared for, encouraged marriage and the growth of families in order to strengthen the moral backbone of Rome.

"Be careful where you say that." Valens closed the satchel and set it aside. "The Praetorians are quite jumpy as of late."

"Of *late*?" Cato chuckled. "Isn't that a prerequisite to join?" He clapped Valens on the shoulder. "Come on, let's eat."

Low tables sprawled in the courtyard, piled with food and surrounded by colorful dining couches. High-pitched squeals and shrieks of laughter split the hum of conversation.

"The girls are here." Cato's lips tugged up in amusement as he watched his little daughters dodging his father's swinging arms, their black curls bouncing.

"Try to get me, Pappouli!" Lalia, the oldest, ran straight into Marius's arms.

"Get me, 'Pouli!" The little one, Rue, ran back and forth, well out of reach.

"Hello, Marius." Valens walked toward the older man, seated on a cushioned bench.

Marius used his whole body to nod and lifted a hand. "My boy." His voice boomed and his stomach contracted with each word as if it took every muscle in his body to speak. He must be in pain again.

"Uncle Val! Uncle Val! Play with us!" Lalia yelled, wiggling out of Marius's arms and running circles around Valens, curling her fingers into claws and holding them up to her eyes. "You're a sea monster and you have to catch us!"

Valens stomped a foot toward her. She screeched and ran off to hide behind a row of tall columns ringing the courtyard.

Rue held up her arms with a singular demand. "Up."

Valens swung her to one hip and stepped closer to Marius. "How are you feeling?"

The man shrugged and tried a grin. "Wonderful, when all I eat is boiled barley and water, like a criminal." He shook his head and watched with a look of longing as a tray of meat pies went by. "Seeing all this fancy food is killing me."

"No, it's not." Cato crossed his arms. "*Eating* it will kill you."

Marius grunted and leaned toward Valens with a conspiratorial gleam in his eye. "If Cato had gone into shipping instead of insisting on being a physician, I'd be a happy, feasting man."

Cato cocked his head. "No, you'd be a dead man."

"Feasting in heaven." Marius winked.

Rue cupped Valens's face in her chubby hands and forced him to look into her large brown and serious eyes. "Poky face." She gave his cheeks a pat.

Valens chuckled. "I need a shave, don't I?"

Cato turned and gave his wife a grin as she arrived with a tray of cups.

"Will you and Beatrix dine with us before the next gathering?" Delphine handed Valens and Cato cups of wine and Marius a cup that steamed. She sent a sideways glance toward her husband as she added, "Cato may have forgotten to invite you."

Cato snaked an arm around her waist. "Actually, I remembered this time."

"He did," Valens confirmed with a nod. "And we would be glad to."

Rue wiggled to be put down and she ran across the courtyard, tromping through a bed of herbs to where Lalia hid.

Delphine pulled out of Cato's grasp and started after her. "Maria Calogara Rue! Do you need to use the latrine?" A chase around the courtyard followed the question, with Rue loudly insisting she did *not*.

Cato chuckled, watching. "Everyone assured me girls would be well-behaved and quiet."

As Valens took a drink, the lovely face of the blind woman in the market rushed his mind with a heaviness that sank his gut. *Help her to find hope in You, Lord,* he prayed. *And if it be Your will, restore her sight for the glory of Your name.*

"And how was the meeting of church leaders?" Marius shifted warm brown eyes to Valens.

Valens dropped onto the bench opposite him and, with an apologetic look, accepted a meat pie from a tray. "Oh, same old arguments." He heaved a weary sigh and took a bite. "But last night I became 'a bane in the church's side.'"

Cato rolled his eyes. "What have you done this time?"

"I opposed Pastor Lucca. Again."

"About what?" This, from Marius.

"The marriage ban and what we should do about it. What stand we should take, if any." Valens lifted his shoulders. "Lucca thinks we can honor God and the edict—and he's not the only one who thinks that."

"What does Bishop Felix say?"

"He's preoccupied with his letter to the bishop of Antioch, who's telling everyone Jesus wasn't God. He thinks this edict is a temporary thing that will blow over."

"I see. And Pastor Lucca thinks we can honor God and the edict how, exactly?" Marius sniffed the steaming mug, grimaced, and rested it on one knee.

"By encouraging couples to abide by the law, commit to each other, live with each other, and marry later when the ban is lifted." Valens raised his hands. "He's afraid to draw attention to the church. There hasn't been a widespread persecution for ten years now, and he's telling everyone to do as we're told and avoid trouble."

"It's not the worst plan." Cato rubbed the back of his neck. "There's nothing in the Scriptures that says marriage must be ordained by the empire."

"True." Valens nodded. "In one sense, marriage *is* a commitment to one another before God. Simple commitment *sounds* fine, but here in Rome, I fear the application would be difficult. Especially if, say, the man were to die."

Cato's eyebrows drew together. "No widows' rights."

"Exactly." Valens knew firsthand why widows' rights were a lifeline of the empire. His aunt Beatrix, who'd raised him, was a widow and therefore bestowed with the right to own property and retain ownership of her husband's perfume business. If his aunt and uncle had not been legally married, both she and Valens would have been destitute after Uncle Lucan's death.

"The empire won't give property or business ownership rights to a woman who is not legally a widow." Marius nodded. "And Pastor Lucca has no problem with this?"

Valens brushed the pie crumbs from his hands. "He thinks it won't be a problem within the church since we take care of our widows. And while I agree with that—"

"There are still scores of women outside of our churches who wouldn't have the same protection." Cato sent a warning glare across the courtyard. Lalia, racing along the path, stopped at her father's look and walked in slow, exaggerated steps.

Valens sighed. "And so we spent the rest of the time arguing whether to speak against the edict or stay silent." He glanced at the fading light overhead and stood. "It'll be dark soon. I should get home before Aunt Bea gives me another lecture."

"On why you still haven't married Hannah?" Marius smirked.

"On why I shouldn't be walking home in the dark." Valens shot him a sharp look and glanced around to ensure Hannah hadn't overheard. The lovely young woman with overt designs on Valens stood near the fountain with her back turned, visiting with the bride.

"Getting all the tips on how to snag you." Cato elbowed Valens's ribs. "You're getting old, Val."

"I'm still younger than you." Valens looped his satchel across his chest.

Cato laughed. "Yes, but at your age, I'd already had three children—" He stopped, and they all went quiet. Valens felt his chest compress as pain flooded Cato's face. His friend pressed his lips together, with a forced smile that didn't reach his eyes. "Well, you know what I mean. I'll walk you out, Val."

Valens said his farewells and met Cato in the clinic at the front of the house. He stood with his back to Valens, hands braced on the edge of the stained operating table.

"We all miss Peter." Valens closed the door behind him. "But I'm sure a father feels the pain more acutely than the rest of us will ever know."

"All the babies, and now Peter—" Cato sucked in a breath and kept his back turned. "I should have made him come with me. But he wanted so badly to play with his friends—I didn't think it would—"

"You couldn't have known what would happen. He was a good helper, wasn't he?"

"The best." Pride shone in Cato's voice. "He never batted an eye during an amputation." He ran a hand over the battered edge of the table. "Unlike *some*."

Valens felt his stomach lurch. "Don't talk about it."

Cato looked over his shoulder. "You going to vomit again?"

"There's a good chance."

"If you do, use the bucket this time."

They laughed. Cato opened the front door and pulled Valens into a hug. "You're a good friend, Val."

Valens slapped Cato's shoulder as they parted. "You'll see your son again, Cato. And in the meantime, Peter will never have to witness any more of the brokenness of this world."

Cato nodded. "Greet Beatrix for us all."

The apartment Valens shared with his aunt sat above the upper levels of the Markets of Trajan. Overlooking Trajan's Forum with all its colorful statuary and the towering white column outlining Emperor Trajan's victory over the Dacians, the view was stunning and almost worth the number of stairs.

Aunt Bea hovered on the balcony, bent over a high table strewn with ornate glass and clay bottles. Draped in a garish orange-and-pink chiton trimmed in yellow embroidery, she looked as if she belonged in one of her flowerpots. With the assistance of a funnel, Bea filled a small blue glass bottle from a larger amphora, stoppered it, and looked up with an energetic smile.

"Valens, come and smell this. I've made a new thing." She pushed her fingers into the bundle of springy salt-and-pepper curls tied low at her neck. The short curls ringing her face sprang upright again as she bounced on her toes, waiting for Valens to smell her latest concoction.

His aunt and uncle had owned a perfumery in the Markets of Trajan for as long as Valens could remember. After Uncle Lucan's death, the shop's ownership had legally transferred to his widow. Aunt Bea had taken over with the same gusto she'd used to match most of the singles in her acquaintance. A fact she pointed out to Valens often.

Valens took a tentative sniff and prepared for another instant headache.

"It's pomegranate, rosemary, and a hint of citron!" She bit a knuckle. "Well? What do you think?"

"It smells like a summer holiday." The closest thing to a compliment he could come up with.

Bea squealed, triumphant. "Doesn't it *just*? And the perfect time of year for it too, I think—with everyone lamenting the start of autumn, this'll be just the pickup!"

"It's nice, Aunt Bea."

"Wait, don't leave yet." She caught his sleeve before he could escape headache-free. "I have one more I want your opinion on—a man's scent. I think it's wonderfully attractive with a hint of mystery." She sorted through the bottles. "It's perfect for you."

"Yes." He settled a shoulder against the wall and scratched the back of his neck. "*Attractive and mysterious* definitely describes me."

"Well, I wish you'd tell me how you manage to get ink stains on your shoulder." Bea straightened, a green vial in hand.

Valens twisted to inspect the short sleeves of his tunic and grinned. "I'm afraid I can't say. After all, I'm a man of myster—" He choked on the last word as Bea shoved the bottle under his nose.

"That's . . ." His eyes watered.

"Here, try some."

Valens threw his hands up and stepped back. "I think I'll stick with diluted sandalwood."

Beatrix snorted. "Diluted sandalwood. I have a gift for perfumes, and you wear *diluted* sandalwood. You might as well wear chamomile."

"I like chamomile."

"So do cranky babies."

Valens grinned and dropped onto the pink-cushioned couch, hands propped beneath his head.

"You didn't come home for the midday meal again." Bea carefully stoppered the bottles and placed them in a wooden box specially made with small compartments to keep the bottles upright.

Yawning, Valens pinched the bridge of his nose. "Haldas kept us working through it. We were backed up on contracts."

"Because of the ban?"

He nodded. "Everyone's rushing to marry before tomorrow."

"Not *everyone*." Bea sent him a pointed look.

He sighed.

"I've made you too comfortable here." She quirked a brow in thought and in the same breath asked, "What would you like for dinner tomorrow?"

"We're eating at Marius and Martha's before the gathering, remember?"

"Oh yes." Bea tucked a curl behind one ear and sent a sideways glance toward Valens. "Will Hannah be there?"

Valens groaned and raked his hands through his hair. "Auntie, I've told you: Judith and Pennia and Hannah and all the rest were—are— lovely. I just—they're not what I'm looking for."

"What *are* you looking for?" She dropped on the couch opposite him. "I can help you find her."

"I don't know." He pushed to his feet. "But when I do, you'll be the first to know." He planted a kiss on her cheek. "Good night."

Later, Valens lay on his bed in the dark, hands locked behind his head. This "last" wedding had disquieted him. Banning marriage to prevent a way out of a military draft was one thing. But Valens felt the societal repercussions would be much deeper. He flipped on his side. Marriage ban or not, soldiers would still take lovers, and the lovers would still bear children and be supported by the soldiers—so long as they stayed faithful and alive. But lovers of dead soldiers were not awarded widows' status and rights to own property or businesses.

An unmarried woman with children and no income had roughly one option for employment. The thought sickened him.

Valens rolled to his back again and ran his hands over his face. He wasn't sure why the ban bothered him so much. There was nothing he could do about it. He wasn't an adviser or a senator or anyone whose opinion the emperor would respect. He sat at a desk and scribbled out contracts and wills and deeds for property sales. He was a nobody.

Unbidden, the image of the young woman from the market sprang into his mind again—clearer this time. Dark waves of hair peeking out from under that bright red-orange palla draped over her head and shoulders. The vibrant color set off her skin's warm tones and hid everything but full lips quirked into a playful grin. Edict or not, blindness alone was enough to ban her from marriage. What would happen to a girl like that? His heart twisted, and he prayed for her again. The ban would not bring good, but it would not last forever. And it could be worse.

At least he didn't have someone he wanted to marry.

IV

PAULINA WAS TALKING DOWN a protesting Epimandos when Iris entered the bakery through the back door. The warmth of the proofing ovens instantly dissipated the early morning chill. The air inside billowed with aromatic spices and yeast from the dough Epimandos had already mixed.

"It can't be helped, Epimandos. You'll have to greet the customers." Paulina's tone meant business. Iris hung her palla on a peg by the door and tied an apron around her waist. "I don't care if you don't like people. Do you like having a roof over your head? Food in your belly?"

"What about *her*?" Epimandos asked in his heavily accented Gallic whine.

Paulina heaved an exasperated sigh. "Good morning, Iris."

"Good morning, Paulina, Epimandos."

The slave grunted in reply. Iris heard him scooping flour and knocking spice jars against the rim of a wooden mixing bowl.

Paulina's voice aimed at her. "My bakers' guild is meeting with the Guild of Grain Millers. The millers are trying to raise prices and limit our purchase amounts." She nudged a bowl of premeasured ingredients against Iris's arm. Iris took the bowl and set it on the kneading counter. "They're idiots if they think we'll agree to that! They'll put half the bakers in Rome out of business by month's end."

Iris ran her hands through the mixture until it clung together in shaggy clumps, then dumped the contents on the wooden counter. She began to knead. "How long will you be away?"

"Today, tomorrow, however many days it takes for those stubborn, pigheaded, greedy, foul-bellied, fist-clenching—" the colorful diatribe continued until Paulina ran out of breath and ended with—"idiots to bend to my will."

"We should close shop while you are away," Epimandos said.

Paulina ignored him. "Speaking of stubborn and pigheaded men, Epimandos will still have to run the deliveries when the baking is complete, which leaves only you to watch the front counter while he's away."

Unease prickled her gut, but Iris kept her reservations to herself. Arguing hadn't done Epimandos any good. "All right."

"But who is going to watch *her* if I am gone?" Epimandos protested. "She is going to give wrong change, and everyone will think we are cheating them—or we will be robbed, and she will not even know."

"Iris is perfectly capable." Paulina snapped a palla around her head and shoulders. "There's a bell on the door. She'll know when customers come and go. She knows where all the bread is and how much everything costs. She's counted end-of-day earnings for me before—with fewer mistakes than you, I might add. But to set your worries at ease, you can take over as soon as you're back."

Iris stifled a giggle at Epimandos's horrified squeak.

"I'll be back when those dull brains come to their senses."

One did not cross Paulina. She would get what she wanted or wouldn't set foot in the bakery until she did. Paulina was fierce and shrewd. A widow who operated a business where men ran the world had to be. Iris wasn't sure why Paulina put up with the sniveling whine of her slave but knew she trusted Epimandos more than any other person. She never listened to him, but she did trust him.

"If she makes idiots bend to her will, what does that make us?" Epimandos muttered. Iris let him complain and focused on the dough. This one was especially nutty.

Iris guessed aloud, "Pistachio and dried cherry. These must be the hand buns."

"Do not overknead it, or they will not be soft, and no one will come back to buy them, and we will go out of business and starve to death."

"You're a dear little ray of midnight this morning." Iris smiled since it would irritate him. "You must have slept well."

"This will end terribly."

"You're right. Perhaps we should slit our wrists and give up now." Iris flipped the dough and shoved the heel of her hand through the middle.

"I am going to check the outdoor ovens." He moaned. "By now they are probably too hot, and everything will burn."

Iris sighed as the door shut behind him and turned her attention to the dough. She loved the bakery. The routine, precision, independence, and aside from this morning, there were never any surprises. They made the same bread every day in the same order. In Paulina's Bakery, she found security, purpose, control. The market outside might change daily, new stands cropping up to trip her, a table jutting out where there hadn't been one before, but here? Never.

Until today.

Her stomach prickled again. The dough went baby-skin smooth beneath her hands. She gave it one last pat and dropped it into the dough bowl, ready for the proofing oven Epimandos had developed. The long, low brick tunnel had a door on each end, and every night Epimandos built a fire inside the tunnel to heat the plaster-covered bricks just enough to allow the dough they placed inside to rise without baking. No other bakers in Rome had developed such a thing, and the bread and pastries from Paulina's were famous for their pillowy softness.

Iris pushed the bowl into the proofing tunnel as far as her arm could reach and replaced the wooden door. As she kneaded, she slid bowls of dough through the tunnel one after the other until they emerged from the other end. By the time each bowl reached the far door, the dough had risen enough to punch and shape. Over the years, she and Epimandos had honed the timing as perfectly as the changing of the Praetorian Palace guards.

As she replaced the proofing door, Epimandos handed her another bowl. They worked in silence. The only sounds were the creak of Epimandos's scales, the scraping as he mixed the dough into shaggy crumbs, and the rhythmic thump of Iris's kneading.

"Do you want to hear something strange?"

"No." Epimandos clacked a lid onto a jar. "But why do I have the feeling you are going to tell me anyway?"

His attitude would not deter her today. Her heart beat harder at the memory. "The other day, as I went home, I met a Christian in the market. He said he would pray for me to see again."

Epimandos snorted. "Did he not know your father is the carcer jailor?"

"That's not even the strange part. I told him not to bother praying but he said he would anyway."

"Like when I say I do not want to talk, and you insist on talking? I know the feeling."

Iris paused her kneading. "I watered the plants on the balcony when I got home, and suddenly . . . I could see." Her scalp prickled as she said the words aloud for the first time.

"Well." He paused as if studying her. "It obviously did not last. You brought your walking stick today."

Iris continued kneading. "I saw my feet and my hands and the boards of the floor. A bird's shadow as it flew."

"You dreamed it." He set another bowl on the counter beside her. "Last one."

She slid her finished dough toward him. "It was no dream."

"Did you tell your father?"

She dumped the bowl's contents on the counter and gathered the crumbs together. "No. He's been staying at the carcer since it happened. With the ban going into effect and the rioting, I'm not certain when I'll see him."

"What happened to your hand?"

"Is it bleeding again?" She touched the tender patch on her knuckles.

"No. It is mostly scabbed."

"The—I tripped." She didn't tell him she'd tripped because the gods had been removed from their niche and strewn across the floor. Had her father done that? She couldn't imagine it, but there could be no other explanation.

Epimandos slid the bowl inside the proofing tunnel with a clunk. He shuffled to the far end and pulled out the first batch of dough, now ready to be shaped into loaves. She and Epimandos didn't speak any more about her sight. Or anything at all. As Epimandos formed the *quadratus* loaves and carried them to the outside ovens, Iris set to work shaping loaves, buns, and hand pastries.

Outside the front door, the multilevel Markets of Trajan came awake with the dawn. Wooden wheels of delivery carts ground over the paving stones in a rush to get out of the city before the sun rose and Urban Guards began handing out fines. Shop shutters banged open and the aromas of fresh fruit and hanging meat and fish burst into the covered walkways between shops. Iris finished shaping the last few batches of dough and, with Epimandos's help, stocked the bread baskets behind the front counters and unlocked the front door. Iris positioned herself behind the counter, quaking beneath the weight of Paulina's trust.

Two women entered, chattering and carrying with them a lingering fragrance of sandalwood, rosemary, and citrus.

"Do you like it?" one of the women asked. "I'm calling it Summer Holiday—what do you think?" Glass bottles tinkled as the speaker set a wooden box on the counter.

"It *is* rather nice, Bea," the other woman said.

"Good morning, dear." The woman called Bea directed her voice toward Iris. "I'll take one of those raisin buns—they're a hug for my soul! Or my hips, rather. That's where it'll end up!"

"Sounds lovely! Make it two," the other woman said. They cackled.

Iris grinned and moved to the shelf where the raisin buns were piled and fetched two.

The bottles in the box clinked as someone dug through them. "Gah! What is this?"

"My new scent for men," Bea said. Coins clicked against the countertop. "It's so mysterious and exotic, don't you think?"

"You might have better luck selling it to the Urban Guards as riot control. One sprinkle of this and anyone would run."

Bea sighed. "My nephew doesn't like it much either." She took the buns from Iris, who ran her fingertips over the counter to find the coins.

"You must be new, dear," Bea said. "I've never seen you up front before."

Iris's face flushed with heat. "Paulina is away today. I—I'm usually in the back." She ran her thumb over the coins, hoping the images weren't too worn for her to feel. Exact change.

Relieved, she dropped it in the money box.

"You'll do brilliantly, I'm sure," Bea gushed. "You have a wonderful day now."

"And you." A bit of the weight lifted. She could do this.

Bea removed the smelly box from the counter, and the bell gave a tinny clank as the women left. The morning passed with snatches of gossip from the other market vendors who stopped in for their usual morning pastries before the public opening of the market. *So-and-so's daughter is pregnant. Did you hear the apartment on Via Delmari caught fire last night? Child playing with the brazier. The Urban Guards got it put out and no one died.* But news of the emperor's edict outlawing all marriages prevailed over the normal gossip. Iris wasn't sure why she felt her stomach sink. Edict or not, she was well past the age when most girls married, and even if her age did not disqualify her, her blindness certainly did. Still, it was yet one more thing stolen from her.

The temperature rose with the sun. Epimandos left to make deliveries and the gossip lessened as the shoppers increased. Some were less than thrilled to find Paulina out and a new girl in her place. When some discovered Iris's blindness, they were gracious and overly helpful.

Others were not.

"Where's my change?"

Iris handed the customer his honey pistachio pastry as her heart started an anxious thrum.

He'd given her the exact amount. She was sure of it and told him so.

"You owe me three sestertii. Don't play stupid with me, girl."

Iris's face went hot. "I—I'm not stupid, sir."

"Then give me my change, or I won't be back!"

"She doesn't owe you anything and you know it."

This voice sounded familiar, but Iris couldn't place it. After a tense pause, the man left. If footsteps could sound sulky, his certainly did.

"Thank you, sir," Iris said. She took a steadying breath. "What can I get for you?"

"Hello," he said. "We met at the charm seller's booth. I didn't know you worked here."

Recognition flooded her. "Valentine."

She heard a smile in his voice as he sighed. "If you insist. I prefer Valens or Val."

Iris tilted her head, considering. "I don't," she said with what she hoped was an impish grin. "Valentine suits you."

He laughed. "Fine. I'll be Valentine if you like."

"Thank you." She faltered and tucked a strand of hair behind her ear. "I mean, for what you did. Just now."

The quiet of the shop signaled Valentine as the sole customer.

"Have you worked here long?" Fabric rustled against wood as he leaned against the counter.

She slid a hand over the edge, brushing crumbs away. "Six years."

"Six years?" he repeated. "I'm in here nearly every morning. I've never seen you. I would have remembered."

She felt her face grow warm. "I'm usually in the back."

A beat of silence. She shifted. "Can I get you anything?"

"I usually get a raisin pastry, but—"

"We're out. You're too late." She'd never been sorrier to sell out of pastries.

"That's usually my problem." He chuckled. "What else do you recommend?"

"The dried cherry and pistachio ones aren't bad. They're no raisin pastry, of course, but—"

"I'll do that then."

She turned to the rows of baskets behind her and located the triangle pastries. The bell jangled and a pair of feet shuffled in. Iris held out the pastry and Valentine took it, placing the coin in her hand instead of leaving it on the counter for her to find. His fingers were smooth as they brushed her palm. The small gesture brought a smile to her lips.

"I've been praying for you." His voice was low.

She froze, stunned by his admission, and then her thoughts began to race. She wanted to ask him a thousand questions. To tell him about the flash of sight. To demand to know if his god was responsible or if hers were beginning to listen.

Instead, she simply said, "I know."

"Excuse me?" A set of knuckles rapped the counter. "Excuse me, miss. I need three quadratii. I'm in a hurry."

Iris dropped Valentine's coin into the money box and straightened. "Yes, of course." Her voice sounded too loud and overbright. She winced.

"See you tomorrow?" Valentine asked.

He wanted to see her? She shrugged, trying not to let the surprise show. "Maybe. If you're not too late." And if Paulina hadn't finished with the Guild of Grain Millers.

"I'll do my best."

The bell clanged again as Valentine left. The remaining customer cleared her throat.

"Right." Iris smoothed a hand over the sudden jitters in her stomach and turned toward the sound. "What can I get you?"

A sharp sigh. "Oh, just forget it!"

"But—"

Sandals slapped the brick floor and the bell clanked.

"I knew this would happen. How many customers have walked out today?"

Iris whirled around. She hadn't heard Epimandos return. "All of them, obviously. How long have you been here?"

"Long enough to know if Paulina does not come back soon, we will go out of business," came the nasally whine. "Who's your friend?"

"My what?"

"The man staring at you like you were the goddess Venus. Or a raisin pastry." He snickered.

Her mouth dropped. "You've been here *that* long and didn't bother to step in and help?"

"I do not think he wanted *my* help." Baskets crackled as Epimandos peered inside, taking stock of what remained.

"But the other customer needed quadratii."

"I do not like people, and she looked angry."

"Do I look angry, Epimandos?"

He paused. "You look embarrassed."

Iris's face heated. *Had* Valentine really been staring at her? Staring at her scars, no doubt. She ran a hand over her hair, tugging a few strands loose to better hide the marred skin at her temple, and ducked past Epimandos into the back room.

"I'll see you tomorrow, Epimandos."

Panic laced his voice. "Where are you going?"

She undid her apron and slung it over the peg by the door, exchanging it for her palla. "Paulina said I had to be up front until you got back. You're back. I'm going home." Iris arranged the palla over her head and shoulders, careful to pull it low over her forehead to hide her wandering eyes. She gathered the two misshapen loaves Epimandos set aside for her and bundled them into a corner of the palla.

"That is not fair," Epimandos protested. "You know I do not like people."

Iris picked up her walking stick. "Don't worry. They're not fond of you either."

Epimandos made a sound that might have been a chuckle had he been in the habit of laughing. "Thank you. Enjoy your evening, but

I think it is going to rain. I will remember to keep quiet tomorrow. Perhaps I will nap."

"I think a nap would do you good." Iris left. A crisp breeze offset the warmth of the afternoon sun and carried with it all the smells from the various cafés and taverns along the Via Biberatica. Oysters, wine, quadratii, fish stew, meat pies. Her stomach rumbled. Maybe things would be calm enough in the Forum to bring the evening meal to the prison and eat with Pater tonight. Iris fingered the meager coins in her purse and almost reconsidered. She could afford only one place. At the end of the street, where the Via Biberatica left the Markets of Trajan and joined the main road, Iris took a risk and stepped into Minotaur's Table. What were the chances hair ended up in *every* pie?

With food in hand, Iris set out across the streets of the Forum, crossing between the cool shadows of the Basilica Aemilia and the Curia Julia. She wasn't sure what to tell Pater about the flash of sight she'd had or about meeting Valentine in the market and his offer of prayer. Surely if she told him about one, she'd have to tell him about the other. Unease cramped her stomach. Proselytizing was illegal for Christians, as was converting to Christianity. But she'd not converted, nor had Valentine tried to convert her. Not exactly. She tripped over an uneven paving stone and trotted a few steps to regain her balance.

It had only been a flash. A mere blink of sight. Nothing said Valentine or his god was the cause of it.

Senators argued on the steps of the Curia Julia as she passed. Valentine had said he would be back tomorrow. She'd ask for answers then. She wouldn't raise her or her pater's hopes until she knew more. Until then, she decided, she would keep Valentine to herself.

V

THE CHAIR SCREECHED across the tiles behind him as Quintus stood and pounded a fist to his heart in salute. Tribune Lucius Braccus strode into the carcer unannounced.

"At ease, Jailor." The tribune turned and motioned for Markos, the day guard, to close the door behind him.

Quintus slid a "wanted" notice over the set of dice and the scrawled record of the game he and Helix had not finished the night before and waited for the tribune to tell him the reason for his visit. The rioters arrested today? Surely he would have sent a message instead of bothering to come himself.

"Will you not ask me to sit?"

Quintus limped away from his chair—the only chair in the office, unless one counted the extra stool propping up one corner of his desk—and offered it to the tribune with a bow. The tribune gathered his midnight-blue cloak in one hand and sat. The fading afternoon light trickled through the small, barred window and caught in his pale-blue eyes. Tribune Braccus, although a few years older, lacked Quintus's wine-inflated girth and the gray streaking his temples.

"I presume you know why I am here."

Quintus would not presume anything, although he had his suspicions. He tipped his head in cringing deference. "No, sir." His eyes fixed on his chipped and filthy nails.

"I am here to help you."

43

Quintus felt his muscles coil. "Sir?"

Braccus leaned the wrong way in the chair and Quintus tried not to let the amusement show when the tribune gave a hiss of pain as the broken slat in the seat pinched him. "I've been thinking about your situation."

"If I could just have more time—" Quintus began, but Tribune Braccus cut him off.

"You must know, with the state of the empire and the wars, that more time will not be possible."

"No, sir. Of course not." Quintus forced his shoulders to remain rigid and his face expressionless, even though he felt himself falling into a deep pit.

"As I said before, I've come to help." Braccus laced his fingers together and settled his hands on the desk. "You are a good man and a loyal soldier, so I will offer to pay your debts, free and clear."

Quintus wasn't sure why the announcement felt like a punch to the stomach. "Thank you for your generosity, sir. I—I will repay you."

The tribune waved his hand. "I'm afraid I did not make myself clear." He shook his head. "I will cover your debts in exchange for your daughter."

"My daughter?" Quintus's gut rolled. It was no secret around the Praetorian Fortress that the tribune had strange appetites when it came to women. The prostitutes fetched to and from the man's chambers were maimed or disfigured—some of them emerged from his quarters that way. He couldn't allow Iris to join the flock.

Quintus attempted ignorance. "My daughter is blind, sir. She will not be a good servant."

Tribune Braccus blinked, and his lips twisted into a slow smile. "Forgive my frankness, but it is not the use of her eyes that interests me."

Bile rose in the back of his throat. They were talking about his daughter—his little girl.

How could he consider such a thing? He shook his head, barely aware of doing so.

"I know." Tribune Braccus leaned forward. "It's quite sudden, but you must consider the other option. If you do not accept my offer, both you and your daughter will be sold to a debtors' work camp until you pay off your debts. You and I know very well a woman with her condition will not be sentenced to a limestone quarry or an olive grove." His eyes took on a hungry light. "She would be sentenced to physical labor of a different sort."

Quintus felt the blood drop from his face. "Is your proposal so different, sir?"

"As different as a cyclops and a Minotaur."

Both were monsters. Yet what choice did he have but to choose the lesser of two beasts?

Braccus squinted. "Is my offer so despicable that you would rather your daughter be a common whore on the streets? I offer food in her belly, a roof over her head. Two things even you, her own father, cannot guarantee her."

Quintus chose his words with care. "She does not know you as I do, sir. She will not take the news easily."

"She doesn't know me." Braccus shrugged. "It matters not in marriage, nor any other contractual relationship. Why should it matter here?"

"Forgive me, sir, but her position would be more precarious than that of a wife." A bead of sweat slipped along his spine, catching on the fabric bundled around his waist from his military belt.

"Let us dispense with formalities, Quintus, and speak plainly." Braccus thrummed his fingers slowly on the desk as if ticking off the seconds. "Has your daughter other offers?"

The keys on his belt clinked as Quintus shifted. "No, sir."

"In her present condition and advanced age, is she likely to receive any?"

"It is not impossible, sir."

Braccus raised a brow. "Within four months?"

The tension in Quintus's shoulders drooped. "No . . . sir." His leg ached from standing so long.

"Have you family who would take her in when you die?"

Quintus swallowed the retort that, based on age, the tribune was more likely to die first. His lips pinched. "Not by blood, sir."

The tribune nodded, his eyes alight with understanding. "Ah, you refer to the son of Acius Didius Liberare—may he rest in the Elysian Fields. Titus is an intelligent young man. His determination and reputation will earn him a promising career if he continues as he has." The tribune's eyes narrowed. "But Titus cannot marry her. Nor is he likely to when he reaches higher rank—not with her condition."

Quintus shifted his weight off his sore leg and sighed. "Forgive my hesitancy, sir. This is a large matter to consider."

"I need not remind you of the size of your debts. You have nothing with which to repay them, and nonpayment puts both of you in labor camps. For all your efforts to restore her sight, your daughter will be destitute. I am offering her safety. Food. Shelter."

Shame.

"If I may be so bold, sir: Why would you do this for Iris? Why *her*? You can have your pick of any other young woman."

Braccus jerked forward in his seat, resting his forearms on the desk. "Because she is *exquisite*. And since I first laid eyes on her, I can think of having no one else."

Not true—if the nightly troupe of mangled women was any indicator. How long would the tribune's infatuation last? Quintus said nothing.

A single knock at the main door preceded the messenger who stopped on the threshold and bowed toward the tribune.

"You're needed at the Castra Praetoria, Tribune. A matter of urgent importance."

Braccus stood. "Think on it." He locked gazes with Quintus. "It is her life."

Tribune Braccus followed the messenger out. Shaking, Quintus wobbled toward the chair and collapsed into it. His mind ran circles around the tribune's proposition. How could the man be so bold as to suggest such a thing? How could Quintus be so depraved as to consider it? Even so, the tribune was not all empty words. Iris *was* exquisite, as he said. Even more beautiful than her long-departed mother, if that were possible, given the scars twisting her face. But she was also blind, and no man would ask for a wife so unlucky. Not even Titus, though Quintus often wished he could. Quintus rubbed his hands over his face. He should be grateful that the subject of his fears could be so easily relieved. Instead, he felt sick.

⬤

Quintus sat at his desk with a half-empty amphora when Iris arrived. Markos swung the door open and Iris breezed inside, carrying with her the scents of evening dew and meat pies and bread.

"Hello, Pater." Iris grinned and stopped just inside the doorway. "Is everything in its place?"

"It is." Quintus tossed back the remainder of his wine as Iris crossed the room, confidence in her quick steps. She skirted the desk without so much as brushing it and kissed his cheek. Her face shone.

"Hello, my girl. How was the bakery?"

"Long." Iris heaved a sigh. "I've been there all day till just now. Paulina is away; her bakers' guild had a meeting with the Guild of Grain Millers. I worked out front." She unwrapped herself from the dusky-orange palla covering her head and shoulders and handed him a bundle tied into one corner of it. He set out the meat pies and bread, then stood, taking her shoulders and moving her in front of the chair.

"Here. Sit and tell me about your day."

As she recounted the day's events and the market gossip, Quintus poured two cups of wine and added water to Iris's.

"Cyrus nearly drowned yesterday." Iris's eyes drifted somewhere far to the right. "His nephew ran the fishing boat into the reef. It sank and now Cyrus has nothing."

Quintus was glad Iris couldn't see his face. Cyrus supplied the carcer with lobster for the prisoners' fare and better fish for the guards—and at a good price too. He didn't want to take on finding a new supplier just now, nor did he wish to bargain with Tribune Braccus to increase the ration allotment. The wars in the north were expensive. Priorities did not include allocating extra monies for fish to feed prisoners and citadel guards living in safety. And worse, Quintus couldn't ask. Wouldn't ask. Because the tribune would do anything so long as Quintus gave him Iris. He would rather starve them both.

"Pater?"

"Yes?"

"Did you hear me?"

"Yes. How unfortunate about Cyrus."

Her dark brows puckered. "I asked how your day fared. I heard there was rioting yesterday and this morning, but the Forum is quiet now." Wisps of deep-brown hair slid across her cheek where it had come free from the thick braids twisted and pinned to the back of her head.

He stared at Iris, seeing her not as his little girl, scampering about the jail, challenging the guards to sparring matches so she could laugh at their exaggerated expressions while they pretended to die at her hands. The beautiful woman reclining in his chair like a queen was not his little child any longer, nor did he have many years left to care for her. Yet he couldn't make his mouth repeat Tribune Braccus's offer.

"My day was fine. The Praetorians made quick work of the riots, as you can imagine. The back cell's full but they'll be released tomorrow. What did you bring for dinner? I'm famished."

"Bread and meat pies."

He noticed dark scabs on her knuckles as she handed him a pie. "What happened to your hand?"

She ran one hand over the other. "I tripped yesterday morning. Did you put all the gods on the floor?"

Quintus took a bite of his pie and pulled a long black hair from his mouth before answering. "Is that what you tripped over? I'm sorry." He shook his head. He couldn't even protect his own daughter in their own home. "I . . ." He couldn't think of a way to tell her about the seer and her strange message, and just as well, because Iris wasn't listening.

"Anyway, I wanted to tell you . . ." Iris twisted her fingers in her lap, her dinner untouched. "The day before yesterday, when I got home, I went onto the balcony to water the plants and all of a sudden—just for a moment—I could see."

Quintus choked and dropped his cup on the desk. "You what?" His eyes watered—from the emotion or the food lodged in his throat, he wasn't sure. He pounded his chest.

Iris gave a giddy laugh and nodded. "I saw my feet, the floor, the shadow of a bird flying overhead."

"A bird?" Hope surged through him. "That is a good omen, I think. We should buy a meeting with the augurs. Perhaps they can interpret what this means. Do you know what kind of bird you saw?"

She shook her head. "It was just a shadow. When I blinked, it was all gone." Iris reached out and he gripped her hands. "I'd forgotten how badly I want to see until that moment. But *oh*." She sighed, face glowing. "It was glorious!"

Quintus silently cursed as he calculated. The flash of sight had happened prior to his decluttering of the shrine. What if his actions had displeased the gods again? "We will keep praying and offering incense." He gave her hands a squeeze. "And I will bribe a meeting with the augurs as soon as I can. Perhaps they can interpret the sign of the bird."

Iris nodded. "I think I interrupted you before all that. What were you going to tell me?"

"Nothing." He released her hands before she felt how damp his palms had suddenly become. "It isn't important."

VI

The couple sat before him, pale and pleading.

"Hector, Lillith, I'm sorry." Valens kept his voice low and glanced at the desks around him. The Hall of Notarii was a grand name for the desk-cluttered back room in the far corner of the Basilica Julia. Slaves in short gray tunics traded rolls of fresh parchment for completed contracts ready to be delivered. The other notarii were too engaged in their own meetings and scribbles to notice his.

"No one is exempt from the edict. There's nothing I can do for you until it is revoked."

The woman, seated across from Valens, pressed trembling lips together and sent a questioning look at the man beside her before producing a wooden tile from her purse. Her fingers shook as she slid it toward Valens. It appeared to be a ticket to a play at the Theatre of Marcellus. A very old ticket.

"Bribing me won't change the law." According to the faded ink, the play had staged nearly thirty years ago. Confusion puckered his forehead.

Lillith pushed the tile closer. "Just look at it."

He took the tile and flipped it over, squinting at the misspelled words written on the back in rudimentary scrawl: *WIL YU MAREE ME?*

Valens looked up. "I don't understand."

"Hector wrote it hisself." She beamed and Hector looked down, ears reddening. "He gave this to me when we was just children. Before he joined the legions."

"We grew up next door in the same insula across from the Baths of Decius." Hector raised his chin. "Our families are still there. We've known each other since . . . forever."

Lillith looked at Hector. "Loved each other our whole lives."

Hector took her hand and squeezed it, his gaze on her blazing with affection.

Valens cleared his throat, reminding them of his presence.

Lillith took a steadying breath and kept her voice low. "Hector joined the legions—he's been fighting in Germania for twenty-five years and only been home four times." She brushed the back of her hand over her cheek and met Valens's eyes with a look of determination. "He said he'd marry me when he got out, so I waited for him—do you know how hard that was on my pater? I'm an old woman and a burden to my family."

"Prettiest old woman I ever saw." Hector tugged her against his side. She elbowed him but couldn't hide her smile.

This is a trick. A test of loyalty. Valens glanced around. No one appeared to be watching him. Perhaps Hector would report on him later.

Lillith continued. "Hector's term ended a month ago and he got home last night. He came to my parents' apartment and asked me if I remembered the note he wrote all them years ago when we was children." She smiled. "I did, because I kept it tucked away under my pallet."

Hector turned his gaze on Valens, the soft love his eyes held for Lillith hardening to anger. "I kept my vow to serve the empire." The muscles in his jaw bulged as he struggled to keep his voice down. "I served my *full* twenty-five-year term. I wasn't the one stabbing myself in the foot so I could get an early leave—and this is how the emperor repays my service? By denying me the right of *connubium* and the ability to rear legal heirs?" His voice dropped to a pitiful whisper.

Valens's heart pinched. Emperor Claudius II Gothicus would not remain popular with his troops by enforcing such laws. To forbid legionnaires to marry while in service was one thing, but to deny them still once they completed their service? Cruel. *Still, this is only a test.* When most Romans were used to couples acting married without a contract, he wondered why these two insisted on one. Yes, definitely a trap.

Lillith lifted her chin. "I didn't wait all them years to be a kept woman or a wife by *usus*. I will hold my head high and be a proper wife and shut up all them whispers they speak behind my back. All the gossip about why no one wanted me." She sniffed and looked away.

"Have you heard the screams of barbarians in the night as they surround your camp? Held your friend as he dies in your arms?" Hector leaned forward. "I risked the best years of my life for the emperor, for the empire—for *you*. So *you* could sit at this desk and scribble and live in peace and safety with your wife and family."

Valens lowered his chin, shame flooding him. How could he refuse this simple request from a man who had risked so much? *Trap. Trap. Trap.* "I have neither wife nor family."

Hector nodded as if the admission were just. "Then you know how it feels to spend your life alone. You know the longing to hold the one who loves you in your arms every night. The aching loneliness that eats at your gut and keeps you awake long after the world sleeps."

"Yes," Valens admitted in a whisper. "I know it well." He saw a spark of hope in their eyes and took a breath. "But you are asking me to commit treason—punishable by death. Would you risk your lives for this?"

"I've risked my life already." Hector crossed his arms, showing off jagged red scars. "And I'd do it a thousand times over to be with my Lillith."

Valens ran both hands through his hair. The power to grant their request lay in the pen and ink at his fingertips, yet he sat powerless to pick them up. "I—I'm sorry." He gripped the edges of his desk. "I cannot break the law. But the edict will not remain forever."

"An hour feels like forever when you're separated from the one you love." Hector stood and took Lillith's hand. "But you'd never know that, would you?"

Lillith snatched the tile from the desk, as if Valens might try to keep it, and secured it in her purse once more. She sent a look of mingled sadness and anger in Valens's direction.

"I hope you fall in love." Her words, spoken softly, felt like a curse.

Valens watched them leave, nausea circling his gut. He dropped his forehead into one hand and told himself he'd won. He'd passed the test and his supervisor would be over soon to congratulate him. So why did he feel so guilty? Why the heaviness in his chest that told him he'd done something very wrong?

He shoved back his chair and stood, aware of the sweat sticking his tunic to his back. He could use some fresh air. Two clerks marched past his desk, arms full of scrolls. His colleagues worked steadily around him, unaware of the trial he'd endured and passed. Valens caught the eye of his supervisor, Orane Haldas, who stalked between the notarii to ensure everything ran as it ought and to lend his advice on questions of the law. He raised his eyebrows in a look that told Valens to get busy.

Valens resumed his seat and hailed the next person in line. Fresh air would have to wait. He spent the rest of the day writing documents for three warehouse rent adjustments and the sale of an inn. As afternoon reached for evening, the patrons waned, and as Valens prepared to leave, Haldas stopped him. Surely to congratulate him.

"The merchant Ganesh Musa Ravi sent a messenger asking for you to meet him at his villa to organize the sale of an apartment block." Haldas swiped a dingy cloth over the sheen on his bald head. "He'll see you first thing in the morning, so take your things with you now. Good evening then."

Haldas moved on and Valens offered his "Good evening, sir," to his back.

Still disturbed by the couple, and humming a discordant tune, Valens gathered a roll of parchment, a reed pen, ink, and his official notarius seal. Before dropping it into his satchel, he turned the brass stamp over to study the image of the emperor. The bearded profile of Claudius II Gothicus stared straight ahead, looking rather pleased with himself. It looked curiously like the old stamp and profile of the previous emperor, Gallienus. Only the name and beard differed. Valens dropped it into his bag and marched outside with a glance at the sky, hoping he would not be late again.

❖

Lalia and Rue launched themselves at Valens the moment he and Beatrix entered the dining room. Marius, Martha, and their sons and daughter-in-law sat on the dining couches.

"Uncle Val! Up!" Rue accentuated her demand by holding both little arms straight up at Valens.

Lalia tugged his hand, pulling him toward the opposing wall, where three sets of double doors opened to the balcony overlooking a small public garden. "Come see the trees with me! I know all their names."

"I'm hungry," Rue announced as Valens hoisted her to his hip.

"Me too."

"So good to see you, dear!" Bea swept over to Martha and kissed both her cheeks. "I've brought sweet pastries from Paulina's for after dinner."

"How wonderful!" Martha made room on the low table for Bea's basket. "Nothing rivals sweets from Paulina's."

Cato followed Valens as Lalia dragged him to the balcony.

"Don't drop me!" Rue squeezed his neck until he choked.

Valens tugged at her arms to loosen her grip. "I'd never do that."

Lalia hung over the marble railing, pointing out and naming the different trees and shrubs.

"You're very smart."

"I *am* four." She looked up at Valens, hands on her hips.

Cato shot him a look of mock sternness. "She *is* four."

"Forgive me, my lady. I forgot how grown-up you are." Valens bit back a grin and gave Lalia a deep bow, much to Rue's delight. She squealed and threw back her head of springy black curls. Valens barely caught her before she tumbled out of his arms.

Lalia rolled her eyes. "I'm not a lady. I'm a girl."

Valens straightened and glanced at Cato, who shrugged and shook his head. "There's no winning with women." He ruffled Lalia's curls. "The sooner you realize that, the sooner you'll find one."

Valens groaned. "Not from you too."

"Sorry. Do you have time to come with me on a call tomorrow? There's a fisherman by the docks in a bad way."

"I can in the afternoon, if that isn't too late."

"Should be fine. Meet me here."

"So I can carry all your things? You need to get yourself a basket."

"*Fffft.*" Cato waved a hand. "I don't need a basket when you always show up to carry everything."

"Someday I won't be available to help. You need a plan."

"Threats, threats." Cato rested a hip against the railing. "You always say that, and yet you show up every time. How was the office?"

Valens let out a long breath. "When I got there, it was full of people nearing a riot. The supervisor dismissed us till after lunch and then called the Urban Guard to dispel the crowd."

"Were they rioting about the marriage edict or something else?"

Tiring of the trees, Lalia began to twirl.

"The edict, yes. But now the priests have banded together and—"

"They're actually cooperating with each other?"

It was no secret that the priests of the varying gods and goddesses competed for the popularity of their patron deity.

Valens nodded. "More than cooperating. They've been petitioning for everyone to offer compulsory sacrifices and offerings to end the war. They've got quite a following of the people and now they're trying to get approval to be able to fine anyone who refuses to sacrifice. On grounds of treason."

Cato watched Lalia spin, his expression tight. "Do you think they'll get it?"

Valens shrugged as Rue patted his cheeks and reminded him they were prickly. "The emperor banned marriage. *Marriage.* If he can do that, there's nothing to stop him from pushing other policies."

"If he lasts long enough. I heard he was ill."

True. Seven emperors had risen and fallen in the previous twenty years, each one bringing with him new policies and edicts, established one year and ignored the next.

"Do you think the priests will get approval for punishments harsher than a fine?" Cato jerked to one side as Lalia swung on his hand.

Again, Valens shrugged. "I hope not, but who can tell anymore? The mob today will either get them dismissed or taken seriously. Who knows which it'll be."

"Cato? Valens?" Delphine stood in the doorway. "The others will arrive soon."

Cato swung Lalia onto his back. "All right. We've shown Uncle Val the trees; now let's show him how well you can eat your dinner."

Rue lifted her tiny chin as Valens turned back inside. "Not hungry."

Cato twisted around. "You just said you were."

"Not hungry." She shook her head, black ringlets flopping.

Valens grinned. "What'd you say? You can't win with women?"

"Valentine would have made a wonderful father." Bea spoke in a mournful tone as the men and children entered. Valens rolled his eyes and pried Rue's arms from around his neck.

"Bea." He groaned. "I'm thirty-two. I'm not dead yet, and—" Valens glanced between the three women, two of whom were staring at him in mock sternness. "Can we stop discussing this already?" He turned to Marius. "How are you?"

It took all the willpower Valens had not to respond when Bea did not drop her voice and spoke in a conspiratorial tone. "He needs help."

Lord, help me.

"It's going to rain tonight." Marius peered toward the open doors, squinting at the sky.

"Hopefully it holds off until later." Valens nodded, grateful for the change of subject, even if it was weather.

Two servants entered with trays of food and the women rose to help lay it on the table. While the women prepared the meal, others arrived in twos and threes until thirty or so filled the room. Valens greeted them all by name as they trickled in and found seats. He'd grown up beside many of them, under the guidance of the older ones. Never had he been more humbled and overwhelmed than when the elders had brought him before Bishop Dionysius and appointed him to be a church leader. He'd remained under Bishop Dionysius's tutelage for several years before the bishop died and the other church leaders deemed Valens ready to lead. They'd prayed and laid hands on him and finally sent him off.

The anti-riot policies left over from long ago forbade religious gatherings of large groups, forcing churches to splinter into small "dinner parties" in various homes across the city. Marius and Martha opened their home to his church immediately. Attendance swelled and ebbed as believers grew and went out into other parts to spread the message. Valens would have it no other way.

Two young men, Linus and Pax, escorted Alesia, a pretty, young widow, and her two small children, a boy and girl. Valens ruffled the boy's already-wild hair and tweaked the tiny girl's nose. She giggled and hid her face in her mother's skirt.

"Welcome, Alesia, Linus, Pax."

They returned the greeting and the children took their place at Alesia's feet when she sat next to Bea. Bea hugged her and sent a questioning look to Valens, who shot her a look of warning in response. Leave it to his aunt to try pairing him with Alesia next. Others joined the company, and Valens moved through the chattering groups, encouraging them to head to the tables and eat. Once everyone had eaten, the room fell into whispers and rustles as people settled on chairs and couches and the floor. Cato and his brothers closed the balcony doors and pulled curtains across the windows.

Valens perched on a stool as Alesia began to sing in a sweet, trembling tone that grew stronger as the others joined in with voices full of passion and conviction.

> *"He was manifested in the flesh,*
>   *amen, amen.*
> *Vindicated by the Spirit,*
>   *amen.*

Seen by angels, proclaimed among the nations,
  amen, amen.
Believed on in the world and taken up in glory,
  amen."

The singing fell away to murmurs of praise and thankfulness that morphed into heartfelt prayer. When one voice faded, another took its place. They prayed for unbelieving neighbors, for the senate and the emperor. They prayed for opportunities to show love and share hope. And they prayed for courage, for boldness to speak truth and act on it, no matter the consequences. Valens prayed aloud for Iris and the others joined in.

The light had gone by the time they'd finished, and Delphine and the servant Phoebe rose to light the lamps.

"I lost my job." Pax rubbed the bruise on his forehead, eyes trained on the ground. He was—or had been—a city messenger, carrying letters to and from people within the city. "I thought my supervisor was a friend. That he might listen—understand—if I shared the Good News, but he called it a favor, letting me go instead of turning me in." His eyes flashed with hurt and anger in the lamplight.

Valens prayed for wisdom as he began to speak to his little flock of believers. "We were never promised an easy life as followers of Jesus. Just the opposite, in fact." The stool creaked as he shifted his weight. "Paul wrote in his letter to the church in Ephesus that we wage a battle not against flesh and blood, but against spiritual forces. And we must put on the armor of God to withstand the darts of the enemy. They come at us in many forms. Discouragements and doubts, the loss of a job or health or a family member. The little voice that tells us to give up, that God doesn't see. That He doesn't care."

Marius gripped Pax's shoulder and gave it a gentle shake. "You've done well, my boy. Trust God to provide a new job for you, and at present, if you have need of anything, we are all here to support and care for each other. We are not here with words only."

A man cleared his throat. "I—I've been on the lookout for a

delivery lad." Novus, a metalworker, straightened from where he leaned against the back wall. "The job's yours if you want it. You already know the city."

Pax's mouth dropped as the room burst into laughter.

Later, after they shared the bread and wine and everyone had returned to their homes, Valens lay awake, staring at the cracked plaster above his bed. The market below the apartment remained just as noisy at night, filled with thumps and shouts and the squeaking wheels of delivery carts unloading goods into the market shops. A smile played at his lips as he thought of the way God had provided for Pax. How the church had come together as He had designed it to. Members working together to support and care for one another, creating a body that was healthy and strong.

"If anyone has the world's goods and sees his brother in need, yet closes his heart against him, how does God's love abide in him? Little children, let us not love in word or talk but in deed and in truth."

Hector and Lillith.

The sudden change of thought sent his gut churning. He couldn't chase the couple from his mind. What would it be like, he wondered, to love someone from childhood? To love someone so fiercely as to risk treason and death just to marry?

Thunder rumbled, shaking the whole building in a deep thumping roll. Rain battered the street like an upended waterpot. Valens threw the blanket from him and crossed the room to the window, leaning out to close the shutters against the rain. He shivered and lit the clay lamp, then fetched the cloth from the washstand to dry his arms and hair. The lamp bathed the room in wavering orange light and shadows. It revealed his narrow bed, the washstand with a red-glazed basin and pitcher, a table and small chair.

He poured himself a cup of water and sat in the chair, squirming to get comfortable on the lumpy pink cushion. Pulling it out from under him, he tossed it on the floor. Bea's love of the garish had somehow infiltrated his space. His leather satchel sat in the middle of the table, holding the tools of his trade. He stared at it, thrumming his fingers on his thigh and taking a sip of water. It was one thing to agree to marry couples he knew. To do the same for complete strangers was something else entirely.

Rushing blood laced his limbs with quivering energy. Valens reached for the bag, flipped back the flap, and spilled the contents on the table.

He froze as something scuttled over the roof tiles. Just a rat.

Feeling foolish, he let out a breath and took the pen and ink. He pinned the curling papyrus beneath his left hand and began writing.

Hector son of Apollonius and Lillith daughter of Apion agree that they have come together to share a common life.

His shaking fingers steadied as he wrote the familiar lines, and by the time he'd finished, the lamp had begun to gutter and hiss, and the rain had slowed to a dull popping on the roof.

Valens stood and crossed to the washstand, where he splashed cool water over his face and hair, rubbing away the burning in his eyes. He braced his hands on the stand, gripping the wood until his knuckles turned white. He looked over his shoulder to where the marriage contract lay nearly complete, lacking just two signatures and his seal. He swallowed, trying to calm the ball of snakes roiling in his gut. He could burn it now and no one would ever know. The temptation to hold the papyrus over the dying flame was strong, but he held back, watching, weighing, debating. Valens dropped his chin and stared at the reflection in the basin. His black hair seemed to disappear into the darkness, leaving a face that wavered in the warm light and turned his eyes into deep hollows. He straightened. He would not burn the contract. He would deliver it to the apartment building across from the Baths of Decius, the one Hector had mentioned.

If it had been a test, they would not be there.

If it wasn't a test, they would be married.

VII

THE OVERPOWERING SCENT of cheap floral bath soap assaulted Iris's nose as she slipped the shuttle of orange linen thread between the warp threads of her loom. She knew it was orange because her father said so. But which shade? The vibrant red-orange of mullet roe? Pale and soft as peach flesh? The powdery ochre of an alley cat? When she'd asked, he'd hesitated and repeated, *orange*.

Iris battened the row of thread and lifted damp hair from her hot neck, twisting it into a coil with a sigh. The cool air relieved her clammy skin. Old Dorma had accompanied Iris to the baths after she'd come home that afternoon. Iris sniffed. The sickly sweet smells of her bath oils weren't going to last long with the neighbor's cooking tonight. Curried fish cakes and fried olive bread would hang on her until the next trip to the baths. But considering the poor choice of soap, the smell of curried fish wasn't a terrible alternative.

She continued weaving, her movements swift, rote, controlled. She liked weaving, creating smoothness and order from a chaotic bundle of thread. If only life were as simple and easily manipulated. She ran her fingers over the softness of the completed fabric, which she'd make into a warm wrap for the coming winter. Nearly done. She quickened her pace, falling into the movements and letting her mind wander.

The husband and wife across the hall were arguing again and the single man below banged on the ceiling and inserted his own opinions. Valentine had not returned to the bakery for several days—or at least, not while she'd been up front. Iris hadn't realized how much she'd been looking forward to talking with him again until Epimandos had returned and Valentine had yet to arrive. She tried staying later and even offered to watch the front so Epimandos could rest. When he'd guessed that Valentine hadn't come yet and started to tease, she left in a rush, feeling anxious and a little despairing. The guild meetings would end soon and Iris would go back to kneading and never meet Valentine again. The thought disturbed her more than it had a right to.

Dust from the threads burned in the back of her throat. Iris stood, stretching, and went to pour a cup of water. She was proud of the way she could move through the apartment with ease, skirting furniture without stumbling, her hands falling on the cup and pitcher as easily as if she could see them. Everything was in its proper place—including the gods and goddesses which she had replaced in the lararium, even though she hadn't bothered to pray. She took a drink, wondering about Valentine's "one god." *One* god! How could anyone believe such a thing? Certainly everyone had a *favorite* god or goddess they invoked a little more than the rest, but one god in sum? Absurd. Still, she wrestled with the desire to learn more, even as she tried to convince herself that Valentine and his god had nothing to do with that flash of sight.

The man across the hall slammed his door and thumped down the stairs, yelling curses up at his wife, who shouted some choice ones back at him. He'd be back in a few hours, teary and penitent.

The racket nearly muffled the knock at her own door. Iris set the cup on the table and moved toward the door as the knock came again. More insistent.

"Who is it?" Her fingers paused on the lock.

"Tribune Lucius Braccus."

Her heart began a wild rhythm. Her father had spoken of Tribune Braccus before. He was one of nine Praetorian tribunes and second in command under the Praetorian prefect who ruled Rome in the absence of the emperor. Was her father all right? Surely if he were not, they would have simply sent a messenger with news or, if they were desperate, a centurion—but certainly not a man as important as the tribune.

"My pater is not home, I'm afraid." She spoke against the door. "He's been called away. I will let him know you were looking for him."

"I'm not here to see your father," came the voice. "I'm here to speak with you."

"Is Pater all right?"

"Won't you let me in?" he asked. "There is a matter of a delicate nature I must discuss with you."

Dread pooled in her stomach. Something terrible must have happened. She hesitated a moment more, then flipped back the lock and opened the door.

"Tribune." Iris bowed, clasping her hands together so they wouldn't shake. "Is my pater well?"

He brushed past her. "I'm thirsty."

"Oh. Um, of—of course." She faltered, taken aback by his terse greeting. "I think we may have wine." She left the door wide-open to preserve propriety and moved to set an amphora of watered wine and another clay cup on the table.

"Won't you ask me to sit?"

Iris's smile wobbled. "Forgive me. Will you sit, Tribune?"

"In a moment."

Irritation flared but she squashed it. She would not make a scene before her father's superior. Tribune Braccus's hobnailed boots clacked across the floor, the sound familiar, his gait less so. The door shut with a thump as loud as her heart sounded in her ears.

"Tribune, surely there is no need for—"

The latch clicked into place. She swallowed and hoped her face did not betray her fear.

"No need to fear. Your father is fine." The tribune's voice was smooth and dark as a cobra and just as dangerous. He filled the cup, took a deep draft, and replaced the cup on the table with a tink. "He has spoken with you, no doubt?"

She forced a pleasant tone. "He is my father, Tribune. We speak every day."

He gave an acquiescing chuckle. "About my proposition," he clarified in a flatter voice.

Her throat went tight, yet she forced her voice to stay light and pleasant. "I—I'm afraid that has not come up."

"Indeed? That interests me because your father seems to feel you adamantly oppose the idea."

"I—I, that is—my pater . . . ," Iris stumbled and stopped.

"Then allow me to inform you of what he has neglected to tell you."

Iris shut her mouth, determined to remain pleasant. She couldn't make him leave without disgracing her father, and where could she go that the tribune wouldn't follow? Why had he shut and latched the door? She would have to handle him carefully. *Pater, please come home soon.*

"You are blind."

How observant.

"Which is why you're old and unmarried."

Her mouth dropped.

"What will you do when your pater dies? Have you family who would take care of you?"

Fresh anger fought old fears. Horrible man! How dare he barge into her home and rip the coverings off her worst anxieties? Iris lifted her chin, about to inform him that she could earn her own living, when he continued.

"If you think you can support yourself by kneading a few loaves of bread, you're mistaken. Where would you live? You could no more feed yourself than pay rent. You would be destitute."

Iris fought to keep the anger from her voice. "Thank you, Tribune. Your concern is overwhelming." She took a step toward the door. "But you must forgive me—I was just about to leave."

The couch creaked as he stood and cut off her escape, stepping too close. "I have not finished."

She stiffened as he ran his fingers along her upper arm, the heat of him radiating toward her.

"You need not be destitute. I have spoken with your father about an arrangement that would ensure your care."

Iris took a step back and angled her face away from him. "My father cares for me very well. I have no complaints."

He stilled and drew his hand away. "So he has not told you this either?"

Iris remained silent.

"I regret to be the one to inform you that your father is deeply in debt." He spoke the words crisply, dropping them into her gut like marble blocks. He didn't sound regretful. "His debt is so great he could not possibly repay it if he had four years to do so, much less a mere four months."

Liar. She would have known. Her father would have said something. He'd just spoken of buying a meeting with the augurs. He wouldn't have suggested it if they had no money. Yet she felt strangely out of breath as she whispered, "That is not true."

"It most certainly is." He lowered his lips toward her ear. "He's borrowed hundreds of *aurei* to pay for your healing charms and physicians. And you will both pay the price unless you agree to my proposal."

She tried to swallow but her throat was tight and dry. "And your proposal would cover my father's debts?"

"All of them."

The pieces slowly fitted together. "In return for me? I confess, I am confused, sir. I cannot cook or—"

His voice went husky; lips caressed her jaw. "I do not want you to cook." He ran his hands down her arms to further illustrate his intent. She shuddered and stepped back, bumping the high worktable behind her and lurching forward to keep her balance. The tribune wrapped one arm around her, pulling her tight against him, pinning both arms to her sides. He buried his face in her neck and raked his free hand through her hair, following it as it tumbled free to the small of her back.

She twisted away. "Please, stop, Tribune. You've given your speech and I must speak with my father before—stop, please!" She wrenched to the side, trying to remember what Titus had told her to do in a situation like this. Her action freed one arm, which she swung toward his face. He caught her wrist and slammed her back against the counter, sending the jars rattling and one crashing to the floor.

"Pater will be back soon," she gasped, shoving his hand from her thigh. "He could legally kill you for this."

"He wouldn't dare." He gripped her wrist until the bones ground together and she cried out.

Iris brought up her knee as hard as she could, but he sidestepped and slapped her face.

Her head snapped back, unable to brace for the blow. She could not hold him off.

"Dorma?" She shrieked the first name that came to mind. *"Dorma!"*

Tribune Braccus tried to cover her mouth with his as the door hit the wall with a noise like a crack of lightning.

"Tribune!"

Titus.

Iris sagged in relief as Braccus released her and took a step back. She sank to the floor, shaking.

Titus's voice was tight with anger or urgency. "I'm glad I found you, sir; you're needed at the Castra Praetoria immediately."

The tribune hesitated and cleared his throat, his voice turning toward Iris. "Think about what I said."

Titus stood at the door until the tribune's boots retreated down the steps, then bolted across the room sending shards of broken pottery skittering across the floor.

"I'll kill him. Are you all right?" He touched her burning face and she flinched away from him. "Did he hurt you?"

Iris pressed her lips together and shook her head. "I'm fine." She reached a hand in his direction. Titus took it and she latched on to him with both hands. "Don't leave." She fought rising panic that he would leave her alone. She began to suck in air, too fast. "Don't leave—I'm fine."

He eased down beside her, and she turned in to him, her whole body shaking uncontrollably as tears came. He wrapped his arms around her.

"Shhh, I won't leave." He stroked her head clumsily, strands of hair catching in the calluses on his hand. "I won't leave you."

As Iris calmed and relaxed against him, she could feel his body stiffening with anger. She pulled away, wrapping her arms around herself. Titus smeared wet strands of hair out of her face.

"I'll kill him," he muttered again.

She caught his hand. "They'll k-kill you if you even th-think it."

"It'd be worth it."

"N-not to me."

"What did he want?"

She tilted her face away. "A mistress."

Titus went still as she explained the proposition and her father's financial situation as per the tribune. He stood and paced the room. She heard him rattle the door and curse under his breath. "Who's to say he's not lying?"

"Pater never said anything, but it'd be just like him not to. Especially with it being my fault."

"It's not your fault." The door rattled again. "If it's anyone's fault, it's mine." He sighed. "I broke the door."

She was glad he had.

A pair of old feet shuffled onto the landing and paused. "My dear?" Dorma's voice wobbled. "My dear, did you need something? I heard you call and came as fast as I could. Is Titus bothering you?"

Iris sat, confused for a moment, before realization dawned. She'd called for Dorma.

"No," she said slowly. "No, I'm sorry. I . . ." Dorma had been the only neighbor she could think of at that moment. Thank goodness Titus had come.

"You moved a lot faster when your chicken was lost," Titus snapped.

"That was a matter of life and death." Dorma's voice softened as she spoke to Iris again. "Are you all right, dear? What happened to your face?"

Iris lifted a hand to her cheek, the skin tender and burning. "I'm—I fell. I'm fine."

The old woman's feet shuffled back across the landing and, with painful slowness, down the stairs.

Titus fumbled through the kitchen utensils and went back to the door. "Where's your father?"

"The Castra Praetoria. Weren't you just there?"

"No."

Her forehead wrinkled. "Then how did you know they were looking for Tribune Braccus?"

"They're not." The door thumped and Titus flipped the lock back and forth with a grunt. "When I saw him—it was the only thing I could think of, short of murder."

Iris pulled her hair back and tugged her dress straight. "Will he be angry when he discovers you lied?"

"I don't care. There," he said, satisfied. "Fixed."

She swallowed. "Thank you," she whispered, afraid if she spoke any louder, she would cry again. "Thank you for coming when you did."

"I was on my way to a meeting," he said. "But I had the strangest feeling I needed to come here first. Thank the gods I did."

"Yes." Her voice went soft as she turned her face toward the shrine. "But which one?"

VIII

TITUS LEFT THE APARTMENT much later than he'd anticipated, waiting until Quintus staggered in, too drunk to hold a proper conversation or comprehend what had happened. Anger flooded him at Quintus's carelessness. In his current state, Quintus would be no match for anyone, but Titus knew Tribune Braccus wouldn't be back. Not tonight, at least.

After crossing the Tiber into the slums where men hawked greasy cakes by day and their daughters by night, he looked for the pre-arranged tavern. Curfew fell with the rumble of delivery carts. The crier announced the third watch and Titus hurried. He hoped he wasn't too late. He brushed his hand over the sword strapped discreetly beneath his tunic under his left arm, but his mind was on Iris and not his mission. The image of her battered face and shaking body sent his own hot with anger. He could have torn Braccus limb from limb right then and there. Part of him wished he had.

Titus turned down another street and the smell of tallow, sour beer, and suspicious seafood told him he was close. He had to calm himself. It would not do for him to be riled and distracted. He needed a clear head.

He reached the tavern and judged it to be the right one based on the advertisements and lurid graffiti painted outside. That, and he recognized two of his men planted across the street watching the building. He went in without acknowledging them.

"Wine," he told the busty slave girl who approached him. He seated himself at a grimy table near the counter and waited for his blood to cool. His feelings for Iris could shift from platonic to something much deeper with little encouragement, but he wouldn't—couldn't—allow himself the temptation of those thoughts. The life of a Praetorian *speculatore* was neither safe nor especially long and therefore among the ranks prohibited from marriage. He would gladly see Iris happily married to another man, but to be reduced to the state of a common prostitute? Over his dead body.

Titus thrummed his fingers on the tabletop and cursed when he hit a drop of something sticky. He wiped his fingers on his faded-green civilian tunic, gaze flicking around the room. Situated on the edge of the Tiber near the docks, the tavern attracted all manner of river rats. Most of them were low-ranking sailors, although Titus noticed a few of higher rank gambling at the corner table. None of them matched the description of the captain he sought. But if Titus's men still waited outside, the target hadn't left.

A slave girl clad in a shade of shocking green set two amphoras before him. She poured him a cup of wine and slid the amphora of water in his direction so he could mix it to his liking. He let his eyes linger over her as she leaned farther than necessary to pass him the cup.

"Anything else?" She twirled a strand of dingy hair around one finger, her voice low and suggestive.

He answered with a half smile, his eyes shifting toward the stairs and back to her. "Maybe."

He tossed back the cup and smothered a curse, pressing his fist against his mouth. This place didn't attract its patrons for the wine, that was certain. She took his hand and tugged him out of the chair, leading him toward the stairs. No one seemed to notice except for the other slave, who heaved a sigh at having to cover more tables.

"I'm Artemis." She sent a practiced shy look over her shoulder.

"I'm sure you are." He scanned the dark landing above and counted three doors. Two had light coming through the cracks. He glanced behind. The steepness of the stairs blocked them from view of the tavern below. As Artemis reached the landing, Titus snaked an arm around her neck and pulled her tight against him, lowering his mouth to her ear.

"Move or make a sound and I'll cut your throat," he hissed. She squeaked and went limp, shaking. A flash of guilt went through him. He'd been ready to tear the tribune apart for terrifying Iris—was he so different? He shook his head to clear it. This was about his job, not his pleasure.

"Where is Petrius Convus?"

A burst of laughter erupted below. Artemis didn't move.

"I know he's here because his men are downstairs." Titus kept his voice low and fought the urge to gag at her overpowering perfume. "You point out his room and I won't hurt you."

She started to lift an arm but hesitated when he added, "Point me wrong and you'll feel my dagger first." He pressed the tip of his thumb into her ribs. She gasped and flinched away.

"Well?"

Her hand shook as she pointed to the door on the right, the one without the light. Keeping one arm around Artemis, he nabbed a lamp out of an empty room. Balancing the girl in one hand and the lamp in the other, he got his footing and kicked down the second door of the night. Petrius Convus bolted out of the bed and Titus simultaneously shoved Artemis at him and dropped the lamp on the table, drawing his sword. The tip was at Convus's throat before the man fully pulled his dagger.

"Captain Petrius Convus?"

"Who wants to know?" The man was dressed in the tunic and loose trousers of a seaman. His sunbrowned and unshaven face betrayed him as a man who'd recently arrived in Rome.

Artemis scrambled against the wall, her eyes wide and darting toward the door. Titus sent her a warning look.

"I have orders to kill you." Titus turned his gaze back to the captain.

"For what?"

"Treason." He watched the man's face for confirmation of the rumors he'd heard. "I'm told you plan to side with Zenobia and cut off trade to Rome."

The eastern edge of the empire had fallen out of Claudius II's control and into the hands of a determined and shrewd woman who called herself Queen Zenobia. They'd received snatches of rumors that she planned to march on Egypt next. If she was successful, the grain ships coming into Rome from Egypt would stop.

Artemis looked between them and shifted to a crouch. Convus laughed and relaxed. "And what proof do you have of this *treason?*"

Titus felt the corner of his mouth lift. "I'm a speculatore. I don't need proof of anything to kill you."

Artemis launched herself at Titus with a shriek, teeth bared. He stumbled sideways into the table, knocking the lamp to the floor. The room dropped into darkness for half a breath before the pool of oil ignited in a burst of orange light. Artemis managed to rip out two fistfuls of hair before Titus twisted sideways, slamming her into the wall and off him. Petrius Convus bolted through the flames and made for the stairs. Titus swung after him, lashing out—and missing—with his *gladius.*

As Titus thundered down the stairs after Convus, Artemis jumped him from behind, sending him headfirst into Convus. The three of them tumbled down in a tangle of arms and thrashing legs. When they came to a jarring stop at the bottom of the stairs, the tavern was silent. Titus picked himself up, panting. Blood streaked his arms. Convus lay crumpled at an awkward angle, the hilt of the gladius protruding from his back. Artemis gave a strangled cry and crawled under a table. Near the door, Titus's men held two of Convus's men at sword point. Everyone stared open-mouthed and speechless as Titus bent to retrieve his gladius and wipe it on Convus's tunic.

He sheathed the sword and straightened his tunic as he headed for the door. "There's a fire upstairs."

He'd be reprimanded for killing Convus like that. Titus had hoped to get answers from him first, but running had been confirmation enough of Convus's part in the scheme.

Titus touched the tender spot on his cheekbone. That crazy wench had given him a black eye, jumping him from behind, and his scalp stung. He would leave her out of the report. No one needed to know a woman had inflicted his injuries.

Titus paced his tiny office. Tucked deep into the Castra Praetoria's record building, the "office" was little more than a storage closet crammed with several broken chairs, a wobbly folding desk, and boxes of outdated files written on tablets whose wax had gone too hard to erase and reuse. Titus had arranged it the best he could. He could pace two whole steps before he had to turn and go the other way. Still, having his own private space where he could think was a luxury unafforded in the barrack quarters he shared with nine other men.

Exhaustion weighted his limbs, but he wouldn't be able to sleep if he tried. He had the restlessness that always accompanied a problem without a solution. Quintus might have been the one to run up all his debts, but Titus was the reason he'd had to, and that made it worse. He dropped onto a box of old files and rubbed his hands over his face. He hadn't realized how deep a hole Quintus had dug for himself. Payment was the only way to call off the tribune, but Quintus wouldn't be able to find money of that kind. Unless . . .

Titus fumbled through a crate of tablets, mentally calculating. If he could retrieve his salary from the Praetorian coffers, it might be enough to at least stall. He pulled a tablet out, his name carefully printed on the spine, and flipped it open, scrolling the stacks of numbers until he reached the balance at the bottom. Not as high as he'd hoped. Even if the monies were not frozen due to the war, the pithy sum would do little in the face of Quintus's debt.

Titus replaced the file, wishing he'd taken the physical pay and put it in a bank in the Forum instead of allowing the money to remain in the Praetorian vault. *Foolish.* He left the makeshift office, stomping down the darkened hall, angry with himself. Iris was blind because of him. If he hadn't been showing off . . . He sighed. Now what? There didn't seem to be any other options.

IX

IRIS SAT ON THE BALCONY in the stillness that came long before dawn, waiting. The chill and damp of the night had not yet lifted, nor would it. The air hung heavy with imminent rain. A dove cooed and its mate answered. She relished the quiet before Silvia would begin barking at her slaves in the laundry below, signaling to Iris that she'd best get to the bakery.

Her father groaned. His bed creaked as he rolled upright and climbed from it. First a step, then a shuffle as his weaker leg dragged slightly. The wood floor crackled beneath his weight as he made for the kitchen.

Iris stood. "Good morning, Pater."

"Iris." Quintus's voice was rough with sleep. "You're awake early."

"I'm not usually visited by Tribune Braccus in the evening."

She heard a thump and a creak as he dropped onto the bench. "That was real?"

"Is it true? What he said?" She crossed her arms. Across the hall, a baby sputtered and started to cry.

Her father took a deep breath as if to explain but said only, "What did he say?"

She took a step forward. "That you were in debt because of me. A debt so deep you couldn't pay it in four years, much less in four months." She swallowed and went on when her father did not deny it. "And that he offered to pay the debt in return for me to become his . . . his . . ." She couldn't bring herself to say the word.

He cursed, not quite under his breath. "Come inside and shut that door."

She obeyed but remained on the opposite side of the room.

Her father sighed. "I was going to tell you." She heard the sound of callused hands rubbing against an unshaven face. "But I wanted to wait until I was certain we had no other options."

"And then what? Surprise me on the day he comes to claim me?" She fought panic from her voice as he confirmed her fears. "I thought we did not keep things from each other, Pater." Even as she spoke, she thought about Valentine and guilt pricked her conscience. She pushed it away.

"You shouldn't have to worry about our finances."

"I do when it concerns me being sold to pay your debts."

She heard him rise and potter through the kitchen looking for something to eat. Bread clunked on the table followed by an amphora and two cups.

"*I'll* be sold to a quarry to work off the debts." He sawed at the bread with a knife. "I'm trying to protect you."

"You were not protecting me when the tribune showed up last night and might have forced himself on me if Titus hadn't intervened."

The knife clattered on the table. Her father fell silent. "I'm sorry." His voice cracked and broke. "I did not agree to his offer. I merely listened. He should not have come here. He should not have—"

She moved toward him, shoving her anger beneath a lid of calm. "Is it really as bad as he said?"

Pater was quiet for so long Iris thought he would never answer. "Yes." His voice came low and hoarse. "And I don't know what to do. If I don't agree, I'll be sold to work in the mines and you'll be sold too, but in your condition there's not much for you besides . . . At least the tribune is only *one* man."

The memory of his hands on her set her whole body shaking. "Is there no other way?"

He didn't answer. Fear wrapped around her ribs. She felt as

trapped as she had when she'd awakened to find her world suddenly plunged into a darkness she couldn't escape. She sank onto a stool and gripped the edge of the table, trying to keep the panic at bay as her brain spun for solutions.

"Iris."

She barely heard Pater speak.

"It's going to be all right." His voice sounded far away, like he was talking to her from deep inside the sewer tunnels of the Cloaca Maxima. Echoing, hollow, full of—

"This is all my fault." The words nearly choked her.

"No." Pater spoke in a soothing voice, but he'd hesitated long enough to make tears spill down her cheeks. "*I* borrowed the money."

"But you borrowed it for all the physicians and offerings. You borrowed it for *me*."

"And I'd do it all again." A cup banged on the table in emphasis.

She heard the high-pitched gurgle of liquid poured into a cup and the clunk of the jug being set down again. The sound of him drinking and swallowing.

"Can you renegotiate the repayment time?"

He didn't answer and she assumed he'd shaken his head.

"What can we sell?"

"There is nothing." He sighed, defeated.

"We can't just give up, Pater. There must be something we can do." She shuddered. "I won't go with him. I'll die first."

They sat in silence, thinking.

"Could we run?" Iris asked. If they could run as fast as her whirling thoughts, they might have a chance.

"We don't have the funds to get very far."

"But if we sold our things, ate only the bread Paulina gives me, and saved my earnings?"

Quintus sighed again and she heard him scratching his head. "Perhaps," he wheezed. It took Iris a moment to realize he was crying.

"Pater, please don't." She pressed her lips together, still angry and in no mood to comfort him.

She blinked. Her father's shape swam into focus, bathed in the yellow light of a lamp.

Her heart seized in her chest. She gasped and stared.

He looked just as she remembered him, though lines etched deeper grooves on his face. Gray swaths cut into the short brown hair just above his ears. He needed a shave. A white scar ran through the black stubble across his throat from a prisoner's escape attempt. He pressed the heels of his hands into his eyes, wide shoulders shaking.

"Pater." All anger drained into shock. Her chest began to heave as she realized that what she saw was real. "Pater, I can see you."

His head jerked up. "What?"

"I can see you." Terror that she would blink and lose him again choked her awe.

He leaped to his feet, the battered wooden stool clattering behind him. "But how?" His eyes darted toward the shrine.

She shook her head. "I don't know—but I see you. Your blue tunic is wrinkly. Silvia needs to wash it. You need a shave—"

Iris blinked.

Something like a fish scale dropped over her vision, flickering with light yet clouded and blurred.

"I didn't—I didn't pray yesterday." Confusion masked her father's voice. "I couldn't. I didn't know what to say."

She heard him move around the table. Felt his hands on her shoulders, then cradling her face in their rough gentleness.

"I—It's blurring now." Her mind caught on his words. *He* hadn't prayed. *She* certainly hadn't. But Valentine had said he'd been praying. She blinked again. The scale remained, filtering in the flickering yellow lamplight and dusky shadows and the undefined darkness of her father's face.

"It's black again?" Acute disappointment stung his words. His hands dropped from her face.

She shook her head. "I see a dim light. I just . . . I can't see you anymore."

"This is good. We must be close to appeasement." He moved to the lararium, where she heard him arranging the figures and pouring a libation of wine. Two images played repeatedly before her darkened eyes. The bird's black shadow skittering over her feet and, far dearer, her father's face. The tribune nearly forgotten, giddy excitement coursed through her. Perhaps, perhaps the curse was beginning to lift.

Silvia's screeching from the laundry announced the arrival of dawn. With hurried thanks to the gods, Iris and Quintus left the apartment for Paulina's Bakery. If her feet sprouted wings, Iris doubted she would feel lighter. They chattered the whole way as if repeating what had happened over and over would reassure them that it was real.

A thought flickered to life in the hard layer of parched doubt in her mind. She squashed it.

No.

But when the thought came back, she didn't crush it again. It had taken root. What did she have to lose? Today, if Valentine came into the bakery, she would confront him.

Iris fidgeted. Epimandos would be back soon and Valentine had not come. She'd moved through the morning, distracted and quiet—much to Epimandos's delight, which was rather difficult to discern from his usual gloom and doom. The rain had slowed the late-morning shoppers to a trickle, and Iris stood behind the counter, bored and on edge. The more she longed for Valentine to walk through the door, the more annoyed she became for wanting him to. *He* had obviously not thought about her as much as *she* had thought of him.

The door in the back opened and shut. Epimandos had made his deliveries with surprising speed despite the rain. Disappointment swirled in her gut. Hesitating a moment more, she moved to the back room and traded her apron for her heavy palla. Water dripped from Epimandos as he exchanged his wet tunic for a dry one.

"The street is a river." Epimandos wrung water from his tunic. "My sandals are ruined. I am soaked. I will probably catch cold and die."

"But the shop would be so dreary without you to cheer it up."

Iris wrapped the palla over her head and shoulders. "At least wait until Paulina comes back before you get sick and die. I can't make the deliveries."

Epimandos sniffed and walked past her into the front of the shop. "This place would fall apart without me."

She took her walking stick and followed him, intending to leave through the front door, where she could walk beneath the protection of the barrel-roofed arcade over the market street.

Baskets crackled as Epimandos checked the contents. "Are we having fewer customers? Is it because Paulina is gone? I knew this was going to happen."

"It's probably the rain. No need to tell anyone we're going out of business just yet." Iris opened the door and stepped outside. "Have a good afternoon, Epimandos."

"Hmmm."

She shut the door behind her, leaving the bright warmth of the bakery for the breezy dampness of the Via Biberatica. Iris shuffled her way down the curved street, mentally ticking off the vendors as she passed them. Yanni's Silk Slippers, the sponge and pumice stone shop, Neptune's Oyster Bar, and Praxtus Perfumes across the street—which no one could miss. The door of the perfumery opened and shut, wafting a cloud of mismatched scent into the street. Iris held her breath.

"Iris!"

Her pulse jumped as Valentine's sandals splashed across the street. She paused, concentrating on arranging her features into an expression that didn't appear too eager and relieved to meet him again.

"Shopping for new perfume?" She coughed as Valentine arrived in a haze of burning scent.

"Oh no." He shuddered. "Although my aunt would love nothing more. Are you going home?"

"Yes."

"By yourself?"

"I'm not incapable of navigating."

"Forgive me, I didn't mean—only when I ran into you the first time, the Praetorian came." He trailed off. "I didn't know if you were meeting . . . someone."

"Not this time," she said. "Titus—*the Praetorian*—is an old friend. On the rare occasion he's nearby, he walks me home."

"Do you live near here?"

"Cedar Street. Do you know it?"

"No." Valentine patted something—a satchel? "I'm headed to the Quirinal Hill district. Is it on the way?"

"For part of it."

"Can I walk with you?"

Iris hesitated. She didn't know him, not really, and Tribune Braccus's attack left her uneasy at the thought of even walking on a busy street with a strange man. But she desperately wanted answers— if he could, or would, give them. A busy street was as safe as she was going to get. She started walking. "Why do you talk to me?"

"What do you mean?"

She tucked a loose strand of hair behind her ear and tugged the edge of her palla lower over her face. "Most people ignore me or, if they must talk to me, act as if I am an imbecile."

"That sounds frustrating and lonely."

"Sometimes."

Water ran in rivulets down the street, chilling Iris's feet. She wasn't sure how to broach the subject of his god, so said instead, "You never came back to the bakery."

"I've had early meetings with clients lately. I've been dying for a raisin pastry." There was a dull thumping sound as he patted his stomach. "Though goodness knows I don't need them. As my aunt so kindly reminds me."

Metal pans clanged as they neared Minotaur's Table, warm smells curling through the open doorway and onto the street. Iris's stomach growled.

"You've mentioned your aunt twice now. Does she live with you?" She pressed her arm over her stomach, hoping he hadn't heard.

He hesitated. "I live with *her*, more like. She raised me after my mother died and my pater—well, that's a long story."

"I'm sorry," Iris murmured. "I lost my mother too. Do you work in the market?"

"I'm a notarius. Left or right on Alta?"

"Then you work in the Basilica Julia? Take a right on Alta, left on Cedar Street."

"You know it?"

"It's my favorite building in the Forum." She held up her hand, palm toward him. "The Basilica Aemilia is beautiful, too, with all those pink-and-black-speckled columns, but the Julia holds my heart. Pater used to take me there to watch the trials when I was little."

She sensed his gaze and immediately felt heat climb into her cheeks. "What?"

"Nothing," he said. "I've never met a woman with such passion for architecture before."

"Much less a blind one?"

He didn't say anything.

She traced her finger over the rippled scar on her temple that her palla had slipped back to reveal. "I haven't always been blind, you know. I tried to see the world from the top of an aqueduct and fell." Her stomach rolled the way it had when she'd taken those first hesitant steps after Titus. He'd been right. The city from that perspective did steal her breath. And then the strength in her knees. The sight from her eyes when the view rushed up to meet her.

She stopped in the street and turned to face him. "Which brings me to the questions I have for you."

His swallow sounded like it hurt. "Yes?"

They stood just under the edge of the barrel roof where the Via Biberatica met the main road. Rain poured down, splattering on the street in wet snaps. Iris could feel the drops wetting the hem of her dress. She took a deep breath. Now or never.

"You said you would pray for me." She balled both hands on the top of her walking stick. "Did you? Don't say yes if you didn't. I—I need the truth."

"I did." His voice was low, almost breathless. "Why?"

She sucked in a breath, trying and failing to calm the sudden pounding of her heart. Her voice dropped to a whisper. "Because every time I see you and you promise to pray for me, I've had flashes of sight afterward—just for a few seconds and it's gone again."

There. It was out. She had finally admitted it aloud. Her pulse rushed in her ears. He didn't say anything.

"Was it you?" she asked.

He hesitated. "No."

Her gut plummeted.

"If it was anyone, it was my God."

Tears burned in her throat. "Why would your god do this? Why toy with me?"

Valentine's hand settled on top of hers, warm and solid and kind. Vastly different from the tribune's greedy touch. "He's not toying with you, Iris. He's *calling* you."

"Calling *me*? For what purpose?"

"He calls us all to—" He didn't finish. In the next moment, he'd withdrawn his hand and taken a step back. "I'm sorry." His voice laced with something like panic. "This is Alta Path. Can you find your way home from here?"

Taken aback by his sudden change, she could only stammer in reply.

"There he is!" a new voice growled far to her right. It was unfamiliar, male, and rough.

Footsteps crunched through the rain.

"Go home quickly," Valentine said in a rush. "If I don't see you again soon, find Beatrix—the perfumer. She can help you. And be careful."

Just like that, he left again and took all her answers with him.

X

"Hector." Valens forced a stiff smile. "How's Lillith?" Dread
grew in his gut as he flicked his gaze between Hector and the two
men with shoulders like bulls who flanked the ex-legionnaire. They
were going to clap his wrists in irons; Valens was sure of it. His eyes
darted toward Iris, still standing where he left her, looking as if she
could not decide whether to go home or sit and cry. His heart twisted,
but he would not drag her into whatever this was.

"Not here." Hector's lips barely moved as he spoke. "We need you
to come with us."

Dwarfed by the colossus of the three men, Valens didn't have
much choice but to comply. They surrounded him, one on either side
and one just behind. Iris had begun to pick her way down the edge
of Alta Path. As the three men escorted him away, Valens prayed she
would safely find her way home and find his aunt for her questions.
He might not see her again.

"What is this about?" Valens asked in a feigned tone of innocence.
"Where are we going?"

"Not yet," Hector clipped from behind. They cut between the
forums of Trajan and Augustus where clusters of men argued phi-
losophy under the porticoes near the libraries. Rain plastered his hair
to his forehead and stuck his tunic to his skin. The carcer came into
view and his pulse quickened. This was it. He'd made an illegal contract with a speculatore and now he would pay the price. But they

walked past the prison and kept going. They were not headed in the direction of the Praetorian Fortress, but they could just as easily dispatch him in an empty alley. The white-and-gold temple of Jupiter towered above them on Capitoline Hill, full of figures in flapping robes. He caught a glimpse of several augurs with their curled wands, then turned his focus back to the march. The four kept a quick pace until they'd crossed the white Pons Aemilius bridge. No one spoke. No one took notice of three brutes escorting a man out of the city. Anyone who did notice would probably think he hadn't paid rent and needed to be taught a lesson. They'd kill him quietly outside the city.

The Via Aurelia carried them to a small, run-down inn far outside the walls of the old city—a place for travelers who didn't have the money for an inn closer to the Forum. The three herded Valens into the humid warmth of the adjacent tavern and pushed him to an empty table of greasy dark wood covered in a sticky film. The walls of the place had once been pale-golden block but were stained dark with the grime of smoke, grease, and unwashed hands. The men settled around him, one beside and two across the table. One of the men, not Hector, hailed the tavern keeper for wine.

At this time of day, after lunch and before the midafternoon rush, the tavern was quiet. Two of the four other patrons looked like they'd been drinking since the night before, and the others were silently eating a grayish soup. The tavern keeper, a barrel-shaped man with spindly legs and gray hair matted into long cords, brought them four cups, water, and an amphora of cheap wine.

Surprised and relieved not to have been gutted in an alley, Valens didn't dare refuse the wine. "What is this about?" he asked.

No one answered until they had each taken a drink. Hector flicked his eyes around the room before leaning forward and resting his forearms on the table.

"What you did for Lillith and me. That took courage."

The unease in Valens's gut lifted slightly. That did not sound like the speech of a man about to kill him or drag him to the magistrate. He hazarded a glance toward the other two.

"But?" He waited.

"I don't know what changed your mind." Hector tipped his head and took a drink. "But I won't forget the look on my Lill's face when you came with the contract."

Valens squinted. *All this to say thank you?*

The other two men set their cups on the table and turned questioning looks on Valens.

Hector lowered his voice further. "Will you do it again?"

XI

QUINTUS LURCHED TO HIS FEET with a salute and a deep bow when the old man entered, draped in pristine white robes bearing a red- and purple-striped border. A crow perched on his shoulder, glittering like charred wood. He did not require an introduction.

"It is an honor indeed to be graced with the presence of the chief augur of Jupiter, Best and Greatest." Quintus slowly straightened. "I am in your service."

Gaius Favius Diastema, chief augur and interpreter of the will of Rome's highest deity, glanced around the room before answering. "I would speak with you privately, Jailor." Rain dripped down the sides of his balding head, soaking the neck of his robe. The crow tilted his head, centering Quintus in one obsidian eye.

Quintus nodded. "We are alone."

Favius hesitated, rubbing a liver-spotted thumb along the worn spot on the curved divining rod he held. Quintus waited, hardly believing his good fortune. He'd meant to purchase a meeting with the augurs and have them divine through the flight pattern of the birds whether Iris would see again. He'd never imagined the chief augur would come to *him*. The gods were surely smiling upon him today.

Gaius Favius lifted his chin and took a deep breath. "I need you to arrest someone for me." He kept his voice low. "Off the record."

Quintus waited in vain for the augur to elaborate. "What are the grounds for arrest?"

Favius shifted. "None yet."

"To knowingly arrest and hold an innocent would put my job and reputation at great risk." Quintus's mind raced over the ramifications. No one could be imprisoned on suspicion alone, and besides, the carcer was more of a halfway point between conviction and execution or banishment.

"The arrest must take place under utmost secrecy. There can be no witnesses; do you understand? The arrest happens *sub rosa* or not at all."

Quintus opened his mouth but said nothing. Chief augur or not, how could he risk his reputation, his livelihood, his daughter—for such a venture? Yet perhaps . . .

The augur's eyes narrowed. "I will protect your reputation and reward you, *handsomely*."

At this, Quintus's head lifted. How handsomely? Enough to get him and Iris out of Rome? Enough to pay the debts?

The augur's eyes sparked with triumph and the crow reared his head back with a sharp cackle. Quintus gave a quick nod when Favius named the target and his price.

"I will do it." An idea lit within him. "But my condition is this: You must ask Jupiter, Best and Greatest, if he will restore sight to my daughter. When he answers, I will do as you say."

Irritation flashed through the old man's eyes at the bargaining, but he agreed to perform the auguries.

A week passed before a messenger arrived at the carcer with a single word.

Yes.

Hope surging, Quintus began his search.

XII

VALENS WANDERED THROUGH THE PUBLIC GARDEN covering a large portion of Caelian Hill, looking for the meeting place he'd been directed to. He hadn't told anyone about the ex-legionnaires and thinking about them now only brought his mind back to Iris. He'd tried multiple times in the last week to find her again, but his duties had brought him into the office earlier and earlier and kept him so late in the afternoon that by the time he got to the bakery, Iris had already gone. He prayed the opportunity to speak with her again would come soon and that her willingness to hear the truth would not be hindered by the way he'd left her the last time. He winced at the memory.

Low shrubs wearing the crinkled, wilting leaves of early autumn adorned the terraces cut into the rise of the hill. Cypress and palms stood tall, the untrimmed dead fronds rustling in the damp breeze. Valens hurried toward the cedar grove ahead that provided cover amid the sparse autumnal gardens. That must be it. All thoughts of Iris were put aside for the moment as he entered the ring of trees.

As promised, three couples and two additional men waited in the grove, faces upturned as if wondering if the clouds would empty rain upon them. Better if they did. There would be less chance of anyone else happening upon them.

He lifted a hand, recognizing Hector and Lillith and the two ex-soldiers Hector had introduced at their compulsory meeting.

The brides, in traditional saffron-colored veils, were older than most women entering marriage but still within childbearing age. Valens glanced at the other two men, standing apart, arms crossed. Their presence filled the requirement for five witnesses. Hector didn't bother with introductions but gave Valens a look that assured him they could be trusted.

Valens removed his leather satchel from beneath his cloak and laid it on the round sundial that had no doubt been placed in the grove long before the trees had grown around it, rendering it useless in shadow and green moss. The couples shuffled closer.

"We didn't know if you'd really come." Hector's voice was low.

"I said I would." Valens pulled out two scrolls, a bottle of ink, and a box of reed pens from the bag. "But if you wish to proceed, we will do things my way."

Hector glanced at the two grooms, who nodded but looked wary. Valens lit a small lamp he'd brought and set it on the sundial, although they had no need of light.

"Corbulus and Galatia, yes?" Valens turned to the couple on his right. The one-eyed soldier gave a single nod while the pale-haired woman beside him smiled shyly and leaned into his side.

"And Felix and Vinia?"

"Yes." The barrel-chested soldier put an arm around the woman with graying hair and a young face.

Valens gestured. "Stand here, Felix and Corbulus, and face your intended."

The two men did as they were told and stood shoulder to shoulder, facing the two women, who stood across from them. Lillith and Hector clutched each other's hands and watched from the side. A chill breeze shifted through the grove, causing the cedar branches to lift and droop and the yellowy-orange veils to billow.

"Take each other's hands."

They did as Valens directed. He bowed his head. "Lord God, Creator of heaven and earth, You have made man and woman for each other and for relationship with You. I ask Your blessing on these couples who are here despite a man-made law and have pledged themselves to each other." He opened his eyes and ignored the wide-eyed looks the eight turned on him as he invoked the blessing of a god Rome did not sanction. As long as he was breaking one law, he might as well keep going.

"The path you have chosen is difficult," Valens continued. "What we're doing here is dangerous and illegal. *Treason*—and yet, here you stand, gazing at each other as if death is of little consequence if the alternative is remaining apart." He paused, feeling an uncomfortable flicker of envy as he watched the couples glowing at each other as if unaware he was even speaking.

The sky began to spit.

"Will you, Galatia and Vinia, pledge to remain faithful wives, loving and respecting your husbands until death parts you?"

The women nodded. "I will," they said.

The wind fluttered the contracts on the sundial. Valens reached behind him and held them down with one hand. "And will you, Corbulus and Felix, pledge to remain faithful to your wives, protecting and providing for them, loving them better than yourselves as Christ so loved the world and gave Himself for it?"

Their eyebrows puckered in confusion, but they nodded. "I will," they answered in unison and produced simple iron rings they slipped onto the third fingers of Vinia's and Galatia's left hands.

Valens unrolled the scrolls and heated a stick of imperial red wax above the guttering lamp flame before smearing a glob next to his signature and pressing a fisted hand into it, setting the notarius seal into the wax. The men gathered and mirrored his actions with their own seals.

Valens snuffed the lamp and rolled up the contracts. His lips lifted in a smile as he placed the sundial to his back and faced the couples.

"It is my honor, then, to pronounce you man—*men* and wives."

Hector and Lillith beamed. Galatia smiled without showing her teeth as she leaned against Corbulus. Felix, however, swung Vinia off her feet and lifted her high enough to press an enthusiastic kiss on her mouth.

"All right, you two." Hector laughed and slapped Felix's shoulder. "There'll be time enough for that later."

Valens grinned and handed each couple their rolled contract before packing his things. He tucked the bag over his shoulder beneath his cloak.

"Come with us." Hector gripped Valens's shoulder. "I and some men from my legion have bought a tavern across from the Forum of Augustus. Have a drink with us to celebrate."

Valens smiled but shook his head. "I'd better get home."

Hector's grip tightened, as did his smile. "Please." The other four men watched expectantly. "There is something we must discuss."

A latticework of climbing roses partially covered the open front of the Centaur's Cup. The others had abandoned them at the entrance, and Hector seated Valens at a table near the back with the explanation that women were strictly prohibited.

"Lillith's orders." He shrugged and fetched two cups of wine from the barrels behind the counter. There were few patrons. Outside, the rain began falling in earnest, slapping the paving stones.

"Quintus!" Hector slapped the blue-clad back of a middle-aged man slouched over the counter. "Good to see you. How've you been?" The man, Quintus, mumbled something in response and Hector shook his head. "This one's on me." He refilled the man's cup. Before returning to Valens, Hector caught the server behind the counter and spoke into his ear, flicking glances between Quintus and Valens. When he returned, his grin looked forced.

"We'll have to speak carefully," Hector muttered beneath his breath as he passed Valens a cup and sat across from him. "That's the carcer jailor." He tilted his head toward the man who looked about to fall asleep in his cups.

"What's this about?" Valens asked.

Hector hesitated and took a drink before answering. "Like my friends and I, many of the men from my legion, the Secondus Parthica, have returned home after serving their term. Men who have risked their lives and proven their bravery and loyalty to the empire time and again. Men who have been repaid with dishonor and disrespect." He took a breath and glanced at Quintus, who stumbled toward the door, aided by the server. "You're a good man."

Valens already suspected what request would follow this stroke of his ego and waited for it in silence.

"A brave man," Hector continued, eyeing Quintus, who wove his way outside.

"A stupid man, some would say." Valens shifted in his seat.

Hector's mouth tipped slightly. "You know what I am about to ask, and I assure you, you will have the loyalty and protection of my men if you agree. We've given our best years to serve the empire, and Emperor Claudius Gothicus has rewarded us by withholding our right of connubium and the bearing of legal heirs. I am asking you to show pity on my men and do for them as you've already done for me and my friends."

Valens took a breath. How could he refuse? He'd committed the act of treason already. Still, the consequences of the request weighed heavily and had been sitting not twenty feet from him—albeit drunk. Valens traced his thumbnail over the lines etched into the side of his clay cup. What he'd done was risky, though it hadn't seemed terribly dangerous. But if he continued, would he put Bea at risk?

"If I agree, this cannot be traced to my family." Valens looked up. "I want no messages sent to my home. We do everything at night."

Hector hesitated at the last condition but nodded anyway. "Agreed."

"How do you suggest we communicate?"

Hector brightened. "The tavern is covered with roses." He waved a hand toward the doorway. "When there is a *meeting* for you to attend, I will hang a rose above the door. It will be inconspicuous enough."

Valens looked at the doorway and slowly nodded. Hanging roses above a dinner table or from a tavern ceiling was common enough. To be sub rosa—*under the rose*—meant to maintain a vow of utmost secrecy and confidentiality.

"And where will these *meetings* take place?" Valens asked. "No homes, no apartments—the risk of being overheard is too great."

Hector took a drink. "Public gardens. There are many; we can establish an order and rotate. To offset the danger of being in the city at night, my men will act as escorts and guards, and witnesses when needed."

He'd clearly thought this through.

Valens gave another slow nod. "You trust your men to remain sub rosa?"

"They'd be fools not to be if their names are sealed as witnesses."

"Then I agree." Valens held out his hand and the men gripped arms.

"Watch for the rose."

City of Rome
Ides of Februarius, AD 270

His hands are tied behind his back. Black and purple and swollen
beyond recognition.

His fingers have been crushed one by one. The names demanded
of him left unspoken. He's been beaten, seared with red-hot irons,
stretched on a rack, denied food and water. Still he stands.

Still he refuses to give in. To die.

Even as the stands scream to save their hero, one glance at the
emperor's purple-draped box where the Praetorian prefect sits tells
him he will not be spared. The prefect's arms wave, though he cannot hear the shouted orders. A blue tide sweeps down the aisles of the
stands—Praetorian Guards armed to the teeth and ready to quell the
crowd. They'd kill every person in the stands before the prefect would
let word get to the emperor that he'd let a riot break out. The shouts
begin to die as the guards do their job with clubs and the pommels
of their swords.

His eyes slam shut, lips moving. "Not on my account, Lord.
Don't let anyone die on my account." No one can hear him over the
Praetorians enforcing the quiet that follows.

A trapdoor in the arena floor drops into the underground hypogeum *and three men emerge in studded leather loincloths carrying
clubs stained dark with old blood.*

He is not sorry for what he has done, but he has one regret.

Just one.

XIII

Stomach in knots and sweat on her hairline, Iris entered the perfume shop to a gaggle of high-pitched voices and the clashing aromas of rose and basil. She sneezed.

Valentine had not been back to the bakery, or if he had, Iris had not been aware. Paulina had returned, smug and triumphant, claiming she had single-handedly overthrown the tyranny of the Guild of Grain Millers. Iris had not run into Valentine again, nor had she any other glimpses of sight, despite her renewal of devotion to the gods. She had held off visiting the perfumer, hoping Valentine would show up, but her desperation had won out in the end. She wanted answers. So she'd braved the crowds and cloying smells and stepped inside.

"Good afternoon!" a bright voice called over all the others. "Welcome! I'm having a sale today. Everything on the left side of the shop is half-price." The voice grew quieter as it drew closer. "Ah, you're the girl from Paulina's."

"I'm Iris."

"Beatrix." The woman spoke as if her name was every bit as exciting as the sale. "But most people call me Bea. What can I help you find today? I have a lovely new scent called Summer Holiday."

"Actually . . ." Iris swallowed. A bead of sweat ran down her hairline toward her ear. If Valentine wouldn't answer her questions about the Christian god and had run away instead, how could she be sure the perfumer wouldn't do the same? "I have some questions, but not about—"

"Excuse me? What is the price on this basil balm?" a female voice interrupted.

"One moment." Beatrix patted Iris's arm. Her voice went loud again as she called, "Excellent choice! The basil balm is on sale and one of my most popular scents!" Beatrix moved farther away to collect payment from another customer.

Iris chewed her lip. She didn't like crowded spaces. Nor spaces filled with small breakable things. Someone bumped her shoulder and she shifted out of the way, her hip knocking against the edge of a table. The sound of bottles clinking against each other made her cringe and freeze.

"I'm so sorry." She clutched her walking stick close to her chest and didn't dare to move an inch.

"Excuse me?" A woman tapped her arm. "Excuse me, can you hand me that blue bottle? The one over there with the red stopper?"

"I—me?" Iris's face went hot. "I can't."

"Oh." The woman reached past Iris, jarring her elbow.

Beatrix did not return in "one moment," getting accosted on all sides and bombarded with questions. Iris carefully shuffled toward the door and the fresh air beyond. A sale day was not the time to come asking questions.

"Now, dear—" Beatrix suddenly blocked her exit—"what can I do for you? I'm so sorry for your wait. Today has been a little hectic." She gave a frazzled chuckle.

"Valentine told me you could answer some questions about the Christian god." Iris's voice dropped near a whisper. "But today's not a day for conversation."

Beatrix didn't answer right away, and Iris could feel the weight of her hesitation. Then she took a breath.

"Ladies?" Beatrix turned away, directing her voice back toward the interior. "Forgive me, but I'm going to have to close early today. The sale will still be running in the morning, if you'd like to return."

"Oh, don't close your shop. I'll come back later." Iris turned to leave once more. "It's fine. My questions can wait."

"Nonsense. You're here now. My sale is not as important as your questions."

Despite the moans of protest, the shop emptied quickly. As women filed past her, Iris stood dumbstruck that a stranger would close her bustling shop simply to talk to *her*. No one talked to her. Much less a stranger.

Stillness descended as Beatrix closed the door after the last customer.

"Blessed silence." Beatrix sighed and touched Iris's arm. "Come," she said. "I have some chairs in the back room and we can heat a little water for *calda*. Would you like peppermint or lavender?"

Iris allowed herself to be led, curiosity banishing her unease. "Either one."

In the back room Beatrix released her arm and Iris froze, afraid if she moved and broke something, Bea wouldn't answer her questions. Beatrix fumbled with a little iron brazier, flues screeching open and coals scraping as she poked them and blew them to life.

"Oh, please, sit, *sit*." Water trickled into a kettle.

Iris shifted, uncomfortable. "Where would you like me to sit?"

"Oh, goodness! I'm sorry." Beatrix's hand once again found her arm and she shuffled Iris a few steps. "There, the chair's right behind you."

Iris reached back and felt for the chair, carefully lowering herself into it as Beatrix settled across from her.

"Now." Beatrix heaved a contented sigh. "How do you know my nephew?"

"I met him in the market and then he came into Paulina's."

"I love meeting Val's friends. I fear he doesn't make enough friends his own age, but you must be much younger—how old are you, dear?"

Iris's cheeks warmed. One and twenty wasn't what anyone would call *young*. She answered and Beatrix gushed on, barely stopping for breath. "Valens is two and thirty. You're not that far apart in age; how wonderful."

Whatever Beatrix had interpreted, Iris certainly hadn't gone so far as to compare her and Valentine's age compatibility. She was interested in his *god*. Anxiety prickled her stomach. What if she told Beatrix about the flashes of sight and she didn't believe her? What if she laughed and thought Iris addled in the head?

"I . . ." The word came out on the back of a long exhale. Her mind ran. "I don't even know where to begin." Iris carefully laid her walking stick on the ground at her feet. "Valentine told me the Christian god was calling me. That he could restore my sight."

"Ah." Beatrix elongated the word with understanding. "You're the jailor's daughter, aren't you?"

Iris's hopes sank as she nodded. Beatrix would never answer her questions now.

"How long have you been blind? Don't mind me, I'll just fix our calda."

"Seven years."

Cups clicked as Bea set them down. "You would have been, what, fourteen? That must have been very difficult."

"Yes." It had been difficult. And terrifying, depressing, lonely, achingly sad. And once she'd spiraled to the bottom of that pit, the climb out was long and slow. Some days she still felt herself sliding back in. "But anymore I've grown used to it—thank you." Iris took the warm cup Bea nudged against her knuckles. The sharp scent of peppermint rose on the steam. "I think it bothers other people more. My pater and Titus, they—I can tell they pity me, and I wish they wouldn't."

Beatrix let her talk, encouraging her, asking questions here and there in a kind voice. Iris talked on and on, sipping the calda and beginning to feel safe and comfortable and . . . and strangely enough, loved. By a stranger. When her stomach rumbled loudly, she gasped.

"What time is it? How long have I been here, rambling?"

"It's near dinnertime, I suppose." Beatrix's chair creaked. "Will you eat with me? I'm afraid I've asked you too many questions and you haven't asked me any."

Iris shook her head. "Pater will wonder after me, and I've imposed on you long enough."

"Nonsense. It's been an utter pleasure getting to know you. You're such a sweet thing."

Iris bit her lip; if she didn't ask now, she might never get the nerve again. "Do you believe in the Christian god?"

"I do." Beatrix's voice went low and serious. "His name is Jesus."

"Jesus." A shiver ran down her spine as Iris repeated the name. "Valentine said he could restore my sight."

"Yes, He can." Beatrix's tone implied there was a *but*. Iris waited for her to continue.

"He *can*, but that does not always mean He *will*."

Iris's shoulders sank. "Then he is not so different from all the other gods." She fought irritating tears of disappointment into the back of her throat. "They all *can*, but they don't."

"No," Beatrix said even more softly. "They don't because they can't."

"And yours can but doesn't. How is that different?"

"It is vastly different." Beatrix's cup clinked against a table. "And difficult to understand."

"Valentine told me this—this *Jesus* god could heal me. That he called to me. Why is he calling me? What does he want?"

"Ah." Beatrix's chair creaked as if she settled herself deeper into it. "Now *that* is a question I *can* answer."

Iris waited.

"Long ago God spoke to His people, Israel, through a prophet, revealing who He is and what He has done for all those who choose Him over all other gods. 'But now, O Jacob, listen to the Lord who created you. O Israel, the one who formed you says, "Do not be afraid, for I have ransomed you. I have called you by name; you are mine."'" Beatrix spoke in quiet reverence, and the words echoed deep within Iris with a power that made her scalp prickle. "'"When you go through deep waters, I will be with you. When you go through rivers of difficulty, you will not drown. When you walk through the fire of oppression, you will not be burned up; the flames will not consume you. For I am the Lord your God.""'

Iris's throat burned. As much as she hated to admit it, fear clung to her heart as naturally as weaving came to her fingertips. She found safety in habit and routine. Or at least, she had. This god seemed far, far from safe, yet safety was what he offered? She wanted it, wanted to know more—yet another voice whispered doubts. How could this god offer safety when his followers were thrown into prisons and fed to the arenas? How could this powerlessness help her?

Iris nodded at Beatrix as if she were a madwoman babbling on a street corner. "Thank you." She picked up her cane and stood. "But I should be going now. I will think on what you've said."

"Oh, but there's so much more." Beatrix spoke as if taken aback by her abruptness.

Iris slid her cane in front of her, searching for the doorway. "I have to go; my pater will worry. But thank you for the calda and conversation." She hesitated. "It was very kind of you to stop everything for me."

Beatrix took her arm and together they made for the front of the shop. "Please stop in anytime you like, dear." She took a breath. "My nephew has been very busy lately—working all hours—but he would love to answer your questions, I'm sure."

Iris stepped outside. The wind had picked up since her entrance into the shop. Beatrix followed her out and locked the door behind them.

"Will you find your way home all right?"

"Yes." Iris smiled.

Beatrix clasped Iris's hand in both of hers, her grip warm and firm. "If God is calling you, you are right to seek Him. He is not far from those who seek Him with their whole hearts." She whispered, "I will pray you find Him."

XIV

VALENS'S CHEEK RESTED against his pillow. One eye opened. Shut. Opened again. Jerking upright in a panic, he yanked a tunic over his head and snagged his sandals by the laces, bolting for the door.

"Is there a fire, Valens?" Bea faced the polished bronze mirror set into the wall in the main room where it caught the best morning light.

"Sorry, Aunt Bea, I'm late."

She chuckled and turned a face smothered in white cream toward him. "Late? The market is hours from opening. I just got up."

He stopped as her words registered and ran a hand through his hair, making it stand on end.

Bea waved a hand toward the low dining table between two pink-cushioned couches. "There's breakfast, such as it is."

Valens shuffled toward the couches, exhaustion settling over him as the panic of waking wore off. He sat, realizing he'd forgotten his belt. He dropped his sandals and rubbed his hands over his face, groaning.

Bea moved toward him in a whirl of lemon and basil scent. "What's going on, Valens?" She settled across from him. "You've been out all hours lately. I've hardly seen you but in passing."

Valens rested his chin in his hands, elbows on his knees. "I've taken on some extra work." He hesitated to reveal anything more.

Her head tilted to one side, eyes narrowing beneath the heavy layer of cream. But she didn't press. "I don't like you being out after dark; I worry for you."

"I'll be all right." He surveyed the table before him with an air of casual indifference. Sliced bread, soft white cheese, dates, and honey.

"You've been mugged before."

Valens leaned forward and smeared a piece of bread with cheese and honey, topping it with a date. "Who hasn't?" He forced a grin and took a bite. What he wouldn't give for a raisin pastry.

"I don't like it." Bea's mouth tightened. "I don't sleep well when you're away."

"But hasn't that been your plan all along? To get me out of the house?"

Her brown eyes widened. "Are you courting someone?" Her voice rose to a hopeful squeak. Before he could deny it, she clapped her hands and rushed on. "Oh! That reminds me: your friend stopped by the shop."

Friend? What friend? Heat prickled his neck—shame rather than embarrassment, though Bea wouldn't be able to tell the difference. How long had it been since he'd seen Iris? A week? Two? He hadn't forgotten about her—not exactly—he'd just been preoccupied. Since the meeting with Hector, roses hung above the doorway of the Centaur's Cup every time he'd passed. His evenings were crowded with secret weddings, church gatherings, and sometimes both. He woke so late every morning he hadn't had time to stop for a pastry, much less a conversation.

The cream on Bea's cheek twitched as her lips wrestled into an uncharacteristic grimace. "Do you think that's wise?" Her words were gentle but held a note of censure.

"What?" Valens asked around another mouthful.

"She's lovely, certainly." Bea shifted. "But she's not a believer."

Valens stopped chewing and frowned. It took him a moment to understand what Bea hinted at. "Iris had some questions and I tried to answer them, that's all." He shook his head. "I'm not *courting* her."

Despite her prior objection, Bea had the audacity to look

disappointed. A thin beam of light trickled in through the crack in the closed balcony door, illuminating a horde of dancing dust motes.

"Well." Bea touched her chin, then rubbed the cream into her cheeks. "I don't think I answered her questions very well. She came to the shop once and I haven't seen her since."

Valens slid his feet into his sandals and laced them up. If he left soon, he'd have enough time to swing by Paulina's on his way to the notarii offices. "I'll keep an eye out for her then."

As he went to his room for his belt, Bea called after him, "Your tunic's on backward."

XV

"SPECULATORE DIDIUS LIBERARE!"

Titus swore under his breath. A slave in a brown tunic reached him in the shadow of the arched gateway of the Porta Decumana.

"Centurion Gracilus wishes to speak with you. Immediately."

Titus gave one longing glance toward the city, where he'd hoped for a few minutes to talk to Quintus about his debts. Weeks had gone by without a spare moment to get away from the Castra Praetoria. The last time he'd tried to leave, he'd been rerouted to fight a fire that had jumped to three other buildings and had taken days to put out. He sighed. Thirty seconds more and he could have disappeared for a few hours.

He returned with the slave the way he'd come, weaving past the open training grounds where guards rolled in the dust pounding each other with fists as commanders looked on. Behind the combat training, other guards scaled towers while a group of runners skirted the wall, leaping barrels and barriers. It might have been a training ground for Olympic athletes rather than an elite troop of soldiers who might or might not see combat.

The officers were quartered in a plain building at the crossroads in the center of the fortress. As Titus stepped inside, the warmth of the fading autumn sun vanished. Praetorian cohort standards lined the walls of the hall. The blue-and-gold flags bore images of scorpions, eagles, lions, a winged ram—each paired with the name and number of the nine Praetorian cohorts. At the end of the hall, sun streamed into an open courtyard bustling with harried slaves carrying scrolls and trays of food and wine, weaving around four centurions deep in conversation.

Titus followed the slave through an open doorway and into a large corner room.

Centurion Marcus Gracilus, leader of Titus's century, stood behind a tablet-strewn desk silhouetted by the bright whiteness of the window behind him. To his left stood the trecenarius, Justinian Faustus, commander of three hundred men and leader of the division of speculatores. Because of his unique position as soldier and spy, Titus answered to them both. He slammed a fist to his chest in salute.

"At ease, Speculatore." Trecenarius Faustus, highest in command, led the conversation. "I wanted to congratulate you on the success of your mission to take out Petrius Convus." His eyes and tone darkened. "But these stunts you pull—burning the tavern? You could have brought down the entire Tiberina district!"

But I didn't. Titus stared at a crack in the wall and let Trecenarius Faustus rage on the dangers of fires and how quickly they could spread. On how sections of Rome had been destroyed by fires countless times over the centuries and did Titus want the notoriety of lighting the latest? Had he enjoyed the last few days of fire duty? Did he want to be put on permanent fire duty like a common Vigiles Guard?

Titus took the verbal beating in silence. Eventually Faustus circled around to the real reason he'd summoned him.

"No doubt you've heard of this *Friend of Lovers,* as they call him."

Titus's eyebrows lifted. Everyone was talking about the man who secretly—or not so secretly—married couples despite the emperor's ban. The stories had spread like fleas on a dog. There were none, and then they were everywhere.

Faustus waved a hand. "Truth be told, I would let it go, if not for the prefect's insistence it disappear. The rumors are reaching new heights. The people talk of this *friend* as if he were their hero,

OF LOVE AND TREASON

restoring their rights of citizenship. It's creating a wedge between the emperor and the people, and it's going to get ugly." He paused, glancing at Centurion Gracilus. "In the emperor's absence, it's our job to keep the peace."

Titus shifted his weight, pondering the situation. He knew the Praetorian prefect, Marcus Aurelius Heraclianus, was in a tricky position trying to balance his support of the emperor against the emperor's waning popularity among the citizens. Emperor Claudius's short sights were set on driving out the barbarian invaders and reuniting the splintering regions of the empire, by any means and at all costs. But the love of his subjects faded in light of his temporary edicts.

Titus glanced between the officers. "Won't arresting the people's hero cause greater problems?"

"That is why this must be done carefully. The people are on the verge of unrest. Our goal is unity." Faustus nodded and glanced at Centurion Gracilus. "The emperor is fighting to unite the wayward regions of the empire, and we must wage war of our own. War to unite the people, the gods, and the emperor."

He was selling the importance too hard. Titus suspected punishment. "And how do you propose we do that, sir?"

"Stop the weddings."

Titus fought the urge to roll his eyes. *Weddings?* His jaw went tight as anger flowed through him, swift and hot. "With all due respect, sirs, you're pulling me off the Zenobia mission to investigate *secret weddings*? Half the soldiers in the legions have illegal wives and children. *Mars and Jupiter*—even some of the Praetorians do!"

His commanders ignored the outburst.

"It is not about the *legality* as much as it is about the *principle* of obedience." Faustus braced his hands on the edges of the desk.

Centurion Gracilus gave a nod. "The emperor must be assured we're taking this seriously. How better to do that than put our best man to the job?"

Titus shifted his unimpressed gaze to his centurion. This was punishment for the tavern fire. "You intend to arrest the people's hero and for me to take the fall for it."

"You're our best speculatore." Faustus straightened. "We need this problem to disappear quietly. Find him. Get rid of him. Eventually the rumors will fade. *Pax Romana.*"

Titus crossed his arms, giving them both a stony stare. They stared back, not giving an inch. He sighed. "If they're contracted marriages, we question the scribes and notarii." Titus pinched the bridge of his nose. "Perhaps there are a few idiots unaware of the edict." Although one would have to be deaf, blind, and live in a cave not to have heard of the edict.

"An idiot or a traditionalist willingly superseding it," Faustus said. "Either way, he has a death wish."

"Execution then, sir?"

Faustus nodded. "Sub rosa to the extreme. No witnesses. No burning down inns on your dead bodies."

Titus slammed his fist against his chest in salute. "Yes, sir."

"You will answer directly to me, and you may choose your own force from among the speculatores."

Titus dipped his head. "Yes, sir."

"That will be all."

Titus left the meeting, hot and belittled. After all he'd done in the guard, risking his life to hack the cohort tribune out of the throng of Alemanni during the Battle of Lake Benacus the year before, after his success taking out Captain Petrius Convus—*this* was what they thought of him? They might as well put him on the task force to catch the delinquents chipping the fingers and noses off statues in the Portico of Pompey!

Titus set his teeth and went out to choose his speculatores. The first order of business would be to place a man undercover in the notarii office expressly to inspect the marriage license of any woman who came in to claim the widow's right to inherit property.

He found Adonis sniffing scrolls in the record building. Named after a mythical man of great beauty, Adonis had the most hopeful and delusional mother the world had ever known. With a single tooth in his head and about as much hair, Adonis would blend in with the notarii perfectly. Looks aside, he had an impeccable memory, and if a discrepancy existed in a document, he would find it. Titus recruited two others and they got to work. The sooner they got this over with, the better. It shouldn't take long.

XVI

BEFORE ANYONE COULD HAPPEN A GLANCE, Valens rubbed out the letters in the wax tablet the city messenger had just delivered. His mouth had gone powdery at the words inside, his disappointment over missing Iris the last two mornings forgotten. The handwriting was unfamiliar but the initials at the bottom were not.

They know. Stop before it's too late.

GFD

"I have two announcements."

Valens looked up. His supervisor, Orane Haldas, stood in the middle of the room mopping sweat from his neck and wearing a luxuriant auburn wig to hide the baldness he'd sported the day before. An unwigged balding man wearing canary-yellow shoes stood beside him.

"This is Adonis. He will be working in the legal claims." Haldas pointed to a row of desks along the back wall and motioned for Adonis to join the notarii there. The new notarius moved to his department, his quick dark eyes skittering across the room, taking in everything and everyone.

As Haldas swiped his forehead, skewing the wig, Valens's attention shifted to the three Praetorians standing behind him, gladii strapped high beneath their arms and mostly concealed by their blue tunics.

They were the only ones allowed to bear arms within the confines of the city, but even then, they had to be hidden.

Valens tried to swallow and reached for the cup of water at the edge of his desk. His fingers trembled. The words of the message replayed in his mind. *They know.* He missed Haldas announcing the Praetorian investigator.

"He will speak with each of you privately, and you will answer his questions and go on with your work. No one is to leave the building until further notice."

The head Praetorian stepped to the front and clasped his hands behind his back, feet wide, chest out. Valens returned his gaze to the half-written contract before him and let out a long, slow breath, his heart thudding. What did they know? *How* could they know already? Had Hector trusted the wrong legionnaire? After he'd written the initial three marriage contracts and agreed to work with Hector, word had spread like the Great Fire. In the last week alone he'd performed what, fifteen? Twenty weddings?

Calm. He needed to be calm. Haldas had mentioned nothing about marriage contracts. Or had he?

He dropped his chin and tried to concentrate on the warehouse rent adjustment in front of him. His heart beat too fast, and the stylus trembled violently in his hand. Out of the corner of his eye he watched the Praetorian investigator stop at each desk and question every notarius in turn, taking notes on a wax tablet.

Another Praetorian watched the front and rear entrances while the third snaked through the room, flipping through parchments on desks and unrolling scrolls. The investigator looked younger than Valens, though taller and powerfully built. Pinkish scars crisscrossed muscular forearms. One scar disfigured the lower half of his left ear, running in a jagged line down his neck. Valens had seen him before. In the market with Iris.

With double effort, Valens turned his attention to the contract, but the words seemed foreign. He started reading at the beginning. *Lord, preserve me.* A trickle of sweat slid between his shoulder blades. *I am finished.*

Orane Haldas straightened his wig and intercepted the investigator before he reached Valens's desk. Valens stood and replaced the unfinished contract in the pigeonholed half wall behind him, which separated one row of desks from the next. He kept one eye on the pair as they conferred in tones too low to hear. Haldas mopped sweat from his neck rolls as the Praetorian's eyebrows flickered in a look of surprise. His eyes darted toward Valens, who dropped his gaze and sifted through the piles of scrap parchment tossed on top of the half wall. Valens willed his hands to stop shaking.

"May I have a few minutes?"

Valens inhaled, grabbed the parchment on top of the scrap pile, and turned. "Of course, Investigator, please, sit." He gestured to the chair on the opposite side of his desk, though the investigator had already seated himself. Valens returned to his own chair, laid the parchment carefully on one side of his desk, then noticed it was covered in crude doodles. He flipped it over.

The Praetorian leaned back in the chair. "Your supervisor made me aware of your family connections." His dark-blue eyes settled in Valens's direction. "I apologize for the waste of your time, but you must understand this is standard procedure. I can't have anyone thinking I'm showing preferential treatment."

The tension in his shoulders broke as Valens realized the investigator was nearly giving him a free pass. He hoped the relief did not show on his face. Still, it could be a tactic.

The Praetorian propped a tablet on his lap and settled one ankle on the opposite knee. "What is your full name?"

"Valentine Favius Diastema, but my friends—" He suppressed the urge to continue.

A bronze stylus scraped through the wax tablet, recording Valens's name, living address, education, and years of service as a notarius. Valens relaxed under the easy questions before they took a sharp turn.

"As a notarius, it is required for you to have extensive knowledge of the law."

"Yes, sir."

The investigator's eyes drilled him. "And knowledge of the consequences for disobedience."

Valens's stomach clenched. "Yes, sir."

The investigator shifted. "You are well aware, then, of the marriage ban?"

"Of course, sir." Valens's blood began to race. "One would have to live in the Balkans under a rock not to have heard. None of us were able to come to work for a few days because of the riots."

"Yes, I remember." A corner of the investigator's mouth lifted. "A few days off must have been nice."

"Yes, sir."

"And you are aware that disobedience of the ban is considered treason and punishable by execution?"

"I am."

The investigator set aside the tablet and leaned forward, resting his forearms on his knees. "There are rumors of secret weddings taking place despite the ban." He lowered his voice. "*Legally contracted* weddings."

Valens's eyebrows rose and crinkled in genuine surprise. So word *had* reached the Praetorians after all.

The investigator shrugged. "Someone's probably making a pretty sesterce or two."

"Seems like a risky venture for some coin."

The Praetorian leaned back and locked his hands behind his head. "Maybe he's a traditionalist. Anyone you know having financial difficulties? Or has anyone recently come into money?" His eyes roamed the room.

Valens shook his head, unwilling to cast suspicion on anyone else even if they had mentioned financial issues. "None I can think of at the moment, sir."

The investigator's mouth tipped. "And it wasn't you?"

Valens forced a chuckle. "Well, I might think about it, now that I know there's money to be made off a few ex-legionnaires."

The investigator didn't smile.

Valens sobered and cleared his throat. "I have no burning desire to be executed for treason, sir." That was the truth.

"What about a scribe?" The investigator turned his attention to the group of copiers hard at work in one corner of the room. He scratched the back of his head, brown hair cut short and neat to spite the curl.

Valens shifted, wondering why the man bothered asking his opinion. "They have access to the tools, I suppose." He wouldn't blame an innocent for his own crime. "Have you seen one of the contracts?" He shook his head. "No. If you had, you wouldn't be here. You'd see the notarius's signature and have your man."

The investigator smiled. "You have the makings of an investigator yourself." He pushed to his feet. "If you see anything suspicious or think of anything else, send me word." He tossed a wooden tile onto the desk with a click. Valens took it as the investigator moved to the next desk where Galik wiped his ink-stained hands and invited him to please sit, even though he already had.

Valens turned the tile over.

Titus Didius Liberare, Speculatore, II Gemina
Castra Praetoria, Rome

XVII

IRIS WAITED IN FRONT OF THE LAMP SHOP until the tavern keeper of the Centaur's Cup sent her father outside. She and Hector had worked out a plan to send Quintus across the street to the lamp shop when he spotted Iris waiting. Now she wondered if Hector had seen her at all. She made another careful pass up and down the block, hoping this time the bright orange of her shawl would catch Hector's attention. She sighed in annoyance at the tavern's policy against women. Not that she especially wanted to go inside, but it would certainly save time.

The sharp scent of lamp oil hung in the street, mingling with late-season roses. Iris hadn't visited Bea again, although the questions and half answers ate at her in the quiet moments of the day. Valentine had come to the bakery yesterday morning; she'd caught the sound of his voice and tried to fabricate an excuse to go up front. Refilling bread baskets? By the time she'd found the nerve—and a basket of cheese pastries—he'd gone. The waiting and the whirling of her mind was maddening. She resolved to visit Beatrix again.

Sandals slapped across the street toward the lamp shop, but it was not her father's stumbling limp.

"Iris? It's me, Val—*entine*." He added the last bit with a chuckle.

Her pulse jumped. How, in a city of nearly a million, did Valentine manage to be *here*?

Her mouth turned up in a grin. "Valentine? I haven't run into you in a while."

"I've been working all hours lately. I haven't forgotten about our conversations."

Something warm prickled in her chest.

"Are you selling lamps now?" He stopped beside her, smelling of ink and sandalwood. "Is that why I haven't seen you at the bakery?"

"Do you need a lamp? I hear Galerius has a fine selection." She motioned at the shop behind her.

"It *is*, actually, a very nice selection."

She heard him begin sorting through the table of lamps set against the outside wall of the shop. "Here's a whale with the wick coming from the blowhole." There was a thunk and the sound of fabric sliding on skin as he reached for another. "This one's stamped with bees; I like that. That one's got a mermaid. Here's a foot." *Clink.* "That one's shaped like a—" He turned around again. "You're selling some inappropriate lamps here, miss."

She bit back a laugh and winced. "Could you imagine me working in a lamp shop? Bread is far more forgiving when knocked on the floor. Galerius is kind enough to allow me to loiter in front of his shop while I wait for my father. He's across the street." She felt her face go warm and wondered what Valentine would think when her father came stumbling over—in a jailor's uniform. "Pater has a heavy mind," she tried to explain. "He says the wine helps, but sometimes it's best if I walk him home."

"I see." His voice shifted toward the Centaur's Cup. "What does your father do?"

Her palms went damp. She'd been dreading this question. If she told him the truth, he might not speak to her again. Christians and jailors were not on friendly terms.

"I visited your aunt, the perfumer." Iris smoothed the wide belt at her waist. "She's very kind."

"She is." A smile lit his voice. "She told me you stopped in. Did she answer your questions?"

"Some." Iris nodded. "Others, she said you could answer better."

The breeze, with its smells of herbs, oil, and dust, teased strands of hair around her forehead.

"Oh? Like what?" His sandals scraped as he shifted his weight, appearing to settle in for a conversation.

Iris took a breath. "Beatrix said the gods don't heal me because they can't, but your god *can* heal me but doesn't. If he can, why doesn't he? Why tease me with glimpses here and there, and only when—?"

"Marrrrish!"

The familiar step and scrape of her father's tread stumbled into the street, silencing her question. Her heart sank.

"Excuse me," Iris mumbled. Her face flamed as she turned away from Valentine. "I'm here, Pater." Walking stick in hand, Iris hurried toward the slur of her father's speech.

"Marr—" Quintus stopped, then tried again. "Arr—Irisssh."

Her father slung a heavy arm over Iris's shoulders, nearly toppling them both in the street. Iris's stick jabbed into her ribs.

"Pater, what happened? You're never this bad." She kept her voice low, hoping Valentine had gone.

"Bad?" Quintus shook his head. "I'm shel—shel—*celebrating* our good fortune. I'm very close. Our problems will soon be gone, my girl." He patted the side of her head, knocking her palla back and skewing her hair.

"What do you mean?" She pushed the hair away from her mouth and dug her shoulder into his armpit, hoisting him up.

"If I can arrest—who are *you*?" His face turned away with the question.

Iris's eyebrows crinkled, and she shook her head. Nearly senseless already. She needed to get him home.

"I'm Valentine." Sand on the paving stones screeched as he approached. "But my friends call me Valens or Val."

Iris ducked her head. Could she disappear into an open sewer vent? "Pater's not well. Please excuse us, Valentine. I have to get him home."

"I can help." His voice came from the other side of her father.

"You're so *kind*." Quintus's voice slurred toward Valentine, then swiveled toward her ear. "He's so kind." He laid his head on her shoulder with a sigh.

Hot anger coursed through Iris. She set her mouth in a hard line and refused to speak. This was not the time to mention to her pater that they could save more money for their escape if he would stop drinking it away. In this state, he'd never remember it. She should speak with Hector about refusing to serve him.

Iris shook her head. What good would that do? There was one tavern for every twenty citizens. At least here, she knew where to find him.

They started down the street. Her father stopped talking and grew heavier. Iris shifted her hold, reaching around his back to grip his waist. Her hand bumped Valentine's arm, supporting Quintus from the other side.

"You don't have to do this." Iris raised her chin over her father's head. "I can get him home. I'm used to it."

"Step to the right; there's a sedan chair coming," Valentine directed and added in a quieter voice, "Does this happen often?"

She lifted the shoulder not lodged in her father's armpit. "Only the nights he isn't working."

"Why are you yelling?" Quintus groaned. They fell silent until the noise of the cross traffic signaled the end of the street. Iris directed Valentine to the right.

"How far are you from here?" he whispered.

"Not very." She swallowed. "If you'll leave us at the end of Cedar Street, I can take him from there."

"Are you certain?"

"Yes."

He didn't press, seeming to sense her discomfort. The street dropped into cold shade, and the sharp tang of urine from Silvia's laundry told Iris they were nearly home. She tugged her pater and Valentine to a stop.

"Thank you, Valentine." She hunched beneath the brunt of her father's weight as Valentine released him.

"I hope we can finish our conversation soon."

She nodded. "Me too. Goodbye."

He repeated the farewell, and she listened as his sandals retreated, soon drowned out by the shuffle of other feet. His leaving tightened an ache in her chest, as if he walked away with something she desperately needed. It carved a hole inside her of an unidentifiable shape. She took a breath and trundled her father toward the smell of urine and the three flights of stairs. It was foolish to think that way about Valentine's god. Yet the logic of her mind did nothing to ease the longing in her soul.

XVIII

VALENS SQUINTED AGAINST THE GLARE of the sun and knocked at the *culina* door of Marius and Martha's home. He pinched his eyes, wiping away the burning. Exhaustion weighed his shoulders. Where was everyone? He shifted, shaking the mud off first one foot, then the other. The rains of the past few days had left the streets a sloppy mess of dung and garbage. Yesterday's interrogation left him anxious. If the Praetorians searched the homes of the notarii, they'd find a marriage contract in his. He'd done his best to hide it, but perhaps he should have burned it rather than stashing it under the loose floorboard.

It hadn't helped his anxiety to discover the jailor Hector had pointed out in the tavern was Iris's father. Was the jailor using his daughter as a ploy to find Christians? He didn't want to think so.

Valens knocked again. One of the servants opened the door and stepped wide to let him enter.

"Hello, Phoebe." He smiled, squeezing sideways through the door, lute in hand. "How are you?"

The servant, nearing middle age, smiled back. "I'm fine, Valens." She closed the door behind him. "And you?"

His smile faltered. "Well enough. Is Cato home?" They crossed the kitchen, the smells of fresh bread and spiced chickpeas making his mouth water.

Phoebe ushered him into the courtyard on the other side. "Cato

119

is in his study." She gestured vaguely across the courtyard. "No one else is here yet."

"Thank you. It smells like heaven in here, by the way." Valens crossed the courtyard, sandals snapping on the white marble path. He knocked once on the study door and let himself in.

Cato slouched in a chair, feet on the desk, a medical scroll perched on his knees. Valens set his lute against the wall and claimed the other chair.

"Val, come in, sit down." Cato's mouth twitched but he didn't look up from his reading. He scratched the side of his head, leaving a frizzy bump of curls behind.

"Thank you, I will." Valens flipped through a stack of tablets, hastily scrawled with notes in mostly unintelligible handwriting.

Cato slowly lifted his chin, eyes glued to the scroll, stretching to read the last few words before finally pulling free. "How is the office of late? Anyone bring in sweets?"

Valens gave a carefree shrug. "Fabius brought in some dates he dried on his balcony. Everyone who tried them went on a mass exodus to the latrines. Thankfully, I'd already learned my lesson after his first batch."

"Good for you."

"The speculatores came to question us yesterday."

Cato's eyebrows shot up and he swung his feet to the floor. "What about?"

Valens stood, suddenly restless. He paced the room, poking at books and scrolls shoved haphazardly into the bookcases that covered two whole walls. "They're looking for whoever's writing the illegally legal marriage contracts."

"The Cupid?" Cato straightened.

Valens stopped. "Sorry, the *what*?"

"The Cupid." Cato's eyes bugged as if Valens had just sprouted wings. "You haven't heard? *Everyone's* talking about him."

"I haven't heard him called The Cupid." Valens wasn't sure he liked that.

Cato waved a hand, ticking off the names that had found their way into the everyday gossip of the city over the past month. "Rogue Notarius, Restorer of Rights, Friend of Lovers—I personally like The Cupid. It's easy, and there's the whole forbidden-love thing. So who was it?"

"Who was what?"

"The Cupid, did they find him? Was it the scribe in the corner with the crazy teeth?"

Valens frowned and shook his head, mind racing. *Everyone* was talking about *him*? He'd heard a few things, but between work and church gatherings and the nightly weddings, he'd not been mingling much with the public.

Cato kept guessing. The one with the hair? The one without the hair? Not the date dryer?

"There's no one left." Cato gave up, dropping back in his seat.

Valens rubbed his ear and gave a sheepish smile.

Cato stared at him a moment, then pushed all the air out of his lungs. "No."

When Valens didn't deny it, he jumped to his feet. "Val!" His mouth gaped and shut, searching for words beyond his grasp. "That's a treason charge! It's execution if they find out."

Valens lifted his shoulders. "The investigator seemed to think me incapable of such a crime on account of my family. He asked my opinion on who could have done it."

Cato leaned forward, lacing his fingers and propping his elbows on the desk. "You would accuse an innocent person on your account?"

"Of course not!" Valens shot him a sharp look. "You know me better than that. But I'm not volunteering for the sword either."

"You have to stop."

"What can I do, Cato?" Valens raised his hands. "Most of them are ex-legionnaires who have risked the better part of their lives to keep us safe—yet they're still denied the basic rights of citizenship."

Cato ran a hand through his hair and rubbed the back of his neck. "The Scriptures command us to honor the emperor."

"Yes." Valens nodded. "Honor him as a man made in the image of God. Honor him as a soul Jesus died to save. I will never slur him nor wish him harm, but that does not mean I agree with everything he decrees."

"Do you think it's wise to stir up trouble now?"

"We already had trouble."

"But with the unrest and the war, people are searching for someone to blame. When the war with the Persians went sour ten years ago, it didn't take long for the people to side with Emperor Valerian against the Christians."

Valens fell silent. Cato was right. Perhaps now was not the time to draw attention by taking a stand against the emperor's edict. But why did the thought of staying quiet and safe churn his gut with guilt?

"What are my choices?" Valens lifted his shoulders. "The treason has already been committed. Stopping now won't change my sentence if I'm caught."

"If you stop now, they may not catch you. How often are you performing weddings?"

"Every night."

Cato's mouth tightened. "Val."

"Marriage is a beautiful thing. Ordained by God. It was never meant to be withheld from a man and woman."

Cato pinched the bridge of his nose. "I agree. I can't imagine my life without Delphine. But you can't keep doing this. It cannot be done in secret, not with your name on every contract. If you're caught—" He shook his head. "Stop while you can. Please."

"You would deny others the happiness you have with Delphine?"

Cato squeezed his eyes shut. "You've seen the new orders from the priests? Mandatory offerings to the gods. Noncompliance is viewed as treason and punishable by confiscation of property or death. It's starting again just like it did ten years ago. A lot of believers are leaving Rome. Some have already been imprisoned and pressured to recant."

"I've heard." Valens nodded. "The scribes have been copying the notices for days. Are you leaving?"

"No. Mother and Father moved here expressly to aid believers during times like these." Cato gripped his shoulder. "But you should go with those who are leaving."

"A leader of a church does not run. What sort of shepherd would I be?"

"A live one. Leave the city while you still can."

Delphine poked her head in the door. "Everyone's here." She smiled. "Ah, hello, Val. You brought your lute again, I see."

Valens lifted the instrument. "I brought it to play while we sing."

"You shouldn't have." Cato forced a half-hearted grin. "You're really terrible, you know."

"You're just envious."

Cato threw his head back and laughed. "Bless your delusional heart."

Delphine left, and Valens and Cato followed.

Cato gripped Valens's arm as they crossed the courtyard. "Think about what I said," he pleaded. "Think about Beatrix."

Valens nodded but didn't offer assurances one way or another. Beatrix was the one he most worried about. But he couldn't stop now, and truth be told, he didn't want to. A thrill ran through him each time the contracts were signed and handed off, as if with each one, he set a small bit of the world to rights.

In the *triclinium* on the far side of the courtyard, they met the other believers who had come to eat and worship together. Valens brightened to see the ex-legionnaire Felix and new wife, Vinia, had ventured to join them. The room, vibrating with friendly tones and laughter, swirled with the aromas of fresh bread, curried lentil pottage, marinated artichokes, and roasted fish.

As Valens greeted Felix and Vinia, Pax came and tugged at the lute in Valens's hands.

"I'll take that so you can eat."

Valens released the instrument and Pax stowed it in a dim corner behind Aunt Bea and a throng of older women who shifted their bodies in front of it with conspiratorial nods.

Food eaten and dirty plates stacked on the now-empty table, everyone settled down, some on dining couches, some on stools and the floor while others leaned against the walls. The voices fell away into a gradual and reverent silence.

Valens let the silence linger, quieting his own anxious heart. He prayed silently as many of the others did, preparing his heart both to teach and to learn. One of the women began to sing, softly at first, and the others joined in, their voices filling the room. Valens had always enjoyed singing. Music moved him as nothing else did, and he sang with everything in him, eyes closed.

When the singing fell away, Valens unrolled the scroll he'd nabbed from where it had hidden among Cato's medical scrolls. The second letter the apostle Paul had written to the young leader Timothy was one of Valens's favorites.

Be strong in the grace that is in Christ Jesus.
Entrust the word to faithful men who will continue to teach others.
Share in the suffering as a good soldier of Christ.
A good soldier follows the orders of the one who commands him.

The message flooded his restless heart with peace.

"We are soldiers of Christ. Not the kind to batter our enemies with swords and force, but soldiers who have been given a clear mission. A dangerous mission, to be sure, but one that extends love to our enemies, hope to those we meet." He glanced around the room and let the scroll settle on his lap. "We fight a war which is already won, but that does not guarantee there will be no casualties, no danger. I know many of you are worried about the latest orders from the priests about mandatory offerings and sacrifices. We are commanded to stand firm in the Lord and not to be afraid." He spoke to himself as much as to the rest of them. "God has not given us a spirit of fear, but of power, love, and a sound mind."

Later, as dusk fell and Valens walked Aunt Bea home, he racked his brain to find an excuse to leave and check in with Hector at the tavern. Felix had mentioned that Hector needed to see him before tonight's wedding.

They were halfway to their third-level apartment above the Markets of Trajan when Bea smacked her thigh. "I forgot!" She pulled Valens to a stop.

"What?"

"The box of empty bottles at the shop." She sighed. "I meant to fill them for tomorrow."

Valens straightened. He needn't sneak out or invent a reason to leave after all. "I'll get it. You go on ahead."

"Are you sure? I can go with you." She sounded tired. Even if she hadn't, he would have refused her help.

"We're almost home. You go on; it won't take me long."

He turned and trotted down the steps as Bea called after him, "The box is on the counter next to the door. Do you have your key?"

He held it up and continued down the stairs before crossing the barrel-roofed arcade with its two levels of darkened shops visible from the large open square on the bottom. He cut down the last set of stairs to emerge on the covered street of the shop-and-tavern-lined Via Biberatica, or *Drinking Street*. He paused at the bottom, the perfumery on his left, around the sloping curve of the street. He turned right.

The Centaur's Cup was not far, but Bea would worry anyway when the task took longer than it should have. Perhaps his aptitude for lateness would finally serve him.

Where the Via Biberatica met the main road, the lights died, and darkness settled over the streets. Valens hesitated. Hector had always organized a contingent of his ex-legionnaire friends to act as guards whenever Valens moved about the city after dark. He'd been mugged more times than he cared to recall, and he didn't much care for it to happen again. Still, there were no guards this time and Hector needed to see him.

He'd hardly stepped into the main road when two shadows peeled from the building across the street and moved toward him. In the dimness he couldn't make out their features, but their walk and build betrayed them as soldiers, not common thieves. He relaxed. Hector had sent guards after all.

They stopped in front of him. "We're looking for Valentine Favius Diastema."

"That's me." The tension left his shoulders. "Thank you for—"

"You're under arrest." In one motion they both reached forward and grabbed his arms.

"On what charges?" Valens grunted as his wrists were forced up between his shoulder blades.

"You'll know soon enough."

Fear tightened his spine as he recalled the note. The investigator must have found something. The soldiers jerked him up the street. Valens prayed none of the couples he'd married had been found out.

Thunder rumbled in the distance. The soldiers didn't speak, and Valens didn't press further for an explanation.

They marched down the streets, light spilling in yellow rectangles over square black cobblestones. The night rang with grinding cart wheels, braying donkeys, and bellowing oxen. Carters shouted at each other to quit hogging the street.

God, give me strength. Boldness. Fearlessness that points only to You. The hobnails of the soldiers' boots crunched in his ears. *I am weak. Be my strength.*

They dragged him between colored marble temples of the Forum, light from torches and altars bouncing an eerie orange glow on the pillars. Pushing him up pale marble steps, the men shoved him into an office lit with a single clay lamp. Valens looked around. The dim room contained a broken desk, a mass of messy bookshelves, and two doors: one they had just entered and the other of iron-encased oak, chained and secured with an oversize lock. Valens's stomach began to quiver.

God has not given us a spirit of fear, but of power, love, and a sound mind.

The words came quietly through his mind, immediately silencing the fear that might have taken hold. Valens lifted his head. The man behind the desk occupied the only chair. His gray-streaked head bent over a ledger as he ignored the commotion of three men entering the prison. The jailor finally looked up at the guard on Valens's left.

"Markos. This is the one?" He shifted an unimpressed look in Valens's direction. If the jailor recognized Valens as the man who'd helped Iris bring him home, he did not show it.

The guard gave a single nod. "Yes, sir."

Quintus stood and moved in front of the desk with a dignified gait, despite a heavy limp. He wore a faded-blue tunic and belted baton and held a scroll in one hand. Keys clinked at his waist with every step. He lifted his unshaven chin high with unquestioned authority as he stopped in front of Valens and met his eyes.

"What is your name?"

"Valentine Favius Diastema." He swallowed. "But most people call me Valens. Or Val."

Quintus's eyes narrowed for a moment as if he was trying to decide if Valens was being impertinent. "You're accused of inciting illegal gatherings and leading unsanctioned religious activities."

Valens could have laughed with relief. The married couples were safe then.

"Does that make you happy?" Quintus crossed his arms. "To be labeled a *Christian*?" He spat out the word like a bad fig.

"I *am* a Christian." Valens met Quintus's sharp gaze. "And yes, it does make me very happy."

His head snapped to the left as one of the guards sent a blow to his cheek.

"No bruises, Helix!" Quintus barked as Valens winced and touched his mouth. His fingers came away with blood. "Hit the back of his head next time."

Had Iris told her father about him? Was she his means of hunting Christians?

Quintus's attention shifted to the guards. "Who else knows he's been taken?"

The guard to Valens's left shrugged. "No one. We were discreet."

Quintus nodded. "Good."

Valens's eyebrows pinched. "What is this about?"

Quintus's face hardened. "Do not speak unless questioned."

Valens fought to push aside the fear that snaked around the base of his spine. *Help me be strong. Protect Aunt Bea and the others.*

"Markos." Quintus's dark eyes did not leave Valens's. "Put him in the Tullianum."

Quintus's lips lifted slightly, as if he was satisfied by the look of horror that surely showed on Valens's face. Twelve feet below street level, the domed chamber of the Tullianum had one way in—through a hole in the ceiling—and one way out. As a corpse.

Quintus unlocked the ironclad door. Markos lit a lantern from the table lamp and pushed Valens toward the set of narrow steps descending sharply into slick darkness.

"Will I have a trial?" Valens asked as Markos propelled him forward. He craned his neck and looked back at the jailor, whose face, he thought, held a hint of uncertainty. Quintus didn't speak.

"You'll be given a chance to recant." Markos's voice echoed as he clumped behind Valens. Another shove sent Valens tumbling forward, his feet rushing to keep him from landing on his head at the bottom of the stairs. The odor of unwashed bodies and rot, death and human waste hung in the darkness and set him gagging.

Markos's lantern illuminated a cell of unequal walls meeting at odd angles. Chains dangled from the walls, clasping the wrists and ankles of several prisoners who looked at Valentine with mingled curiosity and pity. Panic scraped in his chest and he fought against it, repeating the Scripture that had come to mind. The words lost their power as fear took hold. They were putting him in a tomb. They would beat him until he died or agreed to give up his God.

Markos hung the lantern on a hook in the block ceiling and shoved a key through a lock on the cell floor. As he slid back the round iron hatch, Valens bent and vomited from the stench. Clearly not all the corpses made it out of the Tullianum. Markos pressed his own lips together and yanked Valens in front of him, facing the hole. He drew a dagger, sliced the ropes binding Valens's hands, and gave him a final shove.

Valens landed in a tomb of darkness, the floor littered with small bones and human filth. His hands and knees stung from the impact and he shot to his feet, shaking his hands free of the revolting litter. The round door above his head slammed shut with the finality of a grave marker.

Blackness. He stumbled backward until the domed walls caught him on the back of his head. He stood shaking, trying to recall passages of Scripture or how to pray. The irony of what he'd just spoken to the group of believers struck him with guilt.

Something moved in the darkness across the room, scraping across the floor in steps that both rattled and squished. An icy hand gripped his arm and Valens jerked away, tripping sideways into the filth of the floor. His hands slipped in something cold and rancid and slick. He vomited again and felt bony hands on his shoulders, tugging him upright.

"Come out of the latrine," a thin, high voice, heavy with phlegm, chided him. "What a strange guest you are to come bumbling into my home, making such a mess."

Valens pulled away from breath that smelled of wet dog and old pork. "I am not here by choice."

The voice cackled. "No one ever is. I am Hades, lord of the underworld. What have you done?"

Insane. The other prisoner was insane, Valens realized, but the knowledge did not calm his pounding heart. "I'm Valentine." He willed his voice to steady. "I'm a Christian."

Hades laid a sympathetic hand on Valens's shoulder, but his words made his blood chill. "Ah, then the executioner will be coming for you soon. But if you prefer, I can end you now with far less pain."

XIX

BEATRIX HAD BEEN UP FRONT for a long time. Iris heard her talking to Paulina, voice quiet one moment, then rising with worry. Iris paused, hands in soapy water, listening as Beatrix's voice wavered in the front room.

"I've been to the Urban Guardhouse and they won't do anything until he's been missing for three days. They say they don't have him." Tears streaked Beatrix's voice.

Iris dried her hands and moved toward the doorway; Paulina said something too low for her to hear.

"I'm so worried!" Beatrix swallowed. "Val never made it to the perfumery—my box was still there."

"Have you checked with the Vigiles?" Paulina's voice soothed and carried a note of confusion.

"Yes." Beatrix's voice dropped, as if sapped of strength. "I don't know what else to do. If the Urbans won't look, I don't know who else to go to."

Another step brought Iris into the doorway and view of the two women, who stopped talking when they noticed her.

"Iris." Beatrix's voice held something like relief. "My nephew Valens went missing the night before last."

Iris's mouth went dry. Valentine was gone? Her heart dropped. "My father may be able to help."

Beatrix made a snuffling snort. "He's the jailor, correct?" Her voice held a note of wavering hope.

The bell above the door jingled as two chattering girls entered.

"Go on," Paulina urged. "I'll be fine." She moved to help the girls.

Iris nodded and lifted her shoulders. "Pater may have a suggestion for where you can look next. Or perhaps he can persuade the Urbans or Vigiles to search for him. I'll get my palla and we'll go now."

"You would do that?"

She smiled. "Of course. It's the least I can do. You closed your entire shop for me."

"Here you are. Two cheese pastries." Paulina's voice swiveled toward the girls, who stopped chattering to count small coins onto the counter in a series of clicks. Iris ducked into the back and exchanged her apron for her palla and cane, meeting Beatrix by the front door.

"Thank you." Beatrix sighed as they set off down the Via Biberatica.

"I hope Pater can help."

The sun warmed Iris's shoulders as the air washed crisp and cool over her face. Beatrix was oddly quiet as they walked. Iris wasn't sure what to say to her, or if she should say anything. What did one say to comfort someone whose loved one had disappeared? Before Iris figured out the answer, they were walking up the carcer steps.

Hobnailed boots descended toward them.

"The gods are smiling on me today."

Iris's knees went liquid at the sound of Tribune Braccus's voice and her fingers tightened around the cane. Beside her, Beatrix flinched and Iris realized she'd squeezed her arm with the same ferocity. She loosened her grip on Beatrix but said nothing as the tribune moved in front of them, forcing them to stop.

"Lovely to see you again, my dear." He spoke in a tender tone that froze the blood in her veins. The breeze brushed her palla against her cheek and Iris reared back, recalling his touch. She stayed on her feet only by Beatrix's grip. Her pulse pounded in her temples.

The tribune chuckled, his boots moving around them. "I can hardly wait until next time." He cooed the words in her ear.

Bile rose in her throat.

Beatrix's arm went around Iris as her knees went woozy. "Are you all right?"

The sound of the tribune's boots faded. Iris pressed her lips together, willing her heart to stop pounding. "I-is he gone?" she stammered, breathing too hard.

"He's gone," Beatrix confirmed. "Are you all right?"

Iris bolted up the stairs. "Let us in, Markos!"

The door opened ahead of her and Iris led Beatrix into the office. Her father had either just finished lunch or was in the middle of eating. The air smelled of cold meat pie and overly herbed gravy that didn't quite hide the sharp tang of rancidity. Beatrix's perfume soon took care of that.

"Iris?" Pater's voice came from behind the desk. "What brings you—? Are you all right?" He let out a breath. "You saw Tribune Braccus, didn't you?"

She nodded and held out a shaking hand, which he grasped in both of his.

"Did he speak to you?"

Again, she could only nod.

Pater cursed. "Pardon me, my lady." His voice turned toward Beatrix. "Can I help you?"

"Pater." Iris latched on to the distraction. "This is Beatrix, the perfumer at the market. Her nephew has disappeared and she's looking for him."

"Ah." Pater's tone went strange and tight.

"Jailor." Beatrix's voice dipped as she bowed. "My nephew disappeared the night before last in the Markets of Trajan. I sent him to fetch something from my shop and he never returned. He never made it to the shop either."

"I see." His tone implied that he didn't. "And you think he may be *here*?"

"I've been everywhere but no one will look for him because he hasn't been missing for three days." Beatrix sucked in a breath and rushed on. "But what if he's hurt? Can you, I don't know, can you look for him? The family name is Favius."

"Favius." Pater repeated the name as if he'd never heard it in his life and shuffled things on his desk.

"Yes," Beatrix said in an eager voice, stepping closer to the desk. "*F-a-v-i-u-s.*"

"I have no record of a Favius here." Pater slid something across the desk with a scuffing sound. "My record book," he said. "See? He disappeared, you say?"

"Yes, the night before last." Beatrix's gown rustled as she bent to inspect the book. "But he wouldn't be in your book. I was hoping you could ask—"

"Have you checked with the Vigiles? The Urban Guards? The Praetorians?" Pater had a disingenuous tone, as if he only asked the questions to placate Bea. A niggling feeling that he was hiding something prickled at Iris's gut.

"I've checked with all of them," Beatrix said. "No one has him and no one will look either."

A bloodcurdling scream rose from the belly of the prison. Iris jumped, bumping Beatrix, who gasped.

"What was that?" Beatrix asked in a breathless whisper.

Her father cleared his throat, his chair creaking as he shifted his weight. "You've heard of the Gothic assassin Grenadix, I assume?"

Beatrix didn't answer, but by the way Pater continued, she must have shaken her head. "He was sent to Rome by his chieftain to assassinate the emperor Valerian. He was caught instead and imprisoned. Valerian died before a grand public execution could be planned. And then Emperor Gallienus had plans to use him in some sort of public exhibit, but the wars started and Gallienus died and now we're saving him for a triumph parade. If—when Emperor Claudius Gothicus has one."

Beatrix's voice sounded weak. "He's been down there for . . ."

"Almost ten years. It's unheard of, I know, for a prisoner to be kept so long, but I don't have orders otherwise. He's insane." Pater's matter-of-fact tone went suddenly dismissive. "I'm sorry I cannot be of more help to you."

"I know something's wrong, but I don't know what to do." Beatrix sounded about to cry. "What if he's dead by the time anyone bothers to look for him?"

"Perhaps he's run off with his lover or taken a trip with friends. Perhaps he doesn't want to be found just now." Impatience sharpened Pater's voice. Iris frowned; it was quite unlike him.

Perhaps he needed a drink.

"He wouldn't do something like that. What if someone took him? What if he's in danger?"

"Have you received a demand for ransom?"

"No." Beatrix's voice broke.

"I'm sorry." Pater shuffled through papers and tablets, either looking for something or attempting to appear busy. "If you'll excuse me."

Iris had spent enough time in the prison to know Pater sat at the desk most of the day perusing old accounts of war history and gambling with the guards. He was never busy. She felt her face flushing at his rudeness but didn't dare call him out in front of Beatrix.

Beside her, Beatrix drew herself upright. "I would like to report a missing person."

"You'll have to see the Urbans for that. This is the carcer."

"Can't you help, Pater?" Iris broke in as Beatrix let out a squeal of frustration. "Can't you call in a favor and have the Urbans look for him before the three days?"

Her father heaved a heavy sigh. "I'll see what I can do, but I can't promise anything."

"Thank you, sir. Bless you." Beatrix's words emerged on a grateful sigh.

Iris stayed with her father after Beatrix marched out of the prison, leaving her dizzying scent behind. She turned toward her father. "What's going on, Pater?"

"What do you mean?"

"Why weren't you kinder to Beatrix?"

He sighed. "If I held the hand of every woman who came in

here looking for a lost man, I'd never get anything done. I did her a kindness."

"*That* was not kindness." She crossed her arms. "What are you hiding? Do you know where he is?"

"I don't have a Favius on my list."

"Pater."

He didn't respond. The scrolls and tablets on his desk rustled.

Another thought prickled the back of her neck. "What was Tribune Braccus doing here?" She shuddered as she spoke his name.

Her father hesitated, then released another long breath. "What did he say to you? You came through the door with wolves on your heels."

"I'd rather face wolves." She wrapped her arms around her waist. She heard her father's swallow from across the room. He stood, his feet scraping a familiar tread to the shelves, where she heard a clink and the bubbling of wine filling a cup.

"Just a few more days, Iris."

She shook her head. What good would a few days do? She hadn't realized she'd spoken aloud until her father answered.

"I can't tell you now. But soon."

His words did nothing to soothe her fears. How many other promises had he broken?

"Are you coming home tonight?" The thought of returning to an empty apartment after running into the tribune made her legs shake.

"No, this is my night to stay."

"Can I stay with you?" She took a tentative step toward the desk. "I won't bother you; I'll sit here on the floor. I just . . ."

"You can stay." He returned the cup to the shelf and took her elbow. "Sit in my chair. I have some things I need to take care of."

XX

VALENS SANK TO THE FLOOR, long past caring about the human filth covering it. The suffocating darkness surrounded him with fear and swirling doubt, threatening to swallow him whole. And then there was Hades, whispering through the darkness, offering repeatedly to end him one moment, then treating him as an honored guest and bestowing him with gifts of moldy bread the next. He prayed Bea would be safe and that she would not do something foolish on his behalf. His late uncle's reason no longer held Beatrix's passion for justice in check. His mind swam with worries and what-ifs. His hands shook. He felt as if someone had him by the ankles, spinning him round and round and round.

"God!" The prayer pushed from somewhere deep in his gut and echoed off the rounded walls. The shrieking hurricane in his mind came to an immediate still. He recalled that this round, tomb-like hole had been the holding place of the disciple Peter before his upside-down crucifixion, and where the apostle Paul awaited his beheading. Those thoughts, dark though they might be, comforted. Valens was neither alone in the belly of the earth nor powerless. The power of the One who formed the stones beneath his head lived within him, and there was no place Valens could go where He would not see or hear. He began to pray. For his friends, his family, the couples he'd married in secret.

As the truth calmed him, Hades began to rage and scream. He

prowled opposite Valens, pacing the circular edge of the domed cell, snarling in the back of his throat like a savage beast. Bones clattered around his feet.

He gave Valens a wide berth.

"Kill him, kill him now," Hades muttered under his breath as he paced. The size of the cell did not allow for things spoken aloud to go unheard. Valens braced himself but didn't stop praying. Hades paced but kept his distance.

A single, small loaf of bread dropped through a sliver of red light in the ceiling, and a skin of water lowered only long enough for each of them to drink once before being retracted. Hades paced himself into a muttering heap along the opposite wall. Food and water came twice, hours and hours and hours passing in between.

From the snatches of sane talk coming from his fellow prisoner, Valens gathered that the man had once been the son of a Gothic chieftain, sent to Rome to kill the emperor before his capture and slow metamorphosis into Hades, god of the underworld. He'd ruled the Tullianum with unquestioned authority for nearly a decade.

How long would it be before Valens became as crazed as Hades?

A scraping noise from above woke him. His stomach stabbed with hunger as he sat up, expecting the usual loaf and waterskin. A blazing half-moon appeared in the center of the black dome, slowly waxing to full and pouring blinding yellow light into the cell.

Hades cowered against the wall, the whites of his eyes wide and flashing. "The executioner comes!" He wheezed and shook a bony finger in Valens's direction. "You should have listened to me! *I* would have killed you gently."

Metallic clicks echoed as a lone chain lowered through the hole, a large metal loop dangling from the end. The executioner should have been lowered on that chain, one foot in the loop, standing and spinning slowly like a sinister circus performer, a leather garrote in hand.

The clicking stopped. The chain swung empty, two feet off the floor.

"Valentine. Grab hold." The voice came from somewhere above.

Valens did as he was told, his hunger-weakened body shaking with the effort to hold on as the metallic clicks came once more, this time withdrawing the chain, and Valens with it, inch by inch. They had not sent an executioner. Perhaps they were letting him go. Perhaps he would be taken to trial. Or perhaps he was to be executed publicly.

His head emerged through the hole in the center of the dome. He squinted against the light of a single lantern and saw the jailor winding the chain with a large wooden crank. Quintus stopped and gestured for Valens to climb out the rest of the way. He complied all too eagerly.

"Strip." Giving Valens a wide berth, Quintus wound the loop of chain up to an iron ring in the ceiling.

Valens yanked the tunic over his head, hard and crusted with filth he did not want to identify. He dropped it on the floor and stood shivering, wondering if this was it. Maybe they strangled prisoners up here. The other prisoners who'd been chained to the walls when he'd first been cast into the Tullianum were gone, shackles dangling empty.

Quintus kicked a grimy bucket toward him. "Wash. But don't drink from it."

Valens knelt and scrubbed his hands and arms, legs and feet. There was no soap. Surely they did not make prisoners wash before executing them. Hope sparked. Perhaps they were releasing him.

Quintus tossed him another tunic of mushroom gray that looked as though someone had died in it. Considering the nature of the prison, that was a good possibility.

"Will you still refuse to give allegiance to the gods of Rome?" Quintus tilted his head, fingering the club at his waist.

Valens stood. "Always." He pulled the tunic over his head.

"You should reconsider."

"I cannot."

Quintus's mouth tightened. "Then kneel."

Valens obeyed. Quintus shackled his wrists to chains dangling from the ceiling and locked his feet into stocks behind him. He would not be able to move from his knees. He needed to use the latrine. Still, this was better than the Tullianum. Better than being strangled.

The jailor dumped Valens's tunic and the contents of the bucket into the Tullianum before securing the cover back in place. He left the lantern hanging from the ceiling and went up the set of stairs, disappearing through the door to the prison office without another word.

Everything went quiet. Valens stared at the shimmering light dancing over the grime-darkened walls. It was warmer here, slightly better-smelling, and best, Hades was no longer begging for permission to wring his neck. Valens took his first deep breath in days as the relief of his new circumstances overcame him. And then, in a barely perceptible whisper, he started to sing.

XXI

WHILE IRIS'S PATER DID SOMETHING in the holding cell that made a lot of clicking sounds, Markos brought in the evening meal and left it on the desk. The barley bread and cold fish cakes sat untouched while Iris paced, waiting for her father to finish.

The office allowed a mere six paces between the front entrance and the door leading to the cells. To be safe, Iris only counted five before turning. Thoughts of Valentine raced through her mind. Where had he gone? Had he taken a trip with friends and forgotten to tell Beatrix? Had he left a note she hadn't found? Or had he run off with his lover, as her father had suggested? An uncalled-for twinge of jealousy snaked through her. She had no right to it, but it rankled all the same.

She couldn't imagine him doing any of those things. Valentine was different. Considerate. He made her feel *seen*. He cared enough to treat her with dignity and speak to her as an equal and not somehow lesser because of her sightlessness. And then he'd revealed that his god had given her the flashes of sight. The subsequent questions would drive her mad if they went unanswered for much longer.

Lost in thought, Iris paced too far and slammed into the wall. Rubbing the sting from her forehead, she muttered beneath her breath. The iron door dragged open, hinges groaning. She could hear Pater's exhaustion in the longer scrape of his limp.

"Markos brought dinner." She moved toward the desk. "Is everything all right?"

Pater snorted as if clearing his nose. "Two days in the Tullianum with Hades is usually enough to make anyone beg to follow the law. Not so with this prisoner." He limped to the desk and sat with a groan. "I hate to have to beat him into obedience, but maybe I'll call Titus to do it. It'd be nice to have him here too. The three of us, like old times." A wistful tone lingered in his words and Iris found herself wondering if the three of them would ever be together again once she and her father left the city. The chair crackled as Pater settled himself into it.

Iris felt for the basket Markos had brought and set out the fish cakes and bread, then measured watered wine into a clay tumbler. She listened to the trickle start with a deep slosh that rose and softened to a bubbly whisper. Setting the amphora down, she took a deep breath. The seeds of a desperate idea had begun their work as she'd paced the office. Iris rushed on before caution could silence her.

"I've been meaning to tell you about the reason for the flashes of sight." She twisted her fingers into the sides of her dress.

"Yes, as the chief augur said, you will see again."

Iris set the tumbler in front of him. "I believe that." She took a deep breath and swallowed. "But not because of Jupiter."

He took a drink. "What do you mean?"

She pressed her fingers into the edge of the desk, drawing a wobbly strength. "I never told you that on the days I had the glimpses, I'd met a man in the bakery and at the market who prayed for me."

Pater stopped chewing. "Who?"

"The same man who helped me walk you home from the tavern."

"I don't remember much from that night."

She shook her head. "It doesn't matter because the last time I saw him, he said *he* wasn't responsible for my sight; his *god* was."

"Which god?" Pater's voice sounded strangely breathless.

She tucked a strand of hair behind her ear. "The Christian god."

"Iris, no. You can't get mixed up with those people. They're dangerous."

"But it's the *one thing* we haven't tried." She heard the muffled gurgles of fish washed down with wine and the high-pitched bubbling of the tumbler being refilled.

"We've been trying to earn the gods' favor for years! Going to the Christians will only set us back further." The amphora thunked onto the desk, rattling stacks of tablets.

Her lips tightened, and her voice dropped. "Yes, well, obviously our loyalty has done us great favors."

He shushed her. "Don't speak like that!" The chair creaked as he leaned forward. "The augurs have read the birds; Jupiter says you'll be healed."

"By which god?"

Pater didn't answer.

"What if the Christian god is the one with all the power?" Her secret thought, finally spoken, came out weak and whispered.

"Don't be ridiculous. If he had any sort of power, his worshipers wouldn't be imprisoned and killed."

Tears heated her eyes. "Please, Pater, we have nothing to lose, and it would put my wonderings to rest."

Her pater did not speak, nor did she hear him eating or drinking. Finally he sighed. "If I let you talk to a Christian, will you stop this nonsense?"

She straightened, hope surging. "Do you mean it? You'll let me go to them? Because I think I know where I can—"

"You're not going anywhere with them," Pater interrupted. "And certainly not to one of their meetings if that's what you were about to say."

Iris went quiet, waiting for his suggestion. Based on the vehemence of his response, she decided not to reveal that her friend Beatrix was a Christian and that Iris had already sought her out.

Pater sighed. "If I let you talk to a Christian, do I have your word that you won't pursue them anymore?"

She nodded, but before she could offer verbal assurances, he cut her off again. "The Christian god is not something to trifle with. Especially now. Christians are not good citizens. They refuse to attend the sacrifices or show proper reverence to the emperor. I don't want you mixing with them."

The hair on Iris's arms rose as Pater spoke, but his warning did not keep the tiny, stunted petals of hope from uncurling in her chest.

"*One* conversation." Pater's voice went steely. "And you'll promise me you won't speak of it again?"

Iris swallowed, feeling her palms grow damp. "I promise."

"Then come with me."

Her breath caught. "*Now?*"

"The sooner the better." His chair scraped across the floor as he stood. "There's a Christian here, but not for much longer."

Elation surged through her, just as quickly squashed by doubts. If this was her one chance, did she want it now? Here? "Do you think a prisoner will agree to invoke his god on behalf of his jailor's daughter?"

"He wouldn't dare refuse." Pater sorted through the mass of jingling keys strapped to his belt. "I would think the fear of punishment would only make his prayers all the more sincere."

He moved toward the ironclad door as fear and hope warred furiously inside her. She nearly called him back. After the hope and longing Valentine had kindled within her toward his god, how could she withstand the bitter crush of another disappointment? Wasn't it better to live with hope?

The key clicked into the lock. Iris couldn't make herself tell her father to stop, but neither could she make her feet move. The door opened again with its familiar groan.

Pater waited. "Are you coming?"

XXII

Titus sat at the rickety desk in his storeroom "office." Outside, the air rumbled with snores rolling from barrack windows like lava from Vesuvius. He should have been asleep too, but something wasn't right. He'd had no word from Adonis since he'd been planted in the notarii office. He'd sent Urian undercover with the guise of a lovestruck man longing for marriage, and paid his street rat, Statian, to keep his ears out for news of recent marriages. If Titus could only find a marriage document, he'd find the scratching quill that created it. With all these pieces set in motion, it chafed to sit and wait.

He reread his notes from the notarii interviews, the feeling that he'd missed something important hanging heavy over him. There was a discrepancy somewhere. He knew it. He could sense it.

He could not find it.

Titus cursed and rubbed his burning eyes. Something one of the notarii had said—perhaps he hadn't written it down. Pulling out his tablets of notes, he began with the first notarius he questioned. Horace Caldarius, the man with the overeager front teeth. Nervous, he recalled, but not suspiciously so. He went down the line, glancing over the notes, recalling what each notarius looked like, how they'd acted as he questioned them.

He paced. The air in the storeroom hung still and close, making his tunic stick to his chest. Titus wished he could just go to sleep. But there'd be no rest until he figured out the problem. His boots kept time with his thoughts. Plowing forward, pivoting as he came to a wall, forward again, wall. He pivoted again, kicking over a box of ex-legionnaires' files as he turned.

He pulled up short. Yes, that was it—something one of them had said.

Titus dug through his notes, careful not to smudge the wax on the tablets. Where was it? Where was—? There. He pulled the tablet free and tipped it toward the lamp, eyes dropping over the hasty scrawl. Something about ex-legionnaires. He hadn't written it down, but he was sure the notarius had mentioned them. Something about making money from marrying ex-legionnaires. An odd enough detail that it was worth looking into. A quick glance at the name dropped a brick into his stomach.

Mars and Jupiter.

He'd have arrested any other notarius without hesitation. But not this one.

He woke the two speculatores he'd recruited for the job. "Ex-legionnaires." He paced as they pulled on tunics and rubbed bloodshot eyes. "Go over the discharge lists and look into them all if need be. I want the names of every recently discharged legionnaire in the city with recent 'wives' or women who could be. And someone alert Statian of this."

A recent discharge might have a greater reason to defy a marriage ban. It would seem unfair. In the same situation, Titus might agree, but that was not his job. His blood pounded; he was onto something. He could feel it.

Grumbling that the files could wait until a decent hour, the two speculatores left to pore over boxes of scrolls while Titus marched to the quarters of Trecenarius Faustus.

"Sir." He beat his chest in salute when he'd been shown inside. "Sorry to intrude at this hour, but I think I've found the notarius I believe is responsible for the contracts."

"If you have your man, why are you here?" Faustus did not appear disgruntled by the unconventional hour and crossed to the washstand, dipping his whole head in the basin, gargling and shaking it before rearing back like a dog, shooting sprays of water in all directions.

Titus winced as flecks hit his face. "The notarius in question is Valentine Favius Diastema."

Faustus raked a towel over his head. "Favius," he repeated. "Surely no relation to—"

"His grandson."

"Oh, gods." Faustus rubbed his temples as Titus filled him in on the interrogation and how Valentine had remarked about ex-legionnaires.

"Seems a thin thread." Faustus shook his head.

Titus tilted his chin. "Sometimes that's all there is to go on."

"Tread carefully." Faustus winced. "We cannot afford a man like his grandfather as an enemy. He wields a lot of power as of late. And to falsely accuse his grandson hangs our careers on a spider's web. Don't do anything without absolute certainty."

"I'll follow him myself."

Faustus nodded. "Keep me informed."

Titus saluted and left.

A city messenger boy waited outside, chest heaving from running. "Speculatore Didius Liberare? You're needed at the carcer." The boy gulped air and braced a hand against the building. "It's urgent."

XXIII

Someone was singing. Iris first heard it after Pater opened the door. She did not recognize the tune—if it *was* a tune—but the voice . . . there was something familiar about the voice.

"Stop." She held out a hand toward Pater. The groan of the hinges ceased, and as he hooked the keys onto his belt, she heard the singing again. The ball of snakes in her stomach roiled. She took a step, the voice louder now.

Pater took her hand. "You don't have to do this."

"I want to know." She shivered. "I *have* to know."

He sighed. "I am only allowing this because I couldn't live with myself if I didn't do everything in my power to help you." He squeezed her hand. "I will never regret spending what I did on cures. I'd do it again. My deepest regret is that you'll have to pay for my indiscretions." He let out a long breath. "It kills me to watch your hopes dashed again and again."

She swallowed. "Then let me do this alone, Pater."

"I can't."

"How many are in there?"

"One."

"Chained?"

"Yes."

"Then what could happen?"

Pater touched the scar on her face, voice dropping with regret. "What could be the harm in a walk to the market, I thought."

"It'll be fine, Pater."

He opened the door wider though neither stepped through it. A voice wove into the room, singing softer now.

"God is our refuge and strength,
    A very present help in trouble.
Therefore we will not fear."

Not ever? Iris rubbed her arms. Not even when imprisoned? Or sentenced to labor in a sweltering quarry? Or forced to be a tribune's mistress?

As if in answer, the singing continued.

"Even though the earth be removed,
    And though the mountains be carried into the midst of the sea . . .
Though the mountains shake with its swelling."

Iris hoped this god was worth the singer's bravery—worth the risk *she* took. Her heart beat like the drums leading an emperor's procession, urging her on, yet she froze, listening. The prisoner kept singing about a god. One seated far above the glory of the skies. A god who looked down on the heavens and the earth. So the Christian god was higher than all the gods on Mount Olympus.

Her legs shook as she started down the steps, her fingers trailing on the damp stone wall, feeling every ripple of the ancient Etruscan chisels that carved out a living tomb long before the Romans settled here. Her feet quivered as she searched and stepped. The sulfur stench of the sewer burned her nose. She'd been in here with Titus as a child, but never since the accident.

The words of the song poured over her with a strange warmth.

"Be still, and know that I am God;
I will be exalted among the nations;

I will be exalted in the earth!
The Lord of hosts is with us;
  The God of Jacob is our refuge."

The song ended just as Iris reached the bottom of the steps. She stopped when it did. The singing did not resume. Pater paused behind her.

Her mouth went dry. What if the Christian refused to pray? What if he prayed and nothing happened? If a god was not powerful enough to keep this devotee out of prison, how could he be powerful enough to restore her sight? This was a mistake. Iris turned, her mouth opening to tell Pater she'd changed her mind.

Another voice spoke before she did. Mild. Clear. *Familiar.*

"Iris?"

She swung her face toward him, the hairs on her arms standing on end. "Valentine?" Her heart dropped. It wasn't possible.

All three were talking at once.

"What are you doing here?"

"Pater, you said you didn't know where Beatrix's nephew was."

"You *know* him?"

"You've seen my aunt? Is she all right?"

"She's well. She's worried." Iris took a step toward Valentine.

"This was a bad idea." Pater took her arm. "We're leaving."

She pulled back. "We can't go now—you promised, and you . . ." She fought her voice into a whisper though it did not mask the accusation in her tone. "You arrested him and lied about it." Iris turned her face toward Valentine. "Why are you here?"

"Not attending sacrifices," Pater supplied. "Leading illegal gatherings, practice of unsanctioned religion."

A rustle of straw and clinking chains sounded from the far wall as Valentine shifted. She wondered how he'd been secured. His voice sounded low to the ground. Upside-down perhaps? Lying flat so the rats could crawl over him at will? Pater had talked about rats getting in through the sewer grate every now and then. She shuddered, pulling her palla tighter around her shoulders.

"We came so I could talk to a Christian." She took two steps toward Valentine. "I didn't know it would be *you*."

"Well." He sighed. "Here I am."

A beat of silence. Iris knew if she didn't broach the subject now, she'd lose her nerve, or Pater would remove her.

"You prayed for me," she blurted.

"I did." Valentine's tone encouraged her to continue. Pater stood still and quiet, although his grip on her arm loosened.

Valentine's admission gave her boldness.

"It's just." She took another step. "Every time I met you and you promised to pray, my eyes were opened. And then you said it was your god and that he was calling me." Iris took three steps toward his voice and dropped to her knees. "My pater and I have prayed to every god we could find, and none listened until you prayed. I'm begging you. Pray to your god again for me so I can see." She stopped as snarls and screeches erupted from somewhere below.

Valentine still hadn't spoken. The hope slipped from her, whirling like a drain at the top of her spine, slowly moving downward and gaining momentum with each second he didn't speak. Her lips trembled.

"*I* cannot heal you." Valentine's voice was barely above a whisper. "But if He chooses, my *God* can."

Her head lifted.

Valentine's voice rose as he continued. "He is the Alpha and Omega, the Beginning and the End. He was, and is, and will always be the One True God. The *only* God. He created everything that exists out of nothing. He spoke and the world came into being, breathed and the stars burst into flame. He called light into existence with a word. He is the All-Powerful One, the All-Knowing One. Creator. Rescuer. Healer."

She could hardly breathe waiting for him to go on.

"I will pray for you, Iris." He paused. "But know this: I am mere clay in the hands of an almighty God. It is in His name and by His design that you are healed. It has nothing to do with me."

She nodded once. Was he protecting himself so he couldn't be blamed if it didn't work? She didn't voice her thoughts. The chains clicked. She closed her eyes—as if it would make a difference.

"Do you believe Jesus Christ, the One True God, can heal you?"

She wouldn't be here if she didn't. "Yes."

He took a deep breath. "Lord God, just as You restored the sight of the blind beggar and many others, restore Iris's sight for the glory of Your name so that all who know her may see You and know You."

That was it. One sentence. No strange incantations. No incense, no money, no blood. The prison dropped into silence broken only by the sound of Valentine's breath. Of hers.

A tingling sensation prickled the top of her head with a warmth like oil running down through her hair. Goose bumps traveled up and down her body.

Iris opened her eyes.

Darkness.

She hadn't realized the extent of her hope until it crumbled around her with that single blink. *Please, God.* Tears flooded her eyes. She blinked them away furiously, not wanting Valentine to see how deep the disappointment cut, how much she'd allowed herself to trust him and his God. As she blinked, a hazy golden spot appeared in the center of the darkness, slowly brightening like polished copper beneath a layer of dust.

Valentine didn't make a sound. Her pater didn't move. The whole prison seemed frozen and silent. The golden spot cleared into an inverted brownish-amber triangle, the lower half of the point darkened with stubble, and then there were eyes above. Eyes and nose and—she blinked once more and the fog lifted completely, revealing a man bathed in a flickering shaft of golden lantern light. He knelt, unshaven and filthy, arms raised toward the ceiling and held there with chains. His eyes were closed.

Iris fell back on her hands, her startled cry jerking Pater into motion. His knees cracked against the stone floor as he dropped beside her.

"Iris?" He cupped her face in his hands, peering hard into her eyes. Iris crumpled and swallowed the hot lump in her throat, managing only to nod as his brown eyes, creased with concern, searched hers.

"Pater, I can—I can see." She reached up and touched his face. So dear, so nearly forgotten. His bristled gray eyebrows rose, and his face wrinkled with understanding as he crushed her to his chest, unable to speak. His shoulders shook, tears plunking into her hair. She stared at the lantern over his shoulder, the orange-and-yellow flame curling and twisting in the darkness. Such a tiny flame, yet so powerful and beautiful. She pulled away from Pater, gripping his hands as she turned back to Valentine.

He knelt, head bowed, black hair gleaming in the light. When he lifted his chin and met her gaze, his eyes shone with barely checked emotion.

"Praise be to God." Valentine spoke through a shuddering exhale.

"Pater." Iris couldn't pull her gaze away from him. "This is Beatrix's nephew. This is Valentine."

"If you must insist." Valentine's lips twitched. "I prefer Valens or Val."

"What magic is this?" Pater asked in awe, twisting to face Valentine.

"You can see." Valentine spoke to Iris, looking as much in shock as they. She nodded, laughing as tears rolled hot down her face.

He grinned back at her, revealing a charming gap in his front teeth, before shifting his gaze to Quintus. "No magic. Your daughter was healed by the power of Jesus Christ."

XXIV

QUINTUS WANTED BOTH TO ARGUE and to listen. He couldn't deny this god's power—nor ignore the danger of it.

Valentine nodded to Iris. "Your daughter's sight is proof of the resurrection and power of Jesus Christ. What other gods have done what *He* has?"

Neither Quintus nor Iris responded. The answer was obvious.

"Who is he?" Quintus asked.

In the orange light, Valentine's eyes took on the hue of polished copper. "Jesus Christ is God. Creator of this world and everything in it. No temple can contain Him. He breathes out stars and life, and yet He is not far from any of us."

"A seer once told me a god she did not know had done me a great service." Quintus shifted his weight. "I have sought this god ever since, but I do not know his name."

"His name is Jesus." Valentine spoke with certainty. "And yes, He has done a great thing for you—for everyone."

Despite the warnings pulsing through his mind, Quintus could not withstand the flood of relief that swept over him at that one name. *Jesus.* Was this truly the god he'd spent years trying to find? The god with enough power to restore Iris's sight—yet unable to keep Valentine from prison? And what was this great service?

"What thing has he done?"

"Pater, can't you release him?"

Quintus turned to see Iris's eyes traveling over Valentine's chains with a look of mingled awe and anguish. Of course. It was the least he could do in the wake of such a miracle. He pushed himself to his feet with a groan. Daggers of pain shot through his leg. He felt for the keys at his belt and limped toward Valentine.

"I'll get food." Iris scrambled to her feet and rushed for the stairs, head tilting this way and that, taking in the dank cell as if it were the most magnificent sculpture in the Portico of Pompey.

Quintus opened the lock on the stocks and Valentine slid his raw ankles free with a groan. "Thank you."

Quintus worked at the lock on his wrist.

"Will you tell me how long I will remain here?"

The lock clicked and Valentine's arm fell to his side. He grunted and slowly flexed his fingers, which were no doubt numb.

How was he going to explain? If he said anything to Valentine about the arrest, about who had ordered it and why, the promised payment would be withheld, and he and Iris could not escape the city. Iris might be able to see now, but without the money, the tribune would still claim her.

"I've been sworn to secrecy on that account." Quintus released the other wrist. "I dare not go against my orders."

Valentine stumbled to his feet, struggling to work feeling into his arms and hands. "You had *orders* to arrest me? From whom?"

"I'm a soldier. I receive orders and I obey."

Speaking of orders, Quintus also couldn't have a prisoner walking around the carcer, free. He gestured to the wall where an ankle shackle lay at the end of a snaking chain. "You'll be more comfortable here at least."

Valentine limped to the wall and slid into a sitting position, legs shaking with the effort.

Quintus closed the iron around his ankle, guilt pricking his conscience. He couldn't leave Valentine here, not after this. But what could he do?

Iris crossed the cell, arms loaded with what remained of their supper. She knelt by Valentine, setting the amphora of wine on the ground beside her and offering him a fish cake, which disappeared in two bites. She poured a cup of watered wine, watching the plum-colored stream like a magic trick. She handed it to Valentine and eyed Quintus.

"Can't you do something, Pater? Can't you get him out of here?" She stood, putting on her best pleading look.

Quintus shifted and shook his head. Miracle or not, releasing Valentine meant no escape for Iris. No matter how grateful he might be, he couldn't take that from her. Quintus met Valentine's eyes with uncomfortable apology. "What you've done is considered treason. I can't release you without a signed document stating you recant your Christian beliefs."

Valentine set the cup beside him, a look of resignation steeling his features. "Well, that isn't going to happen. So what now?"

"*Treason?*" Iris's eyes went wide. "But that means . . ."

Both stared up at him and Quintus felt as if they were on one side, and he, the enemy on the other. Quintus pinched the bridge of his nose. "I will do all I can to get you out of here." It was the best he could promise. "It's the least I can do to repay you for what you've done."

"My God worked here tonight." Valentine tilted his head back against the wall. "But I will not refuse your help."

"God." Quintus repeated the word as if it were foreign. And it might as well have been. *God.* Singular. Strange. "You were about to tell us about your god. About the service he's done."

Valentine started at the beginning, with a creation story Quintus had never heard. Where a god created a perfect world and put a man and woman in charge of it, with a single command not to eat of one tree.

Quintus saw where that was heading.

"They unleashed evil into the world, which separated them from a perfect and holy God. No impurity can stand before Him. He cast them out of the garden forever."

"But it was the god's fault." Iris shook her head, protesting. "If he hadn't made a forbidden tree, all would be well."

Quintus nodded at her observation. The gods were usually blundering things.

"God created people for relationship—with each other and with Him." Valentine shifted and winced but kept on. "Love that has no will of its own is not love at all; it's servitude—worse, it's slavery."

Iris visibly shuddered. Quintus knew she was thinking about the tribune, about their soon-to-be fate if they didn't get out of the city.

He took her cold hand. "Get on to the great service he's done."

Valentine scratched behind his ear. "The penalty for their disobedience was death. Physical death in this world and a death of the soul which permanently separated their spirits from God. That separation passed to their children as well. The only way they could once again rekindle any sort of relationship with God was to obey the laws He gave them."

"All the best stories are about mortals beating the gods at their own games." Quintus gestured for Valentine to continue. "Who did it?"

Valentine shook his head. "There is none righteous, not even one. Whoever keeps all the laws and breaks just one of them is still as guilty as the one who breaks them all. The laws were given to show us that there is nothing we can do to earn our way back into God's good graces."

"So we are doomed?" Iris's whisper did not mask the despair in her tone.

"Yes." Valentine gave a nod. "But not completely." His voice lowered as if about to reveal a great secret. Quintus leaned forward, realizing he was finally about to hear the answer to the question that had nagged at him since he'd been to the seer.

"At just the right moment, God sent His only Son, born of a virgin, born under the laws He'd given, in order to redeem everyone, so that all might receive the right to be called children of God. That right is for everyone who believes on His name."

Iris squinted up at Quintus, who tilted his head.

Valentine explained. "The penalty for sin is death, but God sent

His Son, Jesus, to die in our place so we wouldn't have to. All we have to do is believe that He is our Savior, and we are washed clean before God."

Quintus leaned back on his heels, turning it over in his mind. So much about this god didn't make sense. Yet there was power here. Unlike anything he'd seen before. Though the man chained before him faced torture or death, he was calm and eager to speak of his god. So what was it? What was it that made even women and children walk bravely into arenas, singing until wild dogs tore out their throats? Why didn't the high cost keep them from this dangerous god? Any other sect would have been squashed at the first imprisonment of their leaders. The first martyrs. But for the Christians, persecution was fuel to a flame.

Why?

He'd always wondered. Until tonight. Until he'd seen what their god could do. Other gods held empty promises, but this one . . . Valentine spoke the truth. Quintus knew it suddenly, beyond doubt. He saw himself mired deep, sinking in the quicksand of his efforts to earn the gods' favor. His efforts of piety, of offerings and incense only served to thrash him more deeply in the sludge. He felt in that moment that the Christian God, this *Jesus*, held out a hand toward him. Beckoning. *Come,* He said. *Take My hand, offered for you, and follow Me.*

Quintus's doubts cleared like the banks of the spring-flooded Tiber. "I cannot deny the power of your God." He spoke in a hoarse whisper. "I have searched for years looking for what only your God can offer. I—I don't know what—What do I need to do?"

"Believe on the Lord Jesus Christ and you will be saved."

"I believe." Iris spoke without hesitation and Valentine's gaze shifted to her. His lips parted. Shocked.

Wet glimmers streaked her cheeks as Iris's lips wobbled into a smile. "I believe." She laughed, and Quintus had never before seen such a radiance of joy on her face.

He reached out to take his daughter's hand but in his mind saw himself straining from the muck, reaching for the hand of God.

"Me too." His admission was choked by the flood of peace that rolled over him. It smoothed the tension in his belly, the worries in his mind, like a wave on trampled sand. "I believe."

The lantern hanging from the ceiling flickered violently and dimmed, oil burning low.

Valentine's eyes closed and he tilted his head back. "Praise be to God." He breathed the words, then looked at them once more, serious. "I will not mislead either of you. There is a high cost to following Jesus. It will not make your life easier or safer, especially now. But God promises never to leave you alone, and during your troubles, you will find His overpowering peace."

Quintus already had. He understood now why Valentine and the others could be so serene. God had not used His power to keep Valentine from being arrested but had given him peace instead. A question wiggled its way through the peace. He looked at his daughter. What would this new belief require of them?

Iris gave a nod, eyes wandering the cell. "Even so, I must believe. How can I not?"

The lantern guttered and extinguished, dropping the cell into darkness. Iris let out a strangled squeak. Quintus gripped her hand.

"It's all right," he soothed. "It was just the lantern."

"I thought maybe . . ." Her words came on a relieved breath, but her grip on his hand did not ease as he turned them toward the stairs. Dawn showed itself as a pale-gray rectangle around the edges of the ironclad door. Iris released a long sigh of relief when he pushed it open, gaze darting around the room. She didn't speak until Quintus had closed the cell door.

"What's going on, Pater?" She crossed her arms. "Why didn't you tell Beatrix her nephew was here?"

"I was following orders, Iris." He turned the key in the lock and sighed, resting his forehead against the cold iron of the door. "He was to be arrested for unlawful religious gatherings and held secretly to scare him into recanting."

"Orders from whom?"

"I took a bribe." He squeezed his eyes shut. "If I arrested him, the amount of money they promised would get us out of here. I didn't know it was your friend's nephew."

She was silent for two breaths. "He said he won't recant. What's going to happen to him?"

"I don't know." He hooked the keys back onto his belt.

"We can't just leave him here! Not after what he's done, what he's told us." Her voice was laced with panic that bloomed in her dark eyes.

Quintus glanced toward the front door, where Helix stood guard outside. He lowered his voice. "We'll talk more about this later." He hoped she understood the warning in his tone. They would have to keep this quiet for now. "It's dawn. Go home."

"Pater!" Her eyes went wide. "We have to tell Titus!"

XXV

THE MESSENGER HADN'T GIVEN HIM the reason for the urgency, but Titus rushed anyway. He'd run most of the way at a dead sprint and was out of breath by the time he pounded up the stairs to the carcer. The guard swung the door open before Titus reached the top.

He pushed inside and swept the entire office in a quick glance. "I got your message." No sign of the tribune, nor Quintus for that matter. Iris sat behind the desk. Alone.

"What's going on?" He turned to face her. "I got an urgent message to come here."

Iris stared at him. "I hardly recognize you, but for your voice. You look . . ."

He inhaled to make a quip in response but then noticed her eyes. Pointed at him. And focused. He went still.

"What are you talking about?" His heart began to thrum.

"Older, for one thing." Her voice trembled a little. Then her teeth flashed against her skin in a sudden grin. "You grew into those ears. I was doubtful."

He pinched his earlobe. She was teasing. Had to be. He glanced around again. "What's going on? I ran all the way here."

Iris tugged at her earlobe, mimicking him. She grinned and stood, eyes glistening with unshed tears.

"Mars and Jupiter." His hands fell to his sides. "Can you really see me?"

She nodded and bit her lip, a strangled bubble of laughter escaping. Titus crossed the office in two strides and grabbed her face in his wide hands, staring hard into her deep-brown eyes. "If you're teasing me, I'm going to throw you in the Tullianum with Hades."

Iris laughed and shook her head, a tear escaping each eye. "I'm not."

"Seriously."

"As a Stoic."

Something crumbled in his chest as the reality hit him. She would never pull a prank like this. Titus crushed her to his chest in a hug. "Jupiter Optimus Maximus!" He kissed the top of her head and pushed her back at arm's length to look at her again. "How?"

"It wasn't Jupiter." Her face beamed with a strange inner light. "It was the Christian God, Jesus."

His smile faltered. "The—what?"

"Jesus, the God of the Christians, healed me."

Titus shook his head in disbelief.

She rushed on to tell him the whole story as his mind reeled with the news. He hadn't been sheltered. He knew what the Christians believed. They'd been alternately tolerated and persecuted at intervals since the birth of the religion at the death of its leader. Their refusal to honor the emperor and participate in traditional Roman festivals because they found them in opposition to their invisible god made them insubordinate, unpatriotic, and dangerous in the eyes of good Romans.

But Titus could not deny this one thing: Iris had been blinded because of him. He'd been the one to goad her into climbing the aqueduct with him. Yet here she stood, eyes wide in sight.

"Where's your father?"

"He left. He's trying to find a way to get Valentine released."

"Valentine?" A jolt went through him at the name. "Valentine who?"

Iris rolled her eyes upward, trying to recall. "I can't remember. It's like Flavian or something—but not Flavian." She crossed her arms. "Fla—Fa—Favius! *Favius*. That's it!"

Mars and bloody Jupiter! Something cold settled in the bottom of Titus's stomach. He looked toward the cell door, sitting solid and locked in Quintus's absence. "I want to meet him."

Before Iris could respond, Quintus entered, eyes puffy from lack of sleep, yet sparking with energy.

"Titus." His smile was eager. "You heard the news?"

"It's a miracle, Quintus." Titus nodded and looked at Iris, unable to help the shocked grin. "Praise the gods."

"Praise *the* God," Quintus corrected. He hurried across the room and fumbled through his keys for the one to unlock the iron door.

"Iris told me everything." Titus fought to keep the edge from his voice. "It sounds unbelievable, except for—"

"Except for the fact I can *see!*" Iris sang out, laughing. She grabbed his arm, tugging. "Come and meet Valentine."

Titus snagged the lantern from the desk and led the way as the three descended into the darkness, cloyed with smells of sewer and unwashed bodies.

At the bottom, Titus held the lantern high, swinging it to the left and right, sending streaks of light skittering over the walls. The prisoner, lying on the straw at the back of the cell, rolled over and sat up.

"Come into the light," Titus ordered as Quintus and Iris flanked him.

"Good morning, Valentine." Iris's voice went uncharacteristically shy. Titus's gaze swung from the shadowed prisoner to catch her admiring look. The stab of jealousy froze in his gut as the prisoner spoke.

"Good morning." Valentine looked from Iris to Titus. Recognition flared in his eyes and his calm faltered before his chin dropped in deference. "Investigator." He glanced up from beneath rather large eyebrows. "I am surprised to see you."

"*Are* you?" He didn't mask the accusation in his tone.

Valentine lifted his chin slightly and held his gaze.

"*You* know him *too?*" Quintus looked between the two men in astonishment. Neither answered.

"Titus?"

Valentine's eyes flicked to Iris when she spoke—which Titus found extremely irritating.

"We're briefly acquainted." Titus hung the lantern from the hook in the ceiling. "You healed Iris?"

Valentine's eyebrows lifted and he looked back and forth between all of them. "I—no," he stammered. "My God restored Iris's sight. I am a mere tool in His hands."

Titus bit back a snide remark but couldn't deny his curiosity. If it had been anyone but Iris, he'd have dismissed it as a swindler's trick. He looked at Iris standing beside him and noted again the way her wide brown eyes took in the cell like it was a palace.

He crossed his arms and settled his weight. "Well. Tell me what happened."

They all did. Sometimes Valentine spoke, and then Iris broke in, or Quintus asked Valentine to repeat one of the stories he'd told earlier about Jesus. Titus took it all in, the glowing excitement on Iris's and Quintus's faces and the restored calm of the prisoner. The story was unbelievable at best. Except for the fact that Iris had been blind but now could see. *That*, he could not deny. When the stories turned to center around the exploits of the Christian god, Titus stopped listening. He stood with his arms crossed, the words echoing off the stone walls and low ceiling that brushed against his hair. For a time, all he heard were the echoes as his mind ran.

This was a problem.

"Quintus, I need to talk with you." He spun away. The room went quiet. He felt their eyes on him as he strode toward the stairs, satisfied when two sets of footsteps followed.

"What's wrong, Titus?" Iris's forehead creased as she emerged into the warm humidity of the office.

Titus shoved the iron door shut behind them. "What is he doing here?"

Quintus swallowed. "That's classified."

"I'm a speculatore, Quintus. *Everything* I do is classified." Titus turned to Iris. "Do you mind?" He gestured to the front door.

OF LOVE AND TREASON

"Yes, I do."

He shot her a look that said he wasn't joking. Her lips tightened but she complied with a huff. Titus waited until the door closed on her heels, then whirled on Quintus. "I've got orders to have that man followed and arrested." He pointed toward the cell door.

"*Valentine?* On what charges?" Quintus sputtered. "He healed Iris—you can't arrest him!"

"You already did."

"That was *before!*"

"Who put him here?" Titus wrestled his voice into a deeper tone. "Who else knows what he's done?" His mind ran. Who had solved the case before he had? How had Quintus gotten involved? Would this affect his promotion?

"No one—one person—I don't know. I agreed to a bribe, all right?" Quintus crossed the room and poured himself a drink, hands shaking. "The amount is enough to get me and Iris out of the city, or I wouldn't have risked it."

Titus ran his hands through his hair. That solved one problem—and created another.

"I'm awaiting the order that I can release him." Quintus tossed back the cup and poured a second. "It's the least I can do for the man who healed my daughter and gave us hope."

Titus massaged the back of his neck and turned away, pacing to the front door and back. "He's a notarius."

"I know." Quintus set the amphora back in its place.

"He's been writing marriage contracts despite the emperor's edict."

"*He's* the notarius?" Quintus waved a hand, clarifying. "You're saying *Valentine* is The Cupid? The Friend of Lovers? The one everyone's talking about?"

Titus gritted his teeth. "You mean, *the man committing high treason*? Yes."

Quintus threw back the second cup of wine and set the cup on the shelf. "The people will riot if you arrest him."

Titus shrugged. "No one cared when you did."

"No one knows."

"No one's supposed to know when I take care of him either."

Quintus shook his head. "You can't kill him. Not after what he's done for Iris. We should be lavishing him with gifts, not prison and trial!"

"Oh, there won't be a trial."

"You're certain it's him?"

"Quite." Titus paused and held Quintus's steady gaze. "But I can't do anything without proof—on account of his grandfather."

"Look the other way," Quintus pleaded, limping to his desk and dropping into the chair with a grimace.

"I'm not certain I can. This sort of thing might have slipped through before, but Prefect Heraclianus is a stickler for the law. Not to mention this whole edict is a joint effort between the emperor, augurs, and priests to use the gods to win the war." Titus leaned a shoulder against the iron door and crossed his arms. "Emperor Claudius Gothicus plans to draft all unmarried men. Don't you see? What Valentine is doing directly affects the number of soldiers we'll have and may affect the outcome of the war if other notarii follow suit."

"Still. You can't arrest him after what he's done for Iris."

"I *can't* arrest him." Titus stalked to the shelves across the room. "You've already done that. And as for lavishing him with *gifts*, may I remind you that you have nothing, and I can't retrieve my pay? Between us, we have nothing to offer him."

"Nothing but his freedom."

"I've already told my trecenarius it was him." Titus shook his head. "Even if you release him, he'll still be arrested for questioning as soon as he returns to work."

Quintus crossed his arms, speaking between gritted teeth. "Then we'll have to think of something, because you know as well as I do, we will *not* murder the man who healed Iris."

Titus's jaw tightened. Quintus was right. He should be grateful that his part in the accident need not continue to eat at him day after day. He heaved a sigh of relent. "If we get caught helping a man guilty of treason, we'll face the same fate."

Quintus lifted his chin. "I am in his debt. So be it."

Titus raked his hands through his hair and cursed. "Easy for you to say, when you're planning to disappear. I'm grateful to him but I don't know if I'm ready to throw away my career as a thank-you."

"Then what do you suggest?"

There was only one option.

Quintus tipped his head toward the ironclad door and chewed the side of his thumb.

Titus yanked open the door, his hobnailed boots screeching against the stone steps as he descended. The sound hurt his teeth.

Valentine sat leaning against the wall, legs straight out before him, head lowered, fingers steepled in his lap. As Titus approached, he looked up.

"Investigator." He stood with a wary look.

Titus crossed his arms, the lantern light catching the gold ring on his middle finger as it curled over the swell of his bicep. His father's ring. It bore the image of the Praetorian lioness hunched for attack, surrounded by a wreath of laurels. *IX* had been etched into the ring beneath the laurel wreath. The Ninth. His father's cohort. Titus lifted his fingers; the slight motion caught the light again and illuminated the engraving. If he let Valentine go, he might as well release his dream of being a Praetorian tribune like his father. This was his chance to prove himself. To stomp treason beneath his boot with the single-minded brutality of a guard, loyal to none but the emperor.

Titus sighed and shut his eyes. He was not only loyal to the emperor. "You healed my dearest friend."

"My God did."

Titus fought the urge to roll his eyes and gave a curt nod. "As you say." He lowered his gaze, meeting the calm eyes of the prisoner nearly a full head shorter. "I know what you've done, Notarius." He waited for the usual look of guilty fear, but it did not cross Valentine's face.

Valentine met his gaze, unflinching. Calling his bluff. "Is that why you're here?"

Titus shook his head, lips quirking in a wry smile as he scratched the back of his neck. "No." He gave a huffing laugh. "I'm here because of Iris." He turned and paced the distance to the stairs and back. They were alone. No one would hear this conversation, and even if Quintus overheard, he wouldn't speak of it. He turned back to Valentine.

"I am grateful that Iris's sight has been restored." Titus hesitated and spoke the next words grudgingly. "I cannot in good conscience repay you by bringing you to the Castra Praetoria." He gritted his teeth. "So I'm offering you time to depart. *One day.*"

He didn't elaborate. A notarius would know what he meant. Often, instead of capital punishment, criminals were exiled outside of the empire. It was cheaper and there was that alluring bit of not having to deal with a dead body.

Valentine squinted, a wary look in his eyes, as if waiting for the catch in Titus's offer.

"My men are already looking for you, Notarius." Not the truth, but close enough. "If Quintus can find a way to release you, you will not return home or to your job. You will not stop to say goodbye to your family, your friends, your lover. You will leave the city immediately and never return and certainly never work as a notarius again." Titus lowered his voice and stepped inches from Valentine, who did not shrink back. "If you stay, gods help me, I will do everything in my power to hunt you down and arrest you on charges of treason. Charges punishable by death. Are we clear?"

Valentine gave a single nod.

"Then may your god find a way to get you out of this hellhole."

Deal made, Titus spun on his heel and marched out of the prison, certain he would regret it.

XXVI

After Titus left, Valens let out a long breath and slid down the wall on shaking legs. His thoughts spun. He knew he should feel at least a little concerned about Titus's threats, but he couldn't. Not yet. The fear that had plagued him since his imprisonment had long vanished and in its stead, awe swelled inside of him. God had worked a miracle through his prayer. *His* prayer. And now, not only were Iris's eyes opened, but both she and her father believed. Even if he never saw daylight again, that alone had been worth it.

Unable to sit still any longer, he stood and paced the few steps his ankle chain would allow, praising God for the wonder of it all. Yet the investigator's warning rang in his ears. He would have to leave the city, quite possibly the peninsula. If he didn't, he would find himself back here facing the real charges.

Back. That assumed they would release him.

The door groaned with the effort of admitting a visitor. No hobnails screeched on the stones, and Valens's chin lifted with the hope that perhaps his aunt or Cato had come. He was not disappointed when the lantern light illuminated Iris instead.

He smiled. "You're back."

"I hope I'm not bothering you." She set down a basket and a bucket of water, which she slid toward him.

He shrugged. "I suppose I can put my very important pacing on hold for a few minutes."

She glanced toward the door. "Pater's trying to get you out."

"Did he lose his keys?" His lips lifted in a half-hearted smile.

"It's not that simple, apparently." She avoided his gaze and tucked a strand of dark hair behind her ear. A tiny gold loop strung with small green beads dangled from the lobe.

"You probably shouldn't be in here."

Iris quirked a brow. "Neither should you. Here." She produced a cake of gray soap and a sponge from the basket. "Now you can wash."

Valens vowed never to take soap for granted again. "Thank you." He stooped and dipped the sponge into the bucket, scrubbing his hands and arms, face and neck. Water soaked the neckline of the old tunic Quintus had given him, but he didn't care; washing at least some of the filth away felt too good.

"Have you seen my aunt Bea?"

"She came into the bakery yesterday afternoon." Iris kept her eyes on the basket she was sorting through. "She'd gone to the Urbans and the Vigiles looking for you, but you hadn't been gone long enough for them to bother searching." She paused. "I brought her here, hoping Pater could help, but he couldn't say anything." Her eyes met his then, deep and brown and apologetic. "Would you like me to tell her?"

An ache settled in Valens's chest as he recalled Titus's warning. Would he not be able to say goodbye to Aunt Bea? Perhaps he could send her a note—but no, she'd be off finding lawyers in a minute, consumed with proving his innocence, which was impossible.

"No." Not now at least. "But perhaps when I—if I'm released, you will deliver a message for me?"

She nodded but didn't ask the questions written on her face. "I'll bring you a tablet next time."

"Thank you." Valens ducked his head and focused on washing. "So you know the investigator?" He slanted a glance in her direction as he scrubbed the back of his neck. She was cutting bread and cheese. His mouth watered.

"Titus? Yes." She answered without looking up. "Both his father and mine were in the Ninth. During the civilian siege of the Castra

Praetoria, Pater was wounded and Titus's pater was killed. Pater took Titus and his mother in after that. His mother is remarried and gone to Ostia now, but Titus is like a brother to me."

Valens didn't argue, but they didn't call him The Cupid for nothing. He'd noticed the way Titus had watched her, and it was with something deeper than brotherly affection. Iris seemed unaware of her own loveliness. Her orange palla, no longer hiding her face, was draped around her shoulders instead, revealing deep-brown hair twisted into a simple braid pinned to the back of her head. The dusky hues in her skin and the shape of her cheekbones hinted at Eastern blood. But it was her eyes that captured him: brown and bottomless. Even the scar mottling her temple and cheekbone did not diminish her beauty.

She lifted a small jar of olives from the basket, a smile softening her face when her eyes met his. His face went hot. She'd caught him staring at her with the sponge frozen against his neck.

"You must be starving." She held out the bread.

He let out an invisible sigh of relief. *Thank the Lord.* She thought he'd been staring at the food. He dropped the sponge and took the bread, grateful for the distraction as much as the bread. He groaned as he ate. It was simple fare but surely the softest bread, most flavorful cheese, and best olives he'd ever tasted.

"I should have brought more." Iris's forehead wrinkled as she passed him a red clay cup of well-watered wine.

He was too aware of his fingers clumsily sliding over hers as he accepted the cup. "This is perfect. You are very sweet." He tilted the cup back to cover the flush of embarrassment.

Kind. He should have said *kind.* What was *wrong* with him?

"I wanted to do something to thank you." Iris tugged her palla closer around her shoulders. "You saw me when no one else did. You didn't have to talk to me, to pray for me, but you did." Her voice went soft. "You could have kept your hope to yourself, but you shared it instead. And at great risk." She pulled a rolled blanket from the basket and held it out.

"Well." He wrapped the blanket around his shoulders with a sigh of relief. "When you put it that way, it's a shame I didn't get thrown in here long ago." They shared a chuckle.

"Why does God do this?" Iris shook her head as though realizing she'd asked the wrong question but didn't know what the right one was. "I mean, He's *powerful*, I know that now, and yet here *you* are— in prison. I'm . . ." She tucked a strand of hair behind her ear. "I'm trying to make sense of Him."

"Aren't we all?"

She tilted her head, waiting for him to explain.

He shook his slowly. "I cannot pretend to know the mind of God or tell you what He plans. All I know is that He does not see the world as we do—only seeing what concerns us right now." Valens spread his hands wide. "He sees all of it, the now and the future. Because of that, He can make sense of all that seems senseless in the world."

He told her the story of Joseph, sold into slavery by his brothers, wrongfully accused and thrown into prison. How God had not forgotten him even when Joseph perhaps felt He had. And how in the end, Joseph not only saved his family from starvation and death, but all of Egypt.

"So God threw you into prison?" Iris looked more confused now than she had when he'd started explaining.

Valens shook his head but knew what questions she was trying to untangle. "No." He thought of the demons of fear and doubt that had pummeled him in the darkness of the Tullianum. "I don't believe *He* did that." He rubbed the back of his neck. "There are still evil forces in the world that try to destroy our faith in God. To make us doubt His goodness and His love. God knew Joseph could—and would— save His family and the world when the time was right. God saw all that Joseph could not. The forces of evil sought to destroy a man—a family—yet God turned what was meant to destroy into something that saved them all."

Iris nodded, her face smoothing with understanding. "Joseph wouldn't have known that in prison." Her eyes flickered to meet his. "Neither did you know that you would bring salvation to my father and me."

"No." Valens's throat constricted at the thought that God would use his trial for something so great. They fell into thoughtful silence.

"Can I ask you a question now?" Valens asked after a moment.

"Yes."

"Did Titus say anything about me?"

"Nothing to do with the reason you're here. He and Pater made me leave when they spoke." She collected the empty olive jar and crumb-covered cloths and nestled them back in the basket. "He's going to help Pater get you out. It would be very unlike him not to."

Valens was less certain of this than she seemed to be, but he didn't mention the bargain he and Titus had struck. Titus had come to him alone.

He pushed himself to his feet as Iris rose, hooking the basket over her elbow.

"Before you leave . . ." Valens took a deep breath. He needed to make sure Iris and her father would be connected to the church before he escaped Rome. *If* he escaped. "There is a gathering of believers tomorrow night. They are my friends. Tell them what God has done for you and they will welcome you and your father." He gave her the address.

"Thank you." She left him, face full of unspoken questions.

Loneliness cloaked him as the door shut behind her—which, of course, was only because he'd been in prison for days and hers was the first friendly face he'd seen. He glanced around in the guttering lantern light to see if she'd left anything behind and might return. False hope. He sighed and settled back in his spot against the wall as Titus's bargain came to mind and buried all thoughts of Iris.

XXVII

Titus marched through the city, headed back toward the Praetorian Fortress. His mind reeled.

Iris could see.

See.

No matter how many times he repeated the words, they seemed just that. Words. Three times as he walked away, he'd wanted to turn back just to make sure he hadn't made it up. This kind of thing didn't happen in anything other than myths, or perhaps in a traveling "healer's" show. His legs took on the shake of new recruits who'd completed their first twenty-mile run.

He was not alone in his rote rituals to the gods of Rome. He believed in upholding tradition, not that the gods wielded actual power. The priests, priestesses, and augurs carried political control from their positions rather than from the deities they served. Wars were won by feats of strength and manpower. Not because Mars sat on Olympus.

Even as a young boy, Titus had played his part out of Roman duty rather than any true hope or belief in the gods. After all, what kind of gods would allow his father to die and refuse to heal Iris? And for that matter, what kind of *one* god would heal her after years of worship to *other* gods? He struggled to make sense of such a response from a god at the behest of a treasonous public notarius. Of all people!

He swerved around a gaggle of teenage girls gathered around a

173

street vendor selling purses of all colors and sizes. It made no sense. Even if Titus believed in such things, Valentine was no priest or magician. According to Iris and Quintus, he'd spoken no incantation, offered no sacrifice, no libation, hadn't given Iris any potion—just prayed simple words. "Like one would speak to a friend," Quintus had said. An unfamiliar feeling quavered in the bottom of his gut.

Something like fear—which was, of course, ridiculous.

His father's memory was the closest thing Titus had to a god. Acius Didius Liberare, fallen hero at the civilian siege of the Castra Praetoria, was renowned in life and near worshiped in death, and not only by his son. Titus had no memory of his father but hearing the tales of his bravery and courage lifted his chin with pride and pricked his heart with fear of failure. He was the son of Acius Didius Liberare—"the liberator." A hero's blood flowed in his veins. Would his efforts bring pride to his father's name? Or shame?

As he left the heart of the city and marched past the Servian Walls, the road turned to a slopping mess of manure, rotting garbage, and broken pottery—all that remained from the hurried evacuation of delivery carts the previous night. The cleanup crews were slacking. His boots were caked with something that looked like mud but wasn't.

I will not shame my pater. He clenched his fists. His father and Quintus had been blood-oath brothers. Quintus had proven his loyalty to Acius by taking in his son and getting him placed into the guard. Titus had repaid him with unquestioned loyalty of his own. Until now.

Titus's loyalty to Quintus had, for the first time, come into conflict with his oath of allegiance to the emperor. Were it only friendship between him and the jailor, Titus could have gladly dragged Valentine before Trecenarius Faustus. Had Valentine healed Iris of a common cold or even nursed her to health after a bout of Tiber fever, Titus would have done his duty and removed him that moment. But restoring her sight? Impossible.

The accident had been his fault. How could he punish the man who had undone his guilt?

He squeezed his eyes shut, the familiar shame shrouding him as the memories surfaced.

He'd been showing off. Worse, he'd been showing *her* off. *How stupid.* How arrogant and selfish. He might have been the youngest Praetorian recruit, but none of the other men could boast a girl like Iris. So, perhaps she wasn't his girl—not like that—but one could dream, pretend, and Iris had never balked at exploring the city with him and his friends. She'd regarded him with such trust in her eyes when he assured her that walking along the top of the Aqua Marcia was perfectly safe, that they would only climb the low portion, that the view of the Basilica Julia from the top of the aqueduct would thrill her. That others did it all the time. And she'd taken his hand and followed him.

His stomach rolled and sweat beaded his neck.

They'd not gone far when she'd tugged at him to stop, and when he'd glanced over his shoulder, her face was white, body trembling, then crumpling. The memory blurred, shards remaining. Her hand jerking from his. The flash of pale-orange fabric disappearing over the edge. The scream—hers, or his—dying with a sickening thud from below.

He thought he'd killed her. After all this time, the fear and shame still drowned him afresh as he recalled the image of her face, purple and swollen beyond recognition. Why Quintus had allowed him to remain in his house after that baffled him still. And now Valentine had returned what Titus had taken away. Even as a wave of envy swept over him, he knew he could not repay that gift with a charge of treason and a death sentence. What would his father have done? The lawful thing? Or the merciful thing? Why did they seem to be at odds?

Titus would have to divert the investigation away from Valentine somehow. At any rate, he couldn't tell the trecenarius that his suspect already sat in prison. He needed to get Valentine out of prison and out of the city before anyone found out.

When Titus muttered the password at the gate of the Castra Praetoria, the guard responded that he was needed at the prison block. Titus crossed the forty-acre compound at a jog, warding off the absurd feeling that he was going to his own punishment. Now, surrounded by the strength of Rome's army, his decision to give Valentine time to depart seemed foolish.

The prison warden masked his twisted upper lip by letting the hair grow over it in a bushy black line.

"Name?" the mustache asked.

Mars and Jupiter. "You know who I am, Sidus."

"Just following procedure." Sidus shrugged. "If we don't have law and order, we have nothing. Name?"

Titus twisted past him and strode down the hall as Trecenarius Faustus stepped through a doorway, shutting the door behind him.

Faustus grinned. "Got us a centaur."

It took Titus a moment to realize he was referring to the standard of the II Parthica legion.

"Found him mouthing off in a tavern about The Cupid. Thought you might find out what he knows. We've given him the preliminary beating."

Titus gave a nod and swung open the door to the questioning room. Every imaginable instrument of torture covered the walls. A man hung in the center of the room, wrists shackled to short chains above his head. The red welts covering him from head to toe streamed with blood and slowly purpled. Trecenarius Faustus shut the door behind Titus but didn't join him inside.

Titus and the prisoner were alone.

"What's your name?" Titus kept his back turned and studied a neat row of short-bladed daggers resting in a leather case on the wall.

"Petro," the man grunted. "I am a freeman, not a slave. It's against the law to torture me."

"Not where treason is concerned. You've been talking about The Cupid?"

A defiant tilt of his chin. "Everyone's been talking about The Cupid."

Titus shrugged and trailed a finger down the row of stained handles. "But not everyone has been brought here."

"Question away, Speculatore. I don't know anything."

"No?" Titus turned away from the daggers and shifted his attention to the brazier of coals. He gave the bellows a few pumps until they glowed red-hot and selected a brand from the wall, shoving it into the coals. "Have you been released from your legion?"

"I served my twenty-five-year term." The words came slightly slurred through his swollen lip. "I've been a good soldier. I haven't done anything deserving of this."

"The trecenarius seems to think otherwise." Titus pumped the bellows again, feeling the heat roll toward him, singeing the hairs on his arms. He lifted the brand, the end glowing yellow.

The ex-soldier licked his lips and watched the end of the brand as Titus twirled it carelessly.

"I said The Cupid was a good man, whoever he is." The man didn't take his eyes off the brand. "The legionnaires are going to have a difficult time fighting for an emperor who will not respect their rights of citizenshi—" The last word ended in a roar as Titus jabbed the poker beneath his arm.

"Guard your tongue when you speak of the emperor," Titus growled. Yet the man spoke truth. Emperor Claudius Gothicus, though he'd started as a general himself, would not long hold the loyalty of his legions if he continued with the marriage ban. Titus didn't understand why he did not hurry to pass the draft. Perhaps the illness had addled his mind.

Titus questioned the ex-soldier only until it was clear the man did not know the identity of The Cupid. Before, Titus might have pressed harder out of frustration, out of duty. But the man was not a slave, and therefore capable of speaking the truth without torture. Titus did not need the truth anyway. He needed a cover-up.

XXVIII

I RIS CLUNG TO HER PATER'S ARM as they followed Valentine's directions. Her stomach tumbled with nerves. Valentine seemed certain his friends would accept them, that they would gladly teach them more about Jesus. But would these strangers let them in? Would they talk to the carcer jailor? She sneaked a glance at Pater to see if the same questions plagued him. She could not read his expression, but he wore only a plain brown tunic and regular sandals. Nothing about him other than his posture might betray him as military, unless one already knew.

Outside the Servian Walls, gated villas and shop fronts lined the Via Flaminia. Iris devoured the sights, marveling at tattered furniture in the secondhand shops, a potter's simple red-glazed dishes, a tavern and bakery on the same corner that housed a public courtyard lined with a dozen ovens. Farther down, sagging-headed donkeys made endless laps, revolving a huge millstone round and round over heads of grain. A moneylender's office painted the color of summer palms stood beside a strong-smelling salon. A few workers were still employed on the street, lacquering nails, while dyes, curls, and braids were applied to heads inside.

Iris sidestepped to let a slave loaded with sacks of chickpeas grumble by. Ahead, a sign hanging over the street announced a clinic. The sign and the door had the symbol of a snake draped not over the rod of Aesculapius, but around a cross. A strange symbol of healing if she ever saw one.

Pater knocked twice. A young man dressed in a Roman tunic with Persian embroidery opened the door. His dark eyes flickered between the two.

"Can I help you? I'm afraid the clinic is closed now, but if it's urgent . . ."

"We are looking for Marius." Pater's voice faltered. "We were told there was a meeting here?" He tilted his head back to look at the sign, as if to be certain they were at the right address.

"Valentine sent us," Iris added in a soft voice. She felt Pater's arm tense beneath her hand as if in warning.

"Val?" The man's eyebrows shot up and he swung the door wide. "Come in, come in." He stepped back and gestured them inside. "Is he with you?" He glanced out at the street as if expecting Valentine to be right behind.

Pater shook his head. "I am Quintus Magius." He touched his chest and gestured to Iris. "My daughter, Quinta Magia."

The young man shut the door. "I'm Abachum. Marius is my father. No one's heard from Valens in days. How is he? *Where* is he?"

Pater looked down uncomfortably. "I cannot say."

"The whole thing's strange." Abachum shook his head. "But welcome. Any friend of Val's is a friend of ours."

Iris wasn't so sure.

"Your timing is wonderful. The meeting hasn't yet begun." Abachum led them quickly through a cluttered clinic, chattering all the while.

Iris's shoulders released some of their tension. She'd not expected so quick and kind a welcome. The door in the back of the clinic opened into a large square courtyard with a bubbling fountain and the rustle of date palms overhead. Two shrieking blurs of black curls and matching dresses raced across the courtyard toward them, barreling into Abachum's knees.

"Uncle Bach, have sweet?" The littlest one spoke first, then hid her face in his shoulder when he scooped her up and she noticed the strangers.

"Not this time, Rue." He glanced toward Quintus and Iris. "We have new friends. Can you say hello?"

"My name's Lalia." The older one grinned at Iris and Quintus as if bursting with exciting news. "I am *four*."

Abachum grinned too. "These are my nieces, Lalia and Rue. Now come, I'll introduce you to the others."

Iris did not notice the rest of the house as Rue, slung over her uncle's shoulder, locked dark eyes on her and stared, unblinking and unsmiling. She wrapped one arm around "Uncle Bach's" neck and popped two fingers in her mouth. Iris smiled at her. Rue buried her face and peeked through the tangle of ringlets. Pater suppressed a chuckle.

At the far side of the courtyard, Abachum swept through an open doorway and stepped aside, revealing a group of people in a dining room crammed with too many couches and an odd assortment of chairs, as if they'd been gathered from every corner of the house. The chatter went quiet as they all turned to stare. Iris's face heated and her stomach tightened.

Abachum did the talking. "This is Quintus Magius and his daughter, Quinta Magia. Val sent them."

"*Iris?*"

Her gut plummeted at the voice. No. It couldn't be.

No one else got a chance to speak as an unfamiliar figure, dressed in turmeric yellow and sunset pink, rose from a couch near the window. Iris struggled to make her mouth work as all the air seemed sucked from the room. The figure might be unfamiliar, but the voice was not.

"Beatrix." The blood drained from Iris's face.

The woman crossed the room, springy salt-and-pepper curls frizzing around her temples. A smell, overpowering and floral, came with her.

"You've seen Valens?" Dark circles bagged beneath Beatrix's eyes. She glanced at Pater and her expression froze with her feet. Iris's throat closed. They would surely be turned out. No one would accept them once they knew what they'd done to Valentine.

"Jailor." Beatrix's hands rose to cover her nose and mouth. Muffled gasps choked the room although it held less than a dozen people. "You've found him? Where is he?"

Pater swallowed but said nothing. His eyes locked with Beatrix's, full of remorse. "What I reveal cannot leave this room," he said in a low voice, glancing past Beatrix toward the others. "Can we trust them?"

At Beatrix's quick nod, Pater's shoulders relaxed slightly.

An older man with desert skin and white hair threaded with black strands rose and met them where they stood near the door. "I am Marius." He bowed. "Welcome. Please, sit, and we will talk." He held out an arm, gesturing toward the conglomeration of seats.

Beatrix said nothing as she led the way to the circle of couches, but her hands trembled at her sides. Marius introduced his wife, Martha, and three sons and daughter-in law. Iris struggled to remember the foreign-sounding names. Lalia and Rue, whom she'd already met, dashed across the marble tiles with squeals of "Mama" and "Baba," throwing themselves at the younger couple. Abachum closed the door behind them. Iris's legs shook as she lowered herself to an empty couch. Beside her, Pater sat stiff.

"You've seen Valens?" Beatrix asked again. Her knees bent and she dropped onto a chair with such force the legs screeched against the tiles.

Quintus nodded.

"You must have spoken with the Urbans or Vigiles." Beatrix leaned forward in her seat. "Is he well? Where is he?"

"The carcer." Pater choked the words in a voice full of apology. Iris had never seen him without his mask of courage and confidence.

"*All this time?*" Beatrix squeaked, voice trembling with barely checked emotion. "Or is this recent?"

Iris's heart began to race. Valentine had told her to tell her story. But what if these people did not believe her? Surely Beatrix would. She'd known Iris before. Perspiration prickled her forehead. She took a breath.

"Valentine told us to come." Iris flicked a glance at Beatrix. "He *is* in the carcer, though I did not know it when I brought you there."

Beatrix's lips pressed into a line, but she said nothing, waiting for the explanation. Her dark eyes flicked back and forth between Iris and Quintus, gratefulness and betrayal warring in her expression.

Iris chewed her lip, the story she had rehearsed on the way fleeing. "I was blind." She faltered, pulse flooding her face with heat. Everyone's eyes snapped to her as the words began pouring out in a nervous rush. "I work in the back of Paulina's Bakery and met Valentine several times, in the bakery and around the market. He said he was a Christian, and he prayed to the One God, Jesus. Twice after I saw him and he said he'd pray for me, I had flashes of sight for a few seconds."

Surprise and awe flickered across the faces in the room. No one moved. Iris continued the story, her pulse gradually slowing. When she mentioned Valentine singing as she and her father had gone to the prison, the three brothers exchanged amused looks and even Beatrix cracked a smile.

Iris kept on, fighting the quavering in her voice. "I—I begged Valentine to pray for me, and he did."

"And?" Marius's wife breathed.

Iris's lips trembled as she gave a little laugh. "I can see."

Beatrix pressed a hand over her mouth, tears rolling unchecked down her cheeks.

Marius's wife nodded, closing her eyes, and Marius bellowed, "God be praised!"

"He spoke with us all night," Pater said. "He told us about Jesus, who died for the sins of everyone . . . and we believed."

Their reaction to this news was even greater than when they'd heard of her miraculous healing. Beatrix leaned over the arm of her chair and threw her arms around Iris as the family erupted with strange murmurs of "Thank You, Father," and "Hallelujah," and "Amen!"

The immensity of the gift this strange God had bestowed flooded

Iris anew with awe. Sight, love, forgiveness, acceptance. She looked to her pater and saw the same reflected in his face. How could these people, strangers only minutes before, accept them so readily, so joyously? She'd never known familial love from anyone other than her pater, or Titus. She marveled at the warmth of Martha's and Beatrix's hugs, basked in the feeling for a fleeting moment before realizing it would not last. It could not. Not once they found out the rest.

When the room settled, Beatrix asked the dreaded question. "How did Valens come to be in the carcer?"

Iris's stomach dropped as Pater sucked in a breath and swallowed so loudly it could be heard across the room.

"I received orders to arrest him." He spoke in a low voice, staring at his lap.

"Has he been in the carcer all this time?" Beatrix asked, leaning toward Pater. "I've been so worried. Why didn't you tell me?"

Pater twisted his hands in his lap. "I couldn't reveal it. Couldn't put his name on the records."

"Why?" This came from the man who appeared to be the oldest of the three brothers. He might have been thirty, olive-skinned with a head full of longish black curls that hung to his sharp chin. He had scratches on his arms and looked as though he hadn't slept in days.

"My son Cato, the physician." Marius introduced him again.

Pater shifted. "His name is not on the record to protect his reputation. At least that's what I was told when I received the orders."

"Orders from whom?" Cato pressed.

Her father's shoulders seemed to droop. "I have been sworn to silence. I cannot afford the man as an enemy. If I do not follow the instructions to the letter . . . We have troubles enough as it is."

Beatrix, who'd been watching Iris's father as he spoke, sank back with understanding. "It's his grandfather, isn't it?" She leaped to her feet, the pink and yellow of her dress blurring to orange as she began to pace. "I should have known. I should have guessed—he just *can't* leave him alone!" Beatrix collapsed back on her chair, rubbing her temples. Martha put a hand on her arm.

"I'm sorry." Pater's apology sounded simple enough, but Iris had never heard him say those words to anyone else. Much less someone he'd barely met.

Marius let out a long breath and looked at Beatrix. "God allowed the imprisonment for a reason, Beatrix." He gestured toward Iris and Quintus with his other hand. "Perhaps God will use this to bring Val's grandfather to faith."

Beatrix nodded but looked unconvinced.

"I am working to release him. Valens asked us to come here and learn from you. And to ask you to pray for his release." Pater gripped Iris's hand. "But I must beg you to keep this in confidence for now. I know we do not deserve it, but I beg you, if word gets out that I've accepted a bribe—" He stopped as several servants brought in wine and platters of steaming flatbread, cheese, cucumbers, and spiced chickpeas.

Iris's stomach growled as the warm smells curled around the room.

"Then pray we shall." Marius gave a nod. Without further warning, everyone in the room bowed their heads. Iris did not bow her head and instead stared as the old man spoke, gently, reverently, but as one would speak to another person. He spoke to the One God like Valentine did, with no fancy invocations or flattery. It was as if . . . as if the Person he spoke to was in the room with them. She looked around but did not see an altar or an image of any kind. Marius prayed for Valentine, for his strength and health and speedy release. Everyone raised their heads and Iris's cheeks warmed, but the others did not seem to notice.

Further discussion halted as the door opened and other people entered in clusters of twos and threes. Some carried pots of stew and baskets of bread. Iris and her father stayed where they were. A few of the newcomers greeted them and welcomed them to the gathering. Her pater grew more and more tense beside her.

"Perhaps we should go." He tilted his head toward her, speaking in a low voice. "It would have been better to keep this quiet until I had a solution."

Iris leaned closer. "But Valentine said—"

"This is going to get back to the tribune and we'll be in worse trouble than we already are." He glanced around the room, as if debating how best to make an unnoticed exit.

"Pater." Iris placed a hand on his arm. "We've seen the power of God. We must also trust He's able to rescue Valentine and keep us in safety."

"He couldn't even keep Valentine safe."

"Can't we stay a little longer?"

"You can't leave now; we haven't eaten," Beatrix interrupted.

They both looked at her, startled.

She leaned closer. "I won't speak of it again, but . . ." She glanced around the room and lowered her voice to a whisper. "Is he all right?"

Iris nodded. "He is unhurt, fed, and clothed."

"I hope it will not be long. I've requested an audience with his grandfather." Pater paused. "Is he your father?"

"Goodness, no!" Beatrix straightened and waved, offended at the suggestion. "My sister's husband's family—God rest her soul. It was never a good match."

The room went quiet as Marius stood and raised his hands. "Valens could not be here tonight." He glanced toward Quintus and Iris. She felt Pater's tension rise and release as Marius continued. "And as I am not gifted with the ability to teach, I'm afraid our meeting will be more of the practical sort tonight." He bowed his head and blessed the meal they would share.

Once everyone had eaten their fill, Cato stood, neck reddening at the attention directed toward him.

"An insula collapsed three days ago in the Tiberina district." He hooked his thumbs into his belt. "Dozens are dead; more are without homes. I've been there for nearly the whole of it. Such devastation." He swallowed and shifted on his feet, rubbing the scratches on his arms. "The tenants need our help. They need food, water, clothes—anything to help replace the things they lost. And they need help finding new homes." He paused. "I put it forth to you all to decide if this is where our money should go."

Beatrix leaned over to explain in a whisper. "We do not use the banks. Instead we all keep our money together and dole it out to whoever has need. That way everyone's needs are met, and our monies are never sitting idle."

Iris's eyebrows flickered in surprise. They all shared their earnings with each other? She had a hard enough time turning the money she earned over to her own father, much less a group of strangers. Still, she watched curiously as everyone in the room nodded in agreement and called out ways they could help.

Cato nodded. "We will gather here tomorrow with whatever you can bring, and we'll all go together."

Prayers began, voices picking up where one left off like a thread woven from one person to the next, creating a tapestry of praise that soon fell into song. Iris sat bowed through it all, soaking it in. She didn't know the songs, but her heart agreed. Overwhelming peace and love flooded her with the warmth of the sun bursting from behind the clouds. Her eyes overflowed.

Was this what it meant to be loved by God? How foreign. How . . . *wonderful.*

Iris and Pater didn't speak as they walked home later. The sky turned silvery violet and the peace they'd both felt at the gathering lingered still. The silence wrapped around them, warm and sacred, and neither seemed inclined to break it.

When they stepped into the apartment, Iris picked up a message that had been slipped beneath the door.

Pater lit the lamp and scanned it. "I'm needed at the prison."

"Valentine?"

He shook his head. "Will you pack some food? I may not be home tomorrow." He ducked behind the curtain hiding his sleeping area. Clothes rustled as he changed into his uniform.

Iris gathered a sparse bag of hard bread, cheese, olives, and dates.

"Could I go tomorrow and help at the insula?" she called over her shoulder.

"Shouldn't you be at the bakery?" Her father emerged, buckling his sporran belt over his blue tunic. The polished metal studs glinted as the leather straps swung.

"I could bring them bread, after my shift." Something inside thrilled at the idea that *she* could be the one to help for once.

Quintus nodded distractedly. "As long as you're home long before dark."

Iris trussed the food sack and handed it over. "Is everything all right?"

"I don't know."

XXIX

The cell door protested with a groan as it swung wide, a blinding lantern thrust through the opening. Valens winced and squinted.

"Valentine, you've been summoned." Quintus spoke in a low, grim voice.

Hobnails screeched on the stairs. Valens blinked against the light as Quintus released him from the ankle chain and turned him over to two other men dressed in the uniform of doormen, not guards. As he followed them out of the cell, a sick feeling gnawed at his stomach. *God, give me strength.* His hands were bound behind him. *In life or death, let me bring You glory.*

The doormen took his arms, one suppressing a gag as they yanked him out of the carcer and into the street. Night had fallen. A strange time for a release—or a trial. Quintus didn't speak but clutched a scrap of papyrus and watched him leave with a tense look of apology.

The doormen were not gentle escorts. Two other uniformed doormen waited at the bottom of the stairs and the four surrounded him. As one of the doormen tied a rope around his neck, Valens noticed the black raven embroidered on the shoulder of his white tunic. Understanding and irritation struck him in tandem. It all made sense now. He allowed the doormen to truss him up as he stood compliant, anger rising. Quintus had hinted at being given orders to have him arrested, but *this?* The two men in front held the rope secured around his neck and the two behind held the one that bound his hands.

Considering the length of their journey, the precautions they took to secure their prisoner were laughable.

Valens kept his head down as they walked. The smooth flagstones beneath his feet rose and curved as they climbed and circled Capitoline Hill crowned with the temple of Jupiter. *God, give me wisdom.* They stopped at the base of the hill before an iron-barred door. The emblem of an augur's curved *lituus* rod adorned both sides of the gate in a mosaic of colored glass and marble. The doormen stopped, pulled him through the gate, and locked it behind them before loosening his bonds.

Two of the doormen remained at the gate while the other two, who looked as though they begrudged the job, escorted Valens into the white three-storied villa built into the base of Capitoline Hill. The narrow garden between the wall and the villa, empty and silent at this time of night, smelled of fowl.

The doormen paused as they stepped into a foyer lit by several lamps on spindly stands and decorated with a collection of Etruscan antiques. The sight of a large urn set upon a rather delicate table conjured the unwelcome memory of knocking over an urn and table of similar proportions. His palms began to sweat. That was the last time he'd been here.

"Wait here." The doormen disappeared, leaving him alone for only a moment before one of them reappeared and cleared his throat, beckoning Valens to follow. The doorman motioned him into the triclinium, lavishly decorated with plush red-and-gold rugs, blue-cushioned couches, frescoed walls covered by more shelves, and stands and tables cluttered with well-dusted antiques. A peacock dozed on a perch in the corner, and the air held a lingering smell of boiled fish and bird droppings. The doorman left him alone, and Valens allowed his eyes to sweep the room before settling on the blackened crescents of his fingernails.

The air stirred as an old man entered, robed in white linen edged in purple, red, and gold.

He stopped short and stared. Valens felt his lips tilt in a sheepish smile.

"Hello, Grandfather."

Chief augur Gaius Favius Diastema stared at his grandson with a look of shock, pity, and . . . remorse? He swayed on his feet and his neck did a tiny jerking motion as if struggling to hide a gag. Valens must have looked as if he'd bathed in a chamber pot. He certainly smelled like it, but it was also his grandfather's fault.

"Go bathe. We will talk afterward."

Valens raised a brow. As eager as he was for a bath, it didn't seem fair to deprive Grandfather of the consequences of his actions. "Are you certain? We can talk now."

"We will talk when you're comfortable."

"Ah. Suddenly my comfort matters to you?"

"Valens." Censure tightened his grandfather's voice.

Valens dipped his head and turned to leave, Grandfather's old steward meeting him at the door to accompany him. The nearest baths would be closed at this hour, but Valens didn't argue. There would be plenty of that later. Only the steward walked him through the streets this time. The charade was up.

"How are you, Castor?" Valens attempted a carefree tone.

The gray-haired steward took his time responding, perhaps hoping his silence would explain his reluctance to communicate. "I am old."

As they ascended the marble steps to the bathhouse, Valens wondered at the architect who decided marble would be a good material for perpetually wet stairs. He held out an arm for the old man, who took it as if Valens needed help mounting the steps and not him. The baths were empty, and the slaves cleaning and readying it for the morning rush took one look at Valens and were about to protest when Castor set a jingling pouch on the bench. They responded instead with a stack of warm towels and a selection of soaps, scented oils, and a strigil.

"Wash quickly. I will find out which of these slaves is the barber." Castor shuffled away, arms held out from his body for balance.

Valens stripped, leaving his clothes where they lay. Wading into the tiled pool, heated from below by a large furnace, he breathed a prayer of thankfulness as he ducked his head under and scrubbed away the grime of the prison. He completed the circuit of the baths and steam room and was wiping scented oil off his hands when Castor reappeared, a pale-blue tunic draped over his arm and a slave in tow carrying a box of shears and razors.

Valens dropped the tunic over his head, securing it around his waist with the belt Castor provided, and sat in a reclined chair for a shave and haircut.

"Your grandfather has been worried for you." Castor leaned against a pillar and watched as the slave wrapped Valens's face in a hot, damp towel and began snipping away at his hair.

"Has he?" This was a new tactic of Grandfather's: sending his steward to begin the argument. Valens closed his eyes. His grandfather would not relent, but neither would Valens capitulate to his demands. They came at each other time and again, clashing like stones thrown against a wall. Made of the same stuff, yet entirely incompatible for anything other than damage.

"He is old, and you, his only surviving heir. Should you not have pity on his gray hairs?"

"I long for reconciliation as much as he does."

The barber removed the towel from Valens's face and began to shave him.

"But I will not change my beliefs in order for—" He felt a pinch at his neck. The barber cursed under his breath and pressed the towel against the spot. Was he actually a barber? Perhaps Valens ought to fear for his life now that he was out of prison. He didn't dare speak again until the "barber" finished pressing sharp blades against his neck.

As he took Castor's arm to help him back down the steps, dawn broke over the city in cool pale light. The last few delivery carts sped through the roadways, scurrying for the gates.

"Did Grandfather order my arrest?"

Castor only shrugged. "He will explain all, I'm sure."

This time, when Valens entered the triclinium, his grandfather waited on a couch. He gestured to the couch opposite him, a small table between. Valens reclined, his nerves coiling as they always did when he and his grandfather were together. An iridescent black crow perched on the back of his grandfather's couch, eyeing the breakfast laid out on the table but not daring to make a move on it.

"I should disown you." His grandfather broke the silence and held out a steaming cup the serving boy had filled with warmed wine. Valens took it and said nothing. "You put me in a very difficult position, Valentine."

"I am sorry to create difficulty for you, Grandfather." He meant it.

His grandfather did not answer right away and took his time blowing on his wine before taking a tentative sip. Valens studied him. Gaius Favius seemed much older than the last time he'd seen him. Liver spots dotted the backs of his hands and the top of his head, visible through his thinning hair; the skin under his eyes sagged. Those eyes, like pieces of glittering black obsidian, struck Valens in a piercing stare.

"I cannot continue to protect you." He sighed. "Bribing your release from prison, sneaking you out under the cover of darkness . . ." His lips, like strips of dark raw meat, pressed together. "Next time, it will not be so simple. You must see that now. This foolishness with the Christian god must stop."

"I am grateful to be released." Valens noted that while his grandfather took credit for rescuing him, he did not admit to having him arrested in the first place. He met his grandfather's eyes, feeling the familiar challenge rising with the tension in the room. "But you needn't have constructed such an elaborate scheme to get my attention. If you wanted to talk, you could have sent a message instead of pretending to arrest me. I'd have come."

"But would you have listened?"

Valens sighed. "Grandfather, I will not renounce my God. Jesus is the One True and Living God, and I would sooner die than renounce Him."

"And you just might!" Grandfather slammed his cup on the table, wine spattering the shining wood.

Valens took a breath, willing his voice to remain calm. "Then so be it. I've made my choice."

"I am the *paterfamilias*." Grandfather straightened, voice snapping. The crow reared back too. "I am the head of this family and I hold sole authority over whether you live or die. I demand you give up this foolishness!"

Valens closed his eyes. "Grandfather, I cannot."

Gaius Favius groaned and ran his hands over his face in frustration. "I rue the day my son set eyes on your mother. I knew she'd bring nothing but trouble, and I am never wrong."

It wasn't the first time he'd said such things. According to Aunt Beatrix, Gaius Favius had toasted the gods the night Valentine's mother died giving him life. He'd celebrated and then ordered his servants to go seize the infant and expose him on the banks of the Tiber. All because his mother had been a Christian. Beatrix said she'd found Valens crying on her doorstep the following morning. She hadn't known who'd brought him back, until his father showed up fifteen years later to claim him as heir after a second marriage to a more "suitable" bride failed to produce a child. By then Valens had already claimed the faith of his mother and aunt as his own, and neither his father nor grandfather could sway him otherwise— though Grandfather's methods had grown increasingly violent after his father's death.

Grandfather heaved a sigh. "If you insist upon this civil disobedience, I must demand you keep it quiet." He leveled a stern gaze at Valens. "Do not think you are safe because the eye of the emperor is on the barbarians. The Senate and Praetorian prefect, with pressure from the priests, are adamant about upholding the matters of state and the city. They will not see it fall into anarchy because the emperor is away."

Valens's brow furrowed. Did he refer to his faith or—? No. He couldn't possibly know about the contracts. The note he'd sent to the notarii office must have been simply a warning away from preaching. Sweat prickled his hairline and he resisted the urge to shift. He took a slow, deep breath.

Grandfather continued, dropping his gaze to his hands. "You have heard, I'm sure, that Emperor Claudius will enforce the anti-Christian policies of Emperor Septimius Severus?"

Valens nodded.

"Rome has long been successful in battle when we faithfully worshiped the gods. There has been a great falling away of late, and it shows in the weakness of the empire." He hesitated a moment, then went on with a pointed look. "While the emperor battles the enemies outside, it is the duty of every good Roman to protect the mother-city from the enemy within."

The news took a moment to sink in.

"Grandfather, the Christians are no threat to anyone. We are commanded to love the Lord our God and to love our neighbors."

"Yet who do you proclaim as god?" Grandfather tore a piece of bread from the loaf on the table between them.

His grandfather already knew what he would say. The argument was an old one, deeply rutted on both sides.

"Jesus the Christ is God and there is no other."

"And therein lies the problem. The emperor will not share his glory with a god who does not acknowledge his deity."

"And God does not share *His* glory with a mere man."

"Confound you, Valentine." Grandfather threw the bread on the table. It bounced off and flopped to the floor. The crow lurched for it in a rush of obsidian wings, and the peacock woke with a screech. "I cannot save you again. I cannot." He swung his feet to the floor and straightened, his voice rising in agitation.

"Again?" Valens's anger rose. "Wasn't it your idea to have me arrested in the first place? How was that *saving* me?"

"It was a warning. Showing you what could happen—what *will* happen if you continue on this course." Grandfather's face darkened, spit forming in the corners of his mouth. He beat a shaking fist against his chest. "I am the chief augur. I interpret the will of Jupiter, Best and Greatest. Your disbelief threatens everything—my position, my wealth, my very life." He shook a crooked finger in Valens's direction. "And do you care? No. You're reckless and defiant. Don't you understand I'm trying to help, to—to save you from yourself?"

Valens leaned forward. "I have been saved already, Grandfather."

"Valentine, *please*. You must stop this nonsense." His voice dropped, suddenly weary, and he twisted gnarled hands in his lap. "Things have been set in motion that I cannot undo. I do not know how soon the Severan policies will be in full effect. Perhaps tomorrow, perhaps next month."

Normally Valens would be among the first to know. "Which of his policies?" Valens tore off a bit of bread, smothered it in a spread of goat cheese and mashed fig, and shoved it in his mouth.

"An edict to outlaw the spread of Christianity."

Valens swallowed too soon, and the softness of the bread went down with the ease of a mountain. "That is already in effect." He winced, touching his throat and taking a sip of wine.

"Not like this." Grandfather shook his head. "*This* time it will be subtle, underhand."

"What can they do that they haven't already done? I've already been imprisoned. That didn't seem *subtle* to me."

His grandfather's eyes swept away with a flicker of guilt, but he did not hesitate when he spoke. "Merchants will no longer serve known Christians. Good Romans will be forbidden to patronize the shops of known Christians. Doctors and apothecaries will be forbidden to admit and care for them. When a Christian's shop is identified, so also will all those who enter the shop be. Quietly marked. Every last one of you. And once the prefect can get the emperor to agree, it will not be forced labor in the stone quarries and galley ships; it will be execution for you all."

Valens closed his eyes. *God, give us strength. The ability to trust You completely, no matter what.*

"The signs from Jupiter favor these policies. Please, Valentine." His voice cracked. "I have lost your father—my only son. A man should not have to lose both son and grandson. I *can* save you, but only if you recant." His voice dropped to a whisper. "Please. You're all I have left."

"I am sorry to cause you pain, Grandfather." Valens's chest went tight until he thought it might crush him. "But I cannot, and will not, renounce my God."

Grandfather swallowed. Straightened his shoulders. Refused to meet his eye. "Then I disown you this day. You are no longer heir to all I own, but a stranger to me."

Valens sat stunned for a moment. His grandfather kept his gaze averted. They had never been close—Valens's faith a constant warp in their relationship—but never had it separated them with such permanence. Valens returned his cup to the table and stood, trying to catch his grandfather's eye, stubbornly set on the dozing peacock.

"Very well." The words came out husky and choked. Valens hesitated a moment, swallowing back the emotion burning his throat, then bowed and left, closing the door behind him.

XXX

NEWS SPREAD QUICKLY through the market. Even before she reached Paulina's Bakery, strange faces with familiar voices bombarded Iris, all clamoring to hug her and offer congratulations—and to ask questions. Iris hadn't realized anyone besides Paulina and Epimandos even knew her name. Not one of these other merchants had ever called out in greeting before.

Beatrix pushed her way through the crowd and took Iris's arm. "Sorry." She grinned, curls frizzing out at her temples. "In my excitement, I may have mentioned your news to a few people."

"A few!" Iris laughed. "Did you post notices on every door?"

"They're all dying to hear it from you, dear."

The throng of shopkeepers followed Iris to the door of the bakery. Iris's heart pounded. She hadn't anticipated this. All eyes trained on her. She scrambled to piece together the story without naming Valentine—a difficult task anyway, but had there always been so many colors? Sunlight streamed in golden bars through the pergola over the street, illuminating faces and clothes in a dozen shades. Her mouth went floury and her hands started to shake. What was the question?

"Well?" The hairy man who'd stepped out of Minotaur's Table spoke first. "Is it true?"

Iris gave a halting nod. "I—I was blind," she stammered and took a breath. "For seven years. You all know that."

197

Beatrix took her hand and gave a reassuring squeeze.

"All that time my pater and I tried every cure we could think of, prayed to every god and goddess of healing we could find, but they did not hear." She stopped, distracted by two pearl-gray pigeons that fluttered down to perch on the pergola above the herringbone-tiled street. "But then I met a follower of the Christian God. And he prayed for me, that by the power of Jesus Christ my eyes would be restored—and I can see."

There was a moment of complete silence before questions started in earnest. Iris did her best to answer, reassured by the pressure of Beatrix's hand on hers. When the crowd swelled with customers, the shopkeepers dispersed.

Beatrix patted Iris's shoulder. "You spoke wonderfully, my dear."

Iris shook her head, unconvinced. "I didn't explain anything like Valentine would have."

"And you shouldn't. You're not him. God gives each of us the words to say when we speak, and while they'll never be the same as anyone else's words, they will be exactly what someone needs to hear." Beatrix smiled and lowered her voice. "Have you seen him?"

Iris shook her head again. "Pater left last night after the meeting, and I haven't heard if he released Valentine."

Beatrix nodded, her mouth tightening as if to swallow back tears. "Will you go to Marius and Martha's later?" She attempted a bright tone.

Iris nodded.

"Good. Come by my shop after closing and we'll walk together." Beatrix gave her hand one last squeeze and hurried toward her perfumery.

Iris hesitated on the street, wishing she could do something for her new friend as the ache in her chest grew. She shut her eyes, trying to remember the proper way to start a prayer. Did it matter? They'd all spoken to God like a friend. *Please. Please release him.*

Iris opened her eyes. Had the potter across the street always glazed his bowls with blue vines? Sparrows swooped overhead on the lookout for crumbs below. A woman in a yellow dress and gray palla pinned to her lily-orange hair stood waiting for the glass shop to open, a basket on her arm. Two young women tested makeup on the backs of their hands beneath the pink awning of the cosmetic shop, already open and attracting customers. The sun streaking through the window slats high overhead promised an odd autumn day of blue skies, heat, and humidity. Steam already rose from the puddles in the street. Reluctant, Iris turned into the bakery.

Two people whom Iris immediately judged to be Paulina and Epimandos stood inside the door wearing, in turn, expressions of shock and sullen disbelief.

"Well. This is wonderful!" Paulina's round face shone. "I worried when you didn't come yesterday. We thought you might be ill." She tucked a strand of bread-brown hair behind her ear.

Iris worried her hands. "I'm sorry. When it happened, I was so excited and distracted I completely forgot to come in."

Paulina gave a laugh and shook her head, throwing plump arms around Iris in a quick, uncharacteristic hug. "I can only imagine!"

Epimandos cocked his head, stiff black hair shaved short enough to see his golden-brown scalp. "Does this mean she can help with deliveries?" His dark eyes squinted as if he suspected Iris of faking all this time.

"We'll discuss that later." Paulina stepped away from Iris. "There will be nothing to deliver if we don't get a move on."

The three of them worked quickly, trying and failing to make up for hours of lost time. For Iris, everything felt oddly familiar and strange all at once. Seeing the pale dough moving beneath her hands, dotted with the reds, browns, and greens of fruit and nuts, distracted her in a way that made her overwork the dough. After the second scolding from Epimandos, she looked around the shop instead, allowing her fingers to tell her when the dough was ready.

Slowly, as the sun and temperature rose, the volume of the market heightened to a cacophony of voices and clacking sandals. The bread was late, but few seemed to care as Paulina regaled them with the tale of Iris's healing. Several times she had Iris come to the front and tell it herself. The afternoon heat brought a welcome lull to the market so nearly complete that the noise went from a roar to a rustle of leaves and the clicking of pigeon claws on the paving stones.

Iris helped Paulina lower the artichoke-green awning over the doorway.

"You sold out quickly despite the late start." Iris tied down her side.

"Yes. Though I'm sure that had mostly to do with everyone clamoring to get a glimpse of you and hear your story. You're good for business." She winked. "I have half a mind to keep you up front from now on." Paulina wiped her hands on her sleeveless green tunic, smudged with flour. "Where are you off to now? To see all the grand sights?"

Iris shook her head. "I'm going with Beatrix the perfumer to deliver things to the people whose apartment collapsed a few days ago."

"Well." Paulina stared at her a moment. "That's kind. If there's any extra loaves, you may take them."

"Thank you." They went in the back door and Iris tied the overbaked or otherwise-misshapen loaves into her palla.

Paulina settled herself at her desk. "Speaking of Beatrix, has she found her nephew yet?"

Iris focused on the knot, thankful Paulina faced away and could not see her unease. "I don't know." She wondered if Valens had been released. If he had, would she ever see him again? "I don't think so."

"Mmm." Coins clinked as Paulina sorted them. "Pity."

Iris opened the door. "I'll see you tomorrow, Paulina. And thank you again for the bread."

"Goodbye." Paulina twisted around in her chair, eyes sparking with mischief. "Whatever you do, don't let Bea sprinkle you with perfume. She likes to fancy herself a matchmaker and thinks her scents have some love-inducing power. It's probably because they induce fainting." She grinned. "You can tell her I said that. It'll cheer her up."

XXXI

USING THE SPARE KEY AROUND HIS NECK, Valens slipped inside the apartment he shared with his aunt. Quintus had returned his personal belongings before discharging him—all except for his tunic, which he didn't mind losing to the Tullianum. The Markets of Trajan had been crowded, the mass of shoppers providing ample cover for him to move through undetected. He pulled the door shut behind him, pausing to take in the garish couches and floral-frescoed walls of the only home he'd ever known. His chest constricted at the thought of leaving Aunt Bea without saying goodbye.

The Praetorian investigator had warned him to leave the city immediately—but he didn't have a choice. His things from the notarii offices were still in his room along with a completed marriage contract. He couldn't leave that behind, or Bea might find herself in as much trouble as him. Besides, unless they found the contract, the investigator had no proof against him.

Valens went to his room and threw things into a small bag. Nothing large or cumbersome, nothing that would make anyone suspect him as a man leaving for a journey of any kind. He took his quills, rolls of papyrus, and seal, surprised his supervisor had not sent someone to collect them. All the more reason to return. He found the marriage contract hidden beneath his floorboards and straightened, holding it. Should he burn it? Deliver it? He thought of Hector and wondered how many roses he'd missed during his

201

stint in the carcer. He'd have to get a message to him somehow and explain.

Fingering the papyrus, Valens moved to the window and peered out. The back side of the markets, tucked so far into Quirinal Hill to be only two levels above the street, seemed quiet and abandoned, but that didn't make it so. If a person were to wedge himself against the building, he would be hard to spot unless Valens stuck his head and shoulders completely out the window—something he had no intention of doing.

He hesitated a moment longer, then rolled the contract into the thinnest roll he could, secured it with string, and buried it in the bottom of his bag. Damning evidence if he were caught. If it were any other couple, he might have burned it, but he'd watched Danius and Emilia grow up, noticed their shy looks for each other before their parents had. He wouldn't keep them apart. Not if he could help it. Valens looped the strap of the bag over his head and shoulder and opened the door. As he stepped into the hall, he nearly bowled over his aunt.

"Valens? You're back." Bea's hands cupped the sides of his face. "You've had a haircut. Are you all right? Where have you been? You look hungry. Are you hungry? *I've been so worried!*" She threw her arms around him and held him tight.

"I thought you were at the shop." He breathed in the familiar comfort of her overpowering perfume.

She released him. "I forgot my lunch and ran up to get it." Her eyes fell on the bulging bag at his hip and returned to his face, scrunched with concern. "What are you doing?"

"I don't have time to explain everything, Auntie, and it's probably safer for you if I don't." He squeezed the back of his neck. "I've been arrested and ordered to leave the city."

"What about the church?"

"I don't know." He sighed. "I vowed not to abandon them. Yet I cannot live here and put you in danger."

Bea sucked in a breath and let it out in a huff as if she'd been expecting something like this all along. "Where will you go?"

"I'll see if Marius has any ideas."

Her chin wrinkled as she pressed her lips together, propping her hands on her hips. "You were going to leave without a goodbye?"

"I was going to leave a note." His head went to one side. "Don't give me that look, Auntie. I didn't want you to be in trouble if you were questioned."

"Was it your grandfather's doing?" She followed him down the hall.

"Partly." He paused at the front door and hugged her. "Thank you for everything you've done for me, Aunt Bea."

"It's just like you to fly the nest now." She sniffed and held him tight. "I think I've found the perfect girl for you."

Valens rested his hand on the latch. "I'm sure you have," he placated. He leaned down to kiss her forehead, noticing for the first time the deep wrinkles around her eyes and mouth. "Goodbye, Aunt Bea." He swallowed the burning in his throat. "I love you."

Bea's dark eyes glistened. "I love you, my boy." She released him, though the look on her face said every bone in her body protested. "God go with you."

The street behind the market apartments was quiet and none of the people in it appeared to be soldiers. Since the Markets of Trajan abutted the Servian Wall, when Valens left through the back exit, he was already outside of the main city. Sticking to the familiar back roads and alleyways, he reached the small kitchen door of the Calogarus household—distraction-free for once.

Phoebe let him in, then shut and barred the door. "We've been praying for you since the jailor came and told us everything." She crossed the kitchen toward the courtyard door. "Master Marius will be glad to see you free and well."

So Iris and Quintus had gone to the meeting after all. Good. He hoped they'd come again.

He made it halfway across the courtyard before Cato tackled him in a hug.

"Thank God you're alive."

Valens chuckled. "So far." He sobered and dug the contract from the bottom of his bag. "I have to go into hiding. Could you see that Danius and Emilia receive this?"

Cato lifted both hands and backed away. "What are you talking about?"

Valens lowered his voice. "The Praetorians know I'm writing the contracts. But the investigator doesn't have proof, so he gave me time to depart before they find it."

Cato crossed his arms, still refusing to touch the document. "Why would he do that?"

"Valens! Thank God you're all right." Marius winced with every step down the marble walkway, arms open to Valens.

"He's a friend to Quintus and Iris," Valens explained to Cato as he hugged the old man. "But he won't let me off a second time." He waved the contract toward Cato. "Will you?"

"What's going on?" Marius asked, looking between the two.

Cato took the contract and held it between two fingers, shaking his head. "Why were you arrested if they didn't have proof?"

"Grandfather arranged it." Valens sighed. "It's a long story."

"Are you in trouble?" Marius asked.

Cato turned to his father. "He has to go into hiding."

Valens lifted the strap of his bag and rubbed his shoulder.

"Were you followed here?" Marius asked, shifting his gaze back to Valens.

Valens shrugged. "Not that I saw."

Marius nodded. "Then it's settled. You'll stay with us."

"I'm not sure that's a good idea." Valens glanced at Cato, still holding the contract as if it were a dead rat rolled in horse dung. "I can't risk endangering you all."

"It won't be the first time we've hidden someone." Marius looked between the two and frowned at the secrets they were obviously withholding. He crossed his arms, waiting for an answer, an explanation. Valens shut his eyes. Should he open the circle of treason participants to include another?

Cato huffed out a breath. "Pater, Val is The Cupid."

As Valens met Marius's serious gaze, the old man seemed

thoughtful but unsurprised. He nodded once. "Were you followed?" he asked again.

Again, Valens shrugged. He'd been watching. He didn't think so.

Marius's tone left no room for argument. "Then you'll stay here."

XXXII

Iris met Beatrix as she lowered the awning over her locked door.

Beatrix grinned when she saw Iris. "Ah! Perfect timing!" She tied down the last corner of the pink-and-orange-striped awning and straightened. "What have you got there?"

"Extra bread from Paulina for the tenants."

"She's a dear, isn't she?"

Iris struggled to keep up with Beatrix's seemingly endless supply of energy. The woman kept up a brisk walk, climbing the sloping curve of the Via Biberatica to exit the market complex at the north end.

"Tell your father thank you." Beatrix spoke softly, looking straight ahead.

Iris's neck snapped to look at her. "Valentine's free?" She breathed the words, hope rising.

Beatrix nodded, but her lips pressed together in a way that made the news seem not altogether good.

"What's wrong?"

"When I went home for the midday meal, Val was there—only long enough to say goodbye." Beatrix's chin trembled. "He's gone."

The words cut the air from her lungs as effectively as the hilly streets. Valentine gone? Just like that? Regret swirled in her belly. "Where?"

"He wouldn't tell me, said it was best if I didn't know." Beatrix chuckled and sniffed. "Funny. I used to dream of nothing else but marrying him off and getting him out of the house."

Iris cracked a half-hearted smile. "Paulina warned me you liked to sprinkle people with perfume and find them spouses."

Beatrix threw her head back with a sudden burst of laughter. "She knows me too well!" She patted Iris's arm. "But there's no fear of that. I promised Valens I'd stop." She sighed and shook her head. "Val never appreciated my efforts. He's stubborn. Holding out for just the right girl. He's like his father in that way. Val's father had eyes for my sister and no one else would do. The woman who catches Val's eye will be a lucky one."

Iris skirted a pile of dung in the road. There had been several young women at the meeting the other night who were beautiful, slender, and unscarred. Iris had noticed her own body in comparison. Much wider in the hips, arms sculpted and muscular from kneading for hours every day. What kind of girl would capture Valentine's attention? If those willowy, unscarred girls didn't, she certainly would not. She lifted her chin and forced her thoughts elsewhere. It didn't matter anymore. Valentine was gone.

Marius and Martha's home bustled with activity. Caught in the excitement of helping, Iris nearly forgot Valentine and spent the rest of the afternoon carrying donations of clothing and household goods to the dusty heap of rubble that had once been an insula. When the sun began to set, she and Bea left, dusty and sweat-streaked. After a quick trip to the public baths, they parted at the Via Biberatica and Iris plodded toward home, weary and content.

Distracted by the blazing pinks and blues of the sunset, which cast its own gleam on the red, white, and gold temples and basilicas of the Forum, she was unaware of being followed until a man moved beside her.

She jumped, pressing a hand to her chest. "*Titus.* I ought to smack you for sneaking up on me like that."

"Sneaking?" He gave a stomp of his hobnailed boots. "You should have heard me coming from a block away. You're lucky it's me and not a pickpocket or worse."

She'd have to be more careful not to get so distracted. "What are you doing here?"

"Working. You?" He tilted his chin, taking in the vibrant colors streaking the sky beyond the temple of Saturn.

"At the baths." She took a breath and spoke in a lower, more serious tone. "Thank you."

"For what?"

She nearly mouthed the words. "Letting Valentine go."

Titus's eyes narrowed. "How do you know about that?"

"I saw his aunt today; she said you'd given him time to depart." She touched his arm. "She was so happy."

"She'd seen him?" Titus's voice held a strange tightness, but the way he studied the temple kept his face averted from her.

"Yes. She went home for lunch and he was there."

"Mars and Jupiter!"

The venom in his voice stopped her in her tracks. Titus took two more steps before he pivoted and faced her.

"What's wrong, Titus?" Her words came out soft and strangled.

He growled and took her elbow, turning away from the Forum and toward Cedar Street. She trotted to keep pace with his long-legged stride.

"I told him not to go home."

Fear replaced the unease. "Is he in danger?"

Titus turned down Cedar Street and stepped over a broken crate. He seemed hesitant to speak now. The street was empty, save for a cat rubbing its tawny side along a doorpost.

Iris caught his arm, tugging him to a stop. "Titus."

He looked down at her and spoke almost in a whisper. "I don't have proof. But if he doesn't leave Rome before I find it, your healer will be executed."

Iris's heart seized, then pounded. Titus was wrong. He had to be. Only people accused of treason or patricide could be executed.

"He's wanted for treason." Titus answered the question she couldn't bring herself to ask. "I need you to understand." He rubbed the back of his neck and sent her a pleading look. "I tried. He healed you; I let him go. We're even."

She stared at him, trying to follow. "You were looking for him before all this?"

He nodded.

Understanding finally dawned. "And you're still looking for him now? Even though you've given him time?"

"He has until tomorrow. If he doesn't leave and he's caught again, it's his fault. Not mine." He tilted his chin, watching her expression. "Don't be upset with me over this, Iris. It's my job to hunt criminals."

"Valentine is not a—"

He dropped his face close to hers, lips tight over his teeth as he spoke. "Valentine is a traitor to the empire. If he stays, I'll have to arrest him. I let him go for *your sake*. But I can't do it again."

A traitor to the empire. She worried her bottom lip with her teeth. Just what had Valentine done? Titus had risked much in letting Valentine go with a warning. He didn't have the authority to banish anyone, and if word got out that he'd done so—she shuddered to think of his punishment. Of course, Valentine would know only a magistrate could officially banish him, so would he bother listening to Titus? The thought of never seeing Valentine again flooded her with swift disappointment. Titus shifted and crossed his arms, recalling to her mind his questions about whether Beatrix had seen Valentine. He was hunting Valentine and using *her* to do it.

Iris's blood went icy. "I have to go." She turned away, locking eyes on the green door of her insula like a sailor would a lighthouse.

"Iris, it's my *job*."

As if that were explanation enough. He didn't follow her. She didn't turn but thought she might have caught a hint of remorse in his tone. Or frustration.

Back in the quiet of the apartment, Iris couldn't keep her mind from running. She half hoped Valentine would leave the city, be free and safe. The other part of her selfishly wanted to see him again. But what of Titus? He'd helped get Valentine released, and she was grateful, yet Titus was hunting him. How could she feel such grate-fulness mingled with the cut of betrayal? Iris sank onto the couch, the fraying cushions long flattened, and in halting sentences began to pray.

City of Rome
Ides of Februarius, AD 270

The three men stop and look at him, clubs dangling from the ends
of their oiled arms.

They wait for him to quiver, to run. He is still. The crowd seems
to hold its breath. Their hero's life balances on the edge of a finely
honed blade. The shadow of the man behind him raises a club
and strikes him on the shoulder. There is a dull smacking sound.
The crowd gasps but no one dares call for "life" again. Not with
Praetorian swords at the ready. He stumbles forward but remains
on his feet.

His lips still move, whispers escaping. No one can hear him.
Another man smashes a club against his chest. He folds over, gasping.
The third man hits the small of his back and he drops to his knees.
He sucks in a breath and looks up, locking eyes with the man raising
the club for another blow.

"It's all right." The words emerge gurgled and sloppy. "It's all right.
I forgive you."

The man's jaw bulges with tension and the club swings down. At
the sight of blood, the crowd begins to keen. Someone throws a red
rose into the arena.

XXXIII

Feet propped on the desk, Quintus leaned back in his chair and skimmed a missive from the Castra Praetoria. Along with enforcing the anti-Christian policies of Emperor Severus, there were to be stricter visitation rules, no food provided to prisoners unless brought by family members or friends.

His mind wandered to the secret meetings he and Iris had been attending the last three months. Despite the risk of capture, Valentine had remained in Rome to teach any who gathered in the Calogarus house. He'd explained that when he'd become a leader of the church, he'd taken the oath not to abandon his flock to save his life. Until called elsewhere, he would stay. No matter the danger. Quintus scratched his stubbled neck. Did that make Valentine the bravest man he knew or the most foolish?

Winter days had seemed long before, but now, with the gatherings to look forward to each week, the hours dragged. Quintus had never known such a hunger for learning, nor such fullness at the same time. Iris felt the same; he could tell by the raptured way she hung on Valentine's every word. The gatherings were almost enough to distract Quintus from the ever-encroaching ending of his and Iris's freedom. He'd not heard from the chief augur and, despite sending a third message this morning, had yet to receive payment for his part in Valentine's imprisonment.

Quintus looked up. A disturbance outside pulled him from his thoughts. Faint shouts, jeering. He swung his feet down. They were coming closer. He set the missive on his desk as the door opened.

Markos poked his head inside. "Urbans coming. They've got prisoners."

Quintus stood as Markos resumed his post outside. He straightened his tunic, brushed the crumbs off the front, and tucked his baton into his belt. He had just enough time to resume his seat before Markos opened the door once more and six Urban Guards shoved five men, three women, and a handful of children inside.

"Aren't there cells at the Ludus?" Quintus pushed to his feet. "I don't have space to hold all these people! Why are there children?"

The leader of the troop of Urbans stepped forward and tossed a scroll on the desk. "These have been arrested as per the new edict that those who refuse to offer sacrifice, incense, or libation to the gods of Rome be imprisoned and tried for treason and atheism. Prisoners convicted of treason are always brought here."

Quintus took the scroll and scanned it, a thread of fear twisting through him. Romans had always been religious, gods and politics as tightly bound as brick and mortar. Without the two of them in tandem, the whole would crumble. Policies like this had been enforced in the past. Emperors intermittently declared monotheism illegal; some enforced cruel punishments, while others turned a blind eye.

Quintus glanced at the prisoners, calm defiance on the faces of the adults, fear and confusion on the children's. All appeared wealthy—not unexpected. According to the Severan policies, anyone who brought a successful lawsuit against a Christian would acquire all goods and possessions of the accused. Wealthy Christians were popular targets, but they were not usually rounded up in droves. At least, not since he'd been jailor.

"Very well." Quintus dropped the scroll to the pile on his desk and reached for the record book, hoping the Urbans did not notice the slight tremor in his hands. He flipped it open. "Names, ages, occupation, and living address, please."

He wrote the information carefully, listing the adult prisoners one by one, and when he got to the children, he just wrote, *six children.*

Entry paperwork completed, Quintus unlocked the door to the main holding cell Valens had occupied. Today it held two men accused of murder. With an apologetic look, Quintus chained the adults and children as far from the murderers as possible.

"There's already a buyer for the adults. Someone from the Theatre of Marcellus should be in contact soon." The Urban leader leaned a shoulder in the doorway of the cell. "There's a new acting troupe putting on *Hercules and the Lion.* I hear the lions are especially vicious. Should be a good show."

Quintus nodded, hoping the churning in his stomach did not show on his face. "And the children?" he asked as they climbed the stairs. Behind them, one of the children started to cry.

"Slave market most likely." The Urban gave a careless shrug.

Quintus shut the door, cringing that he had not been quick enough to keep the children from hearing the Urban's answer. He forced himself to nod in response. If the authorities made the consequences of lawbreaking painful enough, mass obedience would follow. Pax Romana.

He'd never been so sickened by the thought.

The Urbans left. Quintus dropped into the chair. He'd hauled out the household gods with the rubbish that morning. They'd sat neglected in the lararium for weeks before he'd remembered them. Perhaps he'd been too hasty. What if someone had seen him? Money troubles aside, he and Iris might find themselves in deeper trouble than before. Perhaps it was lucky they were not wealthy targets. Quintus rubbed his temples. He had one week before the tribune called in his debt. If the chief augur did not fulfill his obligation, what was he going to do?

The wine amphora called to him from the shelf. Quintus lifted the missive he'd yet to finish and fought the urge to numb himself. He'd not felt the need to drink these past weeks. Spending his free evenings at the Calogarus house learning from Valens had kept him out of the taverns, and while he'd been surprised at the amount of money retained in his box at home, it wasn't nearly enough to get both Iris and him out of the city.

He forced his thoughts away from the debts—getting harder to do by the day—and focused on the missive. *Stricter prisoner visitation.* His eyes went to the shelf, the amphora cork visible over the top of a stack of tablets. He hooked a foot around the leg of his chair. *No food for the prisoners unless brought by family.* He just needed a drink. Just one. He stood and went to the shelf, a rush of anticipation running through him as his fingers closed over the neck of the amphora.

The door opened and Quintus spun around, more surprised by the sudden flush of guilt he felt than at the appearance of an old man. He shuffled inside, and Quintus's eye caught on the black crow embroidered on the man's shoulder. Quintus bowed, feeling the weight fly from his chest. The chief augur would finally make good on his promise.

"Welcome." Quintus straightened. "You're here with the payment?"

"The deal is off."

"It can't be." Despair prickled the edges of his vision. "I held up my end. I did exactly as I was told."

"Unsuccessfully, from what I understand." The old man crossed his bony arms. "Valentine didn't recant."

"Recanting was never part of the bargain," Quintus argued. "The orders were to hold him, scare him, then release him to the chief augur."

The servant merely lifted his shoulders. "Will you argue with the spokesman of Jupiter, Best and Greatest?"

"This isn't what I agreed upon!" Panic rose in his voice as Quintus's mind began to race. He and Iris couldn't leave the city on foot, not with his leg the way it was. They could try to hide within the city, but there was little chance of hiding when the tribune had dozens of speculatores at his disposal. "I risked my position—*everything* for this. The chief augur will hold up his end of the bargain. He *must.*"

The servant shrugged again, one eyebrow raised in challenge. "Or what?" He shuffled toward the door. "Who are you going to tell?"

Quintus shot out a hand to steady himself on the shelf as the steward left. Paying off the tribune was out of the question now. Running was the only option, but one needed money to travel and survive in the far reaches of the empire. Money he did not have and never would. He turned, arm flailing as he reached for the amphora. Time had run out.

XXXIV

STOMACH JITTERY, Iris rushed for the bakery, shivering in the pre-dawn darkness. She'd not slept well. The deadline for their debts would be upon them in two days, and while she'd not seen Tribune Braccus since the encounter outside the carcer, his imminent presence hung over her future like a shroud. She'd walked her father home from the tavern more than once this past week, too drunk to hold a proper conversation. All she'd been able to deduce was that the plan he'd once had for their escape had fallen through. They would have to do something today, but what? Her father would not make it out of the city on foot, even if he were sober.

What could she do? She'd tried praying. God had not answered her. Perhaps she should go to Valentine again? Yet he'd told her once before that the same Spirit in him was in her. Valens did not hold God's ear more than anyone else. God had simply chosen to answer his prayer in a rather big way.

Iris's eyes felt gritty. Traffic had been extra busy on the Alta Path that morning, the wide street clogged with refuse carts hauling animal dung out of the city, and then there had been the undertaker in his scarlet cloak hemmed with bells, warning everyone to stop and make way for the dead. She moved quickly through the darkened corridors of the market, determination marking her strides. Iris and her pater had tried solutions on their own and failed. She would tell Paulina everything. Perhaps she could help.

The Markets of Trajan were mostly quiet. Screeches and clanks came from inside a few of the shops, the only hints of life within the sleeping complex. A few shopkeepers called greetings to her as they propped awnings above their doors and arranged displays of wares on narrow tables outside the shops. Outside of Yanni's Silk Slippers, a pair of sandals dyed a deep vermilion snagged her eye, prickling her with a longing she shoved away. Now was not the time to think about shoes.

Warmth washed over her as she stepped inside the cozy glow of the bakery room.

Epimandos kept his back to her as Iris crossed the room.

"Good morning!" Her voice sounded strange and forced, her belly knotting with nerves over her task. Paulina did not part with money easily. Especially if there was no return on it. Iris tossed her palla on the peg by the door and reached for her apron. Her fingers met with empty air. Epimandos didn't offer his normal objections to her "good" morning. Odd.

"Where's my apron?" Iris turned around as Paulina entered the back room, a wiry teenage boy in tow. Iris's apron was wrapped around his middle. Epimandos paused his mixing, lips twisted in discomfort as he looked from Iris to Paulina.

At first no one spoke. Then Paulina took a breath and stepped forward, lifting her chin. "Iris." She clasped her hands in front of her, unsure and uncomfortable. "I've bought a new slave."

Iris looked at the boy, who wore a bewildered and half-panicked expression as his gaze swung around at all the work to be done. He would enjoy the work eventually. Perhaps in time, he would do the deliveries. She thought Epimandos should look a little more pleased than he did.

She smiled. "Hello, I'm Iris."

"I won't need your help anymore."

Paulina's words froze the smile on Iris's lips. The announcement was more shocking than it had a right to be since Iris had wrestled with how to tell Paulina she would be leaving. Her mouth dropped. Iris glanced from Paulina to Epimandos, who, for once, looked sorry.

He stared at her, the lamplight catching the shine of his scalp beneath his prickly black hair.

"I don't understand." Her thoughts began to spin. If Paulina let her go, would she refuse Iris's request for help as well? "Have I done something wrong?"

Paulina shook her head. "The Severan policies are in full effect with several new additions. The market manager is very devout and is forcing all merchants in the Markets of Trajan to prohibit the sale of goods to and from known Christians. I—I'm sorry. Since everyone knows you're a—well, you're a liability now." She twisted her hands together, looking pained. "What has happened to you is miraculous, truly. I'm thrilled for you, but I have my business to think about. I've sacrificed much for it already." Paulina looked away.

Iris couldn't respond. She'd known of the policies but it had never occurred to her she might lose her job because of them. She *had* been excitedly vocal. But who wouldn't have been? Everyone in the market had heard of her miraculous healing at the hands of the Christian God.

She'd been prepared to tell Paulina she'd be leaving. She should be relieved. Instead, her words seemed stuck behind the growing lump in her throat.

"I see."

"You understand then?"

Iris gave a single nod.

"Good." Paulina turned and rummaged through her coin box. "You've been a good worker." She skirted the proofing oven and held out a small bag of coins.

Iris's vision blurred and Paulina's eyebrows wrinkled.

"I wish you well." Paulina pressed her lips together and took a step back, her voice taking on a forced brightness. "Besides, now that you can see, I would have lost you anyway—some man's bound to come along and swoop you up."

How right she was. Iris fought the urge to spill the meager contents of her stomach, her arm waving toward the hook on the wall that held her palla. Now that the shock had worn off, her mind began running, calculating. The coins would be enough to bribe a delivery cart to carry her father out of the city at dawn. Iris could trot along beside it. They would not get far, but perhaps there would be enough to get them to a place where they could hide and work while they saved a bit to go farther. A foolish hope, but all they had. Iris took her palla and tucked it under her arm. After twelve years, she left the shop with a scoop of small coins and a dazed goodbye.

She bumped her way through the scrambled chaos of the early morning market, hardly paying attention to the citrus seller with the familiar voice and strange face who called out a greeting. She left the Markets of Trajan through the back entrance that opened to Quirinal Hill. Low clouds spat mist as she left the covered arcade of the Via Biberatica and moved up the street where women and slaves heaved water jars to the nearest fountain and children hurried to school—or at least gave a good impression of doing so. A bump from behind sent her stumbling into the path of a slave herding three oxen through the middle of the street toward the meat market.

It was too much. Iris scrambled out of the way, squeezing her eyes shut against the swirling colors and people whirling in all directions. The darkness calmed her with its familiarity. She began walking, her fingers trailing along the wall as she moved away from the market entrance. Propping herself against the damp stone wall, she balled her hands at her sides.

"What now?" She could hardly manage the words as heat rose hard and tight in her chest and forced tears from her eyes. She sucked in a breath, swallowing back the emotion. She wouldn't cry. Not here.

A light touch on her shoulder. "Iris?"

She opened her eyes. Beatrix's face, creased in concern, leaped into view, shadowed by a rose-colored palla.

"Are you all right?"

"A bit overwhelmed." She didn't trust her emotions to remain in check if she revealed the truth.

Beatrix studied her a moment, then took her hand. "Me too. Come with me."

Iris didn't protest as Beatrix led her up the steep residential streets of Quirinal Hill. Here single dwellings lined the streets, hidden behind high stucco and marble-tiled walls.

After laboring a few blocks, Iris trusted her voice enough to speak. "Shouldn't you be opening your shop?"

"Not this morning." Puffing, Beatrix paused on a corner to catch her breath and let a slave laden with full water jars pass. "I had an eviction notice on my door. The market office is turning out all Christian shopkeepers." She let out a long breath. "After nearly twenty years, they're closing my shop."

"Can't you fight it?" Iris's problems seemed to pale in comparison. Beatrix's shop was her only source of income. Especially important now that Valentine could not return to the notarii office.

Beatrix shook her head. "The only way to fight it is to bring proof of my participation in one of the sacrifices." She sighed. "I won't do that, so I'll lose the shop."

"Paulina let me go today." In the wake of Beatrix's news, it didn't seem as terrible.

"I suspected as much. I couldn't buy a raisin bun this morning."

"*Now* this truly *is* a terrible day."

They both managed a laugh. Beatrix wiped a hand over the wetness on her own cheek and knocked at an unobtrusive door in the side of a white-painted wall.

"I'm sorry." Iris touched her arm. "You must be devastated."

"I am sad." Beatrix hesitated. "But I feel a bit of relief, oddly enough. Though I'm not sure why." She looked at Iris thoughtfully as the door opened.

"Hello, Phoebe." Beatrix greeted the servant and attempted a bright smile. She stepped inside and tugged Iris into a warm kitchen. "Sorry to burst into your culina like this—is Martha awake?"

Phoebe bowed. "Welcome, Beatrix." She smiled. "The family is about to break their fast. Come, they will be happy for you to join."

It wasn't until they stepped out of the culina and into a lush and damp courtyard that Iris realized they were in the home of Marius and Martha. She'd never entered it other than through the front clinic. The courtyard was quiet aside from the birds singing in the palms overhead, flitting down to the branches of the potted almond tree. Phoebe left them alone in the blue triclinium, with a promise to alert Martha.

Beatrix settled on a couch. Iris followed suit. Would Valentine join them? Part of her wished he would leave the city and be safe. The other part longed for him to walk through the door.

Martha and Delphine came instead. Martha's face bunched with concern. Her brown eyes darted between Iris and Beatrix, unsure whom to greet first and how.

"Bea, Iris—what are you doing here?" Martha clasped her hands and hurried toward them. "Is all well?" She glanced at Iris with a trace of alarm in her eyes.

"I think—" Beatrix patted Iris's hand—"we've both had much better days."

"It's not yet breakfast." Martha sat across from them. "What's happened?"

Phoebe entered just long enough to deposit a tray of fruit, pastries, and steaming calda. At the sight of the tray, Iris's stomach growled. Delphine served the calda as Beatrix and Iris shared the woes of their morning. The Calogarus women shook their heads, worry etching deeper lines into Martha's forehead.

"It's starting again just like twenty years ago." Martha spoke softly. "Do you remember it, Bea? When Emperor Decius took control?"

"You probably don't remember the reign of Decius." Beatrix glanced at Iris and Delphine, who had been small girls at the time. "Similar to now, the priests and advisers convinced Emperor Decius that the decay of the empire was linked to the tolerance of non-Roman religions. He commanded everyone to participate in the traditional sacrifices where they received a certificate of compliance. Those who didn't have a certificate were executed."

Iris swallowed. She didn't recall the reign of Decius, but when she was ten, Emperor Valerian took control and began a full campaign against the Christians, ordering the deaths of countless church leaders with the vain hope that by removing the leaders, the followers would disintegrate. Her father had nearly lived at the prison, and Titus had joined the Praetorian legions shortly after.

"More calda?"

Delphine's voice broke through her thoughts. Iris held out her nearly empty cup and Delphine refilled it, the bright aromas of lemon, lavender, and basil rising with the steam.

"Thank you." Iris turned her attention back to Beatrix and Martha, who sadly shook their heads. Delphine resumed her seat as the door opened.

"Aunt Bea?"

Valentine and Abachum stepped through the doorway. Valentine looked as if he'd either just rolled out of bed or hadn't slept in days. His tunic was rumpled, dark circles hung beneath his eyes, and his black hair stood on end in a way Iris found rather charming. His eyes darted to Iris and back to his aunt, face stilling as the oddity of the early visit swept over him.

"What's going on?" He looked at Iris. "Is your pater well?"

"I think so." She hadn't considered whether or not he would also lose his position.

"Come and sit, you two." Delphine flicked a hand toward an empty couch and poured two more cups of calda.

Valentine sat and accepted a cup, his eyes shifting between Beatrix and Iris as they filled him in on the morning's happenings at the market. Valentine's lips went pinched and white when Beatrix said that without proof of sacrifice she'd be evicted not just from her shop but from the apartment as well. He shut his eyes, raking his fingers through his hair.

"I'm sorry, Bea. The perfumery meant everything to you."

"I loved it." She nodded and sounded braver than she looked. "But it did not mean *everything*. I have God and good friends. What more do I need?"

Iris chewed her lip, wishing she could be brave enough to say the same. Valentine only knew the briefest of reasons why her father had accepted a bribe for his arrest, not the whole of everything they'd tried to hide from their new friends. Her shoulders sagged under the ever-building weight of humiliation over her father's debts, dread of her fate with the tribune, the danger of their new faith. Sitting here now, the painful pressure of shame and fear swelled inside her chest, threatening to spill into the light. Iris bent, clamping a hand over her mouth to hold it in. She couldn't do it. She wasn't strong enough. A single strangled sob burst from somewhere deep and hidden.

"Oh, my dear." Beatrix wrapped her arms around her shoulders. "It will all be well in time."

But it wouldn't. Iris pressed the heels of her hands into her eyes, mortification at her lack of strength or faith stealing her words and composure. Beatrix coaxed the story out of her in bits and shards until the whole of it came tumbling out in a flood of congealed relief. The debts, the tribune's proposition, Pater's drinking, her fear. She stared at her feet when she finished, too ashamed to meet anyone's eyes. They were all so good, so strong, so brave, so full of faith.

What must they think of her now?

Beatrix's fingers lifted her chin, forcing Iris to meet her brown eyes, swimming with tears of compassion. "Oh, my dear," she breathed. "What a heavy burden you carry. Thank you for letting us share the weight of it." She wrapped Iris in a hug once more, secure and full of love.

Iris blinked. They were not ashamed? She chanced a glance at Valentine, whose face was an unreadable mix of sadness, anger, revulsion. She dropped her gaze again, face burning.

Perhaps not *all* of them were as understanding as Beatrix.

"What is the amount of the debt?" Valentine asked.

Eyes on her white-knuckled hands, she answered. He didn't say anything, just rose and left the room, Abachum on his heels. Somehow that was worse than if he'd criticized her father's carelessness and her lack of faith.

Her lips trembled. "I—I'm sorry. I'm not strong like you all—I'm—"

"We were made to live life together." Beatrix took her hands and looked into her eyes. "We are not strong all the time. God has graciously made us all different, so when one is weak, those with strength can lift them up. We must carry each other's burdens, not add to them with heaps of guilt."

Delphine prayed. Martha joined in, and as her voice ceased, Beatrix began. Their words covered Iris's aching heart like a balm.

When they finished, Valentine stood in the doorway.

"I'll have to discuss it with the others." He crossed the room to the couch. "But if they all agree to it, there's enough in the offering pool to cover the debt."

Iris sucked in a shuddering gasp, her heart beginning to thump. "You would do that? For us?" She shook her head. "But we have nothing to give in return."

"A gift does not require repayment." Valentine sat and held her gaze with one of determination. "We cannot sit idly by while you and your father are sold." He grimaced.

Iris looked between the three other women, who did not seem surprised in the least by Valentine's announcement.

"That's settled." Beatrix folded her hands. "Now I'll just have to find myself a new apartment and we'll all be set."

"I can help with *that*." Martha slanted a mischievous grin at Valentine. "If you don't mind sharing a roof with a criminal."

XXXV

VALENS PAUSED AT THE DOOR of Cato's office, watching as Iris followed his aunt across the courtyard and into the culina, disappearing with one last flash of a brown, sandaled foot. As saddened as he'd been over Bea's news, he'd felt a measure of relief that she'd be protected under the Calogarus roof. While the nightly weddings had gouged his sleep, so had the worry over her being alone in the apartment.

He'd been truly shaken by Iris's confession. Then angry, first toward Quintus and his carelessness, and then toward a tribune who would take advantage and force such a vile future on Iris. His blood went hot imagining Iris forced to—but he wouldn't imagine it. It would not happen. He would not allow it. At least now Valens understood the desperation that had driven Quintus to accept his grandfather's bribe. In Quintus's place, he might have been tempted to do the same.

Valens let himself into Cato's empty office on a hunt for papyrus. After Iris had revealed the truth of their dire circumstances, Valens had not expected her to volunteer to help Bea pack and move her belongings—and several of his—back to Marius and Martha's home. But she'd insisted on helping, and without the slightest hesitation. If there hadn't been so many eyes in the room who would surely tease him about it later, he might have pulled Iris into his arms in gratitude.

The thought startled him. Where had that come from?

"Don't be a fool, Valens," he muttered under his breath, moving toward Cato's desk. He shook his head. The weddings he'd been performing nearly every night must be affecting him. He was a wanted man, living in hiding. Nothing could be gained from entertaining thoughts like that about Iris. Still, he couldn't deny the way she entered his mind at the oddest of times.

And he liked speaking with her. Her eyes lit with wonder and curiosity when they talked about God and with life and mischief when they spoke of other things. She could tease him, and he enjoyed it.

He rubbed his burning eyes. He really needed sleep.

He shuffled through Cato's desk with renewed purpose. How could Cato find anything in this mess? He unearthed a half sheet of clean papyrus and cleared a space on the desk, moving empty cups to the floor, herbs and wine rings dried to the insides. He sat and began writing a note to the church members, proposing they use the offering funds to redeem two unnamed church members from debt and slave auction.

The door opened and Cato stepped inside, followed by Delphine.

"I borrowed some papyrus."

Cato scrunched his nose. "Has Bea been in here? My office smells like roses."

"That's me." Valens kept writing. "Very funny, switching my diluted sandalwood fragrance for rose concentrate. I used extra, just for you."

Cato smirked. "I'd love the credit, but it wasn't me."

Valens looked up with a slight shake of his head as the two said in unison, "Abachum."

Delphine rolled her eyes and shook her head as they laughed. Cato plunked a small wine amphora on the desk, *C.C.* stamped into the clay side.

"I got another delivery this morning from the Centaur's Cup." Cato dropped a receipt on top of Valens's letter. Valens picked it up, noting the number 1 written next to the type of wine. He rubbed his eyes, relief pouring through him. Only one wedding tonight.

Ever since he'd gone into hiding and no longer walked past the

Centaur's Cup every morning, Valens and Hector had created an alternate communication system. Since physicians often ordered medicinal wine, Hector delivered an amphora to Cato whenever he'd organized a wedding. The receipt listed the number of couples to be wed each night. In the months Valens had been in the Calogarus house, wine had been delivered every morning but two. They'd worked out a rotation of the public gardens they would meet in, unless a location was otherwise specified on the receipt. It saved them from meeting in the same spot twice in a row. Valens glanced at the note scribbled on the bottom designating a delivery address, which usually meant a private home. He memorized it, then scraped the wax tablet clean.

"Thanks."

Cato nodded.

"What needs to be done today, Val?" Delphine clapped her hands together.

Valens held up the finished note. "I need this message spread to the members of our church as soon as possible, and I need their answers." He thought a moment. "Flavia Lucilla—the one on Grata Street—needs help with her rent this month. The food for the widow baskets should be delivered here as usual. I can help pack the baskets if you can organize for delivery. We'll also need a few people to distribute bread to those in the Tiber shanties." He scrunched his face, thinking, then opened one eye. "I think that's it."

Delphine nodded slowly, absorbing the list. "Are there enough funds for everything?"

Valens nodded. Many of the grateful brides and grooms had insisted on giving him gifts, usually monetary, although one had bestowed a kitten. Valens had set the money to work. The kitten he'd given to Lalia and Rue, despite Cato's objections that it would eat all the mice and there would be no more dormouse pie at dinner. He was correct on both counts.

"And I'll be heading out at dusk again." Valens sighed.

"When did you last have a full night's sleep?" Cato arched an eyebrow and ran a hand through his shaggy curls.

Valens shrugged. He tried not to think about it. Things would slow eventually. They had to.

"We'll get it done, Val." Delphine gave a determined nod. "But the widows are disappointed you're no longer delivering the baskets and visiting with them. Most of them aren't able to come to the gatherings and they aren't satisfied with what encouragement I can offer."

Valens nodded, thinking. "I could write notes . . . copy a passage of Scripture or something we can tuck in each basket."

"Perfect." Delphine brightened. "They'll love that, and we can read them to the ones who can't read for themselves."

Valens looked from one to the other. "Thank you for all your help. I wish it didn't have to be this way."

"You're family." Cato slipped an arm around Delphine. "And we couldn't leave you hanging."

"Strangled more like." A wry grin twisted Valens's lips. "Beheaded—possible torture."

Cato nodded. "Torn by beasts, gladiator fodder."

"So many options when you think about it."

"Well, *stop*." Delphine pulled away from Cato with a look of disgust. "Honestly, what's wrong with you two?" She crossed her arms. They all sobered.

"I'm sorry to bring this trouble on you all." Valens sighed, raking his hands through his hair. "I didn't know where else to go."

"You need to make more friends."

"All right." Delphine interrupted and wrangled them back to the matter at hand. "Cato, you see about food for the Tiber shantytown. Val, if you'll write those notes for the widows, I'll get this other message on its way."

XXXVI

IRIS WIGGLED A BLUE GLASS PERFUME BOTTLE into the already-full box and tucked barley straw around it. Helping Beatrix pack had taken longer than she'd anticipated. For all her appearances as a free spirit, Beatrix was incredibly meticulous—and thorough. Iris had been hoping to help her carry a few things back to the Calogarus villa, not pack the entire apartment. It seemed Beatrix had no intention of leaving her home quickly or unencumbered.

"Is that the last of them?" Beatrix swirled into the room, salt-and-pepper curls sprouting wildly above her ears.

Iris brushed her hands together and stood. "I think so. Is that it?"

Beatrix turned and peered through the window. "Marius said he would send the boys and a cart after curfew to help move the boxes." Her brown eyes shimmered as she looked at Iris. "Thank you so much. I couldn't have done this without you." She lifted a hand and traced one of the bright flowers painted on the walls, glowing in the evening's fading golden light. Her tone went wistful with memory. "Lucan and I lived our whole lives together here. We were so happy." She stopped suddenly and picked up the crate of perfumes. Iris followed as she stacked it near the door with the others.

"You should probably get home before it gets dark."

Iris hesitated. She'd offered to help not because she'd particularly wanted to pack boxes, but because it was Pater's night to sleep at the carcer and she had no desire to be in the apartment alone. She tried to keep her tone unaffected as she told Beatrix so.

"Good. We can visit longer then. I'm sure Martha's boys won't mind walking you home later." Beatrix set about finding them something to eat while they waited.

Dusk had fallen when Abachum and Audifax knocked on the door and they all began moving everything but the furniture onto a cart. When they reached the Calogarus villa, Abachum and Audifax pulled the cart around to a larger gate Iris hadn't seen before. It led directly into the courtyard, where Valentine met them, wrapped in a hooded cloak.

"I'm glad you've made it back safely." He kissed Beatrix's cheek and smiled at Iris. He had a satchel looped across his chest.

"Are you leaving?" Beatrix asked.

He nodded. "Just for a bit."

"Would you walk Iris home?"

Iris shook her head in protest. "You shouldn't leave—"

"I'd be glad to."

"Good." Beatrix smiled.

Had this been the woman's plan all along? Surely not. Before Iris could voice another objection to Valentine being on the streets, Beatrix smothered her in a hug.

"Thank you, dear. You've been such a help."

Abachum closed the cart gate behind them as Iris followed Valentine into the alley.

He tugged the hood of his cloak over his head.

"Isn't it dangerous for you to be out?" She hurried to catch up.

Valentine paused at the mouth of the street, looking both ways before emerging. "It's probably more dangerous for *you* to be seen with me." He half turned back. "Perhaps Abachum or Audifax should bring you home."

"You have a hood." Her protest came in a rush. "We'll be fine, so long as you're not recognized."

Valentine gave a single nod.

"I thought you were in hiding. What are you doing, leaving the house at this hour?"

He stepped onto the street and headed in the direction of the Markets of Trajan. "Things." He slanted her a mysterious look.

Two Urban Guards stepped out of a tavern and started down the street toward them.

Valentine took her elbow, turning her around and down a side street they'd nearly passed.

"We'll try this route," he muttered, glancing over his shoulder. He quickened their pace and tugged her down another alley, swinging her into the alcove of a doorway. As her back thumped against the bolted door, her heart lodged just below the base of her throat. Memories of the tribune's unwanted advances rushed to the surface. *Valentine is not the tribune.* Valentine stepped next to her, his shoulder overlapping hers, shielding her from view. He lifted his chin to watch the mouth of the street. Iris hardly dared to breathe.

Seconds passed.

Valentine's gaze remained locked on the street. She couldn't see beyond him, so she studied his profile instead. Thick brows shaded warm eyes above a straight, triangular nose that might have been considered large. Thin upper lip shaped like Cupid's bow. Lower lip fuller and curved down toward a square chin. Did he smell like . . . *roses?*

She leaned toward him, inhaling deeply. Yes, definitely roses.

He turned his head toward her, and she snapped back, heat rolling up her neck. He'd just caught her *smelling* him. What sort of crazy woman did things like that? His eyelids flickered as if surprised by her closeness, but he didn't move away.

"Sorry." He swallowed. "I'm just jumpy, I guess." His breath smelled of chamomile.

"Why do you smell like roses?" Her words came out on the breath of a laugh.

Redness snaked up his neck this time, stopped by the twitching of his lips. "The other option was body odor. So you're welcome." His eyes stayed on her face but took on a thoughtful slant. "Could you—would you want to accompany me for a few hours? A circuitous route might serve us well. But if you'd rather, I'll bring you straight home."

A low rumble of thunder shook in the distance. She hesitated, but it only took one thought of spending the rest of the evening alone in the apartment to make her agree.

"I'll come. You'll be less conspicuous with me." She tilted her head. "If anyone's looking for you, they'll be looking for a man alone."

"That's not why I asked."

"We'd best stay clear of the market and forums." She wrapped her palla more firmly around her head and shoulders. "They're always crawling with Urbans."

"Are you certain?"

She nodded. He gave her a slow smile and swung out of the doorway ahead of her. She struggled to keep up with his fast pace but refused to ask him to slow. The smell of the river grew stronger as they walked, and the Theatre of Marcellus loomed suddenly over their heads, rows of stacked marble-faced arches glittering in the gold of the setting sun. The sign painted near the entrance read *Hercules and the Lion*. The theatre was filling with spectators for the evening show.

"Where are we going?" she gasped, trying to ignore the stitch in her side.

Valentine slowed. He tipped his head casually, looking around before leaning close and whispering, "A wedding."

The words were barely audible. Something in his glance sent her heart skittering. And whether it was the way he looked at her or embarrassment over the feelings the look evoked, she flushed. Then laughed. He was joking.

They took three steps before Valentine spoke in a low voice. "I'm serious."

She felt the blood trickle from her face. His eyes were not teasing as he stopped to face her.

"I'm sorry." Dark eyebrows crinkled together. "I don't know what I was thinking. Forgive me. I'll bring you straight home."

"No, don't." She grabbed his hand without thinking. "I've never been to a wedding." She added the last bit in a whisper. Was it treason to attend? Or only if you were the one getting married? Her pater would never allow it. She bit her lip. Titus would be furious. She shifted.

Neither of them was here right now, and truth be told, she didn't want to go home.

His lips parted as if to protest again but she smiled and continued up the street ahead of him. Deep thunder rumbled to the east, where dark clouds gathered, even as the western horizon blazed with color. Crackles answered the thunder as white fingers of lightning glittered through the piling clouds.

Valentine caught up to her. "Down this way." He took her hand and tugged her up a steep side street past an inn, a pub, a street eatery. Turning sideways down an alley, Valentine knocked at a small door and they were let immediately into a steamy kitchen.

"Valens?"

Valentine released Iris's hand as a woman hugged him. She had a wide, matronly face, black hair streaked with gray, and a hairy brown mole on her chin.

"Lenia?"

Iris looked between the two. For all of Valentine's confidence in where they were going, he seemed surprised at where they'd ended up.

"What are you doing here?" Lenia dropped her voice. "We heard you were in hiding."

Valentine swallowed. "I'm here with a delivery." He emphasized the last word. "Did you order something?"

"You?" Lenia's eyebrows lifted. "The *Friend*?"

"I don't really like—"

"Well, God be praised!" She shook her head, wide face transforming from shock to glee. "Who would have thought it was you all this time?"

Iris looked from one to the other as if they'd suddenly shifted into a bizarre language.

Valentine turned to her. "Iris, this is Lenia." He gestured toward the woman. "Lenia and her family once attended the gathering at

Marius and Martha's home, but when they moved across the city, they joined the church in the Tiberina district."

"Pleased as pears to meet you." Lenia looked at Iris, her eyes warming. "We're glad to have any friend of Val's here tonight."

The house was small and did not have a courtyard, at least not a private one. Lenia brought Iris and Valentine into the adjoining room, which was not much larger than the kitchen but glowed with rosy lamplight and murmured voices. In the corner, an old man strummed a slightly out-of-tune lyre. The room held few people, but Valentine greeted each with familiar hugs and introduced Iris, who was met with the same welcome, as if they'd always known her.

Any awkwardness she might have felt intruding upon such an occasion melted in the warmth of friendly conversation. Valentine moved toward a young man, nervously twisting his hands together. Iris decided he must be the groom and looked for the bride, whom she didn't see. Another older man entered and clapped Valentine and the groom on the back and said something that made the groom turn a deep shade of red.

Valentine laughed and raised his hands. "Let's get started."

The few guests stepped away from the groom and Iris followed suit before realizing Valentine had remained with him. She waited for him to join her along the edge of the room, but he didn't. Conversations fell into a rustling stillness broken only by the old man with the lyre as the door across the room opened and a saffron-veiled bride entered. Iris glanced back toward Valentine and noticed the pomegranate-faced groom, whose tight smile struggled to keep the glint of tears well within his eyes. Valentine caught her eye and winked. Her stomach did a flip as he turned back to the young couple before him.

"We are gathered today to celebrate the much-anticipated union of Farro and Livia, who decided their love for one another was worth breaking the law." Though Valentine spoke with a glint in his eye and a half smile, the mood of the room remained solemn. The music faded away and only Valentine's voice carried through the room. Solemn now, as the occasion deemed. Iris caught her breath. It couldn't be . . . He'd said *wedding* but she'd thought—what *had* she thought, exactly?

Valentine continued. "Farro and Livia, what you two are doing today can never be undone. Not on earth, nor in the eyes of God. You pledge yourselves together for times of plenty and times of want. Danger and peace. Health and illness. Life and death."

The couple faced each other and stood in the traditional marriage pose, right hands joined and Livia's left hand resting on Farro's shoulder. As Iris watched, a thread of longing swept through her. Would she ever stand like that? Gazing into a face shining with love?

"Farro, before this crowd of witnesses and an even greater cloud of witnesses above, do you join yourself to Livia, until death parts you? To love her and protect her, to deny yourself in preference of her, to love her as greatly as God loved us—enough to give Himself up to death as a ransom?"

Farro swallowed and nodded. "I pledge myself."

Valentine turned toward the woman, her face still covered by the orangey-yellow veil. "And you, Livia, before this crowd of witnesses and an even greater cloud of witnesses above, do you join yourself to Farro, until death parts you? To honor him, to respect him, to deny yourself in preference to him, to love him and follow him as we all ought to love and follow Christ our God?"

"I pledge myself." The bride's soft voice quivered with barely checked emotion.

Valentine's amber eyes flicked toward Iris. "God created marriage as a picture of His love for us. He loves each of us with a love so deep He gave His own life for ours. When a marriage follows God's plan, we become a picture of His love to the world around us. And yet, that picture is easily destroyed by selfishness, by putting one's own needs above another's, making them feel unloved, disrespected, domineered—and that selfishness ruins the beauty of what God created marriage to be."

He broke her gaze and looked at Farro and Livia again. "But if we confess our sins, He is faithful to forgive us, and so you two must forgive each other and humble yourselves to ask for forgiveness when you fail each other—and you will."

There were chuckles as Lenia elbowed a short man beside her who grinned and sent her a pointed look.

"So love one another, forgive each other, and fulfill God's plan for your lives." Valentine swept a hand behind him, where a papyrus scroll lay unfurled on a table. "The marriage contract has been ratified by your fathers, so there is nothing left to be done but to bless you both."

As Valentine laid his hands on the couple's heads and prayed over them, Iris felt certain that in all the temples and offerings she'd witnessed, there had never been a more holy sight than this. She bowed her head and couldn't help but think of what would happen if the church would not agree to give up their funds and she and her father could not devise another plan to pay their debts or leave the city. *Lord Jesus, rescue us from Tribune Braccus's grip.*

She looked up as Valentine twisted his shoulders through the cluster of well-wishers crowding the bride and groom and made his way toward her. His eyes were warm and steady as they locked with hers. A tingling swirled in her belly.

"You were a little distracting back here." His voice was low. "I almost wished—" Stopping with something like a look of panic, Valentine swiped two glazed cakes off a tray, shoved one in his mouth, and offered the second to her.

"Cake?" He spoke with his mouth full.

Not sure whether to laugh at the sudden change of subject or be embarrassed he'd noticed her watching him, Iris held out her hand. What had he almost wished? Whatever it was, he didn't want to talk about it.

"You're—you . . ." She couldn't bring herself to say it. *The Cupid.* Valentine. She stared at him, trying to reconcile the man who stood before her, mouth stuffed with cake, as . . . an outlaw.

A crack of a smile lit his mouth. "Are you going to eat that? Because if not—"

She held it out, but he didn't take it. "You're *him*," she whispered even though everyone else in the room knew already. "It's illegal, what you're doing. Everyone here could probably be fined or imprisoned, and you—you're already in enough trouble."

Valentine brushed his hands together, clearing the crumbs. His face sobered, voice quieting. "They know the risk." The gleam of mischief returned as he winked. "And it most certainly *is* legal. Just not emperor approved." He crossed his arms and looked over his shoulder at the two families now joined by the laughing couple in the center of the cluster.

"Whatever his goal, the emperor can't outlaw love." He turned back to her. "The two families agree even with the risk. Farro is a legionnaire and he will still leave with his cohort as planned, but he will be fighting *for* his wife instead of—Why are you smiling like that?"

"This is a crucifiable offense." Her voice dropped to a whisper.

He raised an eyebrow. "And that amuses you?"

"No." Iris shook her head, her palla slipping to her shoulders. "You're in all this trouble—you're in hiding because you're a *romantic*."

His face lost the amusement and gained gravity. "I believe in love as God intended it to be. A man and woman bound together until death parts them. To love, serve, and honor each other, becoming a picture of Christ and His love for all of us. Loyal, steady, consuming." He locked her gaze.

Her mouth went dry.

"No man-made law should prohibit what God designed."

"Why haven't you married then?" She took his offered hand and tried to keep her voice light.

He tugged her toward a table laden with more food than the few people in attendance would eat in an evening. He helped himself to a hard-boiled egg filled with a brown paste and drizzled in *garum*, a fermented fish sauce. "The same reason you haven't."

"Have you been blind too?"

He grinned and swallowed the egg. "Maybe."

She took a bite of the cake she still held. Sweet and light, it dissolved in her mouth around the caramel gooeyness of dates. Heavenly.

"Keeping her all to yourself, eh?" The old man who'd been strumming the lyre approached, an elderly woman on his elbow. He handed Valentine a cup of watered wine.

Valentine angled toward Iris as he made the introductions. "The bride's grandparents Hezra and Luppina. This is Quinta Magia, called Iris."

The old woman took both of Iris's hands in rather cold and wrinkly ones and looked deep into her eyes. "It's so good to meet you. We've been praying for Valentine to find someone for *years*!"

"Oh, we're not—I—I'm just—" Iris stuttered as Luppina leaned in conspiratorially and didn't bother to lower her voice.

"He's not a looker like my Hezra, and I worried he might not be able to attract a woman—but look how lovely you are!"

Valentine choked.

Luppina smiled sweetly at Iris as Valentine turned away, coughing and pounding the center of his chest.

Hezra grinned and lifted his cup. "Nice to meet you, miss." He took Luppina's arm.

"Enjoy yourselves." Luppina flashed an approving smile at Valentine and hobbled away.

"Well," Valentine croaked, his eyes watering. "As you can see, Luppina has the gift of encouragement."

"I disagree with her." Iris squinted, pretending to study him. "I don't think it's your looks that are scaring off the women."

His mouth twitched, expression hopeful and wary. "No?"

She shook her head with a mischievous smirk. "I think it's your choice of perfume."

Halfway through the festivities, Hector's two ex-legionnaires showed up to escort Valens and Iris home. Thunder rumbled as Iris arranged her red-orange palla over her head and shoulders.

"Sorry to drag you out in the rain." Valens peered outside. "We should have left sooner."

Iris shrugged. "People make too much of being warm and dry."

"Do you have a cloak?" He shook his head. "Of course not, you didn't have one earlier."

He removed the brown one he'd already put on and settled it around her shoulders instead, ignoring her protests. No one would be out in this weather to recognize him anyway.

With one ex-soldier in front carrying a shielded lamp and the other acting as rear guard, the four hurried up the street. The mist fused into larger and larger drops that began falling hard and fast, rendering the low spots in the streets into small streams that rushed by, carrying trash and leaves. The rain hit the paving stones in splashes and sharp slaps. Valens caught Iris's arm as she slipped. He glanced at the blackened sky. They'd been at the wedding much longer than he'd thought. Iris must have sensed the same and her pace quickened to match his.

Taking refuge under the dripping awning of a lamp shop, they paused to catch their breath. The soldiers took their duty seriously, standing on either side of them, facing out. Iris wiped back strands of wet hair clinging to her face and the corners of her mouth.

Valens forced his gaze into the street. "I know I don't have to ask, because I'm sure you realize already the importance of keeping what you've just witnessed sub rosa."

She gave a nod and hesitated before speaking. "Does my father know what you've been doing?"

Valens shrugged and avoided her gaze. "Titus knows."

He let out a long breath, steadying his nerves. He'd wanted her to come with him this evening because for some inexplicable reason, he needed her to know. To lay bare the extent of his crimes. Perhaps he hoped to see some glimmer of disappointment in her face that would cut the threads he felt binding him to her.

"Titus told me to leave the city immediately upon my release, and if I didn't, he would be unable to do anything but follow orders and arrest me."

"I know." Iris drew in a breath. "I thought it was because you were a Christian, not . . . This isn't something you can pay off with a bribe or a fine, Valentine." She touched his arm, her eyes going wide. "This is, truly, a crime worthy of crucifixion. I'm not teasing about being a romantic now. This is treason." Her chest rose and fell sharply, her words emerging in fierce whispers.

"I know." He struggled to stay on topic when it seemed every nerve in his body centered on that slight pressure left by her fingers on his arm.

"How can you stay?"

"When the leaders of Rome's churches chose me to lead the church at the Calogarus villa, I took an oath not to abandon them. Even if it means imprisonment."

"Or death?"

"Even then."

She dropped both her gaze and her hand, his every sense already heightened. He smelled the lavender soap she'd used on her hair, heard her breath coming steady and soft amid the rain.

What thoughts ran through her head? Was that sadness in her eyes? Relief? Disappointment?

"We should keep going." The rear guard spoke in a gruff tone. "The rain isn't going to let up."

Valens had forgotten they were here. "Of course."

They set off again, walking in silence and skirting the Forum. At the end of Cedar Street, Iris stopped.

"This is fine." She held out his waterlogged cloak, her dress soaked through and sticking to her skin. "I'll be fine from here. The insula is just there. You shouldn't have even come this far."

"Are you sure?"

She nodded and gripped her elbows, shivering. "Thank you for taking me with you. It was beautiful." She started up the street before turning back to him, rain pelting dark hair to her face and neck. "I will not break your confidence. Your secret, and theirs, is safe with me."

"I didn't doubt it for a moment."

He stayed at the top of the street with the guards, waiting until she was safely inside. As he watched Iris disappear, something inside him shifted—something he'd resisted for a long time and now would have to fight harder than ever.

XXXVII

DAWN BROKE LIKE A BARBARIAN HORDE spreading across the sky, leaving red in its wake. Quintus hurried home as fast as his aching leg would allow. He'd spent the last week wallowing in dread of this day. This last day of freedom before Tribune Braccus would strip them to nothing. Guilt prickled his conscience at the way he'd responded by drinking himself to oblivion just as he used to before Valentine's messages of hope had removed his need for it. It had not occurred to him that God might care as much about his problems as He had about his daughter's. How easily he'd given in to the despair again. It had not been difficult to do when the augur refused to pay him for his false arrest of Valentine. Or last evening, when the *lanista* from the Theatre of Marcellus had come to retrieve the Christian prisoners for execution. Quintus could do nothing but hold back the screaming children as their parents were ripped from their little hands and led away.

Their cries tore the air and his heart to shreds. He'd comforted them the best he could, then left them in the cell to wait for someone from the slave market to fetch them. He'd drained the hidden amphora and had gone to numb himself completely at the Centaur's Cup.

Then Hector had approached him with a note.

"This was left here for you." He'd shrugged when Quintus asked who'd left it.

The note from Valens had given him the hope that the drink couldn't. He'd taken the note to the Calogarus villa instead, with news and renegotiations of his own.

Now he unlocked the apartment and let himself in. Iris waited for him—slumped against her loom snoring, but she'd tried, anyway. He shook her shoulder.

"Iris? Go to bed."

Her eyes flew open and she jerked upright, startling him. "I'm sorry—I'm sorry!"

Her panic struck fear in his core. He darted a quick glance around the darkened apartment. "What's wrong?"

She blinked twice, clarity coming over her features. "Nothing. I thought—I must have been dreaming." She groaned and arched her back, rubbing a kink in her neck.

His heart returned to its normal rhythm and he limped to gather a few splinters of wood and stuff them into the small clay brazier. Iris finished the row and tucked the shuttle of thread where it wouldn't get tangled.

"Valens sent me a note." He lit the wood with a flint, breathing life to flames before shifting a chipped pot of water on top.

Her footsteps shuffled across the room. "What did he say?"

"The church members approved the money being used to redeem us."

Iris gave a little cry and murmured a prayer of thankfulness that seemed natural on her lips.

He shut his eyes, keeping his back turned. "I just met with him and told him I couldn't accept."

"What? Why?"

He gripped the edge of the kitchen worktable and studied the jars on the shelf above it. He'd been elated at first, everything forgotten in the wake of his covered debts and the promise of freedom. But when he'd returned from the tavern, with the cries of the children echoing on the other side of the iron door, Quintus knew he could not take the money.

"The Christians in the prison." He turned and forced his gaze to meet hers. "They were tried and taken to the theatre for execution."

Her lips pressed together.

"I could do nothing for them." Sudden emotion swelled in his throat. "But the children—they'll be sold at auction today, and I cannot accept my own freedom at the expense of theirs."

Iris dropped onto the couch, hands clasped in her lap, brown eyes drilling him. "They will use the money to buy those children instead?" She gave a slow nod, accepting, agreeing with his decision.

He sighed and set two cups on the table. They were dirty, but the calda was hot. He dropped a few crumbled leaves of peppermint into the bottom of each cup and poured the water over. "I spoke with Marius. He's agreed to hide us until his next ship returns to port. When it leaves, he will smuggle us aboard and take us away."

Iris nodded again but said nothing. He sat next to her, holding out the second cup. She took it and leaned her face over the steam.

"It is not without risk. Marius's ship is not due until the ides of Februarius. That's two weeks away. The tribune could still find us, but perhaps not."

"You could not let those children be sold. What you did was right."

"If I am taken, you must—"

She turned to him, eyes sharp. "You won't be." Her chin lifted. "We've prayed about this. God will not let you be taken. He healed me. He has great power—we know this."

Quintus hesitated, then nodded. "Yet we've learned that God is not a magic charm, to do with as we please, to direct as we will, but rather, He directs *us*."

"And He directed you to save those children. He won't punish you for it."

"God is not the one executing Christians."

"What are you saying, Pater?" Iris lowered her cup to her lap and stared at him.

His stomach sank. "It is easy to trust in God when He works miracles, but will we trust Him even if He does not?"

Iris slumped against the arm of the couch, as if realizing the depth of what he asked. Quintus wanted to answer with a resounding yes. He knew he should. But would he? Would she?

The question hung suspended in the air. Neither answered it. Neither could.

"But He *has* answered, Pater," she argued in a whisper. "What you've told me now solves everything."

Quintus nodded, admiring her hopefulness and faith. But despite the neatly packaged plan, he couldn't shake the heavy feeling in his gut.

City of Rome
Ides of Februarius, AD 270

He slumps forward, jaw hanging at an odd angle. There is an empty thud and he is facedown in the sand. The men drop the clubs, grab his arms, and drag him to a post that has shot up through the floor for this purpose. They prop him up on his feet and tie him in place. His head lolls back, sandy red lines running down his face and neck. He is not quite dead.

A small man emerges from a tunnel along the edge of the arena. This one is naked except for a pair of magnificent wings that resemble Cupid's. The winged man carries a bow. The crowd goes restless at the show and the meaning behind it: His crimes will not go unpunished by the emperor nor the gods. The winged man strings an arrow on the bow. Takes aim.

Tied to the post, he watches the winged man through half-closed eyes. His body tenses as the arrow is released. The pain is sharp and numbing as the arrow finds its mark in his chest. He feels the warmth leaving him, running down his chest in hot throbs. His eyes shift upward. Has the sun grown brighter?

The keening wails of the crowd fade. The peace in his eyes turns to glass.

The winged man raises the bow overhead as if some great victory has been won.

XXXVIII

Thunder greeted Iris as she entered the street. Though nearly midday, the sky grew dark and ominous. All was in place. At dusk they would run, but until then all must be as it had been. Pater had returned to his post at the prison after donning thick woolen stockings under his sandals to ward off the chill of the last day of Ianuarius. Iris had found her own stockings and, with them, the bundle of her childhood things that would have been sacrificed at the temple of Juno had she ever married. She'd picked it up. Juno had no need for dolls or clay dogs, but she knew a few children who might.

The cold had seeped into her bones by the time she knocked at the culina door of the Calogarus villa. Wind blasted down the alley, bringing a faint swirling of dry snow. She tucked her chin against her chest and knocked again. This time the door opened, and Iris stepped inside, the heat of the kitchen washing over her in a near-painful relief.

"Goodness, you're frozen through!" Phoebe pulled her toward the hearth. "Stand by the oven and warm yourself. I'm afraid you've caught us in a bit of an uproar. Master Marius went to the auctions this morning and returned with six children." Her eyes filled, and she shook her head. "Those poor babies. Their parents, executed in the theatre."

OF LOVE AND TREASON

Iris couldn't help but wonder if their parents had been killed at the play she and Valentine had passed on their way to the wedding. She held out the little bundle. "It isn't much, but I brought some things for them." The few toys were wholly inadequate considering the tragedy.

Phoebe took the playthings. "How thoughtful."

Iris shuddered as she held her numb fingers over the heat. "What can I do?"

"Warm yourself first." Phoebe lifted a kettle and filled a jar with hot water. "I'll be right back." Taking the jar, the maid swept out of the kitchen and left Iris alone, huddled over the oven's heat.

Iris shivered and let out a long breath. The culina looked as if Phoebe had been in the middle of a dozen chores before being called away with every kitchen lamp. The room was dim, but light and the sound of sloshing water came from an open doorway to the right. Iris poked her head inside, surprised to find Valentine in a room she recognized as a miniature of Silvia's laundry.

Valentine had his back to her, a boiling cauldron on the brazier in front of him. The room smelled of vinegar and hot linen, wet wood, and smoke. Her eyes watered.

Valentine glanced over his shoulder, his look of surprise melting into a grin. "Iris."

"Hello." She eased through the doorway. "What are you doing?"

He gave the cauldron a stir with a wooden paddle. "I have no idea. I'm just following orders. Delphine said to boil the diapers. Does this look right?"

She came closer and peered into the cauldron, the smell of hot vinegar burning in her throat. "They're definitely boiling." She looked at him. "For how long?"

He shrugged. "*Boil* was the extent of my instructions."

She suppressed a grin with mock solemnity. "Then you're doing a wonderful job of it."

The culina door banged open. Iris jumped and whirled as Beatrix paused in the doorway, then turned toward the laundry.

"Valens." Beatrix marched inside and swatted at his arm. "I could smell scorched linen from the courtyard. Let me do that, you're ruining them."

"That's not what I was told." Valentine sent a pointed look in Iris's direction.

Her eyes narrowed, but this time she couldn't hold back the grin. "Good morning, Beatrix. Did you get all your things moved in?"

"*All* being the important word." Valentine gave an exaggerated eye roll. "The childhood memorabilia could have been left behind."

"You *loved* that stuffed ostrich." Beatrix lifted her chin.

Valentine's neck went red and splotchy. "I was *four!*"

"Four*teen*." Beatrix did not quite keep her voice under her breath.

Iris giggled. At Beatrix's direction, Valentine moved an empty pot next to the boiling one and Beatrix ladled the diapers into it one by one.

"There's fresh water for rinsing there, Iris," Beatrix said over her shoulder. "Just pour it in over the top of them. That's it."

Beatrix swirled the diapers in the rinse water and set the paddle aside before crossing the room and tucking a stack of towels under her arm.

"We're just finishing with the baths." Beatrix paused in the doorway. "You two hang those diapers and bring the calda to the triclinium."

"How are the children?" Iris asked when his aunt had gone.

Valentine shook his head and pulled a dripping diaper from the water. "Terrified." He twisted the water from it. Iris followed suit. "Asking about their mothers and fathers."

Iris's heart ached for them. "I can't imagine losing my pater like that." She squeezed her eyes shut. "Poor things."

Valentine flung the diaper over a line stretched across the room. "Your pater is a good man."

Iris wrenched water from another diaper and handed it to Valentine. "He feels terrible he could do nothing for their parents."

"I know. He said as much last night when he came. He's worried about you too."

She shrugged. "All will be well soon. Marius agreed to smuggle us out on his next ship."

Valentine nodded and their eyes tangled. "Where will you go?"

"As far as we can, I suppose."

They finished the laundry in silence and Iris returned to the culina as Valentine emptied the laundry cauldrons into the alley by the bucketful.

She added more water to a nearly dry pot on the brickwork stove and searched the shelves to locate a tray and cups. Beatrix poked her head inside again, looked around, then swung the door open fully, stepping inside when she saw Iris alone.

"Where's Valens?" Her shoulders jerked downward with something like disappointment or irritation. "I thought you were working together."

Iris pointed to the laundry. "He's emptying the wash kettle. Is everything all right?"

"Oh, fine, dear. Just fine. Will you bring the chamomile?" Beatrix swept into the laundry and Iris heard a reproachful "Why aren't you with her?"

The overt matchmaking attempt might have been amusing had Valentine's muffled reply not sounded so defensive and annoyed. Iris felt her cheeks go hot. She tried to ignore the tiny flicker of hurt and busied herself searching for clean cups and trying to leave everything else exactly as she found it.

Beatrix swept out of the laundry room, sweet smile aimed at Iris as she left the culina, closing the door behind her. Valentine emerged from the laundry room after the door shut.

Iris looked up. "Is everything all right?"

With a weary sigh, Valentine braced a hip on the worktable across from Iris and closed his eyes. "I'm sorry." He ran a hand through his hair, making the top swath stand on end. He lifted his hands in surrender and looked at the plaster behind her as he spoke. "I don't know what you heard."

She was about to say she'd heard nothing, but he rushed on, refusing to look at her.

"Bea has been trying to marry me off as long as—well, it feels like forever."

"I know." Iris smiled, hoping to ease his embarrassment. "She came into the bakery every morning. You were all she ever talked about." She lifted a conceding shoulder. "Well, you and perfume." She located a jar of dried chamomile flowers and set it on the tray. "She loves you very much."

"Too much, sometimes." He chuckled, leaning to peer into the pot as a whirl of pale steam rose. He turned his head and met her gaze for the briefest of moments before dropping his to the floor. He swallowed. "I'm a fugitive." He spoke so quietly she had to lean forward to hear him. "Bea doesn't understand that no good would come of any attachments, especially now."

His words cut the breath from her lungs, and yet, why should they? He'd never given her any indication he felt anything deeper than friendship toward her. Everything he said she'd already known. But the finality of his words hurt. Or perhaps it was the regret in his voice when he'd spoken them. She took a breath and let it out slowly, silently, taking a moment to smooth her features into an unaffected smile. He stared at his empty hands.

They stood in an awkward silence, Iris, for once, unable to think of a way to defuse it. Water drops spit against the long brazier as the pot began to boil. Grateful for the distraction, Iris ladled it into a red-glazed carafe.

"Come on. You take the tray and I'll carry the water and get the doors." She nudged Valentine with an elbow as if he'd been Titus and breezed ahead as if she was as unaffected by him as he seemed to be by her.

Iris took her time going home. She'd spent the rest of the morning and afternoon helping with the children. Six of them, under the age of eight. They'd clung to each other, fear and defiance in their eyes as if daring anyone to try to separate them—and no wonder. Finally, after baths and food and chamomile tea, they'd fallen asleep in a tangled heap, even in slumber refusing to lose the touch of another. Iris's heart broke for them. Beatrix and Martha told her that the Scriptures commanded believers to care for orphans and it would not be long before these had loving homes. But first they must heal.

Several of the smallest children seemed particularly taken with Iris, and while not relinquishing their grip on each other, they'd clung to her until they'd fallen asleep. Iris hated for them to wake and find her gone, but Martha assured her all would be well. Iris had to return to the apartment and pack the few things they would take with them before she returned to Marius and Martha's with her father. She might have done it earlier had her hands not been full.

As the temples and public buildings along the Via Sacra came into view, she fought the strange sense of emptiness that had come over her when Valentine spoke. He'd acted as if Beatrix were the one who needed to understand his decision to remain unattached, but the way he'd spoken . . . the words were meant for her. Did he truly feel nothing at all for her? Tears stung her throat.

She tried instead to focus on the weaving project that awaited her at home. She'd finished the winter palla in a shade of soft peach flesh and had begun weaving a new piece of cloth with the vibrant colors of a sunset. She'd mingled the orange and yellow strands for a few rows before switching to all yellow thread. She'd try to bring it with. Beatrix would love it.

Cedar Street hung in hazy shadow when Iris turned onto it. Mind filled with weaving and packing, Iris had no warning when a hand clamped around her arm and jerked her into an alley.

XXXIX

THOUGH TEMPTED TO ACCEPT, Quintus declined the extended wine goblet with a slight shake of his head. Tribune Lucius Braccus shrugged and returned it to the table before settling back in the chair behind his desk. The tribune's sparse office made Quintus feel as though they were on campaign again. It commanded an urgency of obedience—much like the command that had forced him here. The troop of Praetorian Guards that had dragged him to the Castra Praetoria had been none too gentle. His left eye was swelling shut, and blood trickled into his boot from a cut on his knee.

"I'm certain this is a misunderstanding that can be explained." Braccus gestured toward the scroll lying on the desktop between them.

Quintus shifted his weight. If this was about his debts, what could possibly be misunderstood? His leg ached, unaccustomed to the fast march of nearly two uphill miles, all without a rest. Sweat stuck his tunic to the middle of his back. *God, give me wisdom.* The words seemed stuck. His mouth went dry. Perhaps he should not have declined the wine after all.

Braccus tipped his cup to his lips, eyes never once leaving Quintus. They were small and close-set, giving him the appearance of a weasel—shrewd, ready to go for the throat. Light from the sconces on the walls caused the gold signet ring on his first finger to glint. He set the goblet down.

"Well." Braccus laced his fingers together. "Do you have the money?"

"Payment is not due until tomorrow."

Braccus raised a brow. "Do you have it?"

Quintus swallowed. "No."

"I thought as much." Braccus sighed. "I'm disappointed in you, Quintus. Not about the money. I knew you wouldn't get that in time." He waved his hand. "It's the scroll that I find most disappointing."

"What scroll?" Even as he said the words, he knew. Valentine had given him a copy of John's Gospel to read. But it hadn't left his home. Dread curdled his gut.

The tribune slid the scroll toward him and gestured at the chair next to Quintus. "Sit. Have a look. Perhaps it will jog your memory."

Quintus's knees buckled and he sat but made no move to reach for the scroll.

"Please explain how this banned book ended up *beneath your pillow*." Braccus crossed his arms.

Quintus shook his head. "You searched my home?"

"And questioned your neighbors—your landlady was appalled when we showed her the scroll. She had her man change your locks right then and there. Such loyalty to the empire. Pity women aren't allowed into the guard, eh?"

Fear sliced through the center of his chest and left his lungs tight. "Where is my daughter?"

The tribune waved aside the question with a shrug and leaned toward Quintus, clasping his hands between his knees. "I don't care about any of this." Quintus recognized the change in tactics. "You're a good jailor. We have never had an issue with your integrity before. Tell me this is a misunderstanding and we'll pretend it never happened." Braccus picked up the scroll and waved it toward the brazier in the corner, glowing orange through the air holes, the fire inside crackling and giving off too much heat.

A trickle of sweat edged down his hairline. "Where is my daughter?" he asked again.

Braccus pounded a fist into his desk. "Where *is* your daughter?" He repeated the question with a growl. "We had a deal."

Relief crashed through him. "You don't have her?"

"Your inability to pay your debts means all your possessions are forfeit. That includes your daughter." The tribune's lips went thin. "You have no right to hide her."

"Am I here because of my *debts* or because of a scroll?" Quintus scrambled to keep up with the tribune's line of questioning.

Braccus waved the scroll. "This could mean a charge of treason. You took an oath, Quintus Magius. Fealty to the emperor. Fealty to the gods. Fealty to none but Rome. Can you tell me you have not broken your oath and joined rank with the Christians?"

Quintus's mouth felt full of sand. His mind ran. While debts meant slavery, a charge of treason carried a death sentence. He knew he should speak the truth, but what would that mean for his daughter? Would they punish her too? *God, protect her. I cannot.*

"Well?" Braccus tapped the scroll on his palm.

Quintus lifted his chin, feeling a strange but welcome surge of strength. "I will honor the emperor. I will uphold my oath to protect him and to protect Rome."

"Very good." Braccus's smile had the distinct tilt of a cat who'd tired of playing with the mouse and was going in for the kill. "And do you swear loyalty to the gods of Rome?"

"No." Quintus cleared his throat and spoke louder. "I cannot."

A single, thoughtful nod. "I see." The ringed index finger tapped the scroll. "And does Speculatore Titus Didius Liberare share similar beliefs?"

Quintus felt his eyebrows crinkle. No. Unfortunately, Titus did not. He shook his head. What was going on here?

Tribune Braccus tossed the scroll on the table and leaned back in his chair, studying Quintus through half-closed eyes. "It's a pity I can't trust you anymore. *Fortunately*—" he jerked forward and picked up a wax tablet and stylus—"I have a friend I *can* trust, serving on the front in Germania. The fighting is brutal there. Casualties every day. Ambushes on speculatore scouts." He shook his head, grimacing. "Those barbarians are ruthless."

Please, no. "I've been meaning to send him a letter for a while, but now seems like a good time." He straightened the tablet before him. "Reposting Titus Didius Liberare will be no great matter. My friend will be glad for the speculatore fodder, I'm sure." He looked hard into Quintus's eyes. "He'll be dead in a matter of weeks, if he lasts that long."

"Don't do it, sir. I beg you. Titus has nothing to do with this." As he spoke, the way Titus had rescued Iris from the tribune's attack rushed his mind. This had little to do with Quintus and everything to do with revenge.

Braccus wrote quickly, his lips twitching as they formed the words along with the stylus. He slapped the two halves shut, wrapped it in a leather cord, and melted sealing wax across the fold. His signet stamped the red wax with a finality that made Quintus flinch.

"Tribune, please—"

Braccus clapped once and a slave entered. Eyes never leaving Quintus, he swung the letter toward the slave, who took it, though Braccus did not let go. "Perhaps I could spare you too, Quintus. You know what I want."

Quintus clenched his jaw and balled his fists in his lap. "Over my dead body."

Braccus released the missive and stood with a dismissive smile. "Very well." His voice nearly cheerful, Braccus turned to the slave. "This goes out with the next correspondence."

Quintus watched Titus's fate scramble from the room. He stilled as the tribune studied him, slowly circling the chair where he sat. His world had spun out of his grasp. If Iris had not been home when the tribune's men had searched their apartment, she was surely on her way by now. If only he could get her away. Keep her safe. He was powerless, sitting here. *God, please, protect my daughter.*

As if someone had whispered instructions in his ear, he suddenly knew what to do. He took a deep breath.

"Iris can see."

Braccus stopped circling and cocked his head. "I heard rumors. But I'd hoped they weren't true."

"A man prayed for Iris to see again. A *Christian*. The scroll is mine. I hid it."

Braccus stared at him.

"But I will hide it no longer. This God has power unlike any other god. And I would know; I've faithfully worshiped the others without result." Quintus knew he had to tread carefully to keep Valens and the others out of trouble. "I hid the scroll because I wanted—I *needed* to know more. This God is different. He is all backward and upside-down. He doesn't war with other gods, has no weakness for drink or women, like our gods. He doesn't have to scheme for power or work for His deity. He doesn't need temples made by human hands because He made everything."

Braccus remained silent. Quintus continued, emboldened, retelling everything he knew with a clarity he didn't know he had.

The tribune eyed him as he returned to his seat, flicking a hand. "I've heard enough."

He'd listened patiently, his face warring between near interest and scorn. He reached out and picked up the scroll, weighing it in his hands, debating.

"So this 'True God,' this Jesus, as you call him—he is the only god?"

"Yes. The only God. The Creator, all-powerful, all-knowing—"

"Yes, yes. You've already spouted his attributes," Braccus cut him off. "So what of all our gods?"

"Fables."

"Fables. All of them? Even the emperor?"

Quintus held his gaze. "Every one."

Braccus rubbed his chin. "I've had a change of heart. I don't think I will burn this scroll after all." He smiled faintly as a glimmer of hope rose in Quintus's chest. "The council will want it as evidence." He clapped again and this time, instead of the slave, two overbuilt guards entered.

"Quintus Magius, you are under arrest for treason and conspiring against the empire. Take him away."

The guards did as commanded. Quintus didn't fight. The calm that had come over him at first remained with him, solid. He pleaded again for God to protect his daughter.

"Take him to the barrack cells to await trial. I need to meet with the council."

They pulled Quintus toward the door, but Braccus stopped them briefly at the threshold.

"Oh, and when you're through with him, bring me the girl." He smiled as the blood drained from Quintus's head.

"I *will* have her. Willingly or not."

XL

THE SCREAM DIED IN IRIS'S THROAT as Dorma's wrinkled face came into view through the black spots of fear edging her vision.

"Shhh!" the old woman hissed, holding a bony finger over her lips. "You must be quiet, and you must come with me."

Iris sucked in a deep breath, willing her pulse to stop racing.

Dorma tugged her farther down the alley. "Come. Come quickly."

Iris resisted. "I can't. I have to go home."

"You have no home," the woman snapped. "They've taken your pater and there's two guards waiting to take you too."

The blood left her head in a rush. "They took Pater?"

Dorma pulled Iris along behind her. "Come. You must get away from here. Titus made me swear not to let you enter."

"Titus has been here?"

Dorma shook her head in disapproval. "You should have seen him, running through the place shouting for you—like a madman. Priscilla won't lay for a month."

Her mind raced and her heart began to thrum a wild and uneven rhythm. The tribune had arrested her pater and come after her too. Iris shook her head; she'd thought they had until tomorrow morning. Had Pater misremembered the date? What would she do now?

Dorma hurried her along, keeping to alleyways and shadows.

"Where are you taking me?" Iris finally thought to ask.

"Titus said to bring you to the Baths of Agrippa. It's crowded, and you can stay in the women's rooms. He'll send a slave to find you when he comes."

Dorma deposited Iris at the entrance of the women's changing rooms and turned to leave, muttering about having to go comfort her chicken. Iris threw her arms around her before she went.

"Thank you, Dorma." She fought back tears.

The woman gave a smile that looked more like a grimace and patted her hand. "Be careful, my dear. The tribune is a vile man."

Iris found a bench in the women's room and settled herself onto it, thoughts and fears whirling. Would she get to see her pater? Or would he be shipped off to a marble quarry without a goodbye? She fought back the tears that threatened to spill. If she let them go, she'd be completely undone and draw attention. The women around her chattered, voices echoing on the frescoed walls in a cacophony that rang in her ears. Wooden-soled bath shoes clacked across the floor. Bath soaps and scented oils of every variety stung her nose. Several women asked if she was all right and Iris mumbled an excuse of waiting for someone and feeling unwell.

It seemed ages before a pair of bare feet paused in front of her. "You are Iris?" A timid slave girl looked at her in question.

A sliver of fear prickled in her chest. "Who wants to know?"

The girl's ears went red. "There is a very handsome soldier outside looking for you. He said his name was Titus."

Iris lurched to her feet and bolted for the door, ignoring the questioning looks that followed her. Titus stood outside, arms crossed, eyes trained on the door of the women's room, and looking as if he'd burst inside if she didn't come out. His face collapsed in relief when he saw her.

She launched herself at him. "Why did they take Pater? Where is he? Can I see him? Will they let him go?"

He gripped her shoulders, hesitating. "Your father's been arrested for treason. I'm sure it's just a—"

"*Treason?*"

"*Shhhh!*" Titus took her hand and pulled her away from the crush of bathers toward the manicured gardens surrounding the bath complex. He stopped under an empty marble pergola at the collision of four paths.

"Iris, listen to me. Look at me. *Look at me.*" He waited for her to comply, his tone steely. "You cannot go home. Do you understand?" He gave her a little shake until her eyes connected with his. "The tribune has his hands in this and he's looking for you too."

Titus said words but they failed to make any sense. Treason? "Is this about the children?"

Confusion lined his forehead. "What children?"

Iris bit her lip and looked away. Her mind raced. Treason. Was this about Valentine's arrest? The bribe? Their new faith? Or something else? But the reason wasn't so important as the outcome. Her father had been accused of treason. What now? She shut her eyes, trying to block out the answer written on Titus's face.

"Iris, look at me. Shhh, hey." His tone went soft, and he pulled her against him as she began to sob. "Do you have friends you can go to? Friends the tribune will not know about?"

She had friends the tribune shouldn't know about.

"Nowhere near the market or Cedar Street. The tribune has men looking for you." Titus peeled her away from him and drilled her with his eyes. "Do you understand? He *cannot* find you."

Iris nodded and shuddered, memories rising like bile. She understood very well.

"I have a little money." His hand went to the pouch at his belt. "I can hide you at an inn for a few days. Come."

"No, I—I have friends."

"Will you be safe with them?"

She nodded, then hesitated, wondering if her friends would be safe with her.

"Go to them." He glanced at the darkening sky. "Are they close? Can we get there before dark?"

She nodded.

"I'll walk with you."

Numb and reeling, Iris allowed Titus to lead her out of the gardens.

"Which way?"

She pointed. They started walking.

"I'll bring you word as soon as I can."

Iris stopped in the road. What was she doing? She couldn't bring Titus to Marius and Martha's. Not with Valentine there. "I don't think you should know where I am." She gripped her elbows and prepared to argue.

To her surprise, he agreed. "They'll most likely question me anyway." He paused. "Do you know the sculpture garden of Sallust? Between Pincian and Quirinal Hills? I took you there once."

"I remember, but I wouldn't know how to find it."

"Anyone can give you directions; they're well-known. Meet me there tomorrow afternoon. I should be able to get away then. Wait near the entrance to the hedgerow maze." He brought her as far as the arch of Claudius I.

"I can find my way from here." She stopped under the arch. "I'll be fine. Find Pater. Find a way to get him out of this."

He cupped her face in his wide hands and pressed a kiss to her forehead, his blue eyes heavy with the pain she felt. "I will do everything I can, Iris. I promise. Be safe. I will see you tomorrow."

He let her go then and she hurried up the road, pausing once to look behind her. He stood watching, the setting sun casting half of his body in brilliant color and the other in shadows. He lifted a hand. She did the same, then turned around and rushed away, racing against the sun to reach the clinic front of Marius and Martha's villa. Was it a mistake to return? Could she trust Titus not to follow her and discover her friends? She stopped. Her pulse rushed in her ears and her knees felt weak. She could not stay in the street, but did she dare endanger her friends? What if Titus found out that Valentine had remained in the city? Would he turn a blind eye a second time? She couldn't answer with a definite yes.

Yet where else could she go? Paulina would not welcome her, and Beatrix had already left her home. She had nowhere else to turn.

Jesus, what am I to do? Protect Pater and my friends.

Beams of light extended heavenward from the western horizon, striping the sky in purple and orange. A heavy peace draped over her shoulders, warm and secure. And as if someone had spoken both audibly and inside her own head, the words *they are Mine* rumbled around her, at once gentle and raw with power.

The words offered no assurances, but they comforted, nonetheless. Her feet started to move.

The lights in the street-front clinic were dark as Iris reached the high-walled villa. She twisted down the narrow alley and knocked at the culina door. Once, twice, three times.

Phoebe opened the door, wearing a wary expression that softened into surprise. "Quinta Magia." She glanced behind her. "Is your pater with you?"

Iris's lips trembled and she shook her head. Phoebe swung the door open wider and ushered her into the culina. "Are you all right? Come, I'll bring you to the mistress."

The others were sitting in the triclinium when Phoebe entered, Iris in tow. They all froze when she entered, the evening meal spread out before them.

Beatrix, the first to overcome her surprise, leaped to her feet. "Iris, are you all right?" Her eyes crinkled in concern.

Shaking, Iris curled her arms around herself, trying and failing to hold herself together as the tears came.

Beatrix wrapped her arms around Iris's shoulders. "Have you been hurt?" She looked her over.

Iris shook her head, sucking in a shuddering breath. "They . . . took Pater."

XLI

Trapped in the city, the wind held a panicked moan as it sought freedom, blasting around the corners of buildings, shooting through the narrow streets and carrying with it unidentifiable trash that battered Valens's shins as he used Cato's spare key and let himself into the clinic. He sighed, latching the door behind him and shutting out all but the wind's howl. The air in the clinic seemed unearthly still compared to the power in the street.

He scrubbed his hands over his face and yawned. He'd had to leave the villa not long after Iris had come, pale and trembling with the news that her father had been arrested for treason.

Usually he looked forward to his nightly forays into the city—his only means to escape the confines of the villa. Tonight, he could think of nothing but returning. Valens cut through the clinic, emerging into the courtyard, which, while breezy, was protected from the worst of the wind. The stars were out in full force. He tilted his head back, an ache crawling up the center of his chest.

Bookended by two weddings, Valens had attended a meeting of Rome's church leaders. He'd been looking forward to the meeting and camaraderie, the conversations and study of the Scriptures. Instead, Valens had found himself—and his choice to stand against the emperor's marriage ban—the subject of debate, again. The vote had been unanimous. The decision made for him. In the space of a few minutes, Valens had been relieved of his church in the Calogarus

264

villa and reassigned to minister in the Lycian region of Asia Minor along the Anatolian coast. They might as well have banished him to the other side of the world.

Body warmed and blood thumping from the walk, Valens made for the bench nestled on the far side of a concrete planter containing the skeletal remains of an almond tree. His body was tired, but his mind raced. The prospect excited him. At least, the prospect of walking streets in the daylight again, of visiting widows and delivering food baskets. But the thought of leaving Rome, the only city he'd known, a city he loved and served, brought his heart to his throat. He swallowed it down, ticking off the constellations as he walked: Taurus, Orion, Lepus, Caelum—Movement on the bench startled him.

"Iris?" He squinted to be certain. "What are you doing out here?"

The slivered moonlight barely illuminated her face. "Couldn't sleep." She spoke softly, hugging her knees to her chest.

"I wish I knew what I could do to help." He sat beside her. "Tell me again what happened."

She shook her head and rested her chin on her knees. "I told you everything I know." But she repeated it all again, voice trembling with barely checked emotion. He wanted to pull her close, tuck her tight against him, and assure her everything would be fine. Instead, he reached out and found her hand, wrapping it in his. To his surprise, she leaned toward him, arms and legs unfolding. She drew in a ragged breath, and he pulled her against him, cradling her head against his chest as she sobbed. He stroked her hair, the gesture sending up waves of the almond-scented soap she'd used to wash it.

"I'm afraid for him." She struggled to take deep breaths. "I'm sorry my faith is so weak."

He rubbed a thumb over her shoulder blade. "There's always a bit of fear in the unknown." He thought of his own reaction to the church leaders' news. "We will continue to pray for God's strength and peace."

Her fingers released the handful of tunic she'd gripped at his side and she straightened, looking into his eyes. Her face was so close to his. Wide eyes vulnerable. He swallowed. Shifted back slightly.

"Will God get him out?" she whispered. The tension in her body begged for a word of hope.

He let out a breath and raked his fingers through his hair, turning away from her to face the fountain. "We're told that all things work together for the good of those who love God, those who are called according to His purpose." He hesitated. "*All things* might be good things, and they might be terribly difficult things."

"That's not very comforting." She tilted her face away and shivered as a swirl of wind shot over them.

"Maybe not." He shrugged. "And yet it is. Because we have the assurance that no matter what happens—good or bad, by our estimation—anything can always be redeemed by God for good if we trust Him."

Iris continued to shiver.

"Come on." He rose and tugged her to her feet. "It's cold and you should be in bed now, anyway."

She shook her head. "I couldn't sleep if I wanted to."

"Then at least let's go to the culina, where it's warm."

She followed him into the kitchen. The holes in the stovetop glowed orange from the embers inside. Iris held her hands over one while Valens added a few sticks of wood to the other and rubbed his hands together over the warmth.

"Where were you?" The flames sent flickering light over the dim walls and the contours of her face.

Valens shrugged, watching the light dance on her dark hair. "I had a meeting." He forced his gaze back to the fire.

"Another wedding?"

"Two." He sighed. "And a church meeting."

She watched him, waiting for him to continue. He knew he should probably tell Bea first, but she was asleep, and he needed to tell someone.

"Considering my situation, the other leaders decided I'm more fit for mission work. They're sending me somewhere in the Lycian region on the Anatolian coast."

"So far?"

The note of disappointment in her voice warmed him.

"I'll have to speak with Marius and see if he can smuggle me aboard when his next ship leaves."

She pressed her lips together and nodded, tilting her chin toward the fire, no doubt thinking of how she and her father had once had the same plan.

"What happens now?" He crossed his arms, fighting the sudden longing to draw her into an embrace again. "You said the investigator was looking into it?"

Iris dashed the back of her hand over her cheek, squinting. "The investig—oh, *Titus*? Yes. He said he'd meet me tomorrow afternoon to bring news."

Alarm spread through him. "He's coming *here*?"

Iris looked at him quickly. "Of course not. We agreed he wouldn't know where I am—in case they questioned him about Pater. I'm meeting Titus in the sculpture garden of Sallust. Do you know it?"

A popular meeting place for lovers and statuary enthusiasts to wander. He nodded. "I can walk you there."

She looked at him as if he'd sprouted a third eye. "You're not even supposed to be in the city. I don't want you arrested too." She glanced away. "Anyway, Martha already volunteered Abachum."

He still wished it were him escorting her, but she would be safe enough with Abachum.

Iris yawned. "It must be close to dawn. I'm sorry I've kept you up."

"I'm not, and you didn't." He yawned as well.

Iris excused herself with a murmured "Good night."

Valens remained by the stove, the room darker and colder without Iris. Guilt plucked at the edges of his mind. She stirred something in him, and it wasn't simply pastoral concern. He paced the culina, ducking under a leg of cured lamb each time he made a full circuit.

He was attracted to her. But it was more than that, wasn't it? Why bother denying it? He ran his hands through the hair above his ears and locked his fingers behind his head. Nothing could come of it. Not possible.

The objections lost their strength under the realization that Iris and her father had also planned to leave the city on Marius's ship. With Valens free to join them, a relationship with Iris was very possible. So long as Quintus was released. If he wasn't—Valens didn't want to think about it. He wondered if Iris would still leave. Would she leave *with him*?

He could still smell the scent of her hair and recall with startling clarity the feel of her body curled against his. Aunt Bea would be beside herself if she knew someone had finally caught his eye. His heart. Of course, it would happen just as he was forced from the city.

Valens sighed and sank onto a stool. What sort of claim did the investigator have on Iris? She'd always spoken of Titus with affection. How deep did it go? He had a fleeting vision of being called to a wedding only to find Titus and Iris waiting for him. The thought rankled. Until he knew, he would try to distance himself from her.

Easier determined than done. They were both hiding in the same house.

XLII

IRIS FIDGETED AS SHE WAITED near the mouth of the hedgerow maze, where statues of a man and a woman sat on either side of the path, reaching toward each other with longing but never touching. Clouds hung low and thick, their impending doom nearly as heavy as her father's.

Despite her reserved state on the way to the gardens, Abachum had chattered about everything from the weather to imported pottery with hardly space to breathe between subjects. When they reached the sculpture gardens, Iris was ready to split up. Abachum wandered alone but stayed within sight of her.

Marble statues of gods and goddesses and a few heroes of myth and legend dotted the gardens. On nicer, less threatening days, the grounds swarmed with artists and lovers. Iris shifted from one foot to the other. Few wandered the gardens today and none of them were Titus.

He was late.

She paced. Pops and crackles erupted around her and a large raindrop splattered against her cheek. She shifted her palla over her head.

"Iris?"

She turned toward Titus's voice. For a moment she stared, still unused to how his actual form did not match the image she'd held in her mind for the past seven years. His uniform of deep Praetorian blue stretched tight across a broad chest as he walked toward her, shoulders shifting from side to side with each step. He had not shaved and wore bad news along with his uniform. Iris's legs began to shake.

"Sorry I'm late." Titus squinted against the rain. "I only managed to get away now."

Iris took a step toward him, dread coiling at the base of her skull, tightening every second he didn't burst with good news.

"Pater?" Her voice shook. Rain slid down the side of her nose and skirted her mouth.

Titus took her wrist and led her away from the maze where the hedges might hide listening ears—if the rain hadn't already chased them away. He rushed her beneath a round-domed pavilion of pale marble columns ringed by bushes crusted in dead flowers. Thunder rumbled and rain fell in a gray roar.

He gripped her hand. Water dripped from his dark hair, running down his neck and soaking his uniform in midnight streaks. Why wasn't he saying anything?

"Titus."

His chin dropped ever so slightly, and her body began to tremble.

"Tribune Braccus called an emergency council last night." He avoided her eyes as he spoke. "The prefect had a notion to be lenient and was about to cancel your father's debts when Braccus accused him of being a Christian." Titus shook his head and spoke through clenched teeth. "Your father wouldn't deny it. It's all over the barracks how he tried to convert the council. He's going to be sold at week's end. He's lucky they didn't kill him." He gave a roar of frustration and turned away, pacing and locking his hands behind his neck. "This could have all been avoided had he just recanted. It'd be scandalous—admitting to entertaining Christian beliefs—and he'd still lose his post, but now it's his freedom."

"He cannot recant," Iris spoke softly, trying to imagine her pater standing up to the council. "Our God is true." When she said the words aloud, peace smoothed the crumpled tension in her heart, even as her legs still shook.

He swung around, anger twisting his face into a strange shape.

"*Mars and Jupiter*, Iris! You can't be serious." Thunder erupted, covering anything else he said.

"Where's Pater now?" she asked when Titus and the thunder had calmed.

"In the Castra Praetoria prison." He rubbed his chin. "Until the next slave auction."

"Have you seen him? How is he?"

"Worried about you." He avoided her eyes and didn't elaborate.

"Will you take me to see him?" She craned her neck to catch his eye. "Please."

"No." Titus shifted away, massaging the back of one arm. "Because your pater admitted to being a Christian and Tribune Braccus brought the charges against him, the Severan policies dictate that all your father's goods and property be awarded to the tribune. That includes you." A muscle in his jaw ticked. "We've orders to bring you to the tribune as soon as you're found. Your pater would die before he let the tribune lay hands on you. As would I. Swear to me you will stay away."

"I promise." She knew nothing could be done by going to the fortress, but would that mean she never saw her pater again? She pressed her fingers to her forehead, the coldness soothing.

"I'm sorry, Iris." Titus sighed and slipped an arm around her, tugging her shoulder into his chest. The molded leather armor he wore beneath his tunic made the embrace stiff and cold. "Truly, I am. Quintus has been like my own father. This is just as painful for me."

"Which market will they take him to?" She smeared the tears from her cheek with the back of one hand. "Could we . . . if we had the money . . . ?" Her voice broke. Wishful thinking. The money Valentine had offered the first time had saved the six children of the executed Christians. There couldn't possibly be enough left to redeem her father as well. The prefect's decision to sentence her father to labor seemed merciful, yet Iris knew with the state of his leg, Pater would not last long in a marble quarry or an ore mine. That he would die was certain, but it would be slow and painful.

"I don't know yet, but I'll find out and send word when I do." His grip on her tightened. "No offense meant toward your father, but in his physical state, I can't imagine he'd go for much."

She nodded, his words offering a flicker of hope. The rain beat the ground, sending small rivers of water snaking through the grass.

"I have to get back." He pulled his mantle over his head, uncovering the tip of the gladius strapped under his arm. "Are you safe?" His tone gentled as he studied her face.

Iris nodded. "Yes."

"Good. When I find out more about the auction, where shall I send the message?"

Her stomach seized. "I thought we agreed you shouldn't know where I am."

Titus shrugged. "The trial's over and I wasn't called to testify. Danger of questioning is over. I want to be able to reach you quickly if something were to change."

She hesitated.

His eyes narrowed as they fixed on her. "They're Christians, aren't they?" When she did not respond, he swore. "You've got to leave. It's not safe."

"And go where?" she countered. "I can't go home or to the market. Paulina won't have me back, and I have no other friends."

His boots screeched against the marble floor as he shifted his weight. "Christians are now considered traitors against the empire. It's only a matter of time before they're all rounded up." He gave a shake of his head and rubbed wide hands over his face. "You have to get away from them. When the order is given to imprison all Christians, I won't be able to help you. My oaths and orders take precedence over my opinions." His voice sounded strange and pleading.

She'd never known Titus to beg. She said nothing but felt the weight of the implication of his words.

"Your orders take precedence, yet you're not taking me to the tribune now," she whispered, her eyes sliding up to meet his.

Titus kneaded the muscles at the base of his neck and dropped his hands to his sides. His right thumb spun the gold ring that had belonged to his father. He didn't speak.

"You have to make a choice, Titus."

"It's not that simple. I wish it were, but it's not."

He flinched as she touched his arm. "If you see Pater, tell him we're praying for him."

Titus bit back a sharp laugh. "If your god cannot even keep him out of prison, do you think he will save him from slavery?"

"God *is* powerful, Titus. Look into my eyes and tell me He's not."

He gave a derisive snort. "Pray if you must, but do not hope too greatly." He gave her hand a squeeze. "Do you have an escort back? We're a long way from where I left you last night."

"I have someone."

He did a quick scan of the grounds. "The boy?"

She nodded. "He's trustworthy."

Titus did not look convinced. "If you say so."

"I do."

"Where can I send you a message?"

"Titus—"

"If you don't tell me, you know I'll find you anyway."

She sighed, indecision warring and finally losing in the wake of the knowledge that she'd never be able to hide from him. Titus wasn't the best Praetorian speculatore for no reason.

"Leave a message at the clinic of Marius Calogarus Cato on Quirinal Hill. I will fetch it there."

His eyes softened and he reached out and tugged her palla forward to shield her face. "Be safe," he whispered, giving her a long look. "Stay hidden." He took a breath as if to say more but just chucked her chin with a finger and turned away.

Iris watched Titus retreat until a hedgerow swallowed him.

"Well?"

She jumped and turned as Abachum ducked into the pavilion, water streaming into puddles at his feet.

"He'll be sold at auction." She blinked back the heat that stung her eyes. "Let's go back."

This time, Abachum seemed to sense her need for silence and didn't speak as they hurried home. Iris was thankful. The rain had slowed to a spitting mist that swirled through the streets like gray fog.

Any minute. Any minute now she would wake up and it would all be a terrible dream. An earsplitting crack followed by a rumble of thunder shook the cobbles beneath her feet. Her mind felt as numb as her toes. Pater, in prison. Pater, sentenced to be sold as a slave. Her foot sank ankle-deep into an icy puddle and pulled her from her thoughts. Abachum tugged her down the familiar alley as another deep choke of thunder shook them.

Phoebe let them in.

"Come in quickly. Goodness, you're both soaked through! Here, stand by the fire." The maid shuffled the two of them close to the stove and added water to a large clay pot.

"I'll tell everyone we're back." Trails of water splattered in his wake as Abachum left the culina. Behind Iris, Phoebe clattered at the worktable before appearing at her elbow with a steaming cup.

"I'll see about finding you some dry things." She met Iris's troubled face with a look of kind compassion. Phoebe patted her shoulder as Iris murmured a thank-you and wrapped her hands around the cup. The scent of cloves and cinnamon spicing the heated wine enveloped her in comforting warmth, though it would not chase the chill she felt deep in her bones.

Alone, Iris shifted closer to the stove and shivered. She shook her head at the irony of her father imprisoned at the Castra Praetoria. Was he cold? Had they given him anything to eat? Would she see him again? Of course she would one day. Yet if she never saw her father again in this life, if he died in the quarry or mine, she would still have to live out the rest of her days on earth missing him. She wasn't ready to give him up. Their life had been turned upside down. What would she do without the solid safety of her father's presence? Who would she turn to?

Trust Me.

The command twisted inside her chest, fear and longing warring for superiority. Iris stared at the flames licking the inside of the hole in the top of the stove. Could she trust God, even now? The talk with

Pater sprang to mind, so recent, yet it felt like ages ago. Of course she could trust God fully then, when He'd shown His power and restored her sight—but would the price of His healing power be paid with her father's life? Did the Christian God work like the Roman gods, bestowing favors and then extracting payment? That was not how Valentine had explained it, and yet—

Delphine and Phoebe burst through the door then, arms piled with colored linens.

"One of these should do." Delphine bumped the door closed with her hip. She dumped the pile on the table and turned to Iris with a hug. "Abachum told us about the auction. We want to hear everything, but not before you're warm and dry." She gestured to the pile. "No sense in taking them back to your cold room; change here by the fire where it's warm. We'll stand guard at the door. Come, Phoebe." As quickly as they'd burst in, Delphine and Phoebe bustled out, their shadows visible in the crack at the bottom of the door.

Iris stripped off her wet things, draping them over a stool. She rubbed her shivering limbs roughly with a linen towel, drying them as much as coaxing feeling back into them. She was tying undergarments around her waist when voices sounded outside the alley door and the latch jiggled.

"You always exaggerate everything. It wasn't that bad," came Cato's muffled voice.

Valentine's voice exclaimed, "You could have warned me first."

A fist pounding against the door covered Cato's reply. Weren't there other doors to this house? Iris snatched a long tunic the color of amaranth and wrestled it over her head.

"Just a minute!"

The muffled argument continued, sans the pounding. "I thought maybe you wouldn't faint a second time," Cato said.

"You should have learned your lesson after the *first* time."

"Everyone else was gone. Trust me—I didn't want to take you either."

Valentine didn't answer. Iris found the correct opening for her head and shoved her arms through the armholes. The gown fit much tighter around the hips and bust than her own, but at least it covered everything important.

"Will I need stitches?"

Fully dressed, Iris scrambled to slide back the bolt and open the door. Cato and Valentine surged in, streaming water. Cato slopped a dripping sack on the table and Valentine flipped back a soggy hood and unpinned his cloak. He ran a hand through his dripping hair and turned to Iris as she rebolted the door. A split in his chin left a trail of blood down the side of his throat.

"What's the news?" he asked, concern weighing his eyebrows. She handed him her towel as Cato opened the culina door and Beatrix, Delphine, and Martha rushed in.

Iris took a deep breath to reply and found she couldn't. Instead, she crossed her arms and bit her lips. Valentine ran the towel over his head and neck, careful to avoid his tender chin. He took a step toward her and stopped as Beatrix rushed to her side.

"Is he all right? Abachum said he's to be sold?"

Iris swallowed. "Titus said Tribune Braccus called an emergency council to try him."

"They've sentenced him already?" Valentine wadded the towel and tossed it on the worktable.

Iris nodded, her eyes burning. "Tribune Braccus wanted execution, but the prefect sentenced him to be sold to a labor camp."

Beatrix's arm went around her shoulders.

"A labor camp." Valentine's eyes shifted as if in thought. "When is the auction?"

She shook her head. "I don't know. Titus said he'd send word. I—I'm sorry. He made me tell him where I was staying. He would have found me anyway."

"It's all right," Martha assured. The others didn't look so convinced.

Valentine turned to Cato. "Doesn't your father have a friend in the auction house?"

Cato shrugged, depositing an armload of dripping herb jars on the counter. "Pater has friends everywhere." He squinted. "Are you thinking to buy him?"

Valentine nodded. "If we can."

Cato looked at Martha. "Where's Pater?"

"Lying down. He wasn't feeling well." Martha shooed them toward the door. "But go wake him, he won't mind."

Valentine and Cato left the women alone, agreeing to gather in the triclinium. Delphine, Martha, and Phoebe piled trays with food and drink. Beatrix tucked back strands of Iris's wet, tangled hair and lifted a camel-colored wool palla from the pile of linens, wrapping it securely around Iris's shoulders. The motherly gesture flooded her with a warmth the fire had been unable to produce. Beatrix had spoken once before about believers bearing one another's burdens. She was glad her father's arrest wasn't one she had to carry alone.

XLIII

MARIUS CONFIRMED AN ACQUAINTANCE in the auction house. While eager to share the news with Iris, Valens forced his feet to keep with Marius's pained pace as they crossed the courtyard.

"What happened to your chin?" Marius gestured toward Valens's face.

"Ask your son." Valens slanted a falsely dark look at Cato.

Cato eyed the cut. "If it opens again and starts bleeding, let me know. I should probably stitch it, but it's scabbing over pretty well."

"What happened?" Marius pressed.

"He fainted." Cato smirked.

"In my defense," Valens protested as Cato swung open the door to the triclinium, "he told me to hold this man's foot—and then pulled out a saw!"

Knowing Martha would not allow such talk over dinner, they quieted as they joined the others in the triclinium. Phoebe fussed over the food, while Bea poured measures of water and wine into cups, and Iris and Martha handed them out. Valens took a seat across from Iris and next to Abachum. The orphans, along with Lalia and Rue, played on a rug in a corner of the room, dolls and wooden blocks and clay animals spread across the floor. The baby snuggled into her chest, Delphine joined Cato on his couch.

Valens looked around. "Where's Audifax?"

"Organizing the goods in the warehouse so as soon as the ship docks, the cargo can be loaded for a quick departure." Marius groaned as he lowered onto an empty couch.

Valens nodded, knowing it was for his benefit. He tried to summon up gratefulness but felt only sadness at the thought of leaving his city, this family. He turned his attention to Iris instead. "What else did Titus say?"

As she repeated the conversation, he tried not to notice the way the wine-colored dress hugged Iris's curves and set off the warm tones of her skin. The lamplight caught damp tendrils of dark hair framing her face and shrinking into waves. He forced his gaze away, making the mistake of catching his aunt's eye, who appeared very interested in his perusal of Iris. He shot her bright-eyed excitement a sharp look of warning.

Iris hugged her elbows and looked at her lap. "That's all I know."

Marius went next, explaining the plan he and Valens and Cato had concocted. If his friend at the auction house could be persuaded to sneak Cato in, they could buy Quintus. He'd have to be pierced as a bondslave—bound to Cato—but Iris agreed that was preferable to a short life in a mine.

"I'll get a message to Titus tomorrow."

Marius nodded. "Then let's pray." While Marius prayed, Valens watched Iris sitting stiffly, not moving at all except for the soft rise and fall of her arms locked across her chest, fingers clutching her elbows in a white-knuckled grip. She looked to be holding herself together. As Marius prayed for Quintus and his release, Valens silently prayed for Iris. Would her faith shatter if the plan did not work? God did not always answer prayers in ways that made sense, at least not by human standards. He prayed she would hold fast, no matter what happened.

As he watched her and prayed, the pinch between her eyebrows softened. Her mouth relaxed, as did the death grip she had on her elbows. Her hands fell open into her lap, palms up.

When his gaze flickered back to her face, her eyes met his. The room went silent. It was Valens's turn.

"The Lord bless you," he spoke softly, not breaking eye contact.

"And be your protector. May the Lord make His face to shine on you and be gracious to you. May the Lord look with favor on you and give you peace."

She shut her eyes, as if drinking in the words and the perfect promise in them. "Amen," she whispered.

XLIV

AFTER THE PRAYER AND EVENING MEAL, where despite the enthusiasm of the orphans, Lalia and Rue declared that they were *not* hungry, the group stayed and visited until the little ones went to bed. Iris enjoyed the easy banter between parents and siblings, Beatrix and Valens. The atmosphere comforted and welcomed her, even if she did not join much in the conversations. Marius looked especially pained after his disturbed rest, and he and Martha excused themselves shortly after dinner. Discussion of her father's arrest had been set aside during the meal and resumed only after Cato and Delphine herded out the children, who rubbed sleepy eyes but at the mention of bed had suddenly become "Vewy, vewy *hungwy!*"

Beatrix sighed as the bedtime protests faded down the hall. "Children long to grow up, yet don't realize that the things they hate most are the very things adults look forward to—eating and bedtime."

They all chuckled.

Phoebe gathered the dishes. Iris rose to join her.

"Sit, sit, you are a guest," the servant protested, but Iris continued stacking bowls, slick with remains of stewed cabbage and garum sauce.

"Let me help. It's the least I can do."

Phoebe protested again when Beatrix gathered the wine cups but gave up when neither would listen. The three carried the dishes to the culina and would have started on the washing but for Phoebe's fierce insistence that she would do the washing if they would bring the calda into the triclinium.

"The young ones sometimes stay up to talk," Phoebe explained.

Bea stifled a yawn. "Well, a young one, I am not," she said. "I'm ready to turn in."

"I'll bring it." Iris reached for the prepared tray. "You go on to bed."

"Stay up as long as you like." Bea patted her arm. "No need to be quiet when you come up. I'm a heavy sleeper. You won't wake me."

Iris lifted the tray and Bea led her out, heading upstairs to the guest room she and Iris shared. Iris went back toward the triclinium, awkwardly balancing the tray and wondering how Phoebe managed it with such ease. Bumping the door open with her hip, she found the room nearly empty. Only Valentine sat on one of the couches, plucking the strings on a lute, head cocked as if trying to decide whether it was in tune or not. He set it aside and straightened as she entered.

"Where is everyone?" Iris slid the tray onto the low table. The room was dim. The bright lamps had been taken by everyone else, which left one near Valentine and two hanging lanterns flickering in dimpled copper shades in the corner.

He shrugged. "Abachum left as soon as I found this sitting in the corner." He waved a hand toward the lute. "Cato and Delphine will be back once the children are asleep."

She sat on the couch nearest his, where the arms met at right angles. "I didn't know you played." She nodded toward the lute. "I had a small harp once, but I was never any good. Will you play something?"

He looked oddly uncomfortable and inclined his head as if deciding how to answer. "I'm not sure that's a good idea."

"Why not?"

He forced a laugh and a light tone, though his eyes remained serious. "Because you just got here, and I don't want to scare you away too."

She squinted, not quite believing him, and noticed a pebble on the floor near the leg of the table. One of the children had likely secreted it inside. With a sudden grin, she scooped it up and turned to Valens, grabbing his hand. His eyes went wide at her touch.

"This, sir, is a magic rock." She lowered her voice and pressed the pebble into his hand. "It will make anyone who touches it play a song on a lute to make me feel better."

Valentine threw his head back and laughed, his fingers wrapping around hers, the pebble trapped between their hands. "Fine. I give in. But I did warn you."

"See? I told you it was a magic rock." She parroted his words back to him, both of them recalling that first meeting in the market. He sent her an amused look, squeezed her fingers, and took the pebble as he released her hand. Iris felt a sudden rush of guilt. What was she doing? Her father was doomed for the auction house and she was here flirting?

Valentine began to strum the instrument, drowning out her thoughts with a tune that was both lilting and mournful. She suddenly missed her old harp and wished she hadn't traded it for yarn. Not that the yarn had done her any good. The tribune owned everything now. Her stomach turned at the thought of him rummaging through the remnants of her old life, deciding what he could sell and what was trash. She focused her attention on Valentine instead.

His dark hair had dried, the front standing up in charming rebellion, and he needed to shave. Even beneath the darkness of the stubble she could tell his chin was bruised. The cut was bleeding again. His eyes closed, a pinch of concentration between his brows as his blunt fingers combed with surprising grace over the strings that were not completely in tune.

Then he began to sing.

She'd heard him sing before, in the prison as she made her way toward him to beg him to pray for her. It seemed a lifetime ago. This time, his voice was quiet, as if he hadn't meant to start but couldn't help it. Then it grew louder as he lost himself in the music. It was a song of lament. A cry to God for help that shifted into a call to remember God's faithfulness.

Faithful. Yes, He was indeed. Iris's mind ran with the faithfulness, the goodness God had shown in the short time she'd believed—and even in the times before.

Slowly, without her really noticing at first, a calm smoothed the tightness in her belly, the lines of worry on her brow. She shut her eyes, her own silent praise echoing Valentine's.

"Thank you," she whispered when he finished. She wiped a hand across her jaw. After the music, the silence was deafening. "That was beautiful."

His eyes flung open, as if he'd forgotten she was still in the room. He squinted suspiciously. "No one's ever said that before."

Footsteps padded across the tile behind them, and a hand reached out of the dimness and snatched the lute from Valentine's grasp.

"Seriously, Val, if Rue wakes up with night terrors after that, you can put her back to bed," Cato growled, then noticed Iris on the other couch. "Oh, sorry." His eyes flicked from Valentine to Iris and back again, widening. "I didn't know . . . you two . . ." He cleared his throat. "I'll just go then. But I'm taking this with me. You shouldn't subject Iris to this kind of torture."

"It was beautiful." Iris twisted around to look at him.

Cato's eyebrows shot up. *"Beautiful?"* He turned to Valentine. Iris felt her neck heat and glanced at Valentine, who was looking at Cato with tight lips and a quick shake of his head.

Cato wiped the grin from his face. "That's wonderful." He held up the lute. "But I'm still taking this. Good night."

"You're not coming back?" Valentine waved at the table. "There's calda."

Cato hesitated, then shook his head. "Putting eight children to bed wears a man out. Delphine and I are turning in. You two carry on. Good night." He hurried back to the door, closing it behind him, but not before Iris heard Delphine's muffled voice in the hall, raised in question.

Valentine let out a long breath. They sat in silence for a moment; then he reached for the tray.

"How are you?" His voice was low as he lifted and turned the jars, reading the labels.

"I'm worried for him." The peace she'd felt moments ago began to recede as she voiced her anxieties. "You all keep telling me to trust God and have faith, but I don't know what that means or how to do it like all of you. I'm afraid you'll be ashamed of my weakness—but I *am* afraid and confused." She paused. "How can God do the impossible and restore my sight, yet He cannot keep Pater from being arrested? I know He is good, but I thought He would protect us."

There. It was out. The whole ugly truth. She couldn't meet his gaze.

Valentine held a jar in each hand, looking at the labels and not at her. His thick eyebrows pressed low over his eyes in concentration. "That is one of the most difficult things to understand. Many in this household have asked the same question, and I don't know the answer myself." He paused. "Peppermint or chamomile?"

She shrugged. Valentine returned one canister to the tray and opened the other, dropping pinches of dried daisylike flowers into two clay cups.

"Cato and Delphine had six children." He spoke in a near whisper.

Iris drew in a breath but didn't say anything as she waited for him to continue.

"Two, they lost at birth; one boy lived a few months . . . and then there was Peter."

Affection softened his voice as he spoke the name. He lifted the jug of hot water and poured a measure into each cup, his lips lifting in a smile of reminiscence. "Peter was . . ." He shook his head. "Full of mischief. He was Cato's shadow and a much better physician's aide at seven than I could ever hope to be." He held out a steaming cup and Iris accepted it, leaning over to inhale the sweet scent.

"What happened?"

Valentine settled back onto his couch, shifting his shoulders so he could see her. "He was playing in the road with some friends, like he did nearly every evening. Out of nowhere a chariot came racing up the street—the horses were out of control or the driver was being careless—no one ever found him. The other boys got out of the way in time, thankfully. But not Peter." Valentine's eyes skittered back and forth across the room and grew shiny. "One of the boys said he tripped and fell." He shook his head and made a snorting noise, dashing the back of one hand across his cheek as he looked away. "He didn't last the night."

"I'm so sorry." Iris touched her lips with her fingertips, stomach clenching at the heartbreak this family had faced not once, but four times. She didn't like where this conversation had gone. Did God not watch over His devoted ones? Had Delphine and Cato not prayed enough? Had Marius and Martha's faith been too weak? Somehow, she doubted that.

"Why does He answer some prayers and not others?"

Valentine shook his head. "I don't know." He took a sip from his cup and gave a painful hiss before resting it back on his knee. "But I do know that this world is bent toward destruction and moved by forces we cannot see. Evil that tries to destroy our faith in God's goodness by delivering senseless acts of pain."

Iris shivered at the thought, but Valentine did not stop there.

"We are told that all things work together for good—we've talked about that before—but whether we will see that good in our lifetime or not, who can know?"

Iris nodded, even though she wasn't sure she fully understood. Couldn't God step in against these evil forces if He was as all-powerful as Valentine said? Yet even as the thought entered her mind, she recalled how God had gifted His creation with the dangerous ability to do as they pleased: to love freely, to do good. And free will that allowed for the purity of good acts also meant there was a second, darker option. People did not always choose well. God did not terrorize people one moment and heal them the next. God *was* the healer, but the free will of people caused the pain.

"God is trustworthy, even when we struggle to trust Him," Valentine said when she did not speak. "You say that you aren't strong like us, but I am far from fearless."

Her eyes snapped to his face, surprised by his admission.

Gaze downcast, he rubbed circles on the side of his cup with his thumb. "When I was thrown in the Tullianum, I—" His voice dropped. "In the space of an hour I'd gone from leading a group of believers, encouraging them to stand strong in their faith, to . . . to cowering in fear as my own faith was tested."

"What did you do? You were singing when I saw you."

"I sat there in the cold dark. Hades kept asking if I wanted him to end my life. And then I started to recall the goodness of God. The faithfulness and mercy He's always shown. He saw me in the pit, was there with me, waiting for me to look up and realize I was not alone." His gaze flickered upward and met hers. "Your pater is not alone either, and neither are you."

She tried to smile, feeling the warmth of that truth beginning to unfurl inside, yet she wondered, if Valentine had felt such fear, what must her pater feel?

He is Mine.

Again, that Voice came, speaking silently and yet rumbling with raw power as it spread a cloak of comfort over her. She shut her eyes, breathing it in, praying her pater would be granted it as well. When she opened her eyes, Valentine held her gaze for a moment before looking away. Iris took a tentative sip of the steaming calda. The warmth spread through her.

"How are you drinking that already? I burned my mouth."

"Pater's a soldier." She shrugged. "We ate everything either cold or scalding hot, no in between." She smiled and gave a conceding tilt of her head. "We also ate everything charred, but that was my fault."

He grinned. "You worked at Paulina's, so I know you couldn't have burned *everything*."

"Ah, but I never did the baking."

"What did you do? I came in nearly every day for a raisin pastry and never saw you but for that one week when you were up front."

She gave a slow shake of her head. "You came in faithfully every morning and never once thought to pray for the poor blind girl kneading dough in the back?" She took a slow drink, watching him over the rim of her cup. He stared back, the crestfallen look on his face changing as one eye twitched.

"In my defense . . ." He paused. "Have you ever had one of

Paulina's raisin buns? I mean, they're *good*. You can taste the love in every bite."

Iris laughed. "I hate to be the bearer of bad news, but that wasn't love you were tasting. Epimandos baked them and he doesn't love anyone."

"Must have been your kneading then."

Iris took another drink, then tapped her chin. "What happened here?"

Valentine touched the redness on his chin and winced at the tenderness. "It's a long story." He sighed. "And rather embarrassing."

"Well, you're in luck." She settled back with a mischievous grin. "Those are my favorite kind."

Valentine groaned and blew on his tea. "Sometimes I go with Cato on his house calls. Usually while he's working, I distract children with stories, or fetch water or groceries, or restring clotheslines. I don't actually help *him*."

She nodded.

"Well, once, he called me over to help. 'Stand by his head and hold his shoulders down,' he says. I do, but then Cato pulls out a pair of shears and snips off the man's infected finger." He set down his cup and made a snipping motion with his fingers on the index finger of his other hand.

Iris pressed a hand over her stomach.

Valentine lifted his cup again. "And I just . . . fell over." He ran a hand through his hair and avoided her eyes, but she had no intention of teasing him over his queasiness. Not when she felt the same. "Then tonight a scaffold of bricks tumbled down on a mason's assistant and crushed his foot. Cato asked me to go along. I should have known better, but I thought perhaps he would warn me if things were going in that direction again. But no. He gives the man some poppy juice and pulls out a saw and then—" He pressed his lips together.

Iris clamped a hand over her mouth. "Don't say it. I can imagine."

He took a tentative sip from his mug, which no longer steamed. "You fainted again?"

"I prefer *blacked out*. It sounds more masculine."

They both laughed. Valentine took a sip and watched her over the rim of his cup, eyes dancing.

"What?"

He shrugged and tipped his head. "I'm wondering how I could have walked into that bakery for years and never known you were there."

She glanced at her lap, then grinned to lighten a mood that suddenly felt too serious.

"That's easy." She set her empty cup on the table and swung her feet off the couch. "You had eyes for raisin pastries."

He laughed fully and she liked the way it clapped out of his chest. She gathered her palla around her shoulders. "Thank you for the calda and embarrassing conversation." She stood. "I feel much better now."

He offered the lamp to her. "Glad to help." His lips tipped in a wry smirk. "Good night, Iris."

She took the lamp, very aware of their fingers brushing in the exchange. "Good night."

She left him alone in the triclinium and made her way to the room she now shared with his aunt. Beatrix snored softly, curled on the far edge of the bed, back to the door. Iris quietly slipped into the undisturbed side of the bed and blew out the lamp. She felt warmed and peaceful and wasn't sure if it was the calda, the conversation, or the company that left her feeling that way.

XLV

"CULL THE PEACHES." Titus muttered the daily password to the guard at the gate. The Praetorian prefect chose the stupidest passwords. Either he was a genuine idiot, or he enjoyed making his men murmur things like "Diana's lip stain" and "bumpy rash" while expecting them to remain stoic.

Titus strode down the cobbled street toward the center of the fortress. The rain had not let up since the afternoon. He pulled his hood up, the smell of damp wool heavy around his face. Quintus had no cloak in his cell and Titus knew his leg would ache in the damp. He'd been allowed to see Quintus once since the rushed trial. Titus shook his head, trying and failing to reconcile the calm, dignified man in chains with the man who'd once drunk himself through the best of days. The change in Quintus had happened suddenly, overnight, around the time Iris had been healed. It didn't make sense. Yes, Iris could see, but now they were in worse trouble than before. If there had ever been cause to make him rage for a drink, it should be now. Perhaps there was more to this god than he'd originally supposed. Even as the thought formed, Titus tried to shove it away. Foolishness.

The record building loomed ahead, stocky walls unadorned with anything of beauty. So unlike Iris. Even though she'd told him where to send a message, after the meeting in the sculpture gardens, he'd followed her and the boy to a house with a dual front clinic and shipping office. His worry eased knowing she was in a fine house and even more because he knew where to find her, if needed. He'd expected her to be hysterical at the news. She'd been shocked at first, certainly, but then had grown eerily calm. It was not lost on him that while this Christian god had been the cause of their problems, neither Quintus nor Iris had renounced him.

Once inside the record building, Titus heard his men celebrating in the hall long before he saw them. As he turned the corner, the three lifted cups and hailed him.

Adonis, whom Titus had relegated to the notarii offices months ago, waved a scroll over his head. "We've got him!" His single-toothed grin flashed. "We've got the proof!"

Titus snatched the scroll from Adonis, who knocked back a cup of celebratory wine and explained while Titus scanned the document.

"I've been watching and waiting, just like you said. Finally, *finally*, a woman comes in with this document and says her husband is dead and she wants the rug shop transferred to her name, as the rightful widow. Look how fresh the ink is." He leaned over and pointed to the stamp and signature at the bottom. "I think this notarius is worth questioning again."

Adonis moved his finger and Titus saw the name. His heart kicked into a victorious rhythm.

Notarius: Valentine Favius Diastema.

Damning evidence.

Titus grinned and clapped Adonis on the shoulder, pitching the man forward. "Well done."

Bato pressed a cup into his hands. They did not celebrate long. As Titus tossed back the cup, he saw a page trotting down the hall toward them.

"Speculatore Didius Liberare, sir. You're wanted in headquarters."

"By whom?"

"Tribune Braccus, sir."

Titus sighed and felt a curl of unease in his gut. He tossed his empty cup at Bato and gave a growl of frustration. "Not a word to the trecenarius until I get back."

Tribune Braccus waited behind his desk looking pleased, which immediately put Titus on edge. He saluted and stood at attention, noticing that his commanding centurion Marcus Gracilus stood in the corner, arms crossed, mouth pinched.

"Speculatore Didius Liberare. You are being transferred to the Ninth Minerva."

The Ninth. His father's cohort. Titus should have been elated. Instead, his gut sank. He looked from Braccus to Centurion Gracilus and back. "Yes, sir. Why, sir?"

"The Ninth needs a good speculatore."

"What of my work here, sir?"

Braccus waved a hand. "What of it? You've had weeks to find a notarius and haven't done a thing. I'm sure Centurion Gracilus can appoint someone more capable."

The insinuation grated. Titus clenched his teeth.

Centurion Gracilus spoke up. "If I may, sir, according to Trecenarius Faustus, Titus is very close to catching the man."

"Actually, sirs—" Titus took a step forward—"I believe we've found our man. There's only to make the arrest now."

"Excellent." Braccus nodded. "The Ninth departs for Gaul the day after the Ides of Februarius. From now on, you'll join them for drills and answer to Centurion Felix Calis. In the meantime, I suggest you make your arrest and say your goodbyes."

Titus's stomach went cold at the mention of Gaul. They were sending him to the front?

"Am I being punished, sir?"

Braccus's eyes went narrow. "Why would you need to be punished, Liberare? Something on your conscience?"

"It isn't common to be transferred to another cohort, sir."

"It isn't common to question your tribune either. Best use your questions to find your notarius."

Titus flicked a glance toward Centurion Gracilus and saluted once more. "Yes, sir."

"You are dismissed."

Titus left the tribune's office, anger growing in his belly with each step. This had to be connected to Quintus and Iris. Instead of returning to the record building where his team celebrated, Titus angled for the gate. He'd meant to send Iris a message about the slave auction, but now, he opted to go in person. Anyway, the tribune had ordered him to say his goodbyes.

XLVI

THREE WIDOWS' NOTES LEFT TO WRITE, and Valens had run out of ink.

He'd scrounged through Cato's office, searching the shelves, the boxes on the floor, under the desk, and in the dusty corners. All he'd turned up were a few styli that looked as though Cato had used them to carve stone instead of wax and two bottles of dried ink with no lids to be found. He did what he could to revive them and left the office to see if Cato had an unneglected bottle in the clinic.

"Medical texts are for physicians," Cato said from behind the drawn curtain. "You shouldn't be reading them. There's nothing wrong with you."

"What about the white spots on my tongue?" The last word came out along with the tongue and sounded like *thung*.

"Completely normal." Cato's pleasant tone grew an edge.

Valens surveyed the shelves of dried herbs and bottled liquids, all labeled in Delphine's handwriting and "organized" in Cato's haphazard style. Poppy and mandrake sat on a high worktable next to a small scale, pill molds, and tiny bottles intended for individual medicines.

Cato pushed back the curtain to reveal a middle-aged woman with faded hair and a smug expression. "You have to take your health into your own hands, I always say." She lifted her chin. "No one else is going to do it for you."

"I still think you would feel better if you got rid of those medical texts." Cato sighed.

She moved toward the door. "Thank you, Doctor. I don't have to pay anything, do I? You didn't do anything, after all."

Cato blinked. "I'll have to be compensated for my time."

"Your *time*?" she repeated, incredulous. "I've never *heard* of such a ridiculous thing."

"You said it was a matter of life or death." He raised an eyebrow. "It wasn't."

"Well, it might have been." She huffed and opened her purse, slapping two coins onto the operating table. "You never know with these things. I'll see you next week."

"That's not necessary."

The woman shut the door on his protest. Cato flopped face-first onto the operating table and let his arms dangle over the sides. "Why me, Lord?" He groaned.

"So," Valens drawled. "I came because there's a callus on my left big toe."

"Go away."

Valens laughed. "I need ink."

"There's some on the desk," came the muffled reply.

"It's dried up."

Cato lifted his head. "Did you add water?"

"Obviously."

"Did you shake it?"

"Of course I shook it; everyone knows you shake it."

Cato let out a long sigh. "Normal people shouldn't be allowed to buy medical texts." He let his head rest on the table again. "They should require a certificate of medical training at the time of purchase."

"But how would anyone take their health into their own hands?"

Cato moaned. "Someday I'm going to move far, far away and live on a farm."

"I've never pictured you as a farmer."

"Beautiful sunsets, goats frolicking on the hillside, good food—"

"That's a picnic. You're thinking of a picnic." Valens walked slowly along the counter, letting his eyes travel over the bottles. "So, about the ink."

"What are you going to do about Iris?" Cato propped his chin on his hands.

A rush went through Valens at the mention of her name. He forced his gaze to remain on the shelves and feigned innocence. "What do you mean?"

Cato sat up with a shuffle. "I've seen how you look at her—like no one else exists when she's in the room. And then your whole *earbleeding* serenade, which she found *beautiful*."

"That was not a serenade."

"Dim lights, you two alone, singing . . . that's a serenade, my friend."

Valens crossed his arms, his heart sinking as he said the words. "The other church leaders are sending me to a church on the Anatolian coast, Cato."

Cato shrugged. "If you haven't noticed, she's hiding too. Once we buy back her father, the least you could do is whisk them away to those white-sand beaches."

The idea was not without appeal, even though his mind ran with all the ways it would never work.

"She could be your Delphine, and you're going to ignore her?" Cato shook his head. "Tell me you're not that stupid."

Valens threw his hands up. "Everyone has been pushing women at me my entire life. I'll find one on my own."

"Well, haven't you?"

Valens turned away. He had and he knew it. The problem was, now that he'd found the one who found her way into his every thought, he wasn't sure what to do about it. He turned toward Cato, about to ask for advice, and noticed his friend watching him and looking—of all things—like he was about to laugh. He lifted his chin and started to speak but Cato stopped him with a raised hand.

"I understand your struggle, Val. I've been there. Every bit."

The compassion in Cato's voice soothed his irritation, although

Valens regarded the sudden helpfulness with suspicion. "What did you do?"

Cato leaned forward as if about to reveal a great secret. "I walked right up to her. Looked her straight in the eye . . . and kissed her breathless."

"Cato."

"Don't argue until you've tried it."

A knock sounded at the clinic door and Cato hopped off the table to answer it.

"What if she doesn't feel the same way?"

Cato paused, his hand on the latch. "If you think that, then you really are stupid, and no one can help you." He swung the door open. "There's ink in the culina. Ask Phoebe for it."

XLVII

IRIS TRIED TO FOCUS on the dough moving and stretching beneath her hands, the one constant in her world. Dough would rise and bake into bread. It always had and always would.

Her movements might have been precise and controlled, but she could not say the same for her mind. She'd sent a message to Titus asking how her pater fared and if there was any word on the auction, but no response had come. Perhaps the message hadn't reached him. She tried not to worry. And failed.

The yeasty smell of bread filled the empty culina. Iris had jumped at the chance to help when she heard Martha directing Phoebe to bake bread for the widows' food baskets. If Iris didn't put her hands to use, she was going to go mad, confined to this house. Bread, at least, was something she knew, something she could control. When half of the loaves had been baked, Phoebe, Martha, and Delphine had gone to deliver the filled baskets, promising to return in a few hours for the rest. With Beatrix watching the children, Iris remained alone in the culina. Perhaps she should have specified that she'd never actually done the *baking*.

The dough went tight and firm beneath her hands. With a wince, Iris plunked it onto the floured counter. Overkneaded. So much for control. It would bake into a brick. She imagined the diatribe Epimandos would have given, the mounting doom of an overkneaded loaf, which would end with eviction and death by starvation for them all. She smiled and almost missed him. Sweat beaded on her upper lip. She wiped it on her shoulder, noticing the front of her amaranth dress covered in flour. She'd discarded her palla long ago and tied her sleeves up to her shoulders but neglected an apron.

Outside in the courtyard, Bea cheered as the troop of children squealed and raced around the covered portico. Iris couldn't help but smile. Delphine and Cato had stepped in seamlessly, ushering all six of the orphans under their wings. They seemed reticent to divide the children into different homes, and after what Valentine had told her, Iris understood the delight the couple found in them.

Iris pulled the wooden oven door open just a hint to see the bread. *Perfectly golden brown,* she'd heard Paulina utter with delight when Epimandos carried in baskets of fresh loaves. Was that golden brown? The inside of the oven was so dark she couldn't tell. Iris shoved a lamp inside. Brown. Definitely brown. Setting the lamp aside, she used a wooden paddle to retrieve the bread, which emerged a solid nut brown with nothing golden about it. It clunked like pottery as she set it on the table to cool. Perfect. A black spot marred the side where she'd scorched it with the lamp.

Iris thought about the poor unlucky widow who would get this loaf. Hopefully she still had a good set of teeth and possibly a chisel. At least it wouldn't spoil quickly. She replaced the oven door and turned back to the table of waiting dough lumps, jumping at the shadow in the doorway.

"You scared me!"

The look on Valentine's face suggested that she'd been the one to startle him. He coughed and settled himself in the open doorway. Behind him, the children shrieked and raced through the courtyard in a tight pack. Bea cheered them on.

"Do you have the rest of the notes?" Iris pointed to his right. "Those baskets there are waiting." She blew at a strand of hair dangling in her eyes, trying to ignore the way his appearance sent her stomach into a confusing tumble.

With a deep breath, Valentine stepped over the threshold as if preparing to do battle. "I ran out of ink." He nudged the door closed with his foot.

Iris tried to ignore the sudden jitters that action sent through her and bent back over the counter, turning her focus on shaping the next loaves. "The ladies will be devastated. Delphine said it's the second thing they all ask: 'Where's Valentine? Did he send a note?' I must admit, I'm a little curious about what these notes entail. Makes me want one of my own." She settled two loaves on the bread paddle.

"I'll keep that in mind." He crossed the room, eyes shifting over the neatly ordered shelves, searching. "Everyone left to deliver baskets?"

"The first half of them." She wiggled the loaves off the paddle and onto the bottom of the oven. "The bread and notes are the last things to go into the rest."

"Makes sense, putting you in charge of the baking." He moved closer, nudging aside jars and bottles on the shelves.

"I'm not sure how sensible it was." She leaned the paddle against the wall and replaced the oven door. "My baking skills are better suited to brick kilns."

He chuckled, moving beside her to peer at the shelves lining the wall above the oven.

She straightened. "This is when you say, 'No, no, I'm sure it's delicious.'"

He smiled in a way that said he hadn't heard her. She frowned, and he flinched when she touched his arm.

"Is something wrong? Are you all right?" She stopped as he turned, his face suddenly inches from hers.

"I'm—" His eyes locked on hers. "Fine. I'm fine." His voice dropped low and husky.

"Are you sure?" She rubbed a lock of hair from her cheek with her shoulder.

He gave a single nod and reached out, curling the hair behind her ear, his fingers tracing the line of her jaw. She sucked in a breath. His thumb brushed over the scar nicking her cheekbone. When she opened her eyes, his had gone dark. She swallowed.

His breath sounded ragged as he let his hand drop. "What is the nature of your relationship with Titus?"

Iris blinked, the turn of the conversation confusing and startling. *"Titus?"* She took a step back and turned to pick up a ball of dough, hoping to mask the way his closeness had made her hands shake. "His father and mine were in the same Praetorian cohort—they were good friends."

Valentine leaned a hip against the table and crossed his arms, watching. The way he'd touched her and the look in his eyes now set her heart in an uneven thumping. He smelled of sandalwood and ink.

She cleared her throat and tried to focus. "They were both stationed at the Castra Praetoria at the time of the civilian siege. Titus's father was killed. My pater took in Titus's mother for a time." She smoothed a new loaf, tucking the rough ends underneath.

"Pater has always been a sort of father to him." She pushed the hair away from her face with the back of her hand and set the loaf on the rising board.

"And you and he are . . ."

"Like brother and sister." She cut another lump of dough free from the bowl and turned to face him. "You can trust him. He'll do all he can to help Pater; I know he will."

Valentine's hand slid around her waist, tugging her toward him. "A brother?" he repeated with something like relief or disbelief. His touch sent her pulse racing.

She didn't resist as he drew her against him, except to say, "My hands are full of flour."

His response of "I don't care" was whispered against her lips. The kiss was short. A mere brush of the lips. Over as soon as it began.

When she opened her eyes, his pupils were wide, ringed by thin bands of amber. Her throat went tight. He kissed her again, like he drank his calda. In tiny, careful sips. Gently. Sweetly. Maddeningly short. She closed her eyes.

When he started to pull away again, she leaned in, flour-caked hands disregarded as they left trails of white on his tunic and in his hair. At her response, he kissed her fully, his lips warm, undemanding and firm.

"Praise the Lord!"

They lurched away from each other. Beatrix stood in the open doorway, hands clasped over her heart, gazing at them as if she'd just seen a batch of brand-new kittens. Iris's face would have felt cooler if she'd stuffed it into the oven.

Valentine cleared his throat and murmured, "Hold on." He brushed past her and moved toward the door.

"Valens, I have *dreamed* of this day." Beatrix's eyes glistened. *"Prayed* for this day. I am so happy—"

"Pardon me, Auntie." Valentine gripped the edge of the door in one hand and Beatrix's elbow in the other and gently escorted her back two steps over the threshold before closing the door on her elated face. He put his back against the door and let out a long breath before looking at Iris with eyes full of mischief.

"Her timing is impeccable as always."

Iris bit her lip, unable to muffle the giggle.

"Come here," he whispered.

Iris skirted the table and moved toward him, watching the mischief leave his gaze. He swallowed.

"When do you leave?" she asked as he took her hands and tugged her closer.

"Whenever you'll agree to go with me."

Her breath caught. "But you said no good would come of any attachments just now."

"I was trying to convince myself more than anything." He rubbed his thumbs over her knuckles. "But try as I might, the thought of spending the rest of my life apart from you gutted me. I'd rather stay here in hiding, no matter the danger, than go to Lycia without you. Unless you don't want me. In which case, it might be a bit awkward to stay." He looked at her with an expression of mingled hope and apology. "I have nothing to offer you."

She tilted her head. "I heard you had a stuffed ostrich."

"You can't have Struthio. Don't change the subject." He was

smiling now. "I know there's a lot of uncertainty with your pater, and I don't expect you to leave him behind."

She pulled her hands free of his and tucked her arms around his neck. "I don't want you to leave me behind either." She kissed him again, and a fist banged against the door.

With a groan, Valentine dropped his forehead into the curve of her neck. "Why can't she mind her own business?"

"She loves you."

"I could do with less love and more privacy."

Ruffling the flour from his hair, she laughed. "No, you couldn't. You're a hopeless romantic."

Between the cracks in the door, Beatrix's voice loudly and carefully enunciated each word. *"I—don't—mean—to—bother—you!"*

Valentine shut his eyes.

"But—is—something—burning?"

"Oh no!" Iris pushed away from him and sprinted to take two blackened loaves from the oven amid billows of smoke. They clattered on the table, chipping like fragile clay. Valentine swung open the shutters and fanned the smoke with a towel.

Iris stared at the bread, hands on her hips. She moaned. "What am I going to tell Phoebe when she sees these?"

He turned from the window and looked at the bread, a mischievous grin playing at his mouth. "I don't know, but I hope Lycia has bakeries."

Stifling a laugh, she grabbed a loaf and raised it, as if to throw it at him. He ducked as the door opened.

Beatrix threw her hands up in defense. "Valens, what have you done now?"

Iris lowered the loaf to the table, charred edges flaking off. "I burned the bread."

Valentine straightened. "It was my fault. I distracted her."

Beatrix beamed at Valentine. "And I'm very proud of you." She turned to Iris, her gaze growing worried. "You need to go to the clinic quickly. Your Praetorian friend is here."

XLVIII

TITUS TAPPED HIS FOOT and stared down the physician, who crossed his arms and looked at the floor. What was taking Iris so long? The clacking of his hobnailed boot on the brick floor grated on Titus's ears but he could tell it annoyed the physician, too, so he kept it up. He'd also annoyed the physician by barging through the door just as he lanced a boil on an old man's foot. The old man had said he didn't mind waiting outside as he scrambled out with barely a limp. Titus wasn't sure why it bothered the physician so much if it didn't bother the old man.

Sandals scraped on the far side of the door the physician had poked his head through earlier, calling for Iris. A timid knock followed, and the physician opened the door cautiously. Titus narrowed his eyes; had he expected someone else?

Iris stepped into the room, face flushed and covered in flour. Her forehead creased. "What are you doing here, Titus?"

He took in her rumpled appearance. "Are they forcing you to work?"

"Forcing—no." She brushed at the flour on her stomach. "I was baking bread. What are you doing here? I thought you were going to send a message."

"I wanted to be sure you were safe." He looked at the physician. "Will you leave us a moment?"

The physician looked at Iris, who nodded and fluttered a hand.

"It's fine, Cato." When they were alone, Iris turned worried eyes on Titus. "What is going on? How is Pater?"

"That's why I came." Titus tore his glare from the door the physician had retreated through. "The auction is this afternoon, and since it involves several prisoners, it's being held in the Castra Praetoria."

She worried her lip. "What can we do?"

Titus fished in his pouch and drew out a small wooden tile. He held it out. "If you can persuade one of your friends to do it, one person can get into the auction with this pass."

Iris took the tile, her eyes going wide. "Right now?"

Titus gave a nod.

"Wait here." Not waiting for him to reply, she fled through the door she'd come in by and, though it was closed, he heard her explaining to the physician in the hall. They both returned, the physician looking torn and hesitant.

"Titus, this is Marius Calogarus Cato," Iris introduced. "Cato, Titus Didius Liberare—I've known him my whole life."

Cato gave a nod. "It's a private auction? I've never heard of an auction taking place in the Castra Praetoria."

Titus lifted a brow. "Are you privy to all the happenings in the Castra Praetoria then?"

"Titus," Iris censured. "Cato is my friend and kindly allows me to stay here with his family in safety. There's no call for rudeness."

Cato stood silently waiting as Titus tried to order his words into something less condescending.

"There are private auctions held in the Castra Praetoria from time to time, for quarry and mine owners only," Titus explained. "These auctions ensure the harshest terms of service for the prisoners sold."

"Harshest terms?" Iris gripped her hands at her waist.

Titus hesitated. "Worked to death as soon as possible."

Iris pressed fingers to her lips.

"And you can get me inside?" Cato asked.

Titus gave him a cursory glance and shook his head. "Not you. Someone older, rougher-looking."

"The only older person here is my pater." Cato shook his head. "But he's unwell."

"I'm fine," an older man grumbled as he pushed open the door and shuffled inside, lifting his chin. "I'll go." The look in his dark eyes dared the others to argue.

Cato took the challenge. "Pater, you can't go. You can barely walk across the house."

"I'll take the sedan chair. Your brothers can carry me. *What other choice do we have?*"

Cato's lips tightened. "Audifax is at the warehouse. Abachum and I will carry the sedan."

Iris faced Titus, worry lining her forehead. "How much will he cost?"

"Not much. These are not long-term workers. And with Quintus's condition, he'll be cheap."

The Calogarus men moved quickly to fetch the money, the other brother, and the sedan chair.

While they waited, Iris gripped her elbows, turning a troubled look on Titus. "Will Marius be all right?"

Titus shrugged. He wasn't confident in the old man's ability to walk into the saleroom, much less perform the part of a slave purchaser. But Cato was too polished, his physician hands slender and smooth, and the other brother was too young. Marius had to do it. They didn't have another option. "For your pater's sake, I hope so."

She touched his arm, tilting her chin up with an imploring look. "They are my friends, Titus. Take care of them."

He committed so much as a nod. The door banged open and Marius and sons reentered, shuffling the sedan between them, curtains swaying from side to side. Marius had changed into a paint-splattered tunic and an old belt. Not a perfect disguise, but it would have to do.

Iris threw her arms around Marius. "Thank you. Know we will be praying for you all."

Titus rolled his eyes and led them out. What good had their god done Quintus? It was Titus who would save him, not their god.

Once outside, the old man climbed into the sedan chair and Cato and Abachum lifted the poles extending from the front and back.

"Take him to the Porta Principalis Sinistra; the guards will let him through there." Titus reached through the curtain and gave the wooden tile to Marius. "Show this to the guards and they'll direct you to the right place." He peered through the curtain, giving the man a hard look. "You don't know me, and you've never seen Quintus. Remember that well or you will not leave the fortress."

With those warnings, Titus headed toward the Castra Praetoria at a run, intending to arrive long before they did.

Titus ducked into the Praetorian gymnasium, trailing a pack of bored guards attending the auction with intentions of betting on the sale price of each prisoner. Racks of weights and wooden swords and training spears of varying sizes had been shoved against the walls to make room for the platform erected in the center court in anticipation of the auction. Titus shifted out of the gambling group and slid into the shadow of one of the pillars ringing the center court where he could see the auction and bidders without being seen. He spotted Marius hunched among the bidders and inwardly cursed himself for not being able to find anyone else. The man was old enough but lacked the ruthless vigor of the other slavers.

The auction began with no fanfare, just a guard shoving a prisoner onto the platform amid shouts and jeers. Titus searched for Quintus in the throng of prisoners prodded through the back entrance and held at spearpoint against the far wall. From where he stood, it was impossible to discern him. The first prisoner sold, then the second and third. When the fourth prisoner shuffled onto the platform, Titus recognized Quintus only by the limp. Sweat broke out beneath his arms as he squinted at the battered form on display. What in the name of Mars had happened to him?

The bidding started with laughter. Titus kept his gaze fastened to Marius, as if by his will alone the old man's hand would lift, no one else would bid, no one would notice the odd slaver purchasing only a single, battered prisoner.

"Liberare?"

He turned at the hand on his shoulder and saw one of his barrack-mates whose name he'd never bothered to remember accurately. Unfortunately, Lucas or Cassius or whatever his name was had not taken the hint.

"What are you doing hiding back here?" Whatever-his-name-was beckoned Titus to follow. "Come join us."

Titus shook his head, glancing back at the platform where Quintus descended the steps. A stab of panic gripped him. Had Marius been successful? He'd turned away too soon. "I came here to exercise," he muttered, stepping away and scanning the front for Marius. "I forgot about all this."

"That's all right. I'll float you a few sesterces."

Titus shouldered past him. "I've got things to do."

He didn't see Marius or Quintus on the court. He circled the outer edge until certain neither remained inside, then pushed his way out of the gymnasium. He did a quick scan of the grounds—there. His tension eased slightly. Marius held the end of the rope tied around Quintus's neck, and for two men in pain, they made good time toward the exit. Titus hung back, waiting until the guard at the gate glanced at Marius's pass and the purchase document before waving them through. He breathed a sigh of relief, then wondered how Cato and Abachum would manage to get both Marius and Quintus back to the house. Neither of the brothers was built for carrying sedan chairs, much less a chair with two grown men inside.

Titus took off at a run toward the Porta Decumana, unwilling to draw suspicion by following Quintus out the same gate. He cut around the outside of the Castra Praetoria and caught up to the four not a block past the gate. They'd shuffled at least out of sight of the guards before stopping. Quintus slumped in the chair with Cato bending over him examining the cuts and bruises.

"I'm fine." Quintus groaned and swatted him away.

"What happened?"

Four faces snapped to Titus, simultaneously relaxing in relief. He scowled. They were lucky he'd come upon them and not a pack of bored guards.

Quintus leaned toward him, holding out his hands. "Titus." He gasped, as if it hurt to speak. "Thank God."

Titus gripped his hands, irritated that Quintus's god had gotten the thanks for Titus's quick thinking. He took in the bruised eyes and blood drying on Quintus's chin and forehead. "What happened?"

Quintus closed his eyes. "Braccus." He pressed a fist to his ribs. "Gave me one last . . . chance to . . . tell him where Iris . . ."

"He's having trouble breathing," Cato broke in. "He's got some broken ribs. I'm not sure what else. We've got to get him home quickly."

It would be dark soon. Titus swore and pointed to Marius. "You, get inside too." He turned to the brothers. "You two take the front. I'll get the back."

XLIX

"GOOD." MARTHA TUCKED HER CHEEK against baby Phineas's fuzzy head and patted his bottom as she bounced and swayed in the easy movement no mother quite forgot. "I think there's enough space for a couch now."

Iris carried out the last crate and set it along the outside wall under the covered portico.

Under Martha's direction, she and Valentine had cleared a storage room in preparation for Quintus's arrival since the guest rooms were already filled to bursting. Three of the oldest children had volunteered to help, but the allure of a rain-drenched courtyard had proven too much for them to resist. Iris pressed her hands into the small of her back and arched as Valentine swept a cloud of dust out of the room and into the bed of herbs across the portico. The children—resilient and loud as ever—shrieked and stomped puddles in the courtyard, trying to see who could get the wettest and be the loudest.

Valentine set the broom aside and called for the strongest of the children to follow him to the triclinium to help move a couch into the newly converted bedchamber. All of them came in a pack, eagerly raising arms to show him the size of their muscles. They grinned proudly when Valentine appeared suitably impressed. Beatrix sighed as she watched Valentine tousling heads and swinging one of the littlest children onto his shoulders. She looked at Iris, as if to ensure that she'd also noticed what a wonderful a father Valentine would be.

Iris's face warmed and she shifted the last crate toward Delphine. "This looks like children's things."

Delphine settled a basket on one hip and leaned over Iris's crate, digging through it with one hand. "Oh!" She lifted a baby tunic. "This is the box I've been looking for."

Martha looked at her tenderly. "You know, dear, it's probably time for us to find families for them."

"Cato and I have been discussing that." Delphine's hands stilled in the crate. "They've been through so much. I can't bear to uproot them again."

Shouts and laughter carried across the dusky courtyard as Valentine emerged from the triclinium, shuffling backward with one end of a couch while the pack of children jostled the other end.

"Look at them." Delphine pointed. "Like they've always been together."

"You mean to keep them all?" Beatrix's mouth dropped.

Delphine nodded and looked at Martha. "I know it's a lot. We've discussed buying a house of our own."

"Pfft!" Martha waved a hand of dismissal and pressed a kiss to the baby's head. "You'll do no such thing!" She grinned and watched the pack shuffling across the courtyard. "I won't have my grandbabies moved out of this house."

Delphine smiled. Iris bit back a laugh as the children discovered they could direct where Valentine stepped by swinging their end of the couch to one side or the other. They immediately forced him into the deepest puddle and dropped their end of the couch, laughing.

"You little Cretans think you're pretty clever, don't you?" Valentine chided, a chuckle breaking through his mock scowl. "Pick up your end, come on." They tried and failed, laughing too hard at their trick.

Iris trotted to the other end of the couch and lifted, meeting Valentine's grin with one of her own. The children danced around her, giggling and asking if she'd seen what happened.

"My sandals are wet." Valentine shook his head. "I should have asked you to help from the start."

She lifted a brow. "You assume I wouldn't have done the same thing?" She jostled her end of the couch.

He chuckled.

The two oldest boys, brown eyes sparkling with mischief, tried to direct them again.

"I'm too smart to fall for your tricks this time." Valentine looked at them and stepped in another puddle. They screamed in laughter and began a game of tag.

Valentine narrowed his eyes at Iris. "You did that on purpose."

"I did not."

He grinned and tugged his end of the couch, sending her skittering toward a puddle. She squealed and wrestled her end of the couch away from it. "You're no match for these arms." Her eyes narrowed in challenge. "Kneading bread has got me built like a gladiator."

He shook his head, fighting to keep a straight face. "If only you could bake."

She gasped in mock offense. "You're lucky they don't have a fishpond."

Beatrix, Martha, and Delphine clustered near the doorway of the guest room, whispering and throwing little glances their way. Iris sobered as her face went warm again.

Valentine followed her gaze, then caught her eye with an apologetic look. "It's Bea." He shrugged a shoulder. "If she has her way, she'll have us married within the week."

"Would that be so bad?"

Valentine didn't answer as they shuffled the couch past the scheming women, but the look in his eyes said a week would be an agonizing wait. Her stomach fluttered. They set the couch against the wall and Iris turned toward the open door, lit a dusky blue-gray from the evening light. Delphine called the children to the culina to wash before the evening meal.

Valentine caught Iris's hand and drew her to him. In the dimness she saw his pulse pounding in his neck.

"I know it was only a kiss." He drew in a shaky breath. "And I have nothing to offer you and no right to ask, but will you—?"

"Yes," she whispered before he could finish. His breath left him in a rush as he pressed his lips to her temple. She shut her eyes, wrapped in the solid warmth of his arms.

"Now that you've agreed never to bake again . . ." He choked back a laugh and wrestled her to stay against his chest as she pushed away. "You will marry me, won't you?"

She swatted him, stilling. "You're terrible."

He grinned but waited expectantly.

"Why me?" Her voice sounded calmer than her stomach and knees felt. "You could have your pick of any other woman."

"I don't want any other woman." He took a half step back and looked into her eyes, swallowing before continuing. "You infuse life and laughter into any room you're in. No matter the task or the conversation, you join in with passion. You are kind and compassionate and caring, and I don't want to miss a single word you say or spend another moment alone, if I could be with you." He let out a shaky breath. "I just want *you*."

She tilted her face back. "I already said yes."

He kissed her, sweet and full of promise, then took her hand, tugging her out of the room before Beatrix could interrupt again. Across the twilit courtyard, the open culina door glowed amber. They hurried toward it, Valentine's sandals squeaking with every step. Four of the children tumbled out the door directed by Martha and followed by Phoebe, who clutched a wooden tablet.

"This just came for you, Valens." She held it out.

He dropped Iris's hand and took the tablet, stepping into the culina and tilting it toward a lamp. "I have to go."

Iris's heart dropped. "Another wedding?"

"Just one." He sent her a look full of mischief and love and anticipation. "Your father will be back soon. I won't be long." He squeezed her hand and left to fetch his cloak and satchel.

Beatrix and Delphine ushered the remaining children out of the culina and toward the triclinium with strict instructions not to jump in the puddles along the way.

Iris turned to Phoebe, who had returned to piling platters of bread and bowls of fish stew onto several trays. "Are these ready to be carried in?"

"Nearly. Grab the jar of salt, will you, dear?"

Iris wiggled the saltcellar between three bowls as a knock came at the culina door. Phoebe rushed to open it. Iris rounded the table as Marius entered, followed by her pater, supported between Titus and Cato. Abachum shut the door as Iris rushed to her pater with a horrified cry.

"What happened to him?"

"Tribune Braccus," Titus spat.

Iris touched Pater's face. His eyelids fluttered, or they might have; the skin around them was bruised and swollen.

"Iris," he breathed. "Thank God you're safe."

"We've got to get him to the clinic." Cato lifted his chin toward the door. "I forgot my key to the front—"

Titus swore.

Iris followed his glare over her shoulder as everything fell silent and still. Valentine froze in the doorway, wrapped in his cloak and satchel. Eyes locked on Titus.

L

"I THOUGHT I TOLD YOU TO LEAVE." Fury poured over Titus with a heat that rivaled Vesuvius.

Iris clutched at his arm. "Leave him be, Titus."

He wouldn't look at her. Couldn't look at her. The others in the room stared wide-eyed and silent.

"I was just going." Valentine took a step toward the door.

Titus let loose a stream of curses. "You should have been gone months ago. So help me—" He started forward.

"Let him go, Titus." Iris lurched to block his way. He shook off her grip, irritated that Valentine did not show a hint of fear. He *should be* afraid. Very afraid.

"I let him go once already." Titus's fists clenched and he stepped toward Valentine, who didn't so much as flinch.

Iris scrambled against him, hands on his chest as if she could hold him back. "Please, Titus, let him be. He *is* leaving, I promise." Her words tumbled out as fast as the rushing of Titus's pulse. "Just let him go."

He ground his teeth. "Give me one good reason why I should let this traitor go free. He's the reason I'm being transferred to the front." He looked at Iris then, the shock of his announcement clear on her face. "I'm being transferred, did you know that? Because I haven't brought this lawbreaking liar to justice." His voice went low, anger steeling him against the panicked tears welling in her eyes. "So give me one good reason why I should let him go."

"I love him," she choked.

Titus stopped. All heads swung to face Iris, who stood her ground and stared up at Titus.

His jaw worked as he met her pleading gaze. "You *love* him." He hated how repeating the words cut the breath from his lungs.

She looked at him steadily. "I do."

Titus took a step back. He turned from Iris to Quintus, whose glazing eyes and battered face held nothing but pain. What could he say? What could he do? Betrayal cut him. They'd betrayed him, betrayed his loyalty. He'd done everything he could to protect them, to keep them safe, to rescue them. *He'd* done it, not their god, not their friends, and certainly *not* Valentine. He took another step back, feeling rage building in his chest, trembling with pressure as it rose.

What would he say when it erupted? What unforgivable things would he do?

Iris stepped toward him, face white. "Titus."

"Don't." He jerked his hands up before she could touch him. *"Don't."* He flailed for the handle behind him, ripped the door open, and stormed into the night. He heard Iris's call echo down the alley.

"Titus? What will you do?"

Titus didn't answer. He didn't know what he was going to do. He only knew he needed to leave before he killed someone.

Moonlight turned the puddles in the street into white luminaries, splashing light onto the buildings on either side. Another night he might have admired it; tonight he didn't bother. The chill air felt good against his anger.

Jupiter Optimus Maximus! He'd always tried to convince himself he would be glad to see Iris fall in love and marry someday. In those thoughts, however, the groom had always been faceless, vague, and above all, not real. Certainly not the most wanted man in the empire. He wouldn't be so upset if she were with some dull barber or a glass-blower, or—

Mars and Jupiter! What was she thinking?

Sweat dampened his back. Not even the dank frostiness of the night had any effect on him until the Castra Praetoria loomed ahead. How could she do this to him? Everything he'd done had been for her—his friend, the only trustworthy constant in his world of back-stabbing rank climbers. He flexed his fingers, half-hoping someone would jump him out of the shadows so he could expend some of the violence he felt. It wasn't about Iris falling in love. But the principle of the thing. The . . . the *principle*.

She knew Titus had been assigned to find Valentine. And all along she'd known—for months she'd known—that Valentine had remained in Rome and had kept it from him. Quintus, too, must have known.

It didn't matter that he couldn't imagine either of them actually turning Valentine in after what he'd done for Iris. Even he hadn't. Still, the secrets they'd kept from him cut. Quintus and Iris against him. When had *he* become the enemy? They'd obviously felt they could not trust him. And now what was he supposed to do? Confirm their suspicions and arrest the man Iris claimed to love? She'd never forgive him. Somehow that prospect seemed worse than losing her to Valentine.

Entering the Castra Praetoria, Titus stormed to his closet office in the record building, barely aware of the strange looks and how his tunic clung to his sweaty body even as white clouds of his breath puffed before him. He'd freeze once he stopped. As he stepped into the darkened halls of the record building, hobnailed footsteps rushed toward him in the dark.

"Liberare?" Bato rounded the corner, lips tight. "We've been looking everywhere for you. Where in hades have you been? You're going to miss it! Everyone else has left already."

"Miss what? What's going on?"

Bato grabbed his arm and spun him back toward the door. "Urian came back right after you left—he's *in*. He's got himself a wedding set for tonight in the Gardens of Maecenas. If you want to be there for the arrest, you'd better pray Mercury lends us wings."

They crashed into the moon-splashed streets, running faster than

LI

Iris tied the ends of her red-orange palla into a neat bundle around the things Delphine had insisted she take with her. A bone comb, two dresses, a heavy woolen palla, a fine linen wrap nearly sheer with lightness. A purse. A pair of beaded sandals. An extra belt.

"Your pater will need some things too." Delphine spread a blanket and added a few of her husband's tunics and belts to the middle.

Overwhelmed by the swiftness with which everything was happening, Iris could only nod her thanks. Cato and Abachum had taken her pater to the clinic, where they remained, cleaning his wounds and stitching cuts. She'd stayed by his side as they all discussed what to do. Cato and Marius insisted that Valentine, Beatrix, Iris, and Quintus leave that night. Marius's ship had not yet arrived, but they could hide in one of the warehouses for a few days until it did. Approving the plan, Valentine had refused to go before he'd performed this final wedding and sent Hector word of his departure. Iris had begged him not to go, but he'd simply kissed her and promised to return soon.

He'd left and returned every night for weeks. Tonight would be no different.

"I wonder how Beatrix is coming along." Iris tried to steer her thoughts away from Valentine and renewed her focus on packing.

Delphine chuckled. "I can only imagine the sorts of *necessities* she's bringing." She tied the bundle for Quintus and lifted it from the bed. "We'd better go help."

Beatrix had several piles strewn over her and Iris's couches and still she dug through the mass of crates and baskets lining the walls in search of more.

"Bea." Delphine surveyed the mounds. "You know you'll only be able to take what you can carry."

"I'm surprisingly strong." Beatrix bent over a crate. "I can't seem to find the bag Lucan gave me for that trip we took after our wedding." Her voice echoed in the crate. "It held everything—ah, here it is!" She held it up, her triumphant smile fading. "I remember it being bigger."

Delphine smiled and turned toward the bed, selecting and folding a pink stola.

"Lucan was a good man." Beatrix took the gown from Delphine and nestled it into the bottom of the bag. "Not a day goes by that I don't think of him, but . . ." She paused and added a second dress of warm pink and a third of a paler shade. "Even in the sadness, God has given me deepest joy."

"How?" Iris folded a garish palla of lemon yellow embroidered with pink-and-orange flowers. It completely suited Beatrix.

"I clung to Him. Tighter than I ever thought possible. I had to. If I didn't, I'd have clung to my grief and turned bitter. I clung to God until He became my everything. And once He was my everything, I needed nothing else."

Iris shot a glance toward the wall of belongings. Beatrix giggled and shrugged. "Well, I didn't say I stopped being sentimental."

"What happened to him?"

Beatrix's smile drooped as she slowly rolled a pair of orange woolen stockings. "The herb supplier for our perfumes has a farm outside of the city—not far, a day's journey if the weather holds, two if it's wet." She took a breath and tucked the stockings deep into the bag. "Lucan made trip after trip without incident, but the last time he went, heavy rains kept him on the farm for a week. The farmer urged him to wait until the roads dried, but Lucan refused and set out anyway."

Iris handed over another set of rolled wool stockings.

Beatrix's voice dropped. "He was found a few days later, dead on the roadside. There was no sign of violence or accident, so . . ." She shrugged. "We figured his heart must have just stopped."

"Oh, Beatrix," Iris breathed. "I'm so sorry."

Beatrix nodded and added three pairs of sandals to the top of the pile. A question had been growing in Iris since she'd heard of Delphine's son Peter, his young life cut short despite their prayers, and now Lucan, by all accounts a good man, also dead. She gave voice to her thoughts.

"How do you cling to God when terrible things happen? He could have stopped them, yet He didn't. How do you keep from . . . from clinging to the grief?"

"Ask yourself what you know is true. God is good." Beatrix's voice rang firm. "Even in loss, even when He does not answer our prayers as we would have Him do, He is good, and we can trust Him."

Iris sighed. She didn't want to argue. She'd experienced the goodness of God more vividly than most—yet the questions lingered. God did good things, but what of all the terrible things that befell His followers?

"How do you know?"

"'You are good and do only good.'" Delphine closed her eyes and drew in a breath. "When Peter died, that was the only passage of Scripture that came to my mind. The only thing I could hold to. I repeated it over and over because I knew if I did not, I would begin to repeat other things. Untrue things, spoken from the depths of my pain."

She swallowed back the emotion in her eyes and sank down onto the edge of the bed. "My Peter is dead because our world is broken, but it took many months of crying to God for me to see that." She stopped, dashing a tear from her cheek. "I long to hold him, to hear his sweet laugh, to smooth those shaggy curls—and the goodness of God made a way for that to happen someday. Just not here."

"Exactly right." Beatrix wrapped Delphine in a hug, tears streaming down her face.

OF LOVE AND TREASON

Iris swiped at her own cheeks with the back of her hand. "I'm not as strong as you are." She shook her head. "I fear if something had happened to my pater, I would have fallen apart."

"Your father cannot hold you together," Delphine said as Beatrix returned to her bag. "But God will. I promise you that."

Iris nodded. She wouldn't know until the time came. Deep down she hoped it never would and she could go on trusting in God's goodness because it was unquestionably evident. Her sight, her father redeemed, Valentine's love—it was all good.

The bag was fair to bursting as Beatrix heaved it to her shoulder with a wheezing groan and lurched forward with a few steadying steps.

Delphine and Iris reached for her. "Are you—do you have it?"

"Like I said—" Beatrix grunted—"I'm surprisingly strong."

"At least you're only walking to the warehouse." Delphine grabbed the bag and eased it from Beatrix's back. "I'm sure Val will insist on carrying it anyway."

"Don't be so sure." Beatrix swiped a curl out of eyes sparkling with mischief. "I haven't even packed for *him* yet."

By the time they'd packed and lugged the bags into a pile outside the culina, Cato shuffled Quintus across the darkened courtyard toward the triclinium. Iris rushed to her father's other side and tucked her shoulder into his armpit, lifting and supporting him.

"Pater?" She ducked her head to peer into his lowered face. "I'm so glad you're safe."

He grunted and gave a weak squeeze to her arm. "Not . . . safe yet." His words were mumbled and slurred. "Not until we get you . . . away from . . . here."

"Shhh." They shimmied sideways through the triclinium door. "We'll be away soon enough. You rest."

She and Cato settled him onto a couch and Beatrix draped a blanket around his shoulders. In the lamplight, the cuts and bruises stood out stark and black against the pallor of his skin. A few held stitches. Quintus closed the swollen slits of his eyes as if too exhausted to even sit. Iris sat beside him and, once Marius had blessed the evening meal, took a small bowl of cabbage and barley soup from the table laden with food. She tested the heat of it and lifted the spoon to her father's lips. He ate half the bowl in small, painstaking bites until he shook his head. Cato gave a nod that it was all right and Iris let him rest while she turned to her own food.

Neither Marius nor Cato spoke. Abachum and Audifax had yet to return from the docks. No one seemed particularly given to conversation—even Beatrix, who ate in silence. Iris followed suit but found she could hardly get more than a few bites into her stomach, which felt all in knots. How long would one wedding take? When would Valentine return? What would Titus do? She didn't think he would call out the guard on them, not after what Marius and his sons had done to rescue Pater. Yet the fury and hurt on his face did not imply reasonability.

Cato stood and walked to the balcony doors, opening one and peering into the night. He shut it and returned to his seat. "Do you think we ought to get everyone to the docks now and let Val meet us there?"

Marius shrugged and looked at Beatrix and Iris as if to gauge their thoughts. He must have sensed hesitation because he said only, "He'll be back soon."

They finished the meal, read a Scripture, and prayed. Still Valentine had not come.

Abachum returned with the news that everything was ready at the warehouse. Cato and Abachum moved Quintus and his couch into the culina, where they would all be ready as soon as Valentine returned.

But he didn't.

No one said anything, but dread curdled in Iris's stomach. Had Titus really left when he stormed out? Had he circled back around and arrested Valentine? She didn't voice her fears; they were already written on everyone else's faces. Phoebe and Delphine served calda, then left with Martha to put the children to bed. Quintus dozed. Beatrix sat on a stool near Iris's perch on a stack of barley sacks, sipping from her cup in silence.

When Cato began to pray aloud for Valentine's speedy and safe return, she clenched the cup, fear swirling. Surely if Cato did not feel the same dread, he would not be praying like this. Her shoulders ached, but as Cato prayed, the tension lessened. The hour and the prayer stretched. She let her head rest against the wall.

The latch on the outside door jiggled. Iris jerked awake at the sound, startled and confused to find herself in the culina. It came back to her in an instant as Cato lurched to his feet. *Valentine.* Relief melted the uncertainty tightening her shoulders as the jiggling latch turned into a pounding fist.

Cato unlatched the door and swung it open. "It's about time, Val. You had us all—" He took a step back. Titus stepped inside and shut the door behind him, but not before Iris noted the pale light of dawn behind him.

She stood, her legs shaking. "What have you done?" she choked. "Where's Valentine?"

LII

When Valens left the Calogarus home, he could not help but wonder if Titus had truly left or if he lingered in the shadows outside, waiting for his chance to arrest him. He'd almost given in to Iris's pleading to stay. They had everything they needed to escape the city. It would have been so easy to take her hand and remain, to marry her then and there in the presence of her father and their friends. He wanted to change his mind and stay, but as the words were on his tongue, a niggling sense of unease filled his gut. How could he marry the woman he loved and be satisfied, knowing he'd broken his word and left another couple waiting in the dark? Did his word mean nothing? So he'd kissed her again and told her he'd return soon.

With a quick prayer, Valens left the safety of the culina and turned down the alley, heading for the public gardens on Esquiline Hill. They were his least favorite of the garden meeting places, located near the city dumping grounds and over what used to be mass burial pits for the poor. Always the gardens carried a stench no amount of flowering shrubbery could hide—even if they were in bloom. Early in the month of Februarius, everything was still stark and bare.

No sign of Titus. Valens pulled his hood up and gripped the edges of his cloak against the wind and set off at a brisk clip. Hector had not sent men to escort him tonight. It rarely happened that he forgot, but there had been a few times he and the ex-legionnaires had been only minutes behind each other. They'd meet eventually. He forged ahead. The Gardens of Maecenas were on the opposite edge of the city from the villa. It'd take him forever to get there and back.

Valens tried to keep alert for movement in the shadows. The hilly streets cast in the silvery-blue moonlight were bright and not wholly abandoned. The people taking advantage of the illumination and milling about the streets gave him a sense of security that allowed his mind to wander back to Iris, the kisses, the promise in her wide brown eyes. He'd marry her tonight if Quintus agreed.

The sound of his footsteps changed from sandals scuffing against cobbles to the crunch of gravel paths. Had he arrived so soon? Valens took a moment to catch his breath and then scanned the gardens. Stone terraces held up copses of trees and bunches of shrubbery that in summer would bloom in brilliant patterns but now seemed haphazard and overgrown. He walked the paths, scanning the stands of trees for figures. They would see him first, standing on the moonlit path, silhouetted by the white gravel. Usually the man emerged first, made certain of Valens's identity before waving his beloved from hiding.

No figure emerged. Had he read the missive correctly? It *had* said the Gardens of Maecenas, had it not? A stick snapped in the clump of cedars ahead. Valens moved toward the sound, feelings of relief and anxiety swirling in his stomach. A shape shifted in the shadows—was that an arm? Waving? A cloud obscured the moonlight for a moment. He tilted his head, squinting. Yes, definitely waving. This couple must be especially cautious. Sandals whispering over dried grass, he left the path, moving toward the figure, which grew in height and girth the closer he came.

His whispered greeting was met with a hissed word that might have been *"Hush!"* or *"Run!"*

The world brightened as the cloud unveiled the moon and the man's face came into view. Valens stopped short.

Titus.

Titus was the groom?

No. No, of course not.

Titus opened his mouth as if to speak, then clamped it shut as guards broke through the thicket behind him and surged toward Valens, spreading and circling. Titus's eyes slammed shut with a look of . . . remorse? Valens's limbs laced with quivering energy, but he didn't move. Even if he could have, there was no way he'd outrun Praetorians. Titus hesitated, the torn look in his face hardening as he shouldered through the saplings separating them. He reached Valens before the others did and gripped his arm as the troop surrounded them.

"You're under arrest," Titus grunted as he twisted Valens's arms behind his back and tied the wrists.

Iris.

Oh, Lord, Lord, *my friends!* Were there guards at the Calogarus house too? Would Marius and Martha be arrested for hiding him? Abachum and Audifax? Cato? Would Titus put Quintus and Iris at risk? He didn't think so, not after what Titus had done to rescue Quintus, but he'd left in a rage. *Lord, protect my friends.*

Valens could think of nothing else as Titus grabbed the back of his neck and one arm and shoved him ahead of the guards, who were whooping and pounding each other's shoulders as if they'd won some hard-fought victory instead of hidden in a few bushes to waylay a single man armed with a pen.

One of the guards stripped him of his satchel and riffled through the contents. He lifted a scroll and unrolled it, tilting it into the moonlight.

"Urian! I've found your marriage contract!"

Urian ripped the scroll out of his hands with a sharp laugh. "What say we let him go and I marry Saphira instead?"

The first guard snatched the scroll back. "She'd never agree to you; she likes me better."

"I tried to warn you," Titus growled in his ear and glanced from side to side at the men surrounding them. He straightened. "I always said I'd get him eventually." His voice was too loud. Confident. Triumphant.

Valens shouldn't have been surprised. He shouldn't have felt the strange sense of betrayal swirling in his gut. Titus owed him nothing. Titus had given him one chance to leave and Valens had not taken it. If Valens was a man true to his word, so was Titus.

With the tip of his gladius, Titus kept Valens at a quick march. The impenetrable walls of the Castra Praetoria loomed ahead in the darkness. Once he entered, there would be no hope for escape. His thoughts centered on Iris and his friends. He prayed constantly, silently, the only thing that kept his feet moving forward as Titus pushed him through the Porta Principalis Sinistra and toward the prison built into the northeastern wall.

Titus turned to the four men still accompanying them. "You go on and celebrate. I'll get him to the prison."

One of them shook his head. "And let you have all the glory when you alert Trecenarius Faustus? Not a chance. We'll celebrate together later."

Titus's mouth tightened and he avoided Valens's eye as they entered the prison. The four guards waited outside as Titus shoved Valens toward the prison warden, a bucktoothed guard with thin hairs slicked over a balding pate, who took his duties overly serious.

"Name." He settled on his chair with a wiggle and inspected the point of his stylus.

"Valentine Favius Diastema in for questioning," Titus answered for him.

Valens felt his eyebrows lift slightly even as his stomach sank. He should be in for execution. He carried evidence of his crimes on his person. Questioning was a light excuse for imprisonment, even if a dreadful prospect.

The warden flipped open a tablet and wrote his name in letters that were painstaking and slow.

Titus shut his eyes. "Curse you for having such a long name."

Valens stared straight ahead down a hall of doors lit at the end by a single torch. "Most people call me Valens, or Val."

"Number twenty-three."

Valens twisted around as Titus prodded him into the cell. The warden locked it and went back to his duties.

Titus hesitated. "I thought you were smarter. I didn't think you'd show."

Valens felt a flicker of surprise.

"You had everything." Titus's voice dropped to a whisper, unable to mask the anger and envy in his tone. "And you gave it up for this." He gestured to the cell.

Valens let out a long breath and looked away, taking in the shadowy grime of the dampened brick walls and the smell of mildew and unwashed bodies. "Do to me what you will, Investigator. You'll have fame enough for bringing me to justice." He shifted his eyes back to Titus, drilling him with a gaze firm and entreating. "But I beg you: leave my friends in peace. They're protecting Iris and Quintus."

LIII

IRIS WOULD NOT LOOK AT TITUS. She couldn't force herself to. Not after what he'd done. After what he'd taken from her.

An agonizing day had passed since Titus had shown up in Valentine's place, warning them all that Valentine had been arrested. Titus had said he'd meant to warn Valentine, but his men had charged out before his signal and he'd had no choice but to aid in Valentine's arrest or be labeled a traitor himself. He'd watched Iris, his posture begging her to understand why he'd had to go through with it. She'd refused to look at him then and she refused now.

"Sit and eat with us." Marius gestured toward an empty couch. Only the four women and Abachum were gathered to break their fasts. Quintus was resting and Cato and Audifax had left on a medical summons. Titus moved into the room and sat on the edge of the couch, looking as though he expected a barbarian attack at any moment. Through the open balcony doors, the children competed for who was the tallest.

Iris gripped the blue-cushioned arm of the couch with a damp hand. Beside her, Beatrix sat stiffly, clutching a steaming cup of calda and staring at Titus.

"How is he?" Beatrix's expression turned tentative.

Titus shrugged. "He's . . . singing like a madman."

His eyes widened and flicked around the room in obvious surprise when everyone chuckled.

"Will they move him to the Tullianum?" Marius asked.

Titus shook his head. "He's been transferred to the Ludus Magnus for questioning, and he'll remain there until the Lupercalia Games."

"Questioning?" Iris's head snapped up then. Beatrix reached over and gripped her hand.

Titus shifted and explained in a voice that said he didn't want to. "That's why I've come." His gaze slid over them all. "The prefect has ordered Valentine's questioning. They don't believe he acted alone and want him to give up the names of anyone who harbored and helped him. And names of the other church leaders and their meeting locations."

Fear tingled in her arms. Iris choked back the lump lodged in her throat. "Who's doing the questioning?"

A muscle twitched in his jaw. "I'm here to warn you all—for your safety and everyone else's. Get out of the city while you can."

"Who's questioning him, Titus?" Her voice grew louder, sharper.

He locked his gaze on Marius, the effort to avoid her question evident in the lines on his face. "You have to leave. Please."

"You're doing it, aren't you?" Acid burned in Iris's throat.

Titus shut his eyes and hung his head. Though he didn't speak, the movement was answer enough.

Her stomach tumbled. She was glad they hadn't eaten yet. "Why bother warning us?"

"To protect you and your father," he admitted quietly. "And to protect the people caring for you both."

Iris opened and shut her mouth, unable to think of anything to say. Did he really think this would make up for Valentine's arrest? For his torture? She pressed her lips together, not trusting herself to speak as anger and grief rolled over her in waves.

Marius leaned forward with a wince and a grunt. "Thank you, son." He reached out and grasped Titus's thick arm, looking him hard in the eyes. "You are not far from the Kingdom, I think."

Titus shrugged free. "I want nothing to do with your beliefs, old man. Don't mistake this warning for anything other than what it is.

My aim has always been to keep Iris and Quintus safe. Will you swear to do that?"

Marius gave a slight incline of his head. "I will do my best, certainly, but it is God who holds each of us. Our days are numbered in His book and there is nothing we can do to add or take away from what He has set."

Titus blinked twice before turning to Iris, jaw hard with anger. "Come with *me* then. I'll take you to my mother in Ostia. I'll arrange a cart for your pater. You'll both be safe there."

Iris leaned away, shaking her head. "I don't want—I want to stay here."

"*He's* not going to protect you." He jerked a hand toward Marius and accentuated every word as if Iris were a child. "These people and their so-called *god* have brought nothing but trouble to you and your pater."

Iris released Beatrix's hand and twisted in her seat to face him. "That's not true, Titus." Her anger clashed with a solid stillness as she spoke. "God restored my sight, freed Pater, gave us peace and hope—"

"*Hope.*" Titus spat out the word like a rancid olive. "Hope for what? Your pater would have been worked to death if *I* hadn't stepped in. Your lover is going to die—and *this* is the god you're choosing for protection?"

Marius and the others said nothing. This was a conversation meant for the two of them, and while none of them could bring themselves to interrupt it enough to leave, they all sat still and silent.

Titus raked his hands through his hair, cursing at them all through gritted teeth. Iris's anger softened, melting into pity. He didn't know. He truly didn't know. He was only acting on what he saw from the outside. The panic she'd felt for Valentine had eased a little with her declaration of God's peace and hope. What Marius said was true. They were all in God's hands and there was no safer place to be. No matter how precarious that appeared from the outside.

Iris stood and skirted the table, approaching Titus with an outstretched hand. "Come with me." She tilted her head toward the door. He followed her into the courtyard, where the sun reflected perfect fragments of the house and sky in the puddles. She stopped near the silent fountain, its basin filled with rainwater and dead leaves.

He crossed his arms, the breeze lifting the short dark hair off his forehead. "Are you going to speak honestly now?"

"I did." Iris tightened her palla around her shoulders.

"You don't have to repeat what they want you to say."

"I'm not." She crossed her arms and struggled to come up with words that would make him understand. "Marius is right. It is God who holds each of us—"

"Well, he's about to drop you all." Titus gripped her arms and gave her a little shake. "Valentine broke the law. *I* have the proof—"

"Valentine didn't do what he did for anarchy's sake." She looked up at him, tone earnest, eyes pleading. "He did it because he believes marriage is what is best for Rome. For families and widow care and property. What he did, he did *for* Rome."

Titus shrugged but kept his hands on her shoulders. "That may be. But you must listen when I tell you that with just a little pressure, Valentine is going to give you all up." His voice dropped low and steely. "That means certain and immediate execution for your pater, for you and everyone else who harbored him. You cannot stay here!"

"Titus—"

He swore and threw his hands up. "I'm asking you—*begging* you to be sensible! You have *two* days." He turned pleading eyes on her. "Convince them to leave. Valentine will be questioned and he's not . . ." He paused, wincing. "He's not the type that can withstand it for long. Believe me, he'll give up your names with the second hot iron and you'll all be taken in. You have to be far away by then."

The courtyard went blurry.

Titus gripped her hands as his voice dropped to a whisper. "Please. I could have borne losing you to him . . . eventually. But I can't lose you like this." He pulled her to him, his embrace apologetic and platonic. She felt his pulse throbbing in his neck, every muscle of his body strung tight and tense as he waited for her to say something.

She could not force her arms to hug him back. "I'll talk to them."

He cupped her face, looking hard into her eyes. "*Convince* them." His hands left her face with a rush of cool air and he turned away, his boots clacking over the pale marble path. Any calm Iris had exhibited in his presence vanished at the slam of the culina door. Her shaking hand shot out and gripped the lip of the fountain. She didn't hear the footsteps approaching until Beatrix put a hand on her arm.

"I'm sorry," Iris choked.

"Oh, my girl." Beatrix wrapped her arms around Iris, her embrace soft and motherly. "Valens was not ignorant of the consequences of his actions. He's been defying the emperor's edict for many months. He knew each time he left there was a risk he would be found out."

"I begged him not to leave." Iris's voice quivered. "Perhaps if I'd been more—"

"Shhh." Beatrix pulled back and shook her head with a sad smile. "It was his choice to make. It was not your fault he left."

"So we do nothing?"

Beatrix took both of her hands in a firm grip. "Nothing's to be fixed by worrying and casting blame on ourselves." Her eyes looked as heavy as Iris's heart. "Those are the tools of the enemy. However difficult, we must pray and trust. God is big enough to rescue Valentine from this. And if He does not . . ." Beatrix tugged her back toward the triclinium, where the breakfast sat cold and untouched on the table.

Beatrix and Iris resumed their places and while no one made a move to eat, Iris told them of Titus's reiterated warning and his urging for them to leave. The room was silent save for the innocent squeals of the children outside.

"What will we do?" Iris asked. "If Titus is right, we're all found out and—" She looked at the children playing outside. Their horrific loss would be repeated a second time.

"Valens would never betray us."

"He wouldn't want to, Beatrix," Iris argued, her voice cracking. "But the Praetorian questioners always get what they want. They'll find a way to break him."

"When the apostle Peter was imprisoned, the believers gathered together and prayed for his release," Marius spoke up.

Hope surged through Iris's chest. She knew that story. "God sent an angel to release him."

Marius nodded. "He did the same thing with Paul and Silas. Only it was an earthquake that time."

"Do you—do you think He would do the same thing for Valentine?" She wasn't sure she wanted them to answer. Her chest felt frozen, emotions locked inside. Their answers might unleash wild hope or despair. She'd seen—literally seen—the power of God. His love, His care, even before she knew Him. How much more would He care for Valentine, a man who followed Him and served others? Beatrix and Martha exchanged glances but neither answered her question.

Marius leaned forward and picked up his bowl of physician-approved breakfast. He grimaced and set the bowl aside.

"I have no doubt God could rescue Valentine if He chose." Marius spoke in a tone that implied his answer would not stop there. "But we must also remember that there came a time when Peter and Paul and Silas were not rescued by earthquakes and angels loosening chains and unlocking gates."

Iris swallowed back the dread stealing over her as Marius continued. "We don't know what God will do," he said. "But right now, we must all pray for Valentine. For his strength, his faith, and if God wills it, his release."

They ate and discussed Titus's demand for them to flee. Cato joined them a while later and they filled him in, weighing the risks. Most spoke for staying, despite the danger. The church had met with more and more irregularity since Valentine's initial arrest, and Marius held that it was time to bring it back together. With persecutions coming again, they must all be strong.

Cato, as much as he'd dreamed of it, didn't want to leave his patients. Delphine and Martha said the widows would be evicted and starve if not for the weekly food basket regime—Valentine covered the rent for many of them. Too much work had to be done, and none of them would shirk their ministries for their own safety.

But they made the decision for Quintus and Iris and Beatrix

to continue with the old plan and leave Rome when Marius's ship departed for the Lycian coast. If they were gone, there would be no evidence of Valentine's connection with the Calogarus family. They would be safe. And if there was a way to free Valentine, they'd send him to Lycia after them. Iris knew it was for the best, yet her throat ached at the thought of leaving Valentine and her friends behind. They'd become family—they *were* family.

After the morning meal, where she'd been unable to eat a thing, Iris wandered into Martha's weaving room and sat before a loom of partly woven green cloth. She studied the threads for a moment, then picked up where the pattern left off and began to weave, relishing the way the pattern followed her direction and plan. As she grew more comfortable, her mind was left free to wander.

"All things work together for the good of those who love God, those who are called according to His purpose." She heard Valentine's voice in her head as clearly as when they'd spoken in the courtyard under the stars. "All things *might be good things, and they might be terribly difficult things."*

The words still weren't comforting. She wanted the good things. Not the difficulties.

"No matter what happens—good or bad, by our estimation—anything can always be redeemed by God for good if we trust Him."

Did she trust God? It had been easy to do so when He'd restored her sight, when He'd given her friends, when He'd allowed their plan to rescue her father to succeed. But now, in the uncertainty, in the danger, with the life of the man she loved dangling in the capricious grip of the Praetorian Guards . . . If Valentine lost his life, could she trust Him still? Could she cling to Him? But if she didn't, what else was there?

LIV

Titus's hands went slick with sweat as he entered the cell followed by Tribune Braccus and a long-fingered scribe. The cells of the three-storied Ludus Magnus lined the edge of an oblong arena with seating for three thousand. Most of the cells contained small but comfortable living quarters for the gladiators who at that moment crowded the arena floor, training for the Lupercalia Games. Titus led the way to the cells on the lowest level. They were reserved for the *noxii* and crowded with the prisoners and criminals condemned to death by the cruelest methods.

The cell Titus turned in to had been built for a singular purpose. He'd been inside many times but never had he felt such a curdling of dread for what lay ahead. Valentine stood in the center of the room, stripped nearly naked, wrists chained overhead.

"Shouldn't I be with the Ninth, sir?" Titus tried to stall. "I've already been pulled from training three times this week."

The tribune closed the door behind them. "No." He gave a benevolent smile. "It's only fair that you have this reward, for a job well done."

The scribe positioned himself and his supplies on a rickety stand in the corner while the tribune circled Valentine slowly—a cat sizing up his prey. Titus's pulse hammered in his ears as he pretended to study the wall of instruments. Whips of varying kinds, long knives, tiny spikelike blades made for nonfatal but extremely painful punctures, pliers for extracting fingernails and teeth, scissors, hooks, branding irons, scourging rods ranging in size from a pinkie's thickness to a club the approximate size of a gladiator's thigh, saws, and several other things that looked terrible but had no real use other than to frighten with sheer imagination.

For the first time, Titus stared at the instruments of torture out of habit rather than planning the approach that would gain the quickest results. This time he wanted no results. He'd received a message from Iris consisting of two words that made him hurl the tablet across the room when he read it.

We stay.

If Titus was successful, Valentine would give away the two people Titus loved most. If Valentine remained silent, the fallback would be on Titus. If Iris knew what he was about to do to the man she claimed to love, she would hate him forever. If she didn't already. He was damned no matter what he did.

"Liberare!"

Titus snapped to attention and turned around. "Yes, sir?"

The tribune settled into a chair, folding one knee over the other and shaking a bag of pistachio nuts into his lap. "I'm rather disappointed at the look of him." He tilted his head toward Valentine. "I thought he'd be taller. More . . . heroic-looking." He cracked a shell and popped the nut into his mouth, crunching with anticipation. The shell clicked against the floor. "Start with the number two rod. We'll warm up slowly, have a bit of sport."

"Yes, sir." Titus reached for the thumb-sized rod. When he turned around, Valentine's eyes were trained on him in an expression Titus couldn't read. The calmness of the look sank into his gut and churned up unease, guilt, and something like fear. He shouldn't be doing this.

Titus tightened his grip on the rod to mask the sudden shaking in his hand. *Don't be foolish.* Valentine had broken the law. On purpose. Again and again. He deserved a good beating for *that* at least. Yet something inside told him this was wrong. He pushed the doubts away and waited for the tribune's cue to begin.

Chewing, Braccus lifted a finger, looking at Valentine. "You're a leader of the Christians, are you not?"

Valentine gave a single nod but said nothing. Titus twirled the rod between his fingers.

Tribune Braccus cracked another nut. "There is no badge of honor here for silence." He popped the nut into his mouth and chewed as he spoke. "Death is inevitable. But you can speak now and spare yourself all this." He wiggled his fingers at the torture devices on the walls.

Valentine shut his eyes and mumbled something under his breath.

The tribune jerked forward in his seat. "What?"

"A good shepherd gives his life for the sheep," Valentine repeated in a louder voice.

The scribe's pen moved across his scroll, recording every word. Valentine's eyes snapped to him, brows flickering with interest.

The tribune laughed. "Likening your people to a bunch of filthy animals?" He paused, considering. "Then you'll also know that sheep will scatter without a shepherd."

Valentine gave a slight shake of his head. "Strike me down." He spoke as if he didn't care. "Someone else will rise and lead them."

The tribune changed tactics. Any other time, Titus would be annoyed with the tribune for taking over *his* interrogation. Not today. Today the man could do the whole blasted thing.

"You think the people love you because they call you The Cupid? Do you think they'll call for your life to be spared when they see their hero in the arena?" The tribune smiled and shook his head. "The crowds are capricious where blood is concerned." He gestured toward the door, where the sounds of the gladiator training filtered through. Crashes of wood and steel. "With one breath they cheer their favorite fighter, and with the second, call for his demise." He let the words sink in. "Your silence will not spare you or your friends, nor will the people. I'll track down every one of your friends and lead them like lambs to the slaughter." He smiled at his own cleverness.

Valentine blinked and shifted his weight from one foot to the other. The chains creaked above his head.

"Impatient to begin, are we?" Braccus dumped a handful of nuts down his throat. "Me too." He waved Titus forward. "Proceed."

Valentine's eyes flicked from the tribune to Titus and his Adam's apple bobbed.

Titus stepped forward, avoiding Valentine's gaze, and instead narrowed his focus to the fleshy part of Valentine's side where the number two rod would elicit the most pain with the least damage. Any hope for Iris's forgiveness crumbled as he swung the rod as hard as he could.

Titus wiped a hand over his forehead, sluicing away the sweat. It ran down the sides of his face and dripped from his jaw. He smeared his hand on his thigh and looked at the tribune, still seated in the folding chair, one knee over the other, cutting his nails with a knife he'd snagged from the wall. He'd lost interest long ago.

"Did he say anything good?" Braccus looked at the scribe.

"Mmm." The scribe scanned the document. "You called him weak. He said, 'God has chosen the weak things of the world to put to shame the things which are mighty.' You told him to shut up." He rolled and unrolled the scroll further down, scanning and reading the lines of scrawl.

Valentine sagged in the shackles, his body covered in cuts and welts that were quickly purpling. His head hung forward. The pain had finally sent him senseless, but it had taken hours. His stamina had surprised Titus and he wished he would have started with more pain earlier, sparing Valentine wounds that would only incriminate Titus further if Iris ever saw them.

The scribe paused. "You asked him how much longer he wanted to suffer. He said, 'Love suffers long and is kind; love does not envy . . . does not seek its own, is not provoked, thinks no evil.'"

Titus remembered those lines. The words had cut him deeper than the blades had cut Valentine. He might have thought he loved Iris, but his actions had not shown it. He'd envied her love for Valentine, lost his temper, sought the advancement of his own career over her desires, and he'd wavered between pleasure and revulsion as he'd beaten Valentine. Love? No. He was despicable. He'd been relieved when the tribune told Valentine to shut up again.

The scribe cleared his throat, continuing. "You asked who had been helping him with the weddings and when he didn't respond, you told Titus to tear out his fingernails. The prisoner said, 'Love "bears all things, believes all things, hopes all things, endures all things. Love never fails."'"

The scribe read the words in monotone, but Titus heard them accentuated with Valentine's groans. The way the words were forced through his teeth as if he couldn't help but speak them. Valentine's eyes never left the scribe as he faithfully copied his words. He'd done it on purpose, knowing they'd later study every word he spoke for clues.

"Should we leave him for now, sir?" Titus hoped the tribune would not require Valentine to be revived so they could continue.

"It would probably be best." Braccus rose and tossed the knife on the chair. He looked at Valentine. "You can try again tomorrow. He'll be good and sore then. Didn't last very long." He shifted his gaze to Titus. "I thought you were better than that."

Titus replaced the instruments in silence after the tribune left. He had underestimated Valentine. Not only had he not said a single name, he'd never once begged for mercy nor cowered as others often did. The eyes that had stared him down with apprehension before he'd begun had grown determined, then steady—calm even, as if nothing Titus could do would break him. Instead of growing weaker with every blow, closer and closer to breaking, something in Valentine had grown stronger, more solid.

The scribe cleared his tools and left. Titus turned to Valentine, hanging in the center of the cell, knees buckled beneath him. Unless he needed the room, Titus usually left them where they were. It had never mattered before whether someone would take them down.

This time, Titus unlocked the shackles and caught Valentine over his shoulder as he dropped. He trundled him out and asked the lanista with the keys for an empty cell. He deposited Valentine as comfortably as he could on the bare floor and, as he left, told the lanista to give him bread and water when he woke.

It was everything he could do.

And it was nothing at all.

LV

"ONE MORE." IRIS PEERED INTO THE BOWL on Quintus's lap. Quintus obediently took the last bite and swallowed. The effort exhausted him, and he sank back against the curved arm of the couch. He looked from Iris to Beatrix, who unwrapped the old dressings on his cut leg.

"Thank you." The words came out on the back of a long sigh. His head ached. He'd felt better since coming here, but the worst had been in the Praetorian prison. He'd paced his cell, agitated and confused, falling in and out of rages and bouts of sobbing. The guards had thought he was going mad. Quintus worried he already had. The dreams had been horrible. Nightmares left him screaming and sweating. But those had gone since he'd come here. He closed his eyes.

What he wouldn't give for just a little drink.

"Can I . . . have a drink?"

Iris lifted a cup to his lips. At the first taste of water, he turned his face away. "A bit of wine," he corrected. "It would help my head."

Iris spoke gently. "Cato said you might ask. He also said you weren't to have any. He said too much wine is what caused your problems in the first place."

He shook his head, ire growing. "Tribune Braccus caused my . . ." He trailed off, suddenly too tired to argue.

"I'm so glad you're here, Pater." Her eyes brimmed with tears.

He forced his lips to tip into a slight smile.

Beatrix smeared honey over the gash on his leg with her fingers. "You're making wonderful improvement." She looked at him over her shoulder. "I wouldn't wonder if a bath and a shave would perk you right up. I have some lovely soap and a new men's scent that's wonderfully attractive with a hint of mystery." She used the back of her hand to brush springy curls away from her large brown eyes and smiled at him. He doubted his body could make a trip to the nearest bathhouse, but he'd go through the effort if it meant she'd keep smiling at him like that. He'd even eat another bowl of whatever that horrible brown mash had been if she'd keep smiling.

"Where did you go this morning, Beatrix?" Iris gathered his bowl and the plates from the dinner she and Bea had eaten at his bedside and stacked them on a tray. "You left and no one knew where you'd gone."

Beatrix paused her ministrations on his leg. "I went to Val's grandfather," she admitted in a low voice.

"The chief augur?" Quintus's voice rasped and cracked. Beatrix's eyes flew to him and she gave a single nod.

"And?" Iris sank down across from Beatrix. "Will he help Valentine?"

"No." Beatrix blinked and renewed her focus on Quintus's leg. "He said he'd already warned Valens something like this would happen. He's washed his hands of him."

"How could he do that to his own flesh and blood?"

Beatrix wiped her fingers on a rag and motioned for Iris to lift Quintus's foot so she could wind the new bandage around his calf. "Valens is a liability to Gaius now. If word spread that the chief augur tried to help his traitorous grandson, he'd lose everything. He's not willing to do that."

Quintus shut his eyes and listened to them fuss over his cuts. He was more sore than hurt, but he let them worry over him. Better they had something to distract them from worrying over Valentine.

The silence stretched. His eyes stayed shut but he did not sleep.

"Are you afraid, Beatrix?" Iris asked.

Beatrix's response was hesitant. "I am terrified."

He opened his eyes just enough to peer through his lashes. The two settled at the foot of his couch.

"That Valentine will give us away?"

"No, no." Beatrix tied the bandage tight enough Quintus winced. "He wouldn't do that, no matter what they did. Valens has always been stubborn—outright defiant sometimes. My, but he used to give me a time!"

"Really?" Iris shook her head, her scar puckering as she smiled softly. "I can't imagine that."

Beatrix chuckled and pressed a hand to her chest. "Used to make my heart just ache, the way he always wanted to help—not that he always *was* a help, mind you. And once he had a mind to do something, heaven and earth couldn't stop him. Nor a good paddling."

Pain shot through his bruised face as Quintus struggled to hold back a smile. He nearly fell asleep listening to Beatrix regale Iris with tales of the young Valentine.

"I am so glad he met you. I worried Valens would go through all of life and never fall in love."

Wait, what? Senses suddenly on the alert, Quintus listened. *Love?* Who? Iris and Valentine? He shouldn't have been surprised, not with the way they'd seemed to get along so well, talking after every meeting for the past—how many months had it been?

Iris took a breath. "Do you think he'll get out? I keep imagining he'll come knocking on the door like that story of Peter."

Peering once more through his lashes, he saw Beatrix smile, though it didn't reach those warm eyes of hers. "I hope so. With all my heart I hope so. And I believe God knows the desires of our hearts and so longs to fulfill them. He is the giver of all good things, but . . ."

The corners of Iris's smile sank.

"We must decide if God is worth trusting, when He does not answer our prayers the way we think He should." Beatrix reached for Iris's hand. "He is." She nodded with assurance, conviction. "I promise, He is worth it."

Iris took a breath to respond when a knock sounded at the door.

Quintus jerked upright, startling the two women. Iris locked gazes with Beatrix, hope lighting in her eyes as she leaped up and flung the door open.

Titus.

His expression deflated with Iris's shoulders. She stumbled back and allowed him to enter. Titus's gaze flicked around the room, taking in Beatrix and Quintus.

"Quintus. How are you?" His words were a whisper. Phoebe, who'd followed Titus to the door, shooed two wide-eyed little boys out of the doorway before closing it behind her.

Iris, swallowing back a disappointed look, answered before he could. "Improving." She turned toward Quintus. "He's eating and his wounds are healing well."

A relieved sigh sank Titus's chest. "Thank the gods."

Beatrix rose, turning her body toward Titus. "Any word on Valens?"

Something shuddered across his face for the briefest of moments before smoothing to stone. "He's still at the Ludus Magnus." Titus hesitated and rubbed the back of his neck. "He made it through two days of questioning and did not breathe a word of any of you."

Beatrix's lips pressed together. Quintus longed to say something comforting but his head had begun to throb. Iris stared at Titus, her back hard and straight. His next words shattered her calm.

"He's sentenced to execution on the second day of the Lupercalia Games. That's the day after tomorrow."

Beatrix's fingers pressed against her lips and her eyes squeezed shut.

"And?" Iris choked. "Do you have a plan to get him out?"

"Iris." Titus swallowed, voice low, expression full of regret. "I cannot get him out. But in the chaos tomorrow, I may be able to get you in to see him. One last time."

Iris pressed a hand over her mouth. The air whooshed out of Quintus's lungs. This couldn't be happening. Not to Valentine. He had God's ear, after all. He'd prayed and healed Iris when no one else could. Where were the angels and the earthquake? Marius had read the stories several times the last few days as the household gathered in Quintus's room to read Scripture in the evenings.

"You should go, Beatrix." Iris wrapped her arms around herself. "You raised him; it's only right."

Titus looked at Beatrix, uncomfortable. "It's the Ludus," he said in explanation. "No one will think twice about a young woman being escorted inside—they're always hanging around the gates watching for a glimpse of their favorite gladiators. But a respectable woman such as yourself would be—"

"I'm too old to pretend to a tryst with a fighter." Tears were thick in Beatrix's voice. "Can I at least send a message with Iris?"

"As long as it doesn't contain information on who or where you are."

Beatrix dropped her chin. "Understood."

Titus turned to Iris, shoulders heavy. "Come to the gates of the Ludus Magnus early tomorrow morning. I'll be waiting for you. The crowds will be thick so you won't have to worry about drawing suspicion." He hesitated. "Dress well. Only the ones with money get in."

She nodded.

Titus's hands twitched, then balled tightly at his sides. "Tomorrow then." He looked at Quintus and gave a nod.

Iris's lips tightened. "I'll be there."

LVI

WITH HIS TONGUE, Valens tested the tender spot where his bottom front teeth had been. The tribune hadn't been impressed by his strength of will. Or his singing voice. Valens wished he could have fainted—blacked out—sooner. The sight of blood had done the trick flawlessly in times past, but apparently the blood had to belong to someone else. How irritating.

He'd awakened propped against the rough stone wall, heavy iron shackles biting into his raw wrists. He made the mistake of shifting his body to relieve the needles in his legs. Pain exploded through his chest and shoulders, sending a jolt of light through his vision. He sagged, panting against welling nausea.

Three sets of footsteps clacked in the corridor. All night the lanistae had been emptying the cells of the noxii, leading them out of the Ludus Magnus and into the bowels of the Flavian Amphitheatre next door. The gladiator training school had fallen eerily silent. The condemned who remained seemed afraid to draw attention to themselves, as if they might be overlooked if they were quiet. The place stank of fear and sweat. The footsteps came closer. He'd been warned the questioners would return one last time and had heard the tribune mutter that they'd better leave enough of him intact for a good show tomorrow. Valens let his head fall forward and prayed for strength enough to protect his friends and stay true to his faith.

Once more, God. Grant me strength.

Keys jingled in the lock on his cell. His heart began to pound. His prayers were cut short as the door swung open on protesting hinges. He bit his lip as his arms quivered in the shackles.

What would they use against him this time? Rods? Fillet knives?

"Valentine?"

His heart stopped.

Dear God. No.

His eyes flew open. Iris ran toward him, a blur of pink and white. The door shut with a solid clunk as she dropped to her knees before him. He moaned, mind whirling. "What are you doing here?" Would they hurt her to break him? "Oh, Lord, no."

Tears coursed over her cheeks. Hands touched his shoulders, his face. "What have they done to you?"

"You shouldn't be here. Why are you here—? Ow!"

"Sorry." She shrank back on her heels. "Titus helped me get in. We've all been praying for your release." As she spoke, her eyes traveled over his bruises and the crusted black slices lacerating his chest and arms. Horror mingled with the pallor of her face.

He attempted distraction. "How is your pater?"

She dragged her gaze to his, shaking her head as if to clear it. "Growing stronger every day." Her lips trembled, eyes slammed shut. She pressed a fist against her mouth, shoulders rigid as she fought for control.

"Don't cry." He longed to draw her into his arms and hold her tight against him. The best he could do was grit his teeth and shift his weight, raising one numb hand to brush against her head, draped in a deep rose-colored palla. He'd never seen her in that color before. It didn't suit her as well as the orange.

"You cannot die, Valentine." Tears rolled over the swells of her cheekbones. "God would not ask it of you."

He dropped his hand. "But He asks it of us all. Death to selfish desires, to pride, to power, to having our own way, to anything that would keep us from following Him with our whole hearts."

"Would He have me give up you?" Her eyes met his, dark, agonized.

His heart ached. "You cannot venerate me over Him. You must not." He shook his head. "I am bound for the arena. There's no escape for me now." He studied her face, drinking in every curve and edge of her features, committing them to memory. She tilted her head and used the edge of the embroidered palla to gently wipe his temple, his jaw, his chin. He leaned toward her touch.

"We must have hope," she whispered.

Hope. Yes. But not for his release.

He closed his eyes as she rested her forehead painfully against his. Suddenly he wanted nothing more than to hear her laugh again. "I know you like a man in chains, but we've really got to stop meeting like this."

She made a small noise, the cross between a laugh and a cry. "This is the last time."

"Yes." Ignoring the pain shooting through him, he lifted his hand to clumsily caress her cheek with fingers stiff and crusted with blackened blood. He longed to feel the softness of her skin but couldn't sense a thing.

"Pray for me, my love." His voice went hoarse. Her eyes opened, clear and brown with black freckles around the pupil he'd never noticed before. He lifted his chin and touched the tip of his nose to hers. "Pray that God would grant me the courage to die well. Pray that He will work something good from my death."

She pressed her lips together and leaned back, pulling a ragged breath through her nose.

"Iris, God is not a magic charm to buy in the market. He hasn't promised to answer every prayer the way we want. There is no release for me this time." He swallowed. "And He's given me peace in accepting it. He'll give you the same if you but ask."

Her face turned, eyes rising to meet his, soul-deep sadness reflected in them.

His lips twitched but didn't quite make it into the shape of a smile. "My one regret is not being thrown into prison years ago, so I could have loved you longer."

Her lips trembled, and she smeared a hand across her wet cheek but didn't answer.

"None of that, my love." He touched her cheek again. He winced as his fingers left a trail of red on her jaw.

She sniffed, reaching up to wrap her fingers around his. The pain of her touch nearly sent him senseless. He fought back the black spots dancing in his vison and gritted his teeth.

"Tell Cato he can have my lyre, to remember me by—I'd give him my satchel to carry his own things, but they took it from me."

Iris sucked in a steadying breath. "That reminds me. I have a message from Beatrix and everyone." She pulled a small tablet from her belt.

"Will you read it to me?" Valens shifted, needles of pain shooting through the lacerations on his legs. He closed his eyes as she read, a pain deeper than his physical wounds stretching in his chest, forcing tears from his eyes. The letter shared prayers and encouraging Scriptures. Everyone sent their love.

Iris set the tablet beside her with a clatter.

"Thank you." The words were choked, difficult to maneuver past the lump in his throat.

The lock clinked with keys.

"Time's up." Titus's low voice came from outside.

Valens's heart began to pound with a sort of panic. "Give them all my love. Tell them to pray for me. Tell Aunt Bea . . . tell her she's been better than any mother to me. Tell her . . . thank you." His lips trembled and he looked hard into her eyes, stretching through the agony to grip her hand. "Keep the faith, no matter what happens. God is good and does only good, even if others don't. We can trust Him."

"Come on, girl." The door swung open, revealing Titus and an armored lanista built like a brown bear who dwarfed even Titus's size.

Iris leaned forward and reached up to cradle his bruised face in her fingertips. He turned his head, kissing her fingers, struggling to breathe. *Please, God, let her be all right. Comfort her.*

Carefully, tenderly, Iris pressed her lips to his. "I love you."

He couldn't speak. Only stared into her eyes hoping she could read in his own everything he wanted to say.

"Girl. You leave now or not at all."

She stood and reached for the tablet.

"Leave it," Valens choked. "Please."

She nodded and stumbled across the cell to where Titus and the lanista waited at the door.

Was that a glimmer of pain on the Praetorian's face? Titus turned away before he could be sure. Iris paused in the passage and turned back, opening her mouth as if to speak. The lanista shut the door too soon.

LVII

I~RIS HELD HER EMOTIONS IN CHECK~ until Titus had paid the lanista and the heavy door shut them onto the raucous street. After the silence of the near-empty Ludus Magnus, the roar of the streets glutted with people celebrating the Lupercalia festivities slammed her ears. Children darted through the crowd wearing wolf masks representing Lupercal, the she-wolf who raised Romulus and Remus, the twin founders of Rome. Everyone had donned their best garments, most in white and shades of red and pink. Those who had attended the sacrifices of the goats and dog at the Lupercal Cave bore splatters of blood on their foreheads for good luck.

Nausea threatened to spill her breakfast on the street. Iris leaned against the side of the Ludus and pressed her hands over her face, bending double and sucking in deep breaths. If it hadn't been for his voice, for the shaft of white light filtering over him from the high, barred window that illuminated his eyes, she might not have recognized him. The questioners had been thorough.

Titus touched her shoulder. "Iris."

"*Don't* touch me." Venom laced her words as she snapped straight and shoved him backward. "How could you do that? How could you make me look at what you've done?" She clapped her hands over her face, sobs rising from somewhere so deep in her body, the moment between the sob and her next breath felt infinite. The crush of the crowd afforded a privacy they would not have had otherwise.

He took a step toward her, touched her shoulder again. "I'm sorry, really—"

She slapped his hand away and slammed a fist into his chest. He wore his leather breastplate beneath his tunic. The sharp pain made her angrier.

"Iris." He caught her other wrist as she swung for him, tears and anger blurring her vision.

"Let me go!"

"You're drawing attention—" Her fist connected with his jaw. The people near them gave a wider berth to the woman assaulting a Praetorian Guard. No one wanted to be near the consequences of that. Iris hit him again, then sagged against the Ludus sobbing, energy spent.

"We should go." Titus frowned at the thickening crowd.

"Make way!" A shout barked through the noise and others joined in. "Make way for the Lupercai!"

The shoving of the crowd grew worse now, forcing them to stay pressed against the Ludus or be crushed. Someone stepped on her foot, shooting pain through her toes. Tears stung her eyes, nothing to what Valentine must feel.

A path opened down the center of the street and everyone fought to be along the inner edge when the priests of Lupercal passed, brandishing long thongs of the sacrificial goatskins to lash any women nearby. A lashing meant good luck and a promise of fertility. The cheering crowds closed in behind the Lupercai, joining the procession as men rattling jars over their heads came next.

"Come, ladies!" The jar-men beckoned. "Write your names on a tile for a pairing with your Lupercalia lover!" The jars rattled with wooden tiles as the men shook them over their heads. Their efforts were immediately rewarded by a swarm of young women eager for men to draw their names out of the jar and be coupled off for the holiday.

The crush of the crowds eased. Iris slid down the side of the Ludus and sat in the dirt. She pulled her knees to her chest and dropped her forehead on top, blocking out the bare legs of men and swirling skirts of women in their best sandals. She sensed Titus drop to a crouch beside her, but he didn't reach for her again.

He took a deep breath as if to speak but didn't as he let it out and drew in another. "I didn't mean to capture him that night."

She squeezed her eyes shut against the dimness created by her drawn-up knees. Did he expect her to believe that? She'd seen his face, his anger.

"I mean . . ." He faltered. "I wanted to—at first. When you said you loved him, I wanted to kill him." The admission came out in a whisper.

Iris stilled.

He kept talking, pouring out the same story he'd told the morning he came to tell them Valentine had been arrested. This time, she listened in silence.

"I knew you'd never forgive me if I arrested him, and no matter how *I* felt about him, your happiness means more to me than my loyalty to—" A swallow. "I tried to intercept him—I promise I did. But I wasn't soon enough."

She lifted her head. "Am I to believe you didn't mean to beat him either? To burn his arms, tear out his nails? Were those accidents too?" The words came with a hard edge.

He pressed his lips together and looked away. "I'm sorry."

"Well, I don't—" She pushed to her feet. "I can't forgive you, not—I don't even want to look at you." She wiped the back of her hand along her jaw and pulled the garish palla over her head, angling her face away from him. She'd trusted Titus, spoken highly of him to her friends, assured them he would help. And he'd betrayed them all—*her* most of all. The anger had left a hollow in her, like Vesuvius, emptied of her molten rock. "Take me back."

Titus walked beside her, until they entered the swell of the crowd again and she nearly lost him. He gripped her wrist then and, without looking at her, tugged her through the tiled plaza around the Flavian Amphitheatre where men selling tickets stood on barrels near the entrances, shouting to be heard over the noise of the crowd.

"I've got tickets for the afternoon gladiator matches!"

"Three tickets here for the morning beast hunts—all with a chance to win a hindquarter of beast!"

"Gladiator matches! Noon show included!"

"Watch a man wrestle a panther!"

Iris clamped her lips against the swells of nausea. Titus maneuvered them swiftly through the crowds until they broke free of them on the Via Flaminia.

"I can make it alone from here." Iris shrugged out of his grip. "You've done enough." The words came out more accusatory than she'd meant them to, but she didn't apologize. That was for him to do.

"I leave tomorrow morning with the Ninth Minerva." He crossed his arms. She felt his gaze on her but wouldn't look up. "I don't know if I'll see you again so—"

"Goodbye." She allowed her eyes to connect with his to convey how little she cared. Titus's expression crushed under the weight of that single clipped word. She almost regretted how harshly the word had come out, but anger refused to let her soften.

He opened his mouth to speak, then shut it and simply nodded. "Goodbye, then." He turned on his heel and shoved his way into the crowd, heading back the way they'd come, wide shoulders bowed as if laden with a weight he could barely carry.

Iris turned toward the villa, ignoring the twinge of her spirit urging her to go after him, to forgive him while she could. She lifted her chin. Whatever weight Titus carried, he'd heaped it upon his own shoulders.

LVIII

TITUS WOVE THROUGH THE HYPOGEUM, a maze of dimly lit corridors hidden beneath the sand of the Colosseum floor. Above him came the thunderous rumble of fifty thousand spectators and the clash of swords and thud of spears and bodies. The Praetorians had been called to the amphitheatre in force. When word had gotten out that the man known as The Cupid would be executed at noon on the second day of the games, outrage swept through the city. How dare the emperor kill the hero of the people? Riots had broken out. The Urban Guards had been ordered to surround the amphitheatre, while Praetorians were stationed inside, lining the interior halls and the aisles in the stands. The departure of the Ninth Minerva had been postponed until the following morning.

A trickle of fine sand seeped through a crack overhead, and somewhere in the shadows a large cat snarled. Titus followed the sound to a large capstan in the center of the underground maze where animal trainers herded a huge striped tiger into a cage. He paused, watching slaves turn the capstan, raising the cage all the way to a trapdoor in the ceiling. A sweat-slicked slave fumbled with a lever as the rest waited, bodies tense. A square of blinding light and a powdery cloud of sand split the ceiling as the trapdoor dropped into the cage like a ramp. Another slave pressed a red-hot poker into the tiger's hindquarters, and with a roar, the tiger leaped up onto the arena floor.

Wild cheers erupted from the stands. The slave with the lever closed the trapdoor once more.

"Station three, ready!" the foreman directed in a shout and everyone scrambled to a capstan in another location of the floor.

Titus tore his eyes away and moved further down the corridor. The Praetorian prefect had found himself in a tight spot, wedged between loyalty to his emperor and maintaining the favor of the people. If he let Valentine live, the emperor would execute *him*. If he obeyed the emperor's directive and executed Valentine, the people would riot and kill him anyway. Titus found himself in a similar spot. If the people found out *he* was behind the arrest of their beloved hero, he would be a dead man too. And if the people didn't kill him, the barbarians waiting at the battlefront would.

He shook his head and focused on the task ahead. Valentine had been moved from the Ludus to the amphitheatre during the prior evening's gladiator matches. Titus hadn't been quick enough to intercept him then. Now he kept to the outer corridors of the hypogeum, where cells studded the outside edge. The close air was humid and stank of sweat, fear, and animal feces. He wasn't sure where the noxii were kept, but he knew an air of pure confidence was key in getting him there.

"You there!" He flagged a lanista with a belt full of keys. "Where are the prisoners for the noon executions?"

The lanista gave a noncommittal wave of his hand. "Around."

"I'm a speculatore, here on behalf of Tribune Lucius Braccus. I need to see one of the noxii. A man by the name of Valentine Favius Diastema. It's urgent."

The lanista studied him a moment, then tipped his head toward an open cell. "Wait here."

Titus waited, feet apart, arms crossed, as the lanista left. A snake of fear coiled in his gut. He jiggled his leg to mask it. He'd agonized over what to do and couldn't be sure this last panicked idea would work. Either way, he was a dead man. So what did it matter?

A low growl from somewhere farther down the tunnels raised the hairs on the back of his neck and arms. The animals were starved, he knew—the lions, wild dogs, tigers—then fed pieces of dead prisoners to help them acquire a taste for human flesh. His stomach churned. This was a terrible idea. He should go. Before he could move toward the exit, the clink of chains announced the return of the lanista who prodded a staggering Valentine into the light of a flickering torch. Head down, he walked past Titus with a shuffling stiffness. The lanista chained him to iron rings in the wall of the open cell and stepped back.

"I'll let you know when I'm through." Titus dropped a few coins into the lanista's palm.

The lanista closed his fist over the coins and left. Titus watched him until he stationed himself at the end of the tunnel just before it curved out of sight. When he turned back, Valentine stared at him.

"Are the others safe?" His raw, bleeding wrists dangled at his sides, secured to the wall by short chains. Blood streaked his swollen fingers and dried down one side of his chin.

"Your friends need you." Titus gritted his teeth. "*Iris* needs you. We don't have much time." He pulled out a thin metal pick and set to work on the iron clamped around Valentine's left wrist. "Listen closely. We'll have to trade places. It—it's the only way. I've received orders to join the fighting at the front with the Ninth Minerva. They leave at dawn. I have the documents with me; they'll get you out of the city and then you can go wherever you please from there. Burn the uniform and no one will be the wiser."

Valentine jerked his wrist from Titus's grasp and clutched it to his chest with a hiss of pain. "They'll execute you if you let me escape."

Titus glanced at the door. "I'm not doing it for you." He paused and took a deep breath. "Iris . . . loves *you*." He hated how his throat constricted over the words.

"And I love her." Valentine shook his head. "But there's no way I'd make it out of here."

"With my uniform and hooded cloak, you'll be fine." Titus hadn't expected it to be so difficult to beg a condemned prisoner to go free.

"Why are you doing this? Wasn't sending me to the executioners your plan all along?"

"Yes." Titus wrestled Valentine's wrist back and concentrated on the lock. "But if I leave you here, Iris will never forgive me." He thought of her angry goodbye yesterday. The pain of it stinging still. "It's the only way out now. We can't both leave. There are armored lanistae everywhere on the lookout for gladiators trying to escape during the chaos. If you take my uniform and pull the hood over your face, no one should stop you."

"What about you?" Valentine squeezed his eyes shut. "You think Iris and I could live happily together knowing you'd been executed for letting me go free? How could she forgive *me*?"

"I would do anything for her—give anything." The locking mechanism clicked but didn't give. Valentine kept trying to pull his arm away. "Stop fighting me. She wants *you* . . . and I can't live with the way she looks at me."

Valentine studied him a long moment before his lips tipped in a sad smile, some realization crossing his face. "There is no greater love than to lay down one's life for one's friends."

"Trust me," Titus growled, "you are *not* my friend."

They didn't have much time. The fighting in the arena above had gone quiet. The floor grated with the sound of pushcarts and the scraping of bodies being cleared from the sand. The noon show would begin soon. Already the stands hummed with boredom. The noon show was neither exciting nor competitive. It was a bloodbath of unarmed noxii against gladiators armed to the teeth. Sometimes the noxii were pitted against beasts. Criminals though they were, and deserving of death, Titus could never quite stomach the noon show. Now he'd be part of it.

The lock gave and Valentine's arm dropped free to his side. Relief and dread rolled over him. Titus reached for the other shackle and Valentine pushed him away, pulling a wooden tablet from his ragged tunic and slapping it against Titus's chest. "Give this to her."

Titus shrugged away from him. "Give it to her yourself."

"I'm not accepting your offer. I can't."

"What do you mean you can't?"

"Must I list the reasons?" Valentine looked incredulous. "For one thing, you'll be executed. Two, you don't believe in God—"

"How could I?" Titus threw his hands up. "You speak of a loving god, yet he sends his faithful ones to go and die! He *afflicts* those he claims to love."

Valentine spoke quickly. "A loyal soldier goes where he's ordered, does he not? Regardless of the risk, of the cost to him?"

Titus looked away. "It's too much to believe in. And not enough."

"Seek Him, Titus, and you'll see He's more than you could hope for. His peace surpasses all unrest around you. His joy overshadows all hurt. His life drowns out all fear of death." Valentine's eyes glowed with earnest passion.

Titus's eyes narrowed. "How can you not fear it?"

"Death is not the end. God promises eternal life through—"

Titus gave a roar of frustration. "You. Are. Going. To. *Die.*" He beat his fist against his chest. *"I'm* the only one who can save you now, *not* your god!" He smacked the heel of his hand against the wall behind Valentine's head.

"No," Valentine spoke quietly. "You're not. My God is powerful enough to save me without condemning you to death in the arena. But even if He doesn't save me from this, He is worthy of my worship, of my devotion, of my very life."

Titus stared at him. "Iris loves you. I'm the one handing you life, and you'd rather die than be with her? Is that what you want me to tell her? 'I offered him a way out and he said he'd rather die'?"

Valentine's chin jerked and his eyes softened and turned down at the edges. "No. Of course not. But what you're proposing I cannot agree to. She will understand that."

Titus's jaw hardened. "Fine." He locked Valentine's wrist back into the shackle and shoved the barred gate open with an ear-piercing squeal.

Valentine sighed. "Titus, wait."

City of Rome
Ides of Februarius, AD 270

He is tied to a post, dying. A Praetorian enters the arena in polished armor and spotless blue tunic and marches toward him. Flowers rain from the stands, not for the fighters, not for the soldier, but for him. Not even the Praetorians can harness the roar of protest as the soldier pulls out a gladius, the short blade gleaming in the bright noon sun. There is no ceremony this time, no showmanship. The soldier grasps a handful of his hair and with a practiced swing and little resistance, his head dangles in the soldier's grip. The stands go deathly still.

A trumpet blares and from beneath the purple awning, the Praetorian prefect shouts for all to hear: "So dies a traitor who dared to defy the empire. Remember this day."

They do.

LIX

Spectators poured from the colossus of the Flavian Amphitheatre as Iris reached it. The sun had just passed its zenith in a blue and cold sky and her breath hung in frosty puffs above her head. She'd left the others gathered in the dimness of her pater's room, praying for Valentine. Iris had grown restless and left as the morning grew late. She couldn't sit anymore. Her heart was breaking in pieces. Surely the God who had healed her and rescued her pater could not mean to let Valentine die. He was a good man. He treated everyone with kindness and compassion. His gap-toothed smile was contagious. She wanted to be here when the earthquake struck, when the angel appeared and broke his chains and led him out. She would be first in line with an *I told you so* grin.

Iris stepped into the wide court around the amphitheatre, pressing against the flood of bodies smelling of sweat and perfume and too much wine. The food stands set up around the four exits were swamped within minutes. Dizzy with the roar of slurred voices and the screech and snap of sandals on flagstones, Iris looked up at the monstrosity of stacked arches and, catching the waning arc of the sun, realized she was too late.

She knew it, and yet she would not allow the flickering spark of hope to extinguish. It was faith, she told herself. Or perhaps denial.

363

Her ears perked toward the conversations, hoping for snatches of a miracle. Perhaps God had shut the mouths of the lions, like he had for Daniel, or opened the doors of the prison as he had for Paul and Silas.

The spectators had a dazed look about them that was not wine induced. Some wailed outright.

Her throat began to burn.

A man draining the last dregs of his wineskin tripped into her, spraying the mouthful over her shoulders and neck. The man swore and apologized, patting at her with a puffy hand. Iris ducked past, hardly noticing. She broke through the thick stream of bodies spilling from the southern gate and moved more quickly as the crowd thinned at the edge of the walkway. Slaves pulling refuse carts entered through an archway hung with iron-barred gates.

Scanning this service entrance, her eye snagged on a flash of Praetorian blue. It wasn't so much the uniform as the way this Praetorian didn't stride or march or swagger. He stumbled forward and swayed. Her heart stopped.

Her steps matched his, tripping, wobbling, jostled by the crowd. The roar of people seemed to fade into a dull hum. Their gazes tangled. She didn't have to ask. His arms hung at his sides, his expression of defeat telling her everything she didn't want to hear.

"Iris," Titus choked. His mouth opened again but nothing came out.

Her breath quickened. In . . . Out . . . In. Out. In-out. Why did it feel like she wasn't breathing at all? She stared at him.

Say something. Say something. Confirm it. Deny it. Say. Something.

"I tried . . ."

Her hands covered her mouth. A sharpness sliced through the center of her chest, cutting off her lungs completely. Titus came forward and caught her arms as her knees went liquid.

"I tried my hardest—you have to believe me." He dropped to his knees with her as she collapsed. The world went mute. She sucked in a shuddering breath, unable to utter anything but the hiss of silent screams.

Valentine was dead.

No matter how many times Iris repeated the words in her head, they didn't seem true. Didn't seem real—wouldn't have seemed real, except for how the pain confirmed it.

Only the occasional sniffle broke the silence in Marius and Martha's triclinium.

Beatrix sat on the couch beside her, stiff, her clammy hand gripped around Iris's. She had not said a word since Titus had returned Iris to the villa with the confirmation.

Valentine was dead.

Titus hadn't stayed.

"'I do not want you to be ignorant, brethren.'" Marius's voice pushed from his chest, straining with effort. "'Concerning those who have fallen asleep, lest . . .'" He swallowed. "'Lest you sorrow as others who have no hope. For—'" His voice broke. "'For if we believe that Jesus died and rose again, even so . . . God will bring with Him those who sleep in Jesus.'"

The door opened and they looked up. Cato shuffled inside, tear-streaked and pale. He'd left at dawn without a word.

"You know," Martha spoke gently.

"I watched." The words were torn from him. Cato let his head fall into his hands, shoulders releasing with deep, groaning sobs. Delphine stood and wrapped her arms around him, tugging him to a couch and holding him. Beatrix sucked in a deep, shuddering breath. Iris gripped her hand tighter as Marius finished quoting the passage about the future and glorious return of God, who would raise the dead with a blast of a trumpet and all believers would be caught up together to meet the Lord in the sky.

"'Therefore comfort one another with these words.'" Marius squeezed his eyes shut, tears tracing the lines of his leathery cheeks.

Iris longed to be comforted. But first, she wanted to scream. To beat her fists into the ground and rage. The ache built inside like a lump of hot marble, pressing at her chest until it seeped over in scalding streams down her face. She couldn't hold it in anymore and left the room, clamping a hand over her mouth. The courtyard was dusky and quiet. The cold felt good against the charred ache in her chest. She sank to the ground beside the potted almond tree, melting beneath the weight of grief too heavy to carry. Her throat was on fire; the smell of tears burned her nose. She finally let them out, sinking as each sob ripped from her gut until her forehead pressed against the coldness of the pot.

Her mind ran with images. Valentine twirling Lalia and Rue. Winking at her from across the crowded room at the secret wedding. His ceaseless care for the poor and widowed, and his kindness in writing notes to them. This day, the world had been gutted of compassion and love.

As the burning sharpened, she recalled a night not so long ago when she'd felt the same sense of crushing hopelessness and Valentine had been there to comfort her. Who would comfort her now?

"No matter what happens—good or bad, by our estimation—it can always be redeemed by God for good if we trust Him." Valentine's voice spoke the words in her head, his mild tone changing ever so slightly with each word. The gentleness remained but the voice grew in power and contained a tremor of wildness that both shook her to her core and left her in a glass-sea calm.

Do you trust Me?

The Voice came from both inside her and out, wild and firm and achingly gentle. The sound of it made her weep. Did she truly trust a God who could open her eyes and yet allow His people to die? Yesterday she had. This morning she had. It had been easy, then. God had shown Himself to her—powerful, kind, good. It was easy to trust God when He did everything *she* wanted Him to. But if she could only trust Him then, who was truly God? *Her?* Or Him?

Do you trust Me?

Did she?

Could she?

Iris curled herself into a tight ball as if the pain would somehow become smaller too.

Could she trust God even now, with all the world throwing stones and no refuge in sight?

Neither Valentine nor her pater nor even answered prayers could be the fortress in which she trusted.

"Yes." She forced the word past her lips on the back of a sob. "You . . . are . . . good."

Those words were even harder to say. She knew they were true, but they didn't *feel* true. "I will trust You. I . . . I don't understand, but You . . . are good."

Curled at the base of the almond tree, she repeated the truths over and over, fighting the despair that roared in her ears with the force of a hurricane.

You are good. I trust You. You are good. I trust You.

Gradually the tears subsided, the pain in her heart subdued—not all the way, not for good, but enough for now. She pushed herself upright, feeling the hardness of a tablet tucked into her sash. Her hand went over the spot. She barely remembered Titus pushing the small tablet into her hands as he left, apologizing over and over. He had to join his cohort. They were leaving at dawn, transferring some-where to the north.

She clutched the tablet in both hands now, suddenly mourning the loss of her oldest friend. Valentine was with God. At peace, in par-adise. But Titus faced battle, devoted to no god, believing that his fate resided firmly in his own hands. She'd refused to extend mercy and forgiveness. She dropped her head, guilt weighing it down. *Forgive me. And help me to forgive.*

She loosened the knot and unwound the cord wrapping the two halves of the tablet together. It was the same one she'd brought to Valentine, but the letter inside was different. For her. The words smudged and crooked as if written in haste and darkness. They blurred a moment before she blinked them clear again.

My dearest Iris,
    Do not despair, whatever happens. My soul is secure in God.
He is the only one who can rescue me now and I wait with

expectant hope; but even if He does not, do not lose faith. Do not lose hope. Our God is bigger than my death. Our God is bigger than the forces rising against us.

Be strong, my love. Hold fast to Him and do not lose heart. I know how it all ends.

We win.

Our God always wins. Our God is living. Our God is reigning. Our God is and will always be victorious. I told you at the beginning that your life as a Christ follower would not be easy. It would not be safe. But through it all you would not be alone. He is with us always, even at the end.

Our story may not have ended happily, but as Christ followers, our lives and stories never truly end. Our lives are but single threads woven into the tapestry of history—of God's story. Who can tell what picture our threads will complete?

I will see you again, my love. My soul and body will soon be separated, but my heart I leave with you.

As I live and die, I remain your true and loving,
Valentine

EPILOGUE

Iris squinted against the brilliant sunlight glittering on the turquoise waves of the Mediterranean Sea and glanced at the port village scattered on the rocky shore. Pater and her new stepmother, Beatrix, made their way down the path toward her, hand in hand, a cluster of Cato and Delphine's children skipping circles around them, laughing and chattering, voices garbled in the wind. Their parents were nowhere in sight, probably enjoying a few minutes of blessed silence.

Iris smiled. In the peace of Myra, the nightmare of Rome seemed a lifetime ago.

They'd left Rome the day after Valentine's death. Somehow, and she never understood how, Abachum and Audifax had managed to steal Valentine's body, which they'd brought back to the villa and buried in the courtyard, planting the potted almond tree above the grave to disguise it. They'd all fled hours later when guards surrounded the home. Iris, Quintus, and Beatrix had managed to escape through the culina door with Cato, Delphine, and the children. Word had reached them later that Marius, Martha, and the two younger sons had not fared so well. The men had been cut down in the streets, Martha drowned in a public fountain. Refusing to let anyone else suffer at the hands of the Praetorians, Cato ordered the sailors to take them aboard his father's merchant ship and leave Rome that night.

369

Iris left the path and scrabbled over the rocks along the harbor village of Andriake where painted fishing boats bobbed behind the breakers or were hauled like beached whales onto the white sand. She settled on a speckled rock, giving her the perfect view of the sea and the dead-flat road that stretched to the large city of Myra at the foot of the Taurus Mountains. A warm breeze lifted the hair on her forehead, and she inhaled the sharp saltiness, basking in the warmth and stillness before tugging the letter from her sash.

The tablet was worn smooth with handling and the wax had long since hardened to permanence, and although she knew the contents of it by heart, she opened it again and read it, heart tightening at the familiar, beloved handwriting. She loved Valentine. Missed him still. But the suffocating crush of loss no longer squeezed the air from her lungs. The five years in Myra had been peaceful ones, healing ones, but not without pangs of loneliness, especially after her father and Beatrix had married—as glad as she was about that.

Iris closed the letter and wrapped it shut with the cord, thankful for the promise that the Lord's faithfulness remained even amid her doubts and questions. He was good. God had made beauty from pain before. She could do nothing more than trust that He would do it again.

Quintus and Beatrix led the children to the water, where they squealed and splashed in the waves. Iris looked back at the road to see if Cato and Delphine were coming and noticed a single speck moving along in the distance. A slow speck. Shuffling in a humped sort of way. As the speck drew closer, it elongated into a rectangle and then into a man carrying a small traveler's sack. He must have come a great distance. Iris replaced the letter into her sash as she stood, preparing to greet the weary stranger and invite him to their home for food and rest as they often did. She skipped across the rocks and hopped onto the road, chiton swirling around her legs.

The stranger had come to a faltering stop in the road. Iris looked up and froze.

The pause felt like minutes before she realized her feet were moving. Running. She nearly bowled him over.

"Titus!" His name emerged in a shriek. "You're alive! You're here!"

He returned her embrace, albeit awkwardly, his right arm bound in filthy bandages. "Iris. You look well."

Her eyes traced the web of red scars twisting across his face. He'd let his beard grow out to cover most of them.

"And you look terrible." She took a step back. "What happened?"

He shrugged. "I got discharged."

"How did you find us?"

"I'm a speculatore." His lips tipped slightly. "It's what I do. Or . . . what I *did*."

She smiled. "I'm glad."

His eyes met hers, surprise and longing intermingled. "Are you?"

"Of course." Anything she might have added was cut off by the happy screams of the children darting out on one of the breakers and diving into the sea while Bea and Quintus cheered.

"Yours?" Titus's eyebrows flickered upward.

She laughed. "Heavens, Titus! That would be a feat indeed, even if I *was* married."

"I'm sorry." His eyes clouded with emotion. "So, so sorry. You have to know . . . I tried everything I could think of to save him."

"It's not your fault, Titus." She looked down. "*I'm* sorry. I was angry and never forgave you before you left."

He shook his head. "You have every right to be angry, and I don't deserve your forgiveness. *I* didn't warn him away in time, *I* arrested him, *I* failed to convince him to trade places with me, *I*—"

She laughed.

He looked at her, startled.

"You thought you could get *Valentine* to trade places with you? So you would die, and he would live? Oh, Titus." Her heart ached for him. What torture he'd put himself through.

"Anyone else in his circumstances would have jumped at the chance. *I* would have." His expression twisted in such guilt and internal torment, she reached out to comfort him, but he pulled away. "I *tortured* him."

Her hand froze, breath catching in her throat as images of Valentine's battered body rose to her mind.

"And the whole time he did nothing but beg me to believe in his god. To believe in the god who did nothing while I tortured him."

"Titus."

"What a waste."

"Not a waste." She reached up and turned his face to look at her. "We've all been touched by Valentine's life. By his deep faith in God, by his kindness to people otherwise ignored, by his taking a stand and refusing to stay silent and safe." Her voice went soft. "He told me once that all things work together for the good of those who love God and are called according to His purpose."

"And what good has come of this?" His look was haunted and hungry with longing to believe her.

"I don't know yet . . . perhaps I never will, not fully. But the people of Rome will not soon forget Valentine, and neither will we. Perhaps . . ." She paused, growing thoughtful. "Perhaps they, too, will befriend an outcast. Perhaps their kindness will change a city."

He followed her gaze toward the beach, where Quintus had turned and was watching them, his body still.

She touched his arm. "For now, all I can do is retell the story."

"Of Valentine?"

Quintus lurched forward, limping gait increasing from a walk to a run as he drew closer, arms outstretched.

"Of God, who is so rich in mercy and great love that He sent Christ so that we may be made alive and saved by His grace. It's what Valentine lived and died for. And as long as we keep telling *that* story, Valentine's life and ours, no matter how long or short, will never be wasted."

"You really believe that?"

"With all my heart."

She took his hand and tugged, but he resisted as he had for so many years, his gaze shifting from her hopeful face to her pater's outstretched arms. His mouth worked, a turmoil of debate, doubts, and longing whirling in his face. And then something gave, a tiny fissure in a wall of granite that sent the whole of it crumbling to dust.

Titus took a step.

Quintus crushed him in a hug.

A Note from the Author

I never really liked Valentine's Day.

You probably weren't expecting to hear that from a person who spent years writing about the origins of the holiday, but there it is. This story had its beginnings in my pride and God's work in humbling me. The research began as my attempt to justify how stupid I thought the holiday was. And then what I found grabbed hold of me and wouldn't let go.

The story is simple, vague at best, first mentioned in history nearly two hundred years after his death. A man named Valentine, outraged at Emperor Claudius II for outlawing marriage, continued to marry couples in secret until his capture. While in prison, he fell in love with the jailor's blind daughter, prayed for her, and her sight was restored. When he was taken away to be executed, he left her a love letter signed, *Love, your Valentine*.

How tragically romantic, right?!

I needed more. I wanted to read this story and searched in vain for the novel someone had to have written about Valentine in the last seventeen centuries. I came up disappointed and empty-handed. But the story wouldn't leave me alone. Images and snippets of conversations found their way into my mind, and I started scribbling out scenes.

Unfortunately, there are no writings left by Valentine, no

contemporaries who mention him in their own works, and even the historical record makes no mention of Emperor Claudius II's marriage ban (although banning marriage for lower-ranking soldiers was common, as was the practice of striking from the record any mention of unpopular emperors or edicts).

Yet somehow, the stories of Valentine persisted over 1,700 years and inspired a holiday well-known and widely celebrated. So it begs the question, are the stories true? And whether one believes they are or not, how could they be true based on the history and culture of that time?

While I tried my best to ensure this story is as historically accurate as possible, I am not an expert on third-century Rome, and I apologize for any mistakes you may find. I first collected the legends as mentioned above (with variations here and there) and compared them against church history and third-century Roman history and culture, and from there I pieced together a story line which became the book you're holding in your hands.

There were discoveries I found fascinating. Like how Romans viewed Christians as a national security threat. Romans believed their power and success came from their devotion to their gods and that decline came upon the empire when they tolerated those who opposed their gods. Christian persecution always seemed to follow the empire's decline or defeat.

There were also discoveries I wish I hadn't made. Namely, the part about Romans refusing burial for Christian martyrs (because if their bones and body parts were scattered or eaten by animals, the Christians couldn't possibly be raised from the dead as they believed they would be).

While Cato and Delphine are fictional characters, Marius, Martha, Abachum, and Audifax were real people said to have been merchant friends of Valentine who worked with him to aid Roman Christians during times of intense persecution. As included in the story, they were all martyred in February of AD 270. Their crime? Burying the body of a Christian martyr . . . I had to wonder, was it Valentine?

After Constantine's rise to power, the Roman Empire struggled to replace pagan worship with Christian worship. In the fifth century, Pope Gelasius renamed the spring fertility festival of Lupercalia "Saint Valentine's Day" to create something wholesome out of what was not. Perhaps it worked. Perhaps not.

My intent in writing this story was never to venerate a saint, but to lift high the God Valentine and so many other martyrs considered worthy of worship. Worthy of risk and hardship and death. Times will come in our lives when we will need to take a stand, risking something in the process. The questions Valentine faced then are the same ones we face today. Will we choose to follow God? Is He worth the risk? Will we trust Him even when things don't turn out the way we want?

I pray the answer is always a resounding yes.

Jamie

Acknowledgments

Stories have surrounded me since I was a child. My parents, Art and Lori Ogle, filled me and my four sisters with Bible stories, stories of missionaries and martyrs, and stories of what God has done in their own lives. My mom taught me to read and write, and both Mom and Dad read and encouraged my early writing and made me believe I could do this. I'm so deeply grateful for you both.

To my best friend, and swoony husband, Phil—you are the best sounding board and encourager. You've supported this crazy author dream of mine from the beginning and never once complained—even when I randomly fret about people and situations that are not real and spend hours writing in the closet and your dinner looks like boiled hot dogs and a pile of raw spinach—thanks for only telling one person about that. You are always my favorite.

Ellery, Maebel, and Henry, you keep life full and funny and invite me to live in the present with you every five minutes—you are the best gifts. I love you.

My critique partners and writing buddies, Chris Posti, Diane Samson, Kristine Delano, Sarah Hanks, Sherry Shindelar, Heather Wood, Carrie Cotten, and all of my Christian Mommy Writer friends—you challenge and encourage me daily and make this journey so much fun and far less lonely.

The gracious authors who've welcomed and encouraged me along the way, Joanna Davidson Politano, Stephanie Landsem, Laura Frantz, Erica Vetsch, Julie Klassen, Jocelyn Green, and so many others—your kind words have meant more than you know!

I am grateful for David Hollander and Cameron Dryden, who graciously answered my questions about ancient Rome and sent waves of books, articles, and information my way.

To my agent, Kristy Cambron, thank you for believing in me and this story from the start. For working to get this novel into the right hands, for being a calming and encouraging voice in the face of my absolute shock and terror that things were actually happening with my stories. Thank you for going on this adventure with me.

To the team at Tyndale House Publishers and my incredible editors Elizabeth Jackson, Stephanie Broene, and Sarah Rische, you took the story of my heart and made it real. Thank you. It's a dream come true to get to work with you all. I'm still pinching myself!

Finally, but always foremost, to God Almighty. All along the rocky way, through the highest highs and plummeting depths, You were there with me. Leading, holding, sustaining. This is all for You. *Soli Deo gloria.*

Discussion Questions

1. Before reading *Of Love and Treason*, how much did you know about the historical St. Valentine? What parts of this story fit with what you knew? What surprised you?

2. When the emperor passes an edict banning marriage, Roman church leaders argue that they can be faithful to God and still follow the new law, while Valens disagrees. Which position did you find yourself agreeing with?

3. As they wrestle with the new edict, Cato says, "The Scriptures command us to honor the emperor." Valens replies, "Yes. . . . Honor him as a man made in the image of God. Honor him as a soul Jesus died to save. I will never slur him nor wish him harm, but that does not mean I agree with everything he decrees." Think of a time when you've disagreed with someone in power. Were you able to honor that person while still holding to your belief? How do you discern when to follow a person, law, or rule and when to take a stand in opposition?

4. The early Roman church looked quite different from most Christian churches today, with believers meeting in small groups and sharing their resources. Are there elements of the early church you'd like to see the modern church return to? What do you prefer about church as it exists now?

5. Before Iris's vision is fully restored, she receives a few brief glimpses of sight. Compare the story in Mark 8:22-26 of Jesus healing a blind man. Why do you think some healings happen immediately and others come more slowly?

6. Iris also questions why she was healed while in other cases, God does not intervene to save or protect those who love Him. How would you answer her? Have you wrestled with the same question? What was the result?

7. Characters like Beatrix and Cato and Delphine have faced devastating losses yet hold on to their faith. How are they able to do so? Are there people in your own life who stand as similar examples?

8. Titus twice gives Valens the chance to escape Rome. Why do you think Valens makes the choice he does each time? Did you understand his reasons?

9. Titus carries the blame for Iris's injury on his own shoulders, along with the belief that he should get the credit for what he has done. In a moment of frustration, he thinks, "He'd done everything he could to protect them, to keep them safe, to rescue them. *He'd* done it, not their god, not their friends, and certainly *not* Valentine." Why do you think Titus finds it so difficult to surrender responsibility for both the good and the bad? Do you imagine he will ever be able to accept grace?

10. Valens tells Iris, "We're told that all things work together for the good of those who love God, those who are called according to His purpose. . . . *All things* might be good things, and they might be terribly difficult things. . . . We have the assurance that no matter what happens—good or bad, by our estimation—anything can always be redeemed by God for good if we trust Him." How does this perspective affect how you view this story's ending? Have there been tragic or difficult circumstances in your own life that God has redeemed for good—or that you are still waiting to see redeemed?

About the Author

JAMIE OGLE is a predawn writer, a homeschool mom by day, and a reader by night. Inspired by her fascination with the storied history of faith, she writes historical fiction infused with hope, adventure, and courageous rebels. A Minnesota native, she now lives in Iowa with her husband and their three children, and she can usually be found gardening, beekeeping, and tromping through the woods. Learn more about Jamie at jamieogle.com.

CONNECT WITH JAMIE ONLINE AT

jamieogle.com

OR FOLLOW HER ON:

f facebook.com/authorjamieogle

⊙ jamie_m_ogle

g jamie-ogle

CP1929